# SHADOW OF THE TOWER

THE SEVEN PORTALS SERIES

ANDRE JONES

ALIEN
PRESS

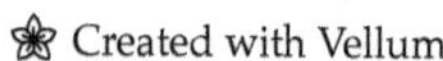 Created with Vellum

# AUTHOR'S NOTE

*'Every cloud has a silver lining'.*

There are two things that have made this book possible with such a quick (for me) turn-around; my retirement, and the current Covid19 lockdown in Melbourne.

Other than my random multi-day runs - which I finished in March 2020 - I don't get out all that much, so many hours have been spent typing, deleting and typing (repeat ad nauseam) to finish. Have no doubt, there has been many an hour with little progress made when I hit a dead-spot and nothing comes to mind.

I am what is known 'in the trade' as 'pantser'; other than having a very broad idea of what the end of the book is like, I really don't know what will appear on the page. (I've even had to change a bit of the storyline because those dastardly characters go off and do something unexpected).

While this book was being edited, I have been working on *Ripples in Time* - Book 3. At the the point of writing these words, I am 65k words in - and recovering from one of those dreaded dead-spots.

I'd like to thank you for purchasing this book - feeding my habit - and I hope it meets your high expectations.

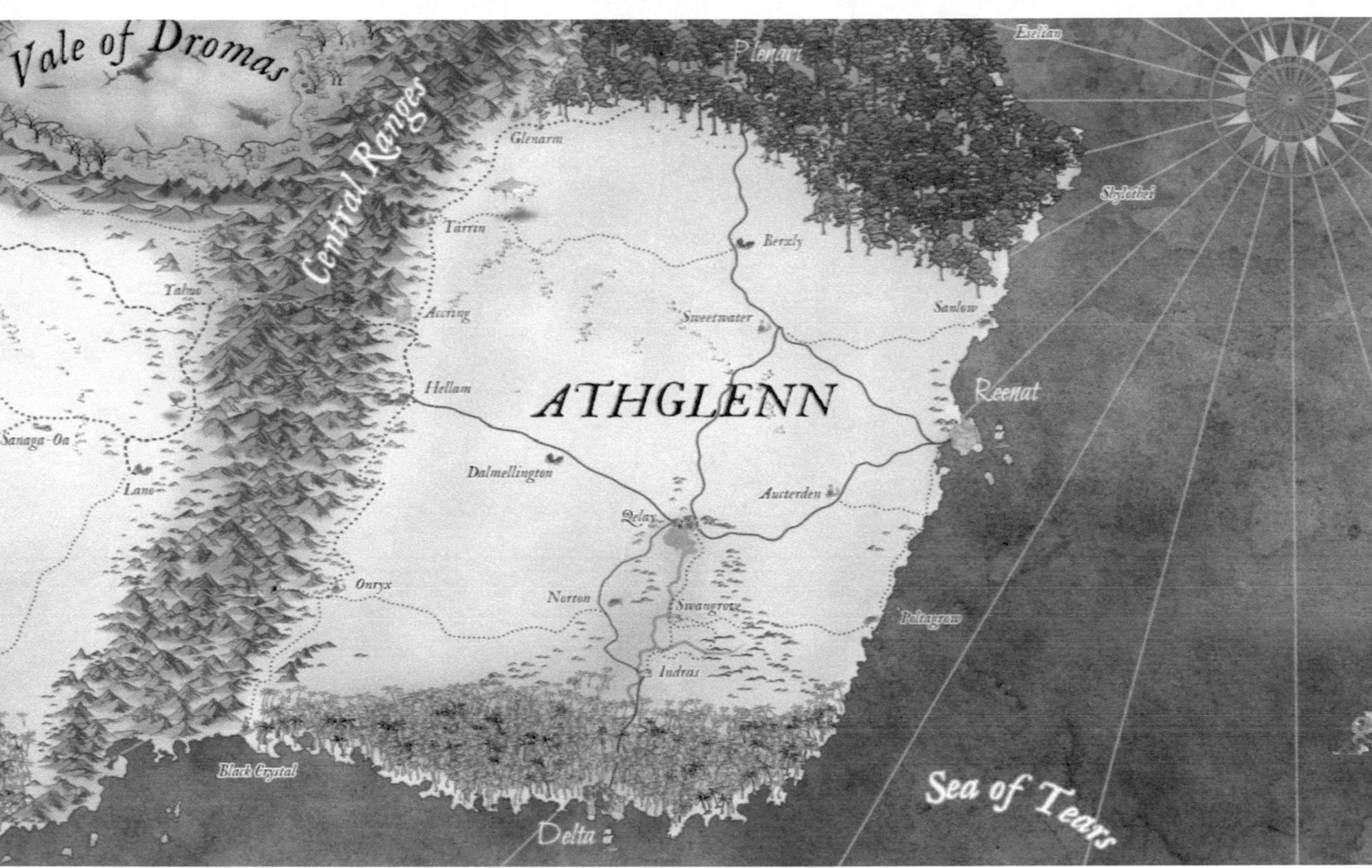

Vale of Dromas
Central Ranges
Plenart
Erelian
Skylethei
Glenarm
Tarrin
Berxly
Accring
Sweetwater
Sanlow
Tahuo
Hellam
ATHGLENN
Reenat
Sanaga-Oa
Dalmellington
Aucterden
Qelay
Lane
Onryx
Norton
Swangrove
Peleagrow
Indras
Black Crystal
Delta s
Sea of Tears

Ogkurr
Chark
Kaliro
Tamroa
Anahlon
Doriel
Irinius
Soolind
Naiser
Ullvaes
FISBANE
Tana
Kemasar
Naran
Belanor
Baseu
Entheas
Iyrenlor
Tiriun
Mylenor

# PART I

# YARNIK

1
———

## A NEW ASSIGNMENT

Enthralled by the blades flashing between three jugglers, the market patrons paid little attention to the cloaked figure weaving through the crowd. The marvellous abilities of the performers from Tesak had spread throughout the city and the plaza was packed.

Try as she might, there was very little chance Leonie could remain indoors for long. She'd have to make doubly-sure to avoid any clerics, regardless of which temple they belonged to. Leonie's high spirits to be outside reflected in the ease with which pouches came into her possession.

To continue the impression of her death, Leonie obscured her feline features by wearing a hooded, dark-green cloak. It was long enough to hide her tail while the hood covered her ears. Oversized clothing concealed her arms and legs while allowing deft fingers when required.

A pair of glins'ool, their long avian necks craning here and there, proved little challenge. Leonie nimbly passed, plucking a small pouch from beneath a wing along the way. Her keen nose picked up a musky scent from another individual, reminding her of Feiron. The eyes of illios were cosmetic; it could be studying her for all she knew. She casually moved on. Pickpocketing a shapechanger made for a short vocation, and sometimes a shorter life. She wondered how Feiron's enrolment into the Guild of Investigators was going.

Emerging from the crowd, she flicked a small part of her recent wealth into the performers' basket. The gold coin glittered as it spun in the torchlight before it clinked with others.

"Thank you," the nearest juggler said in his light Tesakian accent. "Glad you enjoyed the show." He neatly snatched a whirling blade from the air, tossing it back to one of his companions. His voice reminded her of Philbert. *Can't wait to see them again next week.* She was keen to immerse herself in the sensation of flying with the wyverns again.

Continuing on her way, two street urchins chased each other around the market place, their mayhem knocking over a barrel here, or stepping on someone's toes there. When they got closer, the boy ducked behind Leonie, using her bulk to stop the other from tagging him.

"Evening Helen, Sam." She smiled. "One day these stall-holders will put a stop to your antics. It's bad for their business."

"Well," Sam replied, leaping around her as Helen lunged at him. "They have ta catch us first!"

"Good evenin', Leonie," Helen panted, watching Sam intently. She pretended to make another lunge to the right. Sam leapt away, getting tagged when Helen swiftly sidestepped to the left. "Got you! Hah!" She burst with childish glee.

"Now Sam," Leonie admonished gently. "Learn to watch the foot placement."

"How can I watch where 'er feet are if I'm s'posed to be watchin' 'er eyes?" he whined.

"You'll learn with experience. Take it all in. Use your peripheral vision."

"But I don't 'av perifal vision!" he wailed. "I want slit-eyes, like yours."

"Unfortunately, that's beyond me to give. I can only advise

you on how to use your round-eyes better." She tousled his black hair.

"More like he'll get dizzy and trip over his own feet!" Helen called as Sam chased her again. She dodged through the crowd and doubled-back. "By the way," she added, "Jade wants ta see ya."

Leonie nodded at the message, noticing the guards beyond the young girl's view. "There's a new stall on the west side," she continued, "with wonderful scarves all the way from Lyhosa. Best you go that way." She pointed, indicating the approaching guards, angry merchants in their wake. She tossed both youngsters a silver piece. "Now, be off with you both."

The two youngsters sprinted off giggling, dodging through the crowded market place. A couple of stray dogs, sensing a chance to play, yapped excitedly in their wake.

Keen to find out what Jade wanted, Leonie angled away from the guards, stooping slightly to blend more with the crowd. *It better not be a surprise farewell party.*

Her path took her close to the Opsyss temple. Bamboo scaffolding surrounded it. Three nights ago, five Woorin fanatics tried to save a half-rrell sacrifice. Sadly, she wasn't able to save Pasha, her long-lost childhood friend.

The attack resulted in the death of many clerics from both sides and caused massive damage to the temple. Her use of the Jart'lekk blade had diverted any suspicion of the death of Alen, one of the temple's priests. Now the Deathers were hunting assassins; the Flamers thought her dead, putting her in the clear.

Always on the alert for unwanted scrutiny, she took a circuitous route towards Jade's office, the warm evening air another reason for a crowded market. Stallholders called out, and the tumult of hundreds of people wandering the plaza soon faded. She found the sounds of the evening along the waterfront much more relaxing, the creaking of mooring lines as the ships gently rocked with the swell, and the gulls cawing from their perches high up in the rigging. All this quickly faded to silence with the twists and turns of the narrow back streets of the Web, her padded paws soundless on the boardwalk.

Leonie was so engrossed in her thoughts, she almost walked past Jade's office. She ducked down the lane and concentrated. It would be bad enough to be late, let alone having to admit to getting lost. She gave a coded knock on the wooden panel and stepped into the dim interior where Ro, Jade's bodyguard, kept watch. Waving a greeting, she bounded up the stairs, knocking and opening Jade's door at the same time. *No party. Good.*

The new additions to the décor made her wince. The table and chairs were inlaid with silver in a style fashionable about one hundred and fifty years ago. Too ornate for her tastes.

"These are nice," Leonie said, choosing one to sit in.

"Liar." Her boss didn't look up.

Rich tapestries covered the walls, illustrating a variety of scenes from different countries. One showed Plenari, the capital city of Tesak, located in a forest of giant trees. That was a place she'd like to see with her own eyes, and again she considered her pending departure.

Jade glanced up. "How are you feeling?"

"I'm fine." Leonie tried to get comfortable in the chair and failed.

"Ready for your trip?" Jade asked.

"I've got my gear together, and a bit more travelling money from this evening's takings." She placed a pawful of gold coins in a bowl. "And here's the Taker percentage."

One of Jade's eyebrows raised. "Do I need to count it?"

"No point. I didn't." Leonie grinned.

"Seriously though, after the run-in with Dianah and Brendon … their news can't have been good to hear."

Leonie paced the room. Her efforts to gain information about her heritage led to frustration. The answers received during her encounter with Dianah and Brendon created more questions. "Not much I can do about it. Being created as part of an experiment, and not having any real parents is a shock, but … I have to move on."

"And you're happy with that?" Jade asked.

"Of course not. They deserved their deaths and I'm glad I was the one to do it. That will have to be enough." Leonie realised she was clenching the carpet with her claws. "I've got to be practical. I am what they created – unique. I'll have to learn to live with that."

"And this trip?"

"Too many memories here and no telling what those temples are going to do next. Best for all if I move on. As I recall you saying a short while ago, 'There's a whole world out there.' May as well go see it while I can." She changed the subject. "You wanted to see me?"

Jade hesitated. "I've recently accepted a difficult task. I don't want to give it to you, but it's short notice and under the circumstances, you're the best available." Jade stood up with a grimace and hobbled around the table with a walking stick.

"What happened?" Leonie asked, surprised.

"I tripped on the stairs. I'd rather not talk about it." She waved her hand in dismissal. "But clearly, I'm unable to do it. I was hoping you might consider it before you leave."

Leonie suppressed a smile at Jade's reddening cheeks. "I don't know. My boss says I should keep my head down. You know, stay out of trouble—"

"Pfft. When did you ever listen?"

"True. Okay then, I'll do this last job, since you're getting too old."

"Be nice." Jade stopped by an open window overlooking the eastern sector of the Web to peer out. "There's a ship in harbour, the *Tearful Revenge*." She pointed as Leonie came closer. "See it? Blue and white flags. From Ghalena. It's by itself out along the mooring points of Central Canal, though there are still vacant berths along the docks. I'm thinking someone doesn't want any visitors. It also means there'll be a degree of water travel involved." She turned to look at her feline friend. "You're aware of the risks this involves?" Jade continued at her nod. "I'm told there's a particular item on board, a black crystal formed into a sphere the size of a small ball." She made an 'O' with her finger and thumb.

"It's called the Nightsky Orb," Jade continued, "and inlaid with a lot of small but high-quality gems, each one flawless in every regard. The client requires this as soon as possible and is prepared to pay very handsomely if this could be done by tomorrow. Needless to say, anything else you might happen to come across is a bonus. No need to worry about any Taker percentage for this job."

"Hss, it doesn't leave me much time to come up with a decent plan. Why the rush?"

"He has to leave town tomorrow night, and the ship's leaving in a day or so."

Leonie shrugged. "It'll have to be something simple." Hearing a noise beyond the human audio range, Leonie turned to face the door. "Do you know anything about the ship? How many guards and crew?" She waited to see who entered.

"The client informs me—" Jade stopped when the door opened.

Netoha walked in carrying a tray of refreshments consisting of wedges of cheese, slices of meat and a pitcher of ale. Leonie went to the table, moving the scrolls to the side as Ro's wife set the tray down. She thought the plainswoman was looking rosier than usual.

"I reckon there's something someone didn't tell me? When are you due, Nettie?"

"First week in autumn." Netoha beamed.

"Ah." Jade joined them. "We've been so busy of late I forgot you didn't know."

Leonie embraced Nettie with a smile. "At least it'll be a bit cooler for you. I know how you hate this southern heat." She noticed Jade waiting. "You better take good care of her, big boy," she called to Ro, standing by the door. Leonie reached out and clawed a small slice of meat.

'Leaving them to their work, Netoha nodded to them both and took her husband by the arm.

"The client informs me they've been at sea for a few weeks." Jade hobbled back to her chair. "The crew are keen to go ashore, so there will most likely be minimal men remaining onboard. The item we're after is under lock and key in the captain's cabin. I've got a rough sketch of the vessel's layout here somewhere." Shuffling through the scrolls, she handed Leonie a scrap of paper.

"And how accurate is this?" Leonie continued eating, studying the crude hand-drawn map.

"Our contact was a recent passenger." Jade shrugged, mumbling around a mouthful of cheese. "The only other thing he can tell us is the ship-master, Jorak, dislikes anything magical. Some sailor superstition I suppose. Which is good for you, there should be no magical traps to deal with. Ironically, he *does* have a device that warns him of magic – so you can't go there with your ring or harness."

Leonie rolled the sketch and slipped it in her belt under her blouse. "Fair enough. I shouldn't need them for this; the harness is only good for up and down anyway." She grabbed another slice of meat. "If that's all, I better check out the area and come up with an idea on how to pull this job off." With a wave she headed for the door.

Jade called to her. "Get back in one piece and watch out for yourself."

"You worry too much. This place won't fall to pieces without me."

## 2

## THE NIGHTSKY ORB

Leaving Jade's office, Leonie went home to drop off the ring and since the streets still had a bit of activity, she decided to stretch while waiting for a later hour. When the time came, she wound her way through the back lanes in higher spirits than at any time in the past week.

Despite her flippant jokes, she felt good to do this favour for Jade who had looked after her for years. It was also a relief to get back to some serious crime. Plus, this last job might gain her a bit more travelling money; she wanted to be able to pay her way and not be reliant on anyone. Feiron was an old friend, but Phil may not appreciate having a thief working in his company. She had decided recently to change her ways. *After this last job.*

Continuing west, she started following the Bridgeway, almost deserted now that it was night. The road zigzagged across the waterways, weaving in among the warehouses and various businesses of the busy port. From the southeast sector of Dockside and crossing three major islands, the path would finish up on Old Monastery Road at the palace's outer gates. But, to get to the mooring area used by the *Tearful Revenge* near Reed Island, she left the main road and turned north. Some of the connecting bridges were higher and more elaborate than others. Those spanning major waterways reached over a hundred feet in height, allowing access to the larger ships.

Leaving Dockside, Leonie crossed over at Upbridge to Diamond Island before skipping across another bridge to Long Island. From here, a small group of islets were strung together by wooden walkways known locally as 'floats' simply because they were too insignificant to be called anything else. This area was favoured by fishermen and they regularly lined up along the railings during the day.

It was along these floats, the only links between Reed and Marsh Islands, that Leonie got her best view of the mooring points Jade had mentioned. They were a fair distance from the shore, but still out of the main shipping lanes of the wide Central Canal.

Out across the water at its assigned mooring post sat the ship, its blue and white pennants flapping lazily in the evening breeze. She was not a large ship when compared to the three- and four-masted leviathans that pulled in, but looked majestic with the ornate residences of Emerald Island as a backdrop.

Leonie leant on the weather-beaten railings and began to examine the area closely to come up with a plan. Her jobs required stealth and agility and, when she could help it, allowed her to remain dry. She was not skilled in the handling of boats and was not a particularly good swimmer. The few dealings she had had with deep water almost ended with her drowning. Long ago she decided swimming in croc-infested waters wasn't conducive to her good health and long life. And salt water had disastrous effects on her fur.

While considering all these things, Leonie eyed the lone fisherman along the walkway. Idle banter might relax her mind and even get some pertinent information to use. Fishermen had little else to do except talk. Or drink.

She sauntered over. Yammering gulls flew up in a cloud, screeching and squawking before finally settling back down after she passed. Leonie spent a good deal of time with the old angler, who turned out to be a fount of knowledge about the workings of the harbour. As he spoke, she spotted some of the *Revenge's* crew heading into town in the ship's rowboat. She said goodbye to the old man and thanked him for his time with half a silver. Expedient use of the floats allowed her to shadow the crew.

At the Broken Mast, a tavern in the centre of Long Island, the crew settled in for serious drinking and wenching. A few gold coins and a brief message from Leonie to a serving girl ensured a longer and entertaining stay for them. She didn't want them on the ship during her visit. The loosening of the mooring lines of their rowboat would create another delay to their return. That simple task accomplished, she moved on to search for more information.

———

Sitting on her haunches in the shadow of a boatshed on the islet of Reed, Leonie set to work. Beside her were a pair of empty wineskins, two coils of rope and a barrel of a foul-smelling concoction. An old pearl diver swore the stuff was a deterrent to the hungriest of predators. Leonie hoped his advanced years, and the fact he still had all limbs intact, was positive proof of its claimed effectiveness.

The angler she'd spoken to earlier had given her an idea of the workings of the harbour. Shocked someone could live there and not know of these things, he took great delight in sharing his knowledge. Hearing all about currents and tides, Leonie learnt that they were somehow affected by the moons. Who was she to argue? Since the moons were so close together this time of year, the tides would be stronger and higher. In a few days, there'd be an eclipse, bringing a much larger tide, he'd added.

This corresponded with what she overheard about a festival the temples were organising. *I know one temple that won't be celebrating.*

Leonie spent quite a while along the floats and small jetties searching for this specific site. If the current did as the angler said, then from here it should carry her towards the ship.

Waiting for the tide to turn completely, she inflated the wineskins before making her move. After checking the area for activity, she carried her gear to the end of the short, rickety pier. Putting the small barrel down on its side, she worked the stopper loose with her dagger, allowing the noxious fluid to run into the water. A slick established itself along the channel. She tied one end of the rope to a pylon, making sure the knot was tight so it would not come loose when she hauled herself back, then tied the two lengths together then unravelled the coil to prevent tangling. Joining the two wineskins with a small length of cord, she placed them on the very edge of the jetty, within easy reach.

Leonie took off her outer clothing to keep her limbs free and smeared the foul-smelling stuff all over. Her nose wrinkled. "This'd better be worth it," she muttered to the night. "I'll have to bathe every day for a week!"

She tried to move as quickly as possible. If it was up to her, tonight wouldn't have been the night to do this job. Any job. The twin moons, Luminor and Luxor, were up and both were full, giving everything a silvery sheen. Hindrance to her work or not, she had to admit the twin moons were beautiful. Now that she was aware of their movements and significance in such things as tides, she couldn't recall ever seeing them so close before. In her line of work, the darker the better – a shadow among shadows.

Tying the rope end around her waist, she hesitated before lowering herself into the water. Jade had been right about her hating the water, but even hating was an improvement. A few weeks ago, Leonie utterly loathed it. Contemplating such an activity as this would have been an absurdity if not for Styx and the mental training he'd started coaching her through.

Carefully descending the ladder, Leonie avoided any splashing. The water was cold. She shivered as it wormed its way through her fur. Reaching up, she grabbed the bladders and slung them over her shoulder. After catching her breath and adapting to the cold, she descended the last few rungs. Hanging on to the ladder with one arm, the tide slowly pulled at her body.

The cold made her shiver momentarily. Placing the wineskins under her arms, she finally let go of the woodwork. Panic threatened when she realised the only thing between her and sinking to the bottom were these small bladders.

Leaving the work to the incoming tide, she paddled occasionally to keep in line with the *Revenge's* silhouette and, she hoped, within the stream of the deterrent. Halfway to the ship, something brushed against her leg. Her heart leapt to her throat; her head throbbed and her blood pulsed. *Was that a croc?*

She kicked hard. Something struck her leg again, this time wrapping around her ankle. Terror ripped through her as she tried to escape. Leonie thrashed in the water. Trying to contain her fear, she bent over to dig her claws in to remove it. Then she recognised the rough texture.

*Rope!* Convinced her beating heart could be heard across the water, she kept still and tried to slow her breathing. A light flickered in front of her. One of the guards held a lantern up high, but a moment later he lowered it and turned to his companion. No alarm was raised.

Leonie carefully untangled the line from her leg and proceeded with even more caution, noting the bladders weren't holding her as she had expected. She was sure she'd filled and plugged them earlier.

The bubbling was not something she wanted to hear. In her panic, she had pierced the bladders with her claws. Soon all she would be holding would be useless pieces of old goatskin. Putting the renewed shaking of her body down to the coldness of the water, she looked behind to gauge the distance travelled from the pier. The ship was closer.

Drifting towards the stern, she noted the current would take her to one side of the ship. The two guards on the stern and the pair on the bow left a couple more unaccounted for, assuming Jade's informant was correct.

It seemed an eternity before Leonie floated close enough to the ship. With minimal splashing she managed to get hold of the rudder. Gripping it with her foot-claws, she removed the now flaccid wineskins and began untying the rope from around her waist. It was harder than she expected. The water-soaked rope had swollen, causing the knot to tighten.

Once undone, she securely wrapped it around the rudder a few turns and proceeded to climb up the back of the ship using all claws to ensure good purchase. When she was a few feet up she paused to shake excess water from her fur before continuing. She brought the ship's plans to mind as she reached the first set of windows, which would be the captain's quarters. Leonie set to work, blinking away the occasional drop of water running into her eyes.

Selecting which window she would enter was first on the agenda. A brief look at the hinges of both windows indicated which one was used most frequently. The other had salt encrusted in the crevices. Examining the used window carefully, she worked out it was locked but not trapped. A simple latch mechanism secured it shut, so commonplace, that only a few seconds with the appropriate lock-pick opened it. Using minimum force so it wouldn't snap open she slipped her dagger carefully between the woodwork and slid the latch up.

Leonie was in the process of opening the window when the sound of dripping water reached her ears. Closely hugging the side of the ship, she tentatively looked up. One of the guards had chosen this time and place to relieve himself.

*If he wets me, I'll make him a damn eunuch!*

When the sailor finished, she silently climbed through the window and sat on the sill, wiping the seawater off her face and paws with the pathetic excuse for curtains. She surveyed the cabin. It was about five paces deep and seven wide. In the opposite wall was a door with brass hooks for coats. There was also a cupboard with shelving above. Below her, in front of the windows, was a sea chest made from exotic dark wood and bound with metal straps.

Immediately to her left was a large desk with scrolls of various sizes scattered over or stacked untidily on the shelves above. The one parchment currently open showed the delta, with all its sandbars, depths and no-go areas of the aquatic voriens.

To her right was a large bunk, complete with the occupants of the cabin, presumably the captain and his companion. Both were snoring. On the floor, between the bunk and the chest were flasks and goblets. *Maybe they're drunk.* This was turning out even better.

Leonie hopped off the sill, wary of creaking floorboards, and padded across the floor to the door to listen. She heard faint talking from the corridor beyond, the conversation of bored sailors: who did what to whom, how they did it, and how many times. That accounted for the last two of the six guards. Beside the doorjamb was a doorstop, which she put to use. *Just in case.*

Moving directly to the large sea chest, the three large locks she saw meant serious business. She unrolled her favourite fish-skin pouch – purloined from a visiting vorien merchant years ago – selected the required tool and began to work.

It was difficult at first but by the time she got to the third lock, the locks became easier to pick. Pausing now and then, she listened for any hint of alarm. There were faint scuffs of the guards above and other ship noises; groaning woodwork, ropes creaking with wind and wave action, but nothing as yet to cause concern. She would've loved to take one of the locks completely apart to examine their inner workings; however, now wasn't the time.

The chest contained clothing. Delving deeper revealed a scimitar in an ornate scabbard; a weapon she'd heard was favoured in the southern islands. There were also a couple of pouches containing a large number of foreign silver and gold coins and low-quality gems, but nothing resembling the crystal Jade described. The wealth in her paws was enough to make the average thief reasonably happy if the right contacts could be found. She didn't consider herself average but took it all the same. *'If you want to get anywhere in this world,'* Jade had said from the earliest time, *'you'll have to help yourself, especially as a half-breed.'* With nothing else of interest in the chest, no false bottoms or hidden niches, Leonie replaced everything exactly as she found it. As the lid closed, she heard a faint rattle. Turning her head and leaning closer, she opened and closed the lid. Again, the rattle came, though muffled.

Hearing a faint murmur from the bed, she tensed. Belatedly, she realised the snoring had stopped. The bulky figure of the captain moved. Leonie heard a brief whispering, followed by a definite female rebuke. The captain rolled over in a huff. He was now facing Leonie. *If he opens his eyes, he'll see me for sure.* Bracing herself for a dive through the narrow window if need be, she heard the guards outside sniggering.

"Quiet vermin or youse be swimming ashore!" the captain sleepily called out.

Silence followed.

Leonie paused. Her whiskers quivered; her arms strained at the task of holding the heavy lid half-closed. It seemed an interminable time before she heard snoring again. She waited a few heartbeats more before finally closing the lid to begin an inspection.

Concealed within the grain of the wood and the metal straps was a small compartment. Selecting another tool, she undid the screws retaining the metal binding, but not before applying spittle to the metal to prevent any squeaking. Prying open the panel revealed a long metallic box snugly fitting within the hollow. Short work with a smaller lock-pick resulted in a faint click. The inside of the box was lined with velvet and contained a small leather pouch, a necklace of surpassing beauty and something resembling a large marble. It appeared to be black glass with a myriad of small gems embedded within its surface. It was smooth, and extremely cold to touch, very much like a small block of ice she saw once at the Portside markets, only black as night.

Leonie had to marvel at the craftsmanship. This had to be the item in question. She turned to the bed briefly to check on the sleeping couple before continuing. The leather pouch held a dozen fire-gems, amber in colour, with their own internal sparkling light source, and a gold chain interlace necklace forming a web design, with various sizes of sapphires radiating from the centre surrounding the largest sapphire she'd ever seen. She slipped all the jewels into her pouch, replaced the metallic box into the hollow and reattached the bindings. She even took the time to re-lock the three locks to delay any detection of the loss.

Her pouch, now securely tied to her waist belt, contained enough riches to satisfy her immediate needs. As she was about to exit the cabin, she remembered the doorstop. Leonie retraced her steps across the floor, bent down and pulled out the stop, replacing it where she found it.

"Good night and sweet dreams," she whispered to the slumbering pair as she passed.

Continued snoring was the only response.

Ducking her head out to check the guards above weren't about to give her a warm, tingling sensation down her spine, she slipped out, securing the window.

*Slistorf!* Leonie looked down in dismay. The rope had unwound itself from the rudder and was now adrift with the current.

Staying onboard was not an option and nothing back in the cabin could be utilised to help. She didn't relish braving the dark waters of the canal, but there was nothing else for it. The rope was still close enough for her to get to, but her floundering swimming could alert the guards.

Having come to a decision, she still hesitated, hanging onto the window ledge. *Splashing could alert something far worse.* The guards were one thing; crocs were another. She couldn't see the slick of repellent any more. *Is there enough of it still on me to deter their hunger?*

Deciding to climb down to the water and paddle to the rope, the scream from inside the cabin inspired a hasty change of plan. *The whore must've woken.* "Flaming Slistorf's balls!" Leonie cursed under her breath leaping into the night. Her accuracy, if not grace, brought her to the trailing edge of the rope. Gripping it with all her strength, she coughed salty water, all the while quelling the panic.

Swearing and yelling from the ship was a sure sign she'd been heard. Leonie didn't dare look back for fear of losing her resolve. Going against the flow, she started the long haul back to the jetty. The water splashed her face and trickled into her eyes, making her blink. The water also seemed choppier than earlier. *Wonder if that means there's a storm brewing?* She looked at the dark sky. A splash behind her made her cringe. *Daggers? Arrows?* She doubled her efforts to pull herself out of range, kicking her legs since stealth wasn't a requirement anymore.

Within a few moments the splashing was farther behind. With a sense of relief, Leonie decided the time was right to look over her shoulder. There were five guards on the rear of the ship. By the lantern light in the cabin, she could see a couple more figures with their heads out of the window.

*The good captain and his bed partner, no doubt.* "Ha." She allowed herself a smile. Not the best of exits, but under the circumstances, she had what she came after and got away with it.

A jerk of the rope swamped her momentarily, causing her to gag on salt water again. When she surfaced spluttering, she saw a group of men on the jetty. From the glinting of mail by the moonlight, she took them for guards from the local precinct. Two were pulling in her rope; the others were armed with short swords and spears, waiting.

*Maybe,* she decided, *this wasn't such a good plan.*

Her mind raced. Panic almost consumed her. The blackness of despair roamed the edges of her consciousness, threatening to rise like the swell of a spring tide. She cursed herself. *Concentrate.* Everything her mind focused on seemed to have some watery analogy. Her options were clearly; hang on and be captured, locked up in a filthy prison; or escape – meaning, let go and rely on instincts, luck and the tide.

"A fireball would be handy right now," she muttered. With a big breath, she released her end. *Instincts and luck beat being captured by guards anytime.* The incoming tide caught hold, gradually sweeping her back towards the ship. Lying face up, she tried desperately to stay calm and slowed her breathing. She tried to block out all other distractions, but every splash sent her imagination reeling.

She briefly contemplated the idea of going underwater as she drifted within range of the *Tearful Revenge*. A keen-eyed sailor called out, spotting her. *So much for luck.* She heard a loud splash close by and hoped that if it were arrows, their poor eyesight would be enough to save her. Leonie tensed when something landed across her body.

A cheer rose from the ship.

She wiped salty water from her eyes and looked down. A thin rope trailed from the ship to her right. They pulled, dragging it across her ribs and chest. *Surely, they're not trying to snag me with a lasso?* As she reached down to fling off the annoying line, the rope went taut as they pulled. Leonie became painfully aware of their tactics.

*Grappling hook!* A barbed point had caught her in the ribs. As they pulled again, she rolled in the same direction. Swift reflexes prevented the hook piercing her body, but pain still coursed along her side. Her twisting hadn't been enough. The hook tore her fur and skin but snagged on her belt. All tonight's troubles would be for nothing if she lost the pouch. She struggled to release the hook. Undoing the belt would have been easier but the risk of losing the pouch was too high. She choked on seawater again as she grew weary with the effort, not to mention her mental fatigue in staving off the panic. Her situation rapidly deteriorated.

The guards on the pier would have treated her like a common thief. These sailors would be less forgiving. She hated so much to fail and, while she still had breath, resolved within herself that these men would not best her. At all cost, she must not lose the pouch.

Unable to paddle towards the shore, she was slowly hauled closer to the ship. She tried to rest and conserve her waning energy, waiting for a chance to turn the tables. Too soon, the ship's bulk loomed over her, the curve of the hull partially obscuring the crew.

Expecting to be dragged out of the water like a fish, she hung onto the rope grimly.

But they paused. She looked up uncertainly. They were pointing and laughing. Pointing at something else. *Something else in the water!*

*Not me?* A chill coursed up her spine. Her hackles rose. The very fibre of her body screamed out. *CROC!* With a surge of energy, she climbed the rope.

The guards laughed. They released the slack, dumping her.

Another fit of coughing and spluttering assailed her as she went under.

"Now!" one of the guards yelled as a sudden splashing started nearby.

Feeling as if her arms were being pulled out of their sockets, Leonie was tugged out of the water. A gaping maw full of teeth erupted from the dark waters, snapping shut as the huge, scaled bulk flashed past.

The water drowned the sound of their laughter as she was once again unceremoniously dumped back in. Leonie had learnt finally to shut her mouth, but her body and mind couldn't take any more. When she surfaced, a scream ripped from her lungs.

This sent the guards chortling loudly.

*These bastards deserve to die!* All she could think about was getting even. Her mind raced. Leonie frantically scanned the water around her. *Where is it? How soon before the croc turns? How soon will it take to get back?* She had to survive. She wanted to live and wasn't going to give them the satisfaction of screaming again.

With the last dunking, her belt had now become free of the hook. The rope was slack. An impossible idea came into her head. It was so ridiculous it didn't even bear thinking about. No planning. No time, just doing. Her luck had failed her, now it was instinct's turn.

Glancing up for an instant to see where the guards were looking, Leonie saw one of the sailors pointing. Quickly pulling in the slack, she paddled closer to the ship and climbed, digging her claws into the wood, ignoring the cuts from the barnacles. There would be only seconds left and she needed to time this precisely or lose a limb.

It all came down to timing.

She spotted movement. Moments before she heard the sailor call out again, she tossed the hook at the croc. Its reaction was blinding as wild reflexes took over. Jaws snapped open and shut on the hook just as the sailors heaved.

They were expecting Leonie's slight weight, not the bulk of this massive creature. Leonie clung on as the turbulence from the thrashing creature threatened to dislodge her from the algae-covered hull.

Screams were cut off by two quick splashes. A heartbeat of shocked silence followed. Two of the crew had been pulled off-balance and were now thrashing in terror.

*Men could scream as loud,* she thought sadly.

Within moments, more lines were thrown down. One sailor was a few feet from the nearest line. As he reached it, the waters rose around him. There was a terrible frothing, which quickly turned darker in the moonlight. When the water subsided, he was gone.

Calling encouragement, the guards redoubled their efforts to saving their remaining comrade. They dropped other stuff over the side, nets for him to climb, or objects to either keep him afloat or distract the croc. He latched onto a rope and the crew immediately started hauling him in.

Looking over her shoulder, Leonie saw him. His face was pale with shock, his eyes looked sunken and his lips were a dark hue. *He can't be much older than me.* Knowing exactly what was going through his head this instant, she couldn't bring herself to hate him; a flash of conscience and regret.

Their eyes locked. No curses now. No abuse, only a mute stare as he was pulled higher. Leonie wondered if he could see her at all, as he seemed so petrified with fear. She still had to contemplate what her next move would be. Her situation had not greatly improved. If she climbed up, having been responsible for the death of a crewmate, no quarter would be shown by the remainder of the crew. She would have more chance of survival in the water than on deck.

The water erupted again very close to her position.

Leonie gripped the hull tighter, recalling the old pearl diver mentioning a time when he'd seen a croc leap out of the water. She wouldn't have believed it was possible; that something so huge could do it. Now she believed.

She wished she'd remained ignorant.

Jaws closed around the sailor's waist, and he too disappeared into the foaming water, his gurgling shriek cut off as he was dragged below.

Knocked off her precarious hold by the deluge of water, Leonie found herself flailing around in terror. Her mind screamed, telling her to keep still; that her splashing would only indicate her presence. With great resolve, she willed herself to keep still. Her frantic movements quelled, but not her dread.

Her eyes were wide. A primordial sound escaped her clenched teeth. For the first time she could recall, she was in mortal fear, awaiting the inevitable. Nothing more could be done. When she had the presence of mind to look around, the ship was much farther away, the waters much calmer.

Leonie awkwardly turned circles, barely able to keep her head above water while scanning the water around her, wondering when the croc would come. Floating nearby was one of the many items the crew had thrown to help the unfortunate shipmates.

She wrapped her arms around the empty barrel, clasping it to her like the most valuable treasure. Tears of relief mixed with the seawater dripping into her eyes. She found it difficult to keep her eyes open. The water, the cold, sapped her energy. As the current slowly dragged at her, she waited for some sign of the crocodile. Maybe the repellent worked after all.

.  .  .

Not knowing how long she'd been in the water Leonie gradually became aware of her surroundings. She couldn't remember when she had closed her eyes. The *Tearful Revenge*, now lit up with more lanterns, was quite a distance away but no movement could be seen on deck.

The distant jetty where she started tonight's little foray was now abandoned. *Are the guards still looking for me along the shore? Or do they too consider me a corpse?* Right now, that wasn't her concern. Her body was numb from the cold water, fatigue and shock.

She heard soft lapping. Turning, she saw it came from wavelets hitting a nearby float. The first real hope of survival gave her strength and she risked the splashing to reach it. The rough planks of the float were less than a foot above the water level, but it took every ounce of energy to drag herself out of the water to lie gasping on the weathered wood. Even the threat of the guards finding her couldn't motivate her to move at this point. She had survived almost certain death several times tonight and the prospect of lodgings in the local cells would be luxury in comparison.

*What am I thinking?* She berated herself for such thoughts. Maybe she was going mad. With little care for dignity, she crawled off the float until the shadows of a small boatshed obscured her presence. She needed time to determine where she was.

Leonie was surprised at how little the moons had moved. Checking her belt, she was amazed to find the pouch still tied securely, though torn. She sighed with relief, seeing the orb and the gems were still there. All she had on were her leggings and a tight-fitting undershirt, now torn and bloodied. Heading back to the pier to collect her clothes wasn't an option. Only when her teeth began chattering and she shivered did she realise how chilled she'd become. In an effort to get warm, she moved, looking for something to dry herself. Some items of washing left out overnight on a balcony served her purpose, though it was a struggle to get up there. She dropped them over the railing before climbing down. Once on the ground, she donned the oversized shirt and baggy leggings, tucked her tail down a leg, and moved on, wrapping the old cloak around her to retain some warmth.

Always mindful of the obelisks dotting the city and their link back to the Watchers in the palace, she had to take a circuitous route back to Jade's office. She encountered two patrols as they crossed paths. The guards stopped to talk and take swigs from a shared wineskin. Leonie stayed well-hidden between stacks of barrels beside a warehouse until they moved on. There was a brief mention of tonight's theft and search, but little else was useful.

Testament to her weariness, she dozed. Awaking with a start in utter confusion, it took a few minutes for her wits to return. The moons had moved quite a bit and a hint of dawn kissed the horizon. While she cursed herself, she had to admit she felt much better, though her side had stiffened. Now that the area was much quieter it was time to get back to her old stamping ground, the Web. Movement would cause pain, but pain meant life, and she needed to get the blood circulating.

**3**

———

# CAPTURED

Leonie sank deeper into the shadows as another patrol approached. This was the third lot tonight, making Leonie think they were still looking for her. It was not going to be easy. Fortunately, clouds rolled in and she was far more relaxed than before when she had to cross the open spaces of the footbridges.

Almost home. The Web, the name given to the backstreets of Dockside, was where she'd spent all of her life since her mother's death. It didn't look like much, but when it was all you had, you learnt to appreciate it.

Only when the patrol's banter faded did she continue to navigate through the waterfront area. Another shadow among many, she paused occasionally to listen for approaching patrols. She heard a muffled scream from an alleyway ahead.

Leonie considered ignoring it; she was in no condition to get into more trouble. It didn't pay to be too curious around these parts, but it was in her nature. She wouldn't be in the position she was in today if she ignored everything seen or heard. *It's on your way,* she convinced herself. *Just a quick look.* She crept to the corner of the building for a better view.

About ten paces away two men were assaulting a young girl, her clothing mostly ripped. The girl struggled frantically, but when she screamed again, the man undoing his belt struck her, knocking her head back.

"Hold her, Lews!" he hissed fiercely at the man standing behind her.

The scene brought to mind the trauma of her childhood. Circumstances would have been much different if it wasn't for Jade's help, but Jade wasn't here now. *Tonight, it's up to me.*

Overwhelming rage took hold. With fury in her every movement, she silently sped forwards, wondering how best to deal with them. Claw marks would bring too much attention on every rrell in the city. She glanced at the detritus scattered around her. Spying the leg of a broken bar stool, she scooped it up without breaking stride.

Lews, holding the girl's arms, looked around. As he spun he tried to shout a warning but failed when the right side of his face met the length of wood with force. The other attacker reeled back in surprise at seeing Lews topple sideways. He staggered back while reaching for his sword. Tripping over the uneven ground, his cry cut short when his head hit the flagstones with a wet smack. The sword clattered loudly on the cobblestones.

The insignia of Zander's Royal Guard glinted in a stray shaft of moonlight on the dead man's tunic.

"Slistorf!" she hissed. "That's all I need." She was relieved he hadn't had the time to drop his pants.

The young girl swayed on her feet. Leonie barely caught her and lowered her to the ground.

When she was able to sit up, she saw the bodies of the guards. Tears ran down her face.

Gently placing a paw on the girl's shoulder, Leonie tried to comfort her; asking her name and where she was from, to no avail. Looking at the state of the girl, Leonie was glad she intervened, almost ashamed at her earlier hesitation.

"Sussah," the girl mumbled between her sobs.

"Leonie." As Leonie nodded to Sussah, she heard the faint sound of boots and saw the bobbing light of a lantern coming up the lane.

"There's a patrol heading our way." She glanced at the figures lying at their feet. "This could be difficult to explain. Hurry!"

Sussah's eyes remained unfocused. With little sense of urgency in her actions, the girl slowly pulled the ruined clothing up over her shoulders. It was torn open at the front. Leonie used her belt in an attempt to tie it closed, leaving nothing to secure her pouch to. *I'll have to carry it.* By this stage it became obvious both wouldn't escape the patrol.

The young girl was in a stupor or dazed by the punch. Grabbing her by the arm, Leonie pulled her to a shadowed area between a heap of refuse and the wall. When Leonie tried to get her to lie down Sussah began to struggle.

"Listen to me girl!" she hissed. "I'm trying to help you. Look at yourself!"

The thin, damp dress clung to Sussah's comely figure, leaving little to the imagination.

"Do you think these guards will treat you any differently from the first two if they see you like this? Or do you like whoring in alleys?"

Leonie's cheek stung as the young girl's hand whipped up and slapped her. "Good! That's better." Leonie rubbed her face. "Glad to know you're still with me. Sorry I said it. Now, lie down here. I'll hide you under some rubbish and lead them off. When they're gone, get home as quickly as you can. Okay? Here, take this." She handed her the old cloak.

Sussah nodded. "Why are you doing this?" she mumbled from under the trash.

Leonie hesitated before replying. "Because I could. Because no one else would." Glancing over her shoulder, she could see the approaching guards clearly. At the same time, one of them set up a cry of alarm, alerting the others of her presence.

"Slistorf's Balls!" Leonie hissed. "One of them must be a rrell to see so clearly. Keep absolutely quiet and still." She grabbed her pouch and bolted. With a rrell in pursuit, she was going to have to work hard to escape. But true to her words, she slowed down to hurl abuse, thereby ensuring all the guards were after her. She ran down the lane.

After a few minutes, Leonie cast a look behind her. They were now well away from where Sussah was hiding, but the rrell was faster and had closed the distance.

*That bastard's going to be a real pain.* She increased her pace. It had been a long night and considering the ordeals she'd experienced these last weeks, she was tiring quickly. Ahead was an area she knew like the back of her paw. If she got that far with enough of a lead, it would be easy to lose them. Just in case, she considered a back-up plan.

Dodging trash, she fumbled at the drawstrings of the pouch and managed to extract the black orb that was the focus of the night's activities. Leonie snapped the fine chain and popped the orb in her mouth. Her mouth was dry as she tried to swallow. She nearly choked at the size of it but managed to get it down only because of its smoothness.

Racing around a corner, she put on a burst of speed. The next corner led to a warren of warehouses and alleys where she'd be safe. If need be she'd drop the pouch in plain sight of the pursuers. With luck, they'd be more interested in lining their pockets than chasing her. She could always get more gems.

Halfway down the street she started labouring. Her breath came in ragged gasps. She kept pushing, concentrating on the next corner and putting one paw in front of the other.

*A little bit further*, she told herself. *Turn left, then we'll see how good that cat really is—*

She screamed in agony as a crossbow bolt embedded itself into her thigh. She stumbled, crashing into the wall of the warehouse. She dropped the pouch when she flung her arms out to keep from falling, her claws raking the wood. Determined to escape, she turned her mind back to the girl trying to block the pain.

*Hoping that this was worth the effort.*

Step.

*Did Sussah get away?*

Step. Paw on the corner.

THUD.

A bolt protruded from the wall where her head had been seconds before. Close enough for her whiskers to brush along its shaft.

"Next one'll split your whiskers, bitch!" a young voice breathed heavily behind her.

Leonie stopped edging along the wall, very slowly turning around to face her attacker.

The rrell guard approached, his tail twitching as he reloaded. The crossbow glowed faintly. Leonie knew there was no way out of this. Other guards caught up, lungs rasping, leaving little swirls of fog in the cool air. The rrell guard was breathing hard also, but his crossbow didn't waver.

Soon there were four of them gathered around in an arc with their bows out. Their leader finally caught up to them, his chest heaving with the exertion. It was obvious from his sway he was intoxicated.

"Well done, Phellicks," he said. "Pin the murderin' scum t' the wall," he ordered. "Then we can see 'ow many ways we can skin a cat. The rats can 'av wha's left."

The young rrell altered his aim casually and fired without hesitation.

Leonie's right paw slammed back, pinned to the wall. A dark metal shaft protruded from her palm. Her scream cut through the night.

"Bastard!" she hissed through the pain. She locked her knees so she wouldn't collapse. *Not in front of this lot.* The agony was almost unbearable, threatening to engulf her in darkness.

Some of the guards shifted uncomfortably, but Phellicks casually reloaded.

"Don't insult true-bloods. She is half-breed trash," he said.

Leonie glared at him venomously.

"Hah. Still got a spark in 'er," the leader barked, slapping the young rrell on the shoulder causing his crossbow to misfire and splinter the wall beside Leonie's left arm. "Come on Phellicks."

He waved his sword towards her. "I don't wan 'er ta give me a back-scratch. Get tha' other paw pinned down."

The sound of approaching horses reached her ears.

The guards turned as one.

"WHAT'S GOING ON HERE?" A voice boomed from down the street. "And put that sword away you fool," it added. "You'll hurt yourself."

There was only one voice like that in the city. A voice every member of the Royal Guard knew and feared. Captain Levan Macreedy and a small troop of his horsemen made their way along the cobbled lane.

"Cap'n," the slovenly leader croaked, trying to sheath his sword and salute at the same time. "I didn't know you was around."

The captain ignored him and rode through a gap between the guards. The gap widened quickly at the sound of gnashing teeth. His war-horse had the reputation for biting anything it could reach and enjoying it.

The remainder of the mounted troops waited patiently behind him.

Levan looked at the now slumped figure of the female half-rrell surrounded by the spilt gemstones and coins. "Get that woman down!" he ordered two of the nervous guards. They jumped to obey, more so to get away from the temperamental war-horse's teeth. While one took Leonie's weight, the other carefully worked the bolt out of the wall and her paw.

"It's a bit early for target practice, is it not corporal?" Levan addressed the rrell guardsman. "I'm well aware of your background, boy." He leant low in the saddle. "Don't think for a moment your mother's influence will have any effect on how I treat you. That would be your second mistake this morning." Then added in a soft, ominous tone. "Do I make myself clear?"

Even the war-horse seemed to be regarding the young rrell, awaiting a reply.

"Yes, Captain."

The patrol leader, in an attempt to regain some control of the situation, brought himself up to his full height and tried to explain. "We was patrolling the south-east sector of Dockside when we heard a scream. As we went t' investigate, we seen that female half-breed run off. It was then that we come across the bodies of Lews and Oren. With the help of Phellicks' night-vision, we was able to stop the murdering wench from escaping lawful custody. Sir," he added belatedly.

"That's astounding, Sergeant Regor." A semblance of a smile cracked the captain's stern visage. "You actually managed to say all that without slurring."

The sergeant quickly wiped the smile off his face. Before he could respond, his captain continued. "We also rode past the area in question, and can you guess what we found? We found a waif in a ripped and bloodied dress wandering about. She was terrified to see us but managed to tell us two guards attacked her. This woman here," he said pointing to Leonie, now being lowered to the ground, "had apparently saved her from being raped. Considering Oren's state of dress – or undress – I tend to believe her. Lews is unconscious; not dead. You'd know that if you weren't a drunken disgrace. I'll be requiring a full report from you by first light, Regor, to explain your and your men's actions before I decide on the matter. For now, take her into custody for suspected theft, and see to her injuries. However, be aware that I've noted her current wounds. Pray to your deity there are no more."

He then turned his icy-blue eyes back to Phellicks and contin-ued. "I would very strongly suggest you keep your well-known abhorrence for half-breeds in check." His voice dropped to a low rumble. "There have been a number of strange mutilations recently. If I find that you've had anything to do with them, I'll personally make the remainder of your life a living hell." He turned his mount, ordering one of his men to gather the scat-tered gems for evidence. The mounted troops methodically turned as their leader rode past them. The trooper collecting the pouch quickly caught up.

Phellicks sauntered over to the slumped figure and bent over her. "Well men, I suppose we should do what the good captain says."

"Wot you doing now, cat?" Regor asked, watching the rrell.

"Collecting my property." Phellicks turned with the remaining bolt in his paws, glistening red in the moonlight.

## 4

# THE TROUBLE WITH BARDS

Niaarin Grigorid, Second Mage of Delta, was not happy. For the past four weeks her sleep had been broken by visions of a strange landscape. The scene was the same as that damn tapestry in her rooms. Lord Zander gave it to her when she had become a member of the palace retinue. "A reward for your rapid rise in the Arts", her mentor, Kormal, had said when she received it.

"More than likely he couldn't stand it. Too much of a reminder of the disgraced Lord Brendon," she muttered to herself. Woken by another headache, she lay there breathing slowly to begin yet another session of deep meditation. The pounding in her head resolved itself into a soft, persistent knocking on the doors to her chambers.

"Yes." She grimaced, her head throbbing again at the effort to speak. "What is it?"

The ornate doors opened. The chamberlain stepped into the room, seemingly unsure of himself as he dithered in the doorway briefly before moving in at her insistent wave. As the man approached, he seemed to look everywhere but at her.

The spacious room was elegantly furnished with inlaid furniture, imported rugs covered the mosaic-tiled floor. The full-length windows, silk curtains billowing in the morning breeze, opened onto a large balcony full of exotic ferns making it feel a bit more like home.

"M'lady, your breakfast is being served on the balcony as I speak, and the day's agenda awaits your perusal, as per orders."

"Orders?" she murmured in confusion. "What orders?"

"First Mage Kormal, m'lady. As Second Mage you now replace him and his tasks. For the interim, you are Lord Zander's representative in his absence. There is an unscheduled judicial hearing to attend today."

"Yes, yes. Very good, I'll be there." She waved the chamberlain away distantly.

"I shall await you in the reception, m'lady." He bowed, leaving the room quickly.

With a curse, she extracted herself from the tangle of sheets and reached for her robe. Glimpsing herself in the mirror as she stretched, she realised why the chamberlain seemed so disturbed. She'd have to sleep with clothes on next time.

———

Tipp nul Chor Tukk hurried down Sailmaker Lane towards the docks. He'd overslept and now had to contend with the busy streets of Diamond Island. A feeling of inexplicable apprehension had come over him of late, making him somewhat short-tempered, which was totally out of character. In his angst, his feathers were constantly ruffled. He hoped he wasn't coming down with swamp fever. This hustle and bustle did not help matters. Quickly stepping sideways, he managed to avoid having his feet trodden on by an oaf overburdened with goods.

"The drawbacks for avians on the ground," he nattered to himself, "is that suitable footwear cannot be found." Again, he was forced to jump to one side as filthy street children ran out of a nearby alley. When they saw him, they bobbed up and down trying to mimic his gait before dodging a cart being pulled by a di'anth, disappearing up another side street, chortling and carrying on as children do.

Close to him he heard people snigger among themselves. Only then did he become aware of the origins of their mirth. In his efforts to dodge the urchins he had stepped into the fresh droppings of the slowly departing di'anth. With deeply furrowed brows he continued on his way, shaking his foot occasionally.

"For bards I detect little respect!" he angrily clucked. Four weeks ago, he'd been sent to this city-in-a-swamp, leaving his cosy roost in the wonderful city of Reenat. Two weeks by dusty road followed by two useless weeks here trying to research bloody hroltahg prophecy. It had taken a week of bathing and preening to get the road dust out.

Hardly anyone here knew about the hroltahgs, let alone having any knowledge of their foretelling.

"These riddles are dribble!" Tipp snapped his beak in frustration. Two elderly human ladies gaped at him for a second, then hastily moved off. He noticed others glancing his way, no doubt curious as to what he was on about. Doing what any mild-mannered bard would do in this situation, Tipp made a bow to the people on the street, whirling his bright cape with a flourish.

"Just rehearsing for my next play; I hope you all have a pleasant day." Again, he strode on. Key phrases of these prophecies had been going through his head for over a month. They were always in the back of his mind, cropping up at the most inopportune times. It was sending him positively crazy. The council in Reenat had attempted to analyse as many translations as they could find. The chosen phrases appeared to be the most sensible. On this basis, they sent the bards to their assigned regions. Because of some vague references to 'heat' and 'water' in isolated phrases, he'd been sent here.

And for what? To look for some female warrior with a story of power, bad timing and moonlight. He truly had no idea where to start.

But it was his nature and duty to be diligent in his task. He attended every bar, tavern, inn, hostel and brothel – some more than once – to no avail. The woman he sought was nowhere to be found. All he seemed to have accomplished was to get hangovers and moult. He only hoped his fellow bards sent to the other localities had better luck. Too bad the current administrator had banned hroltahgs from his city-state several decades ago. Otherwise, Tipp reflected, he could have consulted one and been on his merry way back to his well-appointed nest.

Perhaps a rollo representative could be persuaded to visit? The thought moved to the back of his mind as a quick survey of his surrounds showed he was nearing his destination. Tipp was passing a herbalist's shop on the corner of Sailmaker Lane when a dark barrel of a man burst out of an alley and barged into him. Unable to use his wings effectively because of his cape the bard fell in a heap.

Tipp had had enough. He was about to unleash a torrent of abuse on this oaf when he recognised Captain Jorak, master of the vessel on which he was currently booked.

"Ah, good captain," he clucked. "Please allow me the chance to amend my stance."

"Morning bard," the ship-master cut in. "Must be off to the plaza garrison to collect some gear that were stole last night. G'day." The captain dipped his hat and quickly strode off in the direction of the Grand Plaza leaving the bird with beak agape.

Tipp managed to get to his feet with some decorum and briskly followed in the captain's wake. The long legs and rapid stride of the glins'ool closed the distance quickly.

"Sorry to hear of the loss of your gear," he chirped, taking position beside the short mariner. "I wanted to know before we go if the arrangements I asked were complete?"

"No worries 'bout it, matey," the captain replied. "Your quarters 'av been modified t' your needs." He doffed his hat to a comely lady as she passed. "That contraption tha' we's made up, is it what youse really wants?"

"Unusual as it may seem to be, for a glins'ool to travel by sea; not by air, so fair and free. These specifications have a great relation with the comfort pertaining to my high station."

"Uh-huh." The captain nodded his balding head as he eyed

some well-endowed ladies leaning out of an upper-floor window, then turned to look at the bard quizzically. "Why do you do that?"

"What did I do?" Tipp asked, confused, craning his long neck around him to see some tell-tale sign of feathers falling out, or worse.

"Why do youse speak tha' way?"

"Oh," Tipp clucked. "How absurd for a bard who is a bird, to speak in a way without rhyming the words. It is our way; my forte." He ruffled his wings. "It's in my nature to do thus – and my job description, do not fuss." The bard bowed briefly to the claps from passers-by.

Captain Jorak kept walking with a bemused look on his face. "This's going ta be a long trip," he muttered to himself.

Tipp pretended not to hear. "May I inquire as to what was taken? Was the culprit apprehended, or is his capture forsaken?"

"The thief took jewellery and stuff tha' I was to bringing for a client in Reenat – some sage or astrol'ger, and yeah, the thief were caught," he explained. "We's nearly had her ourselves. Thought a croc took her. Lost two of me crew too. I went n' tol' the city-watch. Quick-as-a-wink they tells me tha' they nabbed 'er this mornin'."

Tipp listened to all this. *And to think he comments on my speech!*

As they walked and talked, the street became far more crowded. Everyone seemed to be making towards the plaza.

As the crowd grew, Jorak moved across to speak to a dark lad in his native tongue of the southern island-nation of Ghalena. The boy replied in kind and Jorak tossed him a coin before stepping back to the bard.

"Our thief's on trial this mornin'. Word is tha' she killed a royal guard last night. No mention of me stolen gear. I say clamshit! I got to find two more crew now." He walked on using his bulk to clear a path.

Tipp followed though he didn't have the taste for this sort of venue. A bard's job was to gather information and make records of special events as they occurred. Since he was here he may as well witness and record it for future reference.

After shuffling here and there for a prime position Jorak was finally satisfied with the view. Tipp's feeling of apprehension encroached again. He gave up trying to ignore it and went with the flow. Casting his gaze over the heads of the crowd, he began to pick up details of the event and with luck get a grip on what his mind was trying to say.

The plaza was a huge expanse of paved land situated on the west side of Diamond Island, overlooking the Central Canal. On its landward perimeter were the eight main temples of the predominant religions. From here Emerald and Fleet Islands could be easily seen further to the southwest, with a few smaller islets inbetween.

The large gathering boasted a good selection of the major races inhabiting this part of the continent of Shak'aran. A few members of his species were nearby, and a talon of the shorter but fiercer warrior-caste. They contemptuously ignored him.

Tipp was much relieved, not wanting to have to resort to his powers if trouble started. A brood of the reptilian seleth was making its way around the edge of the throng, oblivious to the presence of the talon. *When they encounter each other, there'll be bother.* He was sure it had something to do with them being meat-eaters.

A pod of voriens had recently arrived, indicated by their glistening scales and puddles of water at their webbed feet. Beyond them were a couple of the shape-changing illios: a mentor and student. Tipp only noticed because the student, taking advantage of the gathering and attempting to assimilate the human form, was losing control now and then; various parts reverted to their original shapes and textures.

Scattered among the teeming throng of humans was the occasional rrell, who, despite their fur-clad bodies, enjoyed this climate.

Those damn phrases were coming back again, too.

*'A huntress with a tale … the waning of the moons together …*

*elemental conflux ... of two worlds ... at the accumulation of immense power, she will be powerless.'*

Something was there, but he couldn't grasp it yet.

The Grand Plaza was a venue for markets, festivals, and other forms of entertainment for the masses. Once in a while, when they had someone or something of interest in the city dungeons, the palace would hold a gathering such as this.

Something of note happened. Word must have been about very early, sweeping the town like swamp-gas in a summer storm. Minor trials were already under way, but from the growing anticipation of the crowd, it appeared the main event would soon be forthcoming.

Again, Tipp surveyed the area. A multi-level dais was on the western side of the plaza, theoretically equidistant from all the temples. In events such as this, the accused were brought to the first tier from the rear, up a ramp that led from the garrison dungeon. The judiciary, consisting of representatives from each temple, sat in the middle tier. The presiding judge sat at the top with the advisers. Normally this would be a member of royalty. Since the royal household was away, Tipp didn't know who was taking on this role. From here all he could see was a robed figure, possibly a feline, sitting in the judge's seat. He leant over to ask Jorak if he knew who the presiding judge was.

"A rrell mage from Ghalena," the captain spoke over the noise of the crowd. "Been 'ere a couple o' years, did well for 'erself, now is Second Mage and a priestess for the Eternix temple. Her name's Niaarin Grigorid. From a fairly powerful clan too, so I 'ear."

*'Of two worlds ...'* Two lands, *perhaps?* He thought madly. *Huntress ... Cats are predators. With a strange tale ...* "Tail, perhaps?" he muttered. *Elemental conflux at the waning of the moons together ... A lunar eclipse?*

Tipp needed more information. He looked around frantically, running through key words and phrases. It was on the tip of his beak. *Crowd-trial-water-island-boat-captain-temple-moon. Moons!* He looked up. No moons. Were they waning already?

"I ask a boon, tell me soon about the moons?" he asked the captain.

"Eh? Which one?" Jorak asked.

"Quote both," the bard chirped. "When will they appear to disappear?"

The captain looked at him in confusion.

"Is there an eclipse!" the avian chirped excitedly. He was on to something; he could feel it in his tail-feathers.

"Oh ah, well le' see. What day is it?" Jorak's muttered, furrowing his eyebrows and scratching his head in concentration. "Actually, tonight. Yeah. Strange tha' you mention it now. They be aris'n a while after sunset, but the eclipse s'posed to be around midnight. Very ominous tha'. I've a mind to delay sailin'—"

*Tonight!* The bard's mind screamed. *More.*

His mind raced. *Plaza-crowd-trial-island-river-temples. Temples? Elements! Earth, Air, Water, Fire, Time, Spirit, Life, Death.* "Each temple has a relationship with a particular element," he muttered. *Elemental conflux … Confluence? Union? Meeting?*

*Meeting place of the temples?* "Here? Not enough," he warbled to himself. A surge in the crowd interrupted his concentration. He looked around. The highlight of the trial was coming onto the dais. Tipp caught his breath, not daring to speak, appalled by what he witnessed as well as the people's reaction to it. The accused was a bedraggled rrell half-caste. Jeering and shouting erupted as soon as she appeared on the platform. She was assaulted with fruit and vegetables thrown from the crowd.

He was ashamed to be part of it.

"Flapping spinnakers!" Jorak's exclamation was barely heard in the tumult.

The woman's arms and legs were shackled, but the most degrading aspect was the collar around her neck. It was attached to two poles controlled by burly guards in the livery of the royal household. They used it to move the creature about by alternately pushing and pulling. Twice the poor wretch fell to her knees, but every time she stood back up, staring defiantly at the crowd. It became obvious by her limp that her leg was injured, as well as her paw. Even with all that, the guards were taking few chances.

Tipp's mind wandered again, striving to put various pieces of the puzzle together. *Half-caste, half-breed. Of two worlds? Rrell-cat-feline-female. Female-huntress-cat. Huntress-with-a-tail!* "Tail, idiot, not tale." Like doing a jigsaw in his head, he tried to slide the pieces of information around to make some sense. "Seek the huntress with a tail, for she will be of two worlds. Her time here will end at the waning of both moons together. Her fate and our destinies will be determined at the elemental conflux. At the accumulation of power, she shall be powerless?" *Sorcery? Power? Force?*

"Bard?"

"Erk?" Once again Tipp was dragged from his mental acrobatics, noticing a few people nearby trying to edge away.

"Ye be a mumblin'." Jorak looked at him strangely. "Ye a'right, or coming down with somethin'?"

"Yes! Irk, no! That woman, the defendant; on what will her fate be dependant?"

"Av' youse not been listenin'?"

"I may have missed a few cogent points; on that I would agree—"

"The thievin' bitch claims tha' she was helping a young girl and what happened was self-defence; tha' the other guard died by accident and no' by intent. Still nothing about stealing from me though." Jorak sounded exasperated, shaking his fist at the dais.

"The priests are deliberatin'." The ship-master continued to relate the goings-on. "It should no' be long now though. I hears the dead guard *was* a favourite to join one o' the temple's militia. It does no' bode well for 'er, but they seem ta be arguin'– Hey bard! Where're ye goin'?" he called out as Tipp started the arduous task of pushing his way towards the front.

———

"Has anyone actually investigated this case?" a balding monk inquired.

"Lemnon, I'm sure as much as can be done has been," one of the other judiciary members said.

"And this young girl that was attacked; was she questioned? The accused seems to recall a deep-voiced officer on a huge war-horse. That would surely be Captain Macreedy. Has he been spoken to about this?" He looked about at the faces of his peers.

One of the members spoke up after a pause. "It would seem there was some trouble up-river. Magus Grigorid ordered his immediate attendance. No one here has been able to speak to him yet."

"So, my point remains," Lemnon interjected, "there could be more to this than the simple slaying of a guardsman." He looked at them all in turn as he spoke. Some looked away, some didn't. "Under the circumstances, I feel the right thing – the only thing – for us to do for now would be to wait this out until it can be investigated fully."

Tirruk stood, flicking a lock of brown hair from his face in irritation. A look of disdain marred his pock-marked face. He waved a long finger at the bald Earther monk.

"It would appear to me, monk, you are excessive in your defence of this half-caste creature. She's a thief! She has no morals. Caught red-pawed," he smirked at his witticism. "And attempting to escape lawful custody and killing a guardsman in the process. Come now. Look at her. Do you honestly think this half-breed would bother to save a human girl and risk getting caught with stolen property? I think not."

Other members of the judiciary nodded in agreement at the words of the young Opsyss replacement.

"The trouble with you, young Tirruk, is there's little room for compassion in your heart."

"Your failing, Lemnon," the newest council member retorted, "is that you continue to believe I need it. Great Opsyss sustains me. Compassion is for foolish sops!"

"Gentlemen, gentlemen," Felice, the representative for the

Temple of Life, soothed. "We're not here for a theological discourse. That can be left to debate on long winter nights. We're here to decide on this poor creature's destiny." She looked down to the snarling captive, then swept her gaze over the crowd below. "If there is nothing further to add, I believe it's time to vote. Do we judge her, or do we wait for a retrial?"

After more muttering and murmuring they finally put it to the vote.

"Well then," Felice said after the count. "We have three for judgement; three for retrial and two abstainers. I'll inform Magus Grigorid we have a stalemate. She'll have to cast the deciding vote."

Felice glided to the stairs. Behind her, the priests of the various sects moved apart, congregating into their little groups. Some whispered in low tones, watching the priestess gracefully ascend to the third level. Others nervously looked over to the edge of the large crowd, where it seemed some seleths and glins'ool warriors were quarrelling.

The vorien representative for Water moved closer to Lemnon. "Looksss like the cat'ss dead," Kendallarnick muttered under his breath, the racial lisp evidence of his nervousness. "Niaarin is a devout follower of Eternix. She iss, for the time being, allied with the High Priesst of Woorin and hiss minionss in some essoteric project, or sso I've heard," he said.

Lemnon nodded, listening to the vorien while watching the robed priestess speak to the presiding judge. A nearby disturbance in the crowd distracted him. He looked down. One of the avians, a bard from the style of his dress and plumage, was attempting to make his way to the dais and trying to get their attention. *How odd*.

"Excuse me, Kendal." As he moved away, the monk signalled to the nearest guards, who allowed the bard through their ranks and escorted him to the side of the second level where they met.

The avian bowed deeply and introduced himself. "Greetings and salutations to you, brother. I'm Tipp nul Chor Tukk, there is no other. Of the Reenat Bardic Council Seventh Circle hence, you do me great honour for this impromptu audience."

"May the winds sustain you. The honour is all mine, Bard Chor Tukk. We don't get many of your order down this way. I'm Lemnon of the Earth Temple. How may I assist you?"

"I fear I'm much too late to aid the outcome of that half-rrell's fate." Tipp pointed to the chained captive. "This will seem abstract, on that I will agree, but the events that are now transpiring are foretold in prophecy." As he began to explain to the monk, Tipp glanced up at the mage and the priestess who were still conferring heatedly on the third tier.

**5**

———

# THE HUNT

WITH ANOTHER HEADACHE PENDING AND THE CROWD GETTING restless, Niaarin shifted her parasol to look over them without squinting. She must quickly come to a decision. Below her were hundreds of people; far more than her advisers anticipated. If the citizens were disappointed there'd be riots, which would not sit well with Lord Zander on his imminent return.

Several spells for crowd control came to mind but were discarded for several reasons: those damn Earther monks were always at her door complaining of her use of the power, and any compulsion wouldn't endear her to the citizens. Strangely, she wanted them to like her, or at the least respect her. Remaining popular was needed so she could maintain her status with Lord Zander.

No, she required something else to quell the mounting tension; something more suitable to their liking. Already, from the looks of it, some of the crowd were spoiling for a fight. A squad of guards were pushing through the crowd to curb an outburst on the fringe. A pack of seleth had run into a flock of glins'ool.

Her dilemma was twofold. While most of the people wanted

to see justice – others wanted blood, and she needed to feed a yearning of her own.

Since the judiciary's vote was made public by that annoying bitch Felice, condemning the creature outright was out of the question, but the wretch would die! She would make certain of that. It was the *how* that concerned her.

The vote was tied. Deprived of an outright guilty verdict, she couldn't impose the death penalty without creating an uproar among the council and the judiciary. Looking at the pathetic creature below almost made her sick. The interbreeding of her species and humans, or between any other race for that matter, was something she'd never tolerate.

A life sentence to the dungeons or a public flogging wouldn't satisfy her. What she needed was a way to rid herself of this abomination without upsetting the do-gooders plaguing her, satisfying the crowd, and appeasing her own desires.

So far her latest experiments, even with their faults, had enabled her to eradicate most of the half-breeds from the city. Only a few more to go. Lord Zander would be pleased; no more reminders of the Lady Dianah's abominations.

An onshore breeze picked up, bringing with it the cries of the gulls hovering around the stern of a fishing boat. Niaarin massaged her temples in a vain attempt to alleviate the ache. A thought gradually formed, but she waited to think it through before committing herself.

She let her eyes wander over the sparkling waters whilst contemplating.

The returning fishing vessel, with screeching scavengers in its wake, bobbed around the southern point of Emerald Island. An idea presented itself. She closed her mind to the birds wheeling and diving, to contemplate deeply her burgeoning plans.

Niaarin rose and strode purposefully to her advisers to confirm correct protocol. After a few words, she stepped forward to the edge of the upper tier. By increments, the crowd became silent as they noticed her presence. Their anticipation of judgement was palpable. The mage could feel the tension in the air. Even the participants of the melee seemed to notice a change; quickly the guards moved between them, a physical barrier to further violence.

"Good citizens of Delta," Niaarin called out across the plaza. Risking a rebuke from the Earthers, she enhanced her voice with a minor incantation. "I've been given a sign for our judgement of this accused wretch." She pointed at the manacled thief below. A few voices called out and jeered, but the mage continued. "Since we mere mortals cannot decide the correct verdict, we shall let the Gods themselves decide, as is their right." She continued louder over the rumbles from the crowd. "TONIGHT, THERE SHALL BE … A HUNT!"

The throng erupted into a roar of approval. A hunt had not been called in over a decade. Eventually, the din subsided. Pleased with the outcome, she stepped back from the dais with a wave, leaving the task of explaining the rules of the hunt to one of her advisers.

As his voice boomed overhead, the prisoner was dragged back down the ramp into darkness. Niaarin descended the stairs at the rear of the platform. A boat waited to take her back to the palace and the solitude of her chambers.

Halfway to the pier, she encountered an Earther monk. His name escaped her, but she recognised him as one of the judiciaries. He was accompanied by one of those irritating glins'ool. If she didn't let the Earther speak now, she knew she'd get little rest. Two of her escorts made to intervene, but at a gesture with her parasol, they stepped back, allowing the two men passage.

"Yes, yes. What is it now, monk?" Her tail flicked back and forth in agitation. "I've barely touched the power, so if this is another one of your lectures, you can go now."

"Ah. Good morn Magus Grigorid. I am Lemnon. It has been a while, but this isn't to do with our previous talks."

"Nor am I in the mood for social chit-chat. No offence," she said to the avian before turning back to the monk. "Can't whatever it is wait? I've work to do and a hunt to organise."

"That is precisely the matter we wish to discuss—"

"I won't call it off!" She anticipated his plea, throwing her arms in the air and indicated for the pair to be removed. Two guards stepped up to comply.

"No, no. I fear it's too late for that," Lemnon sighed. "My friend here's a bard from Reenat. He wishes to ask a boon of you; to speak to the accused."

With a word, Niaarin dismissed the guards again and looked more closely at the avian. She'd heard many stories about their abilities and how, in their way, the magic they could wield was rumoured to be as powerful as that of the mages. "For what purpose would you require this interview?" she directed the question to the avian.

Prior to this encounter, Lemnon had informed Tipp of the mage's various tolerances – or lack of – and many prejudices. He suggested the bard try to use the standard Deltan speech. "No rhymes," Lemnon had answered the bard's questioning look.

"My Lady. I am Tipp nul Chor Tukk and honoured to make your acquaintance." He bowed deeply, covertly fingering his medallion as he spoke. "This interview I seek is merely to maintain balance. As you're aware a hunt, nothing less than inspirational, hasn't been called for in over ten years. Such a fine opportunity for the creation of an epic ballad is difficult to pass but to make it more full-bodied, it would need to show at least a semblance of the other side of the story. I can assure you the completed ode would show this fine city, and you in particular as the instigator of this hunt, in a very favourable light."

Niaarin warmed to this fellow immediately. It was a childhood dream of hers to be in a bard's tale, and now it might come to fruition. While she considered the proposal, she heard her retinue murmuring their approval among themselves. She noticed Coundar, bleary-eyed and dishevelled, standing apart from the rest of the retinue shaking his head in disapproval. He had missed the judging, and therefore, his vote. No doubt why she was in this situation now.

The mage came to a decision and faced the bard. "Very well. You may speak with the prisoner, but I trust you'll not interfere.

The hunt will take place as planned. Perhaps, when this ballad is complete, I may hear it?"

"You have my word, as a member of the Bardic Council of Reenat."

She flashed him a smile in acceptance before speaking to one of the guards briefly then turned back to the two scholars. "Young Boran here will take you to the cells," she said. "If that's all gentlemen, I bid you good day."

They bowed as Niaarin, her lackeys following in her wake, made their way past. Some eyed the bard curiously. When the group left, the two scholars turned and followed the guard to the garrison.

Coundar joined with the mage on the pier when the courtiers were encouraged to continue with their own business. "Do you think that wise, mage?" he asked when they finally left.

Niaarin was about to step into her boat waiting alongside but paused on the first step glaring at him. "Do you presume to question me, priest?" she flared back, her tail snaking about her ankles.

"Actually, yes, but I tend to question everyone. It's part of my job."

"The bard can do nothing for her! The Earth monk can do less. We lose nothing by it, and it makes me look good to the people." *And to Lord Zander.*

"Do not underestimate the abilities of the bards," he growled, "or of that interfering prat—"

"And don't underestimate me!" Niaarin's ears lowered in ire. "I am not without certain arcane abilities! The bitch dies tonight by some overzealous hunter; that will be arranged shortly. I understand there's a ship's captain with a personal grudge. I'm sure he will be delighted to be the winner." She turned away and took a deep, calming breath. "Tell me, what of this human girl? Has your searching found her yet?"

"Of course. You know I can be most persuasive," he gloated. "I know of the girl's whereabouts. What about your research; is it progressing as planned?"

"Yes, I believe I have it now," she said, her attitude changing. She twirled the parasol in her paws. "It will work this time. I bet my life and reputation on it."

"Good. I hope your confidence is well-founded; I wouldn't care to be around if it backfires. When can I have a demonstration? I can even supply the subject to test it." He smiled down to her.

"Splendid." Niaarin stepped into the boat, settling on a seat in the centre. "Bring the girl up to my study about an hour before midnight. I'll have everything prepared." She signalled to the boatmen who manoeuvred the craft away from the pier.

Coundar watched the boat begin making its way across the canal. *'Tonight.'* There was a double eclipse tonight, and a sermon to commemorate the event. He had too much at stake to miss this test of Niaarin's. He would simply have to find a replacement to conduct the rituals. Coundar left the stone pier and strode across the plaza to his temple, his cloak whipping in the breeze.

He too had things to prepare.

———

Lemnon wiped his brow as he entered the garrison. He was not as fit as he used to be and the young guard had set a hard pace. Then again upon reflection, he decided he had never really been fit.

Tipp was about to follow when he met Jorak storming out of the garrison main entrance. This time the avian managed to get out of his way before getting bowled over. "Ah, Captain Jorak, about this evening's departure—"

"Sorry bardbird, 'twill 'av to wait 'til the morrow. Not all me gear were returned by that no-good thief! I intend to go hunting tonight to find it for meself!" He stomped off.

"You're travelling by ship?" Lemnon stood in the shaded doorway, fanning himself.

"'Tis a long story-song," Tipp chirped, watching the ship-master move across the plaza and confer with a young rrell guardsman. They were too far away for him to hear anything without using his arts, and the entrance to the constabulary was not the most ideal place to be eavesdropping. He turned and followed Boran down the passages that led to the cells.

They soon found themselves looking into a dark, foetid room in the bowels of the garrison. They could dimly make out the thief's figure lying on the pallet in the back corner.

Lemnon requested the guard leave the lantern behind. "So Bard Chor Tukk can scribe the details of the prisoner's ordeal," Lemnon said. "I seem to recall those were Niaarin's wishes. I'm certain she'd be most put out if we were unable to complete our task. Wouldn't you agree?"

The guard reluctantly did as bid, locking the cell door behind him.

With the aid of the flickering light, the two scholars warily approached the thief. Her left leg was straight out; the thigh bandage had been poorly done, as was the one on her paw. Both were dark with blood.

Lemnon introduced himself and Tipp, who stepped closer with a slight bow.

The bard stopped immediately when she made an ominous hiss. It was not a sound that encouraged stable bladder control. "We haven't much time, so I'll explain as I work." He slowly removed a satchel from under his cape and showed her the bandages and ointments within. "May I dress your wounds properly?"

"For what it's worth." She shrugged, watching his every move.

The monk stood close by, holding the lantern high to cast light on the wounds.

The bard squatted beside her, emptying the satchel's contents between them. He caught his breath, realising the acrid smell came from her.

Leonie saw his head turn away slightly. "Croc repellent," she said. "I didn't want to become a meal during last night's swim."

"Was it worth all that trouble and danger?" Tipp was having difficulty unbinding the sodden bandages.

"Important enough for me, yes." Leonie inserted a claw beneath a fold of the cloth bandage and shredded it effortlessly.

Tipp clucked his thanks to cover his nervous gulp and removed the filthy fabric.

"Care to tell us what transpired?" Lemnon asked.

"What's there to say? I finally ran out of luck." She grimaced as she raised her leg to allow the bird to remove the old dressing from her thigh.

"Apparently so. And?" Tipp asked.

With a shrug, Leonie related the events of the previous evening, in the detail only she could provide.

Tipp listened intently as he cleaned and dressed her wounds. When she had finished, he quickly revealed the real reason for their presence. As he explained, he automatically reverted to his bardic verse. His feathers began quivering at some subsonic signal. He was worried he had contracted some ailment before he realised she was chuckling.

She looked at his face then turned to the monk. "Is your bird-brained friend here serious or did he fall out of his tree? And why can't he speak properly?"

"It matters not a whit, whether you believe it—" the bard started but, seeing her response, took a deep breath and modified his speech. "The point is Leonie, everything prophecy has foretold – or our interpretation of it – has come to fruition, which means tonight at the height of the lunar eclipse something momentous will occur. What that will be is still unclear, but it points to you being at the centre of it all!"

"Who're you kidding?" She slowly stood up and stretched, testing the new dressing. "Tonight, the only *momentous* thing to occur is my inevitable demise. What's uncertain is when, and how many I take with me before that happens. You don't really think they're going to let me go without a surprise or two? I've made a lot of enemies lately." She counted off her accumulated foes. "Now that they know I'm still alive, I'll have the Jart'lekk after my blood; the Deathers are after my soul; the Flamers want any information about the *Seer's Codex*. Somewhere out there is a lunatic killing half-breeds. No doubt most of the Royal Guards will want to have a piece of me for the death of their friend, and the crew of that ship will want what's left!"

"All because of this one job?"

"Ha," she scoffed. "No. Most are after me because of some damn codex, and there's a rogue assassin whose grudge against me is strong enough to raise her from the dead, but I guess she can be lumped in with the Deathers."

Tipp's wings drooped. Despair replaced the hope he held for her. The two scholars looked at each other forlornly. Who were they to try to give this brave victim of such tragic circumstance false hopes?

Leonie saw the look. "Sorry to depress you, but that's the way life is around here for my kind, especially the last couple of weeks." She shrugged. "I don't care for it, but you get used to it. I for one certainly wish it were different. Your healing has turned the odds slightly in my favour." She looked from one to the other. "So then, you wanted to hear my story?"

They nodded mutely as she hobbled around the cramped cell.

"A few weeks ago, I met a rollo."

The men raised their eyebrows. She quickly related her recent travels to them.

"He told me much the same as you; how things would change because of what I'd do; that my life was in danger and anyone trying to help would be also. I even believed him; it's hard not to when a rollo's inside your head." She shrugged again. "I was in a coma most of the time. After being back here for a while it all became less real. Being in danger is sort of an occupational hazard for me."

"And it was you who brought this *Seer's Codex* to Styx?" Tipp asked. "If only I had known, a lot of this may have been avoided. I've studied several similar tomes. This shapechanger friend of yours, Feiron, do you know where he is now?"

"He's out of town and won't be back for a few days."

"Well, maybe I'll find Styx and he can unravel this mystery," Tipp offered. "I'm heading back to Reenat myself shortly."

In the brief silence that followed they heard the footsteps of the returning guard.

"Listen," she sighed. "I really appreciate your help and if I live past this night, I'll try seeking you out and we can discuss this rollo riddle. How's that sound?"

*Maybe there's hope after all.* Tipp wanted to hear more about all of this, perhaps gaining more insight into the prophecies. He made a sudden decision, undoing the clasp that held the torc to his neck. "This is attuned to me. I can sense when it's near," he explained briefly. "If you survive, I will be able to seek you out, or you can find me on the *Tearful Revenge*. I believe you're familiar with it."

"You're on a ship?" she asked incredulously.

"Why is this such a big issue?" He gave Lemnon a hurt look, as if it was the monk's fault, before continuing. "The torc has the motif for the Reenat Bardic Council. Show this to any bard and mention my name. They will endeavour to assist you in any way they can." Tipp then carefully hid it within the bandaging around her thigh.

"Can you get a message out for me?" she whispered.

"Time's up." The guard returned.

"Very good, corporal." Lemnon managed to use his bulk to block the guard's view of the cell. "A bit longer, if you please, to pack up all the inks and let the parchment dry."

The guard stepped back to wait, grumbling about priests and old men.

"Go to the Heart of Gold, a tavern in Dockside," Leonie whispered, helping Tipp put his gear into the satchel.

"I know of it, I visited the establishment last week," Tipp clucked.

"Ask the barkeeper to serve you a Widow-Maker, she'll know what to do." Leonie noticed all the small bottles and jars in his bag. "For a story-teller, you seem to have a lot of medicines."

"Well, in truth this climate doesn't suit me," he chuckled. "I never know what ailment will assail me." He replaced his pack over his shoulder. "I'll see you later maybe?"

"Believe me, I'll do what I can to be there."

The avian stepped towards the narrow doorway to leave.

"Do you happen to be carrying any purgatives?" She winced, rubbing her stomach.

Tipp turned on the threshold of the cell, careful not to knock his beak on the doorframe. "No. My bowel movements don't normally cause me too much problem. Why do you ask?"

"I ate something last night too rich for my diet."

The guard stepped past the bird and pulled the cell door closed before the bard could reply. "Sorry sirs, but I've me orders."

The two scholars called farewell again and strode briskly after the guard.

"I thought bards couldn't lie," Lemnon said to Tipp once the guard showed them out of the gloomy garrison.

They both blinked rapidly as the blazing sunlight caused their eyes to water. The scholars were soon in a park beside the Plaza, nestled between two temples. Slowly they strolled down a path, relieved by the fresh air after the foulness of the dungeon.

"Semantics is an art, which I take to heart," the bard clucked, dabbing his eyes. "Our young mage said, 'I trust you won't interfere. The hunt will take place as planned.'" He mimicked her voice exactly, then changed back to his own. "I believe she does trust me not to interfere, and the hunt will take place as planned here. There's no lie in that, as a matter of fact," he concluded.

The monk's paunch shook with his mirth. "Why not join the priesthood. Then you can really play with semantics. There are a couple of sermons—"

"If I may ask for clarity, you take a vow of chastity?"

The monk shrugged, nodding.

"And there you have it," Tipp replied. "I prefer virility, not senility. It would be a waste for me to be chaste."

"Oh well, maybe in your next life."

"We shall see what will be," Tipp chirped.

After their farewells, Lemnon headed back to his temple to organise the night's sermon, and the bard headed to the Heart of Gold. He had a prophecy to help fulfil.

6

# CITY ON THE PROWL

Leonie listened to her visitors walking away; the stomp of the guard's boots along with the shuffling of the two scholars echoed dimly through the narrow passageways. She unwrapped the torc for a better examination. It was silver, finely made and surprisingly heavy, with a faint aura of magical energy. She secured it within the folds of the bandage again and lay back on her pallet, considering what Tipp said to her, eventually dropping off into a fitful sleep.

She was rudely awoken when the guards roughly bound her limbs. They set to work clipping her claws before tossing her into a sack and then carrying her away in a sealed crate.

From the stench, she didn't want to dwell on the sack's previous use. Leonie tried to estimate what direction they took, but the guards spun and rolled her around every so often, disorienting her.

She was finally released from the crate's confines by being unceremoniously dumped onto the ground. She heard the guards leave, but the sound of their departure faded very quickly. With awkward wriggling, punctuated by stabbing pain from her injuries, she managed to free herself. She breathed in the salty, fresh air with relish and went to work on her bindings, made awkward with only one paw and clipped claws.

With all the rolling about in the sack, the thigh bandage had come loose. The amulet slipped out. When she touched it, she felt a slight stirring within her aching body. "I wonder if the old bird's right about any of this?" she mused. She placed the chain around her neck, slipping the amulet under the remnants of her shirt in case the metal reflected the moonlight, her fur covering the chain.

A quick examination of her wounds showed what she feared; they had reopened and were bleeding again. Little could be done about it now other than wrapping them as best she could with the bloodied bandages.

Carefully standing up, Leonie looked around to gauge her location. Luminor and Luxor bathed the damp foliage surrounding her. Something tickled the back of her mind when she saw them, but this wasn't the time for idle contemplation.

At first, she thought they'd dumped her in the jungles surrounding the city, but this area was too well maintained. *Maybe a park, but where?* She examined the weathered statue a short distance away. Signs of neglect were evident. It depicted three humans, one female and two males, with a faded inscription on one side.

The tolling of the city bells, the signal for the start of the hunt, shook her back to her current situation. She was tired, in pain, suffering from blood loss and couldn't afford to lose concentration. A quick survey showed no other sound or movement, only the faint lapping of waves. She crept in that direction to get her bearings.

It wasn't long before she stood on the pebbled shoreline of an island. Opposite was the Grand Plaza, bathed in moonlight. She could see scattered groups of hunters prowling the opposite shore, waving spears, swords and clubs in the air.

Leonie visualised the location of the city's islands, made easier by her recent map project. If she was right, she was on

Garden Island, which in turn joined with Eel and Emerald, with floats in between. Something wasn't quite right; the amount of time taken to get here wasn't sufficient for travelling through the city streets. It was too risky. Hunters may have spotted them and followed. It wouldn't have been too hard for them to guess what was in the crate on this night. She plainly didn't come across by boat, and she didn't hear the guard's boots stomping along the wooden planking of the floats.

"What sort of idiot do they think I am?" she muttered. "If they didn't use the bridges, and didn't use a boat, then that only leaves tunnels."

"Hello kitt'n."

Leonie whirled as a large, dark figure pushed through the foliage towards her. He uncovered the lantern he was carrying, shedding light over the area.

"Evening, captain. Out for a nightly stroll too?" Leonie recognised the *Revenge's* master. How long had he been there?

"Not quite. I want the orb, wot youse took last night."

"I see." Though his hand rested on his pommel, she noticed his scimitar was still in its scabbard. So, he wasn't out for her blood. Yet. "Under the circumstances, I'd be happy to return it, but as you can see. I've nothing on me." She lifted her arms and turned around to prove it. "What makes you think I'd have anything?"

"Them guards returned me gear, but the orb's still missin'. It be the most valuable item from last night's escapade, as you'd know."

"They took everything from me when I was captured. Perhaps they kept something for themselves?" If Leonie could sow the seed of doubt in his mind, then perhaps no one would have to get hurt. "They even took my claws," she waved her bloodied paw at him.

"And p'raps youse be lyin'."

"Look at me, man. You think after spending a night in the cells, they'd leave me with anything? I didn't have a chance to get rid of it. They took it all last night, I tell you!" She hoped he wouldn't search her, only now remembering the amulet under her tunic. It wasn't what he wanted, but he'd no doubt take it anyway. Her thoughts raced further. *If he finds that, how can I convince him I don't have the orb?* She tensed as Jorak raised his lantern to light up her body.

She saw the look of distaste cross his face. From the change in his stance, Leonie realised the fight left him; he relaxed slightly. Though tough as nails, deep down it seemed he was not a cold-blooded murderer. His hand left his sword. *He's probably as much a victim of tonight as me.*

There was a cry from across the water. Both turned to the plaza. Some sharp-eyed fellow had spotted the lantern and the two of them on the shoreline. The crowd surged towards the nearest bridge. It wouldn't be long until they had company.

Leonie took advantage of Jorak's hesitation and tried to speed things up. She had to get away very soon. "Look, I'll be lucky to live past tonight, especially with half the city out for my blood. If I were you, I'd be wondering why the guards want to get rid of me this way. They told you where I'd be, didn't they?" Her mind raced.

"Yeah, but—"

"So you'd kill me, doing their dirty work. You'll have had your revenge, would leave them alone and not ask questions. I'd hate being used like that. They probably even offered you a reward. You think they'll let you live to collect it? You're a loose end. More likely you'll become an accidental victim." She was making it up as she went along.

Jorak stared at her, his mind working. She could tell because his lips were moving.

"You're on an island with only one exit and a drunken mob clogging the floats. Does that sound like a trap to you?"

He swore to himself, turned abruptly and stomped off back through the bushes.

Leonie was surprised by his reaction but relieved at the

outcome. She was in no condition to fight anyone. She moved back to where she was initially dumped and began a determined search, scouring the area near the monument for a trapdoor of some sort. There wasn't much time left if she wanted to live.

Maybe it was the sound of boots on the bridge that motivated her, but at the same time, she spotted faint scratches in the flagstones indicating a sliding door. Her spirits lifted another notch upon discovering a simple pressure mechanism at the base of the statue hidden within the motif.

The door opened a crack. Gripping it with her good paw she struggled to lever it open. Entering by squeezing through the dark gap, Leonie managed to pull it closed. She was now inside the statue's base, at the top of a stairway leading into darkness. Hearing voices nearby, she held onto the door, thinking frantically for some way of wedging it. If anyone had seen her enter she'd be dead in a minute. As the seconds ticked by no attempt was made to open it.

While waiting for the group to leave, she took stock of her surroundings. There was enough room for her to move without having to stoop too much. Her sensitive nose picked up the recent smell of torches, confirming her suspicions the guards had come this way.

Finally, when the voices faded with distance, she let go of the door with relief. She limped down the roughly hewn stairs one painful step at a time, reaching the bottom after counting fifty. At the base was a tunnel with a solitary torch flickering pitifully. Looking in both directions for any sign of movement, she guessed left headed towards Diamond Island and back to the garrison by the plaza; the other way turned roughly south.

The tunnel ceiling curved above her head. In the centre of the floor was a channel, slimy due to the constant dampness. The walls were rough, either by bad workmanship or age, leaving lots of nooks and crannies. In some places they bulged alarmingly.

Not very encouraging. Silently, still wary of any guards lurking about, Leonie stepped away. After walking south several paces, she sensed the shadow separate from a recess in the uneven wall behind her.

"Ahh. I was hoping we'd meet one last time," a voice purred.

For the second time that night, she almost leapt out of her skin. Leonie immediately hobbled around to meet the new threat.

"YOU!" Leonie spat, recognising the voice. She considered her limited options. Fighting this guy was one she could ill afford, but she could still keep him talking until another idea presented itself. "I see you're still hiding behind your crossbow. You seem to be young for a guardsman, or do they call you guard *boy*?" There'd be no changing his mind about killing her, but if she could taunt him into a rage, he might make a mistake. "Tell me, have you reached puberty yet?"

"Cocky bitch. I'm going to enjoy your death." Phellicks grinned, showing his fangs.

"I've heard that before. Fantasise all you want, *boy*." She edged back and towards the centre for room to move, reminding herself of the slime. "So, what crazy plan did you have?"

"A simple one. A hunter is lucky enough to spot you, though being in here's a new twist. It was all supposed to happen up there. I guess we'll have to drag your corpse back up the stairs. Anyway, he finds you and manages to kill you. He's lucky enough to survive and reap the rewards. I think it'll show the people of this cesspool of a city the Gods are indeed *just*. A fitting end if I must say, and one the city-folk will see as a sure sign of your guilt. My understanding is this particular hunter is very keen to meet you. You still seem to have some of his property. He's truly vexed with you I'm afraid."

"Been there; done that. I just met him. I think he'll be wanting words with you too. Since it was obvious I had nothing on me, he now seems to think maybe some low-life guards took it."

"Poor fool. Looks like he'll be having an accident too."

They both sensed the subtle air movement at the same instant. Someone had opened the statue door. She chanced a look around the tunnel again in case she missed something she could put to use.

"You must be slipping up, bitch, letting someone spot you and the door." His tail lashed from side to side. "Looks like I'll have to tidy up your mess."

She could see he was agitated, regardless of how calm he sounded. Leonie had to think fast. *Did the captain have a change of heart?* she wondered. *Or did someone follow me?* The situation was going to get worse if there were more of them.

Her reverie lasted only a breath. "I thought this'd be a wonderful opportunity for you to finish off what you failed to do last night. Or am I too much for you to handle? I see you haven't got your audience to help you." She moved back further. "Maybe that's why they declawed me, to turn the odds in *your* favour because you're nothing but a mewling, piss-weak kitten."

"Not at all, bitch," he hissed. "Disappointed as I was with the idea of the hunt, this will be much more fun." He raised his dimly glowing crossbow. "I've plenty of bolts. This could take a while." As he brought the bow to his shoulder his body suddenly stiffened.

A dark shape launched itself from the stairway, taking Phellicks to the ground in a flying tackle. He lost his grip on the weapon. It fired when it struck the ground.

Leonie lurched to the side. Too slow!

The bolt struck her as she collapsed. She had difficulty breathing from the bolt's impact in her chest, and the pain in her leg was excruciating. Her vision dimmed as a shadow loomed over her.

"Why is it every time I send you out on a job, you nearly get yourself killed?" a familiar voice said from a few feet away. "You must be losing it."

"Jade?" Leonie croaked, realising she wasn't dead yet.

"Who were you expecting, that bird-bard?" Jade chuckled. "No way he'd come down here. In fact, I'm surprised I'm here."

"In truth, I wasn't expecting anyone," Leonie gasped. As she sat up, the bolt fell to the ground. She pulled the amulet from her shirt. It had a slight dent in its surface, but she'd have been dead if not for the torc. Leonie knew she was far from invincible; she could die like anyone else, but she always managed to stay alive. Lately, things seemed to be getting worse and when all her resources failed, some intervention stopped the fatal blow. Was it luck? Was it really part of this prophecy the bard kept on about?

"You should trust your friends more," Jade admonished.

"I will after this night. How's your leg?"

"I've found some wonderful imported herbs. It takes away all the hurt—"

A groan caused them both to look around.

"And here I was thinking the chit-chat was over." Leonie raised her good paw.

Jade helped Leonie to stand. Together they stumbled across to Phellicks; his breath rasping. Half his body lay in the channel. The water pooled around him before building up to a level where it could flow past his legs.

"Did you know him?" Jade asked.

"He's the guard who shot me last night."

"What a small world."

"Speaking of small worlds, what're you doing here?" Leonie turned to Jade.

"Your bard friend contacted me. How am I supposed to keep tight security when you go telling everyone where I am? Tipp said he spoke to you in the cells and that he could follow you through some torc. He directed me to this island. I was crossing the bridge ahead of a rowdy mob when I met that fat oaf of a captain. He tried to grab me to turn me around, saying there was no one here. He shouldn't have done that. You know how I hate being touched."

"You didn't kill him, did you?"

"No. I nicked his pouch instead when I pushed past. Anyway, I saw a bloodied sack near the base of the statue but couldn't do anything until the mob left the area. Since you didn't pass me and I knew there was no way you were going for another dip in the harbour, there had to be somewhere else for you to go. And here I am to the rescue."

"Not too bad for a human."

"Is that all the thanks I get?"

"Thanks again."

"How are you feeling?" Jade's eyes glittered in the flickering torchlight. "You should get that leg and paw seen to."

"You think so?" Leonie rolled her violet eyes. "I feel like crap."

Jade looked around at the murky water. "You're in the right place for it."

As they talked, Leonie examined Phellicks. He was still alive, a dagger buried deep in his back. He gasped when she pulled it out, wiping it on his tunic before handing it back to her friend.

"Keep it. It may come in handy and you'll need all the help you can get."

"You never know." Leonie slipped it into her belt then bent to pick the faintly glowing crossbow from the floor. It had an inscription along the side.

'*Phellicks Grigorid. May your aim be as true as your blood.*' She stared at it, stunned, muttering the words.

Phellicks's eyes fluttered open as she read it. "I knew … this was a bad … idea," he rasped.

Leonie hissed. "Your mother is Niaarin?"

The young guard nodded weakly. "Not that it counted for anything. I was just another means to her ends." He winced.

"And what would they be?"

"To rid the streets of trash, half-breeds! You. My death won't stop her, only make her more committed, as if that was possible."

"Not if I can help it." Leonie stood up. "Here, take this." She handed the crossbow to Jade. "It's no good to me. A trade for your dagger."

"Not my preferred weapon, but I'm sure to find a use for it." Jade was about to sling it over her shoulder. "Oh, before I forget." She put it down and removed her vest, revealing the harness. "Since we're exchanging gifts, I thought you'd be wanting these back." She handed over the harness and Leonie's ring.

"You think of everything."

"Someone needs to in this outfit."

Once Leonie secured the belt, she turned it on slightly to take the weight off her leg. She turned back to Phellicks. "For what it's worth I'm sorry it ended like this."

"Bitch," he gasped. "It's not finished yet."

Even on the threshold of death, his hatred poured out, like his blood. "For you it is." She shrugged and turned away.

"Not that way. Back up the stairs," Jade whispered, pointing.

"Gods and Goddesses! I want to, but I can't." Leonie's head came up at a faint noise, which quickly resolved into approaching footsteps from the garrison. The group was still out of sight, but the noise echoed in the closed space.

"Time to go," Jade whispered.

"With all the hunters around up there, and me with these wounds, I'd be dead meat before long. You'd have to save me again and I couldn't have that twice in one night. Just lead this lot away."

"And what the hell are you going to do in your condition?" Jade whispered fiercely. "You can hardly walk."

"The harness will help. I thought I'd call in on the palace and give my regards to a certain mage before Zander gets back. She's the one behind tonight and probably all the other half-breed murders. I'm still looking for some answers. I reckon I should give my condolences for her son."

Jade faced her, caught between avoiding the guards and talking her friend out of pure madness. "Are you crazy?"

"No, just extremely annoyed." Her eyes blazed. "And there's a point of honour here too."

"I've seen that look before. Let me help."

"No. You've done enough. You truly have my thanks." Leonie gave her a brief hug with her good arm. "This has become personal. Keeping them," she nodded towards the guards, "off my tail is all I ask. I'm sorry I didn't finish the job you asked. If I can get out of this alive, I'll get that orb back to you somehow."

A cry from the guards warned they had been spotted.

"I have no doubts about that." She looked over her shoulder. "Now's definitely the time for us to go. Good luck," she said, turning to the stairs.

"I've discovered luck's overrated," Leonie said. "Say hello and thanks to Tipp for me. Tell him he saved my life too, and give my love to Netoha and Ro."

"Survive and do it yourself," Jade called back as she ran up the stairs, taking the torch from the sconce and making enough noise to attract the guards.

Leonie felt a tingle in her mind. Looking around, she noticed Phellicks clutching a medallion and mumbling to himself. "You're still hanging on, aren't you." It must've been covered within his tunic, for she hadn't seen it before. It gave off a faint magical aura.

*He's communicating with someone!* The flickering circle of the guard's torchlight approached. She ducked into the dark niche Phellicks had used and held her breath.

"This'un's still breathin'," rasped one of the guards as he arrived.

"Leave 'im. We can do nothin'." His companion hurried past. "It's the other one we want, and she's getting away." Their voices receded as they quickly followed the others up the stairs, leaving the body behind.

Leonie waited until she heard the door above scrape closed. The tunnel was now dark, silent and empty. Just the way she liked it. Phellicks was silent now. Leonie bent over and relieved him of his pouch and amulet, remembering to handle it carefully lest she receive the same treatment as the last time she grabbed an amulet. She examined it briefly after wiping the blood off with a piece of his uniform. It was engraved with the symbol for the temple of Eternix, two circles lying horizontally overlaid by an hourglass. Considering it might come in handy later, she put it inside the pouch. Phellicks had no use for it now.

She slowly edged down the tunnel. If it didn't deviate too much, it should lead somewhere near the palace. "So," she muttered to herself as she crept along, "Niaarin is Phellicks's mother, and she was ridding Delta of my kind. I vowed to try to put a stop to it before, now's my chance." *Maybe my last.*

**7**

---

# APPOINTMENT WITH THE MAGE

THE SLIGHT FIGURE STIRRED, A PAINFUL MOAN PASSING HER DRY LIPS. Her head turned slowly and her eyes gradually opened. Sussah tensed. This wasn't her room. Then she remembered last night. *Was it only that short a time?* The poor cat woman that saved her was now being hunted.

She wanted to help at the trials, but her pleas to her parents fell on deaf ears. Sussah wanted to tell them all the truth about the two guards. Her parents were more concerned about the business if the guards drank elsewhere.

They argued and her father locked her in her room. She removed her ruined clothing and crawled onto her bed, cried herself to sleep. When her father woke her, she saw two female acolytes in pale blue robes standing by her door. They had some story about the judiciary wanting to question her about last night.

*Good,* she thought, still a bit dazed by it all. *I'll set things right and save Leonie from being hunted.* Quickly throwing on a long-sleeved tunic and pulling a belt tightly around her waist she followed them downstairs.

The acolytes took her away in an enclosed carriage of simple design, with a small flask of wine. Since she was still feeling a bit rebellious and elated about being able to help Leonie, she drank deeply.

Sussah found herself on a cold stone floor. She managed to sit up but felt woozy from the effort. There must have been something mixed in the flask, she realised. The small amount of wine shouldn't have affected her so. Not like this. She glanced around.

It was one of the most ornate rooms she had ever seen. The carpets on the curved walls were much nicer than floor carpets, and they had pretty pictures on them. There were lots of candles, crystals and a sweet aroma, like flowers, but very pungent. An open door to the left, framed by billowing curtains, led to what appeared to be a balcony full of plants.

The chalk marks all around the doorway had her wondering. She had learnt her letters and numbers to help her Da in the tavern, but nothing like this. The two other doors on opposite sides of the room were closed. She marvelled at the nearest one; the candlelight made it shimmer like gold.

This place wasn't the garrison; it was not military enough and much too pretty. It had the appearance of a woman's touch, especially with the incense, and was far too richly furnished for anyone she was likely to know.

"Ah, awake are we child?" a voice purred.

A pure-blood rrell glided into the room from the balcony. She was wearing a very thin and revealing pale blue silk robe. She crossed the room and placed a stick of chalk on a tray on the sideboard, wiping the white dust off her paws with a small towel. "You must have fainted with all the excitement," she said to her. "You've been through a lot recently."

"Where am I? Who are you—"

"And what are you doing here?" Niaarin finished for her. "Yes, I thought you might ask that. You know, it's very disheartening not to be recognised by one's citizens, but then you are so young," the mage replied sweetly.

"I'm sorry. I don't get around much, you see. I'm always needed in my da's inn. Are you part of the judiciary?" She only vaguely remembered the acolytes mentioning a meeting and questioning.

"I guess you could say that, yes. I'm Niaarin and I'm told you are Sussah."

"Oh?" Sussah was a bit shaken. She recognised the name. "You're the one who sentenced my friend to death?"

"Well, not to death – it was to test her true innocence. You are at the palace and we are awaiting the arrival of that half—" Niaarin quickly covered the snarl. "Your friend," she finished.

"She's alive?" the girl gasped, delighted. "And she's coming here? Then she made it past the hunters?"

"Yes, to all." The mage showed her teeth in another forced smile.

"But why's she coming here?"

"Why? The young are so inquisitive. To meet up with you of course, and I'd like to get to the bottom of this terrible event also," she lied.

"Oh good," Sussah exclaimed. *Maybe this mage wasn't as bad as everybody said.* "I've not been able to thank her properly. I wanted to go to the trial and stop all this—"

"Well, soon you'll have the chance, but until then here's some food to keep your strength up." Niaarin stepped over to the table and delicately picked at the bowl of sweetmeats. "You must be hungry after all you've been through. Please eat as much as you want."

Sussah sat on one of the comfortable chairs by the table and began experimenting with the new food, delighted at the tastes of the selection of exotic fruits.

Receiving the message about the thief surviving had surprised Niaarin. She wanted the young girl to be relaxed when the thief arrived, otherwise the trap might not work as planned. Pity about poor Phel. She fingered the medallion idly. Even though he was her son, her work prevented her from ever getting too close. It would be a shame to lose him, he showed so much promise for one so young. If he still lived, the temple could always use a pure-blood ...

She dropped heavily into one of the chairs.

Sussah looked up at the sound. "Are you alright?" she asked, food halfway to her mouth.

The mage nodded, eyes closed. "Just a bad headache, child," she forced between breaths. "It comes and goes. How's the fruit?"

"Very nice, my lady." Sussah wiped her mouth with the back of her hand as some juice ran down her chin. "Sorry if I seemed rude earlier, I was surprised and confused at being here."

Niaarin nodded again in response, cradling her head in her paws.

Sussah, having eaten enough for the time being, got up and walked around the room to look at the wonderful tapestries, finally stopping at the largest one. It dominated the room, not only with its size but also with its colour and exquisite detail. It was such a picturesque landscape of undulating plains and rugged mountains in the distance. To one side was a strange circular structure, like a huge ring.

The tapestry seemed to call to her. She felt drawn in. It was so

...

"Lovely isn't it?"

The voice behind her made her jump.

"I can't seem to get that image out of my head," Niaarin continued. "It is so mesmerising."

Hesitating, Sussah considered her words being careful not to offend her host since she had been so nice. "It's strange, but beautiful too. It makes me feel funny. Where did it come from?"

"It was here when I arrived. Personally, I suspect no one else wanted it for the very reasons you find it strange. I think these rooms belonged to Lord Bren before he left ..." Niaarin's voice drifted.

The tapestry showed the image that had been haunting Niaarin for the last few weeks, popping into her head and taking ages to leave. Recently, it had even impinged on her dreams. Maybe she had simply been working too hard on her research, but tonight her heart thumped in anticipation, tonight all the pain and sacrifice would come to fruition, and the girl and the thief would help. Two more to sacrifice ...

"Fresh air might help?" Sussah was standing at her side shaking her.

"What? Oh yes, child. Just distracted ..." Niaarin murmured in response.

"Can we go to the balcony?" Sussah suggested. "The view must be wonderful."

"Hmmm. Yes. Good idea."

They turned to go to the balcony, but at the same time, the mage felt a tingle emanating from her medallion. She tensed briefly in surprise. *She's here!*

"You go ahead, dear one." She recovered her composure quickly. "There's something I must attend to. I promise to join you very shortly. The view is best from the eastern end above the courtyard overlooking the gardens." With that, she swiftly moved to the nearest door, closing it behind her.

Sussah continued to the balcony, unaware of the gilt door opening behind her. Stepping outside into the fresh cool air, she breathed deep. Wandering towards the balcony wall, she wove her way between the many and varied ferns and pruned shrubs.

---

Leonie carefully opened the gold-panelled door and peered in, catching a glimpse of movement beyond the billowing curtains. *The whole room's glowing.* Moving fully into the room as quietly as her wounds would allow, a sudden wave of dizziness came over her, causing her to reach out for something to get her balance. When she had a semblance of control, she made her way past the ornate furnishings that Jade would be able to appreciate, mentally tallying the wealth. Her mind wandered.

She sat down on a chair looking about in confusion. Why all these chalk marks? So much crystal. She couldn't concentrate but knew Jade wouldn't like that big tapestry. It slowly dawned on her that these chairs had been designed for rrells. *At last! I'll have to steal one of these for Jade's office.*

Leonie abruptly lurched up from the chair in disbelief, knocking over a small stand of crystals. "By the Whiskers of Slistorf," she hissed softly. "Why are you sitting down?" She mentally berated herself for her wandering mind. *How could you do that? What were you thinking? Concentrate!* She limped across the room, shaking her head in a vain attempt to clear the fog. The sooner she got this deed over and done with, the sooner she could go home for some well-deserved rest. *I reckon this whole room's a trap.*

Hesitating by the door where she had last seen movement, Leonie took time to catch her breath and to consider, again, what she was about to do. *What lovely curtains …*

She hadn't been up against a mage before and, by all accounts, this one was reputed to be quite powerful and canny. If she didn't end this now, she doubted anyone else would. More lives – more friends – would be needlessly lost. It had to be done, and she had to do it.

Thus, mentally fortified with the *rightness* of her actions, she stepped outside onto the balcony in search of her prey. The crystals out here were arrayed in pretty patterns. Her vision blurred momentarily and she almost stumbled on the step, catching herself before she fell completely in a heap. *Idiot!* She mentally kicked herself for being so clumsy.

In her fatigued state, it took a moment to register something didn't appear right. Everything seemed to be going dimmer. She thought at first, she was about to faint. Leonie looked about. Her gaze was drawn up to the moons and something the bard said earlier came to mind.

Eclipse.

One of the moons was passing across the face of its companion, yet even as she watched, it too was being darkened by yet another shadow. The whole city was slowly going dark! As astounding as this sight was, Leonie tried to drag her befuddled mind back to the task at hand.

*Maybe the loony bard isn't so loony after all.*

---

Astride her flying l'ith, Evlin wheeled and dived above the darkening city, trying to locate her Enemy. The remains of her singed hair fluttered behind, lashed by the wind as they picked up speed. Finally, she felt the tug of the Enemy's presence. It was definitely coming from the palace. All evening she'd been searching, but her ability seemed to have waned recently, and she couldn't fathom what would make it happen. With luck tonight, she'd finally deal the deathblow she'd been so longing for; to avenge the death of her Jart'lekk brothers, to get revenge for her own death, but mainly because it would please her new master.

The last time they met, the Enemy used trickery and magic to thwart her; Evlin wandered lost along the harbour seabed before she found access to dry land. Her life-force was waning, and dawn was threatening with the crimson ribbon along the horizon. Her rage was partially sated when she plunged her dagger into a couple as they slept soundly, tucked up in their beds.

All her efforts for nothing!

Before her full strength returned, along with her seeker talent, she was yet again whisked away to the realm of the dead. Her master's last words were driven into her dark mind like a spike in a crucifix. *Enjoy the rest of your pathetic existence in purgatory – this is your reward for utter failure.*

It had been a surprise when Tirruk approached her. She had no concept of time here. "Lothas has ascended to Our Lord's side," he had said. "I'm your new master and will take on the task he has already set. Go forth on your beast and do Our Lord's bidding."

# 8

# A LAND TOO FAR

THE BALCONY WAS FULL OF EXOTIC PLANTS, MAKING IT DIFFICULT FOR Leonie to spot her target through the foliage. After a brief search, she saw a single figure obscured by large ferns. Leonie rubbed at her eyes in frustration. "Why is everything getting blurry?" she muttered. She hobbled as close as she dared, keeping the plants between them at all times and hoping the mage hadn't set any traps. She'd have enough strength for only one attempt at this and needed to make it count. Extending her ruined claws, Leonie adjusted her stance and bunched her muscles as best she could, blocking out the pain in her thigh. *This isn't going to be pretty.*

Leonie heard noises behind her. A door opening. Footsteps getting closer. Maybe there were guards here after all! She decided the time was now or never. She sprang out to wreak vengeance on her kin's murderer.

At the last possible moment, the figure by the wall turned into Sussah! With no way of stopping her momentum, the confused thief slammed into the startled girl, knocking her over the parapet to fall to the courtyard below.

Lightning reflexes took over. Leonie stretched out and snagged the girl's clothing as she fell from view. The weight dragged the thief into the wall, smashing her already bloody thigh and making a good effort to rip out her foot-claws.

Both screamed; one in agony, the other in sheer terror.

Inching around to try and get a better purchase on the smooth, tiled floor Leonie noticed glyphs and runes drawn around the immediate area, all in chalk.

*More glyphs? Just like inside.*

Sussah's clothing began to rip with her weight.

As the screams subsided, Leonie heard low chuckling behind her. She froze in disbelief.

"Oh bravo, mage. This is a splendid show," Coundar remarked maliciously, raising his wineglass in salute. The pair were standing by the billowing curtains.

"Thank you for the compliment, priest." She made a curtsy. "I couldn't have planned it better myself. However, as much as I'm enjoying this amusement, I don't think the girl's dress will last much longer."

"What do I care about her rags?" he asked.

Niaarin pointed to the struggling Leonie. "If the girl falls, that abomination will be free to attack me. It's dangerous to be disturbed mid-spell. And," she added as an afterthought, "there'd be such a mess in the courtyard below. Lord Zander's due back tomorrow. It could be difficult to explain."

"Then allow me to move aside as you begin." He bowed mockingly, almost spilling his wine in the process. "Rest assured I shall fend off the foul creature if she so much as snarls at you."

Niaarin took a deep breath and started a low chant.

Coundar stepped back and sipped his wine, smiling at the thought of what was about to happen, and if the spell was successful, how he could reap the most benefit out of it. Now he knew where the mage's notes were kept, he could finish off this upstart magician once and for all. Having been so preoccupied in hiding this research from her superiors, she had come to him for assistance instead. The young mage was ambitious, but also too gullible for her own good if she believed that his help was for the furthering of her career. His help came with a price, but not the price she had negotiated. The Woorin High Priest had a different contract in mind.

Smiling again in anticipation, he watched the proceedings. With wine glass halfway to his lips, something about the thief caught his attention but he could not be sure what it was. He looked at her more carefully as she vainly struggled to keep her friend safe. From his limited experiences with these half-breeds, he guessed she was slightly better developed. Jet black, perfect proportions, and more human than the others.

A memory edged his thoughts, about a troublesome half-rrell to the north that killed some of his men. The same one in White Cliffs! She wasn't killed in the Opsyss temple attack? Coundar dropped his forgotten wine. "Great Woorin. NO!" he cried, taking an involuntary step forward. His sandalled feet crushed glass fragments. Could this be the one they had been looking for all this time? He tried to distract the mage, but her eyes were closed and she was already far into her trance. Coundar prayed it wasn't too late and moved closer. He had to question the thief and find out what she knew of the *Seer's Codex*.

Already a dull, pearly glow surrounded the creature and the girl below. If the spell failed, as it had many times before, the thief would more than likely die, taking any information with her, and then she'd be in the realm of the Deathers! They'd learn the secrets of the codex instead.

He couldn't let that happen. Intending to pull her out of the glowing sphere, the High Priest recited a protection chant while he reached in. He felt a strange sensation – an icy tingling along his arms and neck. Time seemed to slow as his hand closed firmly on the thief's shoulder.


"What's happening up there?" Sussah shrieked. The air glowed around her.

"I don't think Niaarin's going to let you fall."

"She's going to help?"

"Not exactly. Climb up!"

"I'll try."

"Just do it!"

Sussah tried to wriggle around to get a grip on the balcony but her dress ripped every time she moved.

"I can't reach," she wailed. "THINK OF SOMETHING!"

"Is there anything you can grab onto?"

"No!"

"Take my arm." Leonie looked about for anything that might aid them. This was playing havoc with her injuries. The harness was jammed against the parapet; she couldn't reach it with her damaged paw even if she tried. She recalled seeing some vines on a trellis from her earlier trip. "Look below you. Can you see vines?"

"They're behind me," she croaked after a brief pause.

Niaarin's chanting got louder, but a new sound made its presence felt, drowning out the mage.

"What's that noise?"

"Nothing good." Leonie braced herself and tried to pull the girl up. It was hopeless. Her mind raged. *It must not end like this!* "I'll try to swing you over." Leonie began shifting her weight slightly to get momentum. Pain lanced through her.

"No! Stop! I'm going to fall."

"One way or the other," Leonie gasped under her breath as she continued.

Something took hold of her shoulder and pulled, causing her grip on Sussah to weaken. Leonie turned and hissed, surprised at the sight of the manic High Priest. She didn't know what he was up to but was sure it wasn't to her benefit. She couldn't use her arms to defend herself, so her jaws were the only option left. Lunging forward she sank her teeth into his forearm. His grip was tenacious; he still refused to let go. The gleam in his eyes told her he was infused with power and it would take more than a bite or two to escape him.

•   •   •

Deep in concentration, Niaarin witnessed the matrix form within her mind. The translocation spell she'd been researching so diligently finally began to take effect; her goddess, Eternix, would surely be pleased. So familiar was she with the spell formula, she was able to modify it on the spot to take into account the extra mass of both Sussah and the thief.

Deep into the spell, her headache forgotten, all daily worries paled into insignificance. She was one with the power. It coursed through her veins making every nerve sing and tingle.

The matrix was now complete. Niaarin envisioned its transference to the chosen location, along with its contents. This was the crucial instant where the translocation of the subjects within the matrix took place. The target area was chosen carefully as no mistakes could be made. Time and again, she'd visited the area to make herself familiar with as many details as possible.

*'A weird landscape of an arid country'* entered her mind.

What? Not the tapestry again!

*'A land of sprawling plains …'*

No! It should be jungle and swamp!

The imagery persisted, infusing it in her mind, replacing her original location.

*'With rugged mountains–'*

WHAT ARE YOU DOING, PRIEST? Her mind raged, becoming aware of his unexpected presence within the matrix. Moments of sheer panic passed.

With her heart in her throat, Niaarin quickly realised she couldn't perceive any flaw in the spell. It adapted, and progressed well, and why not? She knew this landscape as well as her chosen target area. The gut-wrenching trauma of another impending failure was quickly replaced by elation as the spell continued to grow.

*Yes. It's working! Oh yes YESSS …* The power surged through her. Every nerve tingling at its peak. *Ecstasy!* Belatedly she realised much more energy was being channelled than anticipated. She was so overcome by euphoria, she didn't want to stop it, even if she could.

*This must be what it was like to be a powershaper of old! Oh Eternix, you reward me. I give this spell unto you!* One last thought did occur to her in her flash of bliss; *Where exactly is this other place?* She absently hoped it wasn't too far away.

The spell became quasi-sentient; time was its domain, power its life-force. It expanded; began questing for its destination by sending out invisible tendrils of force across the ethereal plane. Further and further it roamed. Stretching out into the void, searching … searching time and space.

The spell required more power to reach fulfilment. It looked for it; found it, took it and continued questing. The plants shrivelled in an instant. Those with more power to give took longer, but all ended the same. The lower half of the priest, still outside the matrix, burst into flame. Niaarin lasted a few seconds before the remainder of her power was sucked dry. The ancient stones of the palace cracked. Fleeting iotas of power from the few remaining guards were whisked away. The spell sensed a greater power within the matrix itself, but beyond reach; the constraints of the spell gave it control only outside. Continuing its expansion required more power. It searched. It spread and found more.

On the ethereal plane, positive signals came back, but at an extreme distance in both time and place … There was another signal, fainter, but closer; a substitute path.

The headland began to shake down to the bedrock as power was sucked from within, delving down to the crystalline structure of the planet's mantle. The southern sector of Portside crumbled and split. The connection broke, as did the source for more power.

The spell arced through the void, its power now all but depleted, barely reaching the substitute path as the matrix began to unravel, those contained within separating before it dissipated completely.

———

Evlin stepped warily onto the balcony, dagger in hand. The scene in front of her was a strange one, but one she could deal with. The instant she touched the palace floor, her strength began to weaken, drained by some unknown force. *What could defy the strength of a god?* But find her she had – surrounded by a white aura, struggling with a black-robed priest by the parapet.

It would be too easy to drain the life-force from the mage, and Evlin wondered how different it would be to thrust the dagger into her with all that power coursing through her. As she stepped forward to slide the dagger between Niaarin's shoulders, an invisible wave of force washed over the balcony. Evlin became disoriented and had to lean against some potted ferns to maintain her balance. The leaves, now dry and fragile, crackled and fell to the floor at her touch.

Looking up in time, she saw the lower half of the priest flare with incandescence. The mage toppled sideways to the floor like a statue, her body also dried and shrivelled. As she watched, the bright light by the railing faded; there was nothing left but scorch marks and slightly melted paving outlining where the legs had been moments before.

The Enemy disappeared! Evlin staggered to the parapet and peered over the edge to see the Enemy's body below; hoping it wasn't too late to stick the dagger into her soft flesh.

"Nothin'!" she screeched. What spell did the mage cast? Evlin whirled around. In a fit of rage, she stumbled to the body of the mage and thrust the knife repeatedly into her chest. There was no life-force left and the skin and fur crumbled like stale bread.

Weak and confused, the assassin staggered to her feet, cursing. She'd find the Enemy, no matter where she was hiding! Kicking the desiccated corpse one final time, she left the balcony and the palace.

# 9

# A VOW ACKNOWLEDGED

PEOPLE RAN OUT INTO THE STREETS, YELLING AND SCREAMING IN confusion and fear. Looking up at the darkening sky only added to their terror; huge clouds churned overhead. Lightning and thunder added to the chaos. Overlaying it all, a deep, groaning sound permeated the air. The ground vibrated. Tiles and bricks from the nearby buildings shook loose, crashing to the streets below.

Within the Earth temple the monks were shaken from their ceremony. They spilled out into the plaza and immediately formed an arrowhead. They were quick and efficient, placing a palm on the shoulder of the monk in front.

At the tip of the arrow, Lemnon shut the surrounding disturbances from his mind and concentrated. His linking with the others seemed to take the longest time. He could not be rushed, for good reason; a mistake could drain dozens of them of power, rendering them mindless, or causing death.

Focusing on the area of disturbance, he sensed the extravagant usage of power. With the combined strength of those behind, he attempted to quell the destructive force. Soon he discovered the spell was out of control. He was uncertain of its purpose but whatever it was, it needed to be stopped, otherwise the entire city risked destruction. Building a sphere of protection around his group, a wall of force curved below his feet, emerging behind to completely enshroud them. Once he was sure there were no gaps, he expanded the sphere as quickly as he dared; too quickly could tear it, rendering it useless. He didn't know if they had the strength to start again.

Anyone with the ability to sense the aura would see a kaleidoscopic wall of energy, fed by the inner powers of the clerics. They'd see the wall move out from the plaza steadily moving in all directions. As it expanded, the shape became flatter on top, to conserve power use and utilise it where it was needed most – on the ground.

———

Tipp had been tracing the aura of his torc, tracking it to the southwestern sector of the city when interrupted by a great disturbance. He quickly made his way to the balcony of his room.

It was much darker than expected before recalling what was to occur tonight. He looked up at the dark circle in the sky. Never had he seen both moons eclipsed simultaneously. It was an awesome sight indeed. If he had been any later, he would have missed it completely.

To the south where the disturbance was strongest, slabs of stone were slowly rising into the air. His bard mind wondered why small pieces of debris rose faster than larger masses. Above the nearest rooftops, the palace came into view.

Tipp thought furiously. Someone, probably Niaarin since she was the only known mage currently at the palace, was using power at a horrendous rate. His studies in history told him the only other time anything like this occurred was in the Power Wars. Another sound impinged on his already overawed mind. The sound of huge volumes of water rushing in to fill the sudden void.

Eager for a better view, he launched off the balcony. With a few awkward flaps of his wings, he landed on the rooftop across the street and watched, horrified, as ships were dragged along the canal, mooring lines snapping. Fast-acting sailors threw grappling hooks to the overhead bridges, then clambered the lines. With another length of rope thrown to them, they started in earnest pulling up nets and other ropes. As each one was secured, crewman swarmed to safety. Then, pulling up the nets before getting tangled in the rigging of the drifting vessel, they lowered them for other similarly stricken crew on other vessels.

He saw the *Tearful Revenge* wallowing in the eddies that had formed from crosscurrents surging around two small islands, but it was still moving towards imminent destruction. Like the other ships, it pitched and yawed wildly. The masts snapped like twigs moments before being sucked into the maelstrom.

Above the city, the palace continued to rise. Around its base, also affected by the sudden draining of power, was a mass of seawater. Even now, however, large drops started to fall back to earth as small amounts of power were slowly re-absorbed from the surrounding environment.

It was fortunate power was normally absorbed slowly, otherwise the city would be awash with a torrential salty downpour. As it was, the evening breeze dispersed the falling drops. Blowing inland, the wind caused a fine shower to moisten the up-turned faces of the city's survivors as they watched the rising of the newest skyland in awe and fear.

Tipp heard cries for help. In the churning water, he saw a couple of heads go under, arms flailing. Without thinking, he leapt off the roof, gliding to the last location of the drowning men. He hovered, flapping awkwardly, unused to this much exertion.

A pair of arms came up again. Tipp clutched one with his foot, careful not to injure with his talons. He was unable to fully pull the fellow out but managed to drag him to the nearest shore.

Several dock-hands and sailors came running over to assist, pulling the man to safety with cheers.

Tipp landed clumsily nearby. He could barely lift his legs to walk, and his wings sagged, he looked back to the water. *Where was the other fellow?*

He struggled to haul himself up only to collapse ungracefully on the path. He was about to try to get up when gentle but firm hands were placed on his shoulders.

"Just relax right there. You've exhausted yourself," a new voice said.

Tipp focused on the figure in front of him, a female glins'ool.

It was only then he noticed the second man next to the first survivor.

"You saved him? Thank you for your assistance," he gasped.

"Accepted," she replied, surveying` the torrent for others. "My name's Biell."

"Our meeting is a good omen, I feel," he replied between breaths, admiring her plumage.

Supported by the crowd, the man he saved stumbled over humbly thanking him, and offering to buy several drinks.

Tipp graciously declined. "Thank you all. We did what anyone else would if they could," he said modestly, catching Biell's eye. "There are those less fortunate all around. What better way to rejoice can be found than to find them, help them and give them aid? This is the stuff from which heroes are made."

The gathering assembly looked to the south where the bulk of the palace filled the sky. Many buildings were in ruins, and small fires from broken oil lamps were starting to spread. In pairs and small groups, they went to help where they could.

The headland where the palace once stood had been completely removed, as had the greater portion of the nearby islands and the southern half of Portside. Chaos and panic reigned. Even in the areas untouched by anything more than a few tremors, people were in the streets.

Around the rim of the new chasm was pile upon pile of collapsed buildings. There were dozens of people searching through the debris for both the innocent victims and those fortunate to survive, whether they be relatives, friends or complete strangers. The whole shattered community worked together.

"Hi there, bard."

Tipp looked around to the owner of the vaguely familiar voice. On the other side of the street was a lithe figure in black leather. She walked over, lightly hopping over some remaining debris, ignoring the wolf-whistles of the sailors who were watching her.

"Well met, Jade. I was going to seek you out later."

"Have you seen Leonie?" She looked about.

Tipp tossed some bricks onto a pile and moved away from the sniggering work group. Jade stepped over with him.

"It is my fear, she is no longer here." He chose his words carefully.

"Damn!" Jade looked away quickly. "Are you sure? I've been searching everywhere. Most of the sewers in this area are now underwater. I hope she got out before this mess happened. The last place she said she was going to was the palace, but I've had the boys combing the streets just in case." She looked up at the new skyland now hovering over the water, blinking back tears.

"I'll look for you up there," the bard offered, following her gaze. "I feel that I should have helped her more, but this wasn't something we foresaw. You know what she's like, how she can be. She was reluctant to even accept help from me."

"Tell me about it." Jade nodded. "I'm sure you did everything you could Tipp, and for that you have my gratitude." She held his hand briefly, then looked around at the chaos. She laughed briefly, causing some peculiar looks from others nearby.

"I told her this place would fall apart without her."

"Don't you hate being prophetic—"

"I'll go with him." Biell stepped up. "He'll probably get lost by himself."

Jade nodded looking from her to him briefly. "Well then, I better get back. Someone's got to keep an eye on the rabble."

"I'll convey what we survey," he said. "One way or another, it's no bother."

"You do that. You know where to find me." She turned away.

"Who's this Leonie?" Biell asked.

"She's half-rrell."

"Which half?"

"Hard to tell." He shrugged again as he changed the subject. "Perhaps we should go to the palace now, before it gets too high."

"Sure. If you're up to it, but it won't be getting much higher in the sky."

"And you know about these things?" He started to make his way to the cliff.

"Yes, as a matter of fact, I do. It's my job to know about them and map their courses too," she called out to his back. "You didn't think that I was some dumb bird latching on to the next cockerel that came around, did you?" She hopped up to join him.

"Perhaps another time we can chatter about this matter," he replied, quickly looking away at the churning water below.

"Did I make the great bard blush?" she teased.

"You could no doubt make the *great bard* do many things." He flexed his wings. "But for now, all I want to do is search the palace. Coming?" Tipp leapt off the ground, flapping his wings for the third time that night.

She quietly launched herself gracefully into the air after him.

------

After the search through the night, the feathered pair slowly spiralled down, navigating between a few smaller lumps of floating rock. The cloud of water from the previous night had dissipated and the destroyed area was plain to see in the daylight. Of the headland where the palace once stood, only the southern-most tip remained, a jagged finger of rock pointing accusingly at the sky.

The southern half of Portside ended abruptly in a wide arc, indicating the extent of the power drain; a few buildings remained precariously balanced on the edge. Both Fleet and Admiral Islands were hanging in the air at about the thousand-foot mark. Most of the naval vessels were destroyed and only a few boats were visible, those remaining only because of the greater distance of their berths from the newly formed abyss, but none appeared to be totally free of damage. The harbour lay strewn with ship wreckage.

"I think travelling to Reenat will be hard," Biell called out over the whistling wind.

"It would certainly seem so, especially for this bard." He unsteadily banked towards Diamond where his lodging was located.

Biell pivoted on a wing and slipped down beside him. "I know of a way to get to Reenat. It won't cost anything, and it will be good for your health."

"If you're suggesting I fly, then I must say goodbye. While I admit to neglecting exercise, I can only hypothesise it would hasten my demise."

"As a ranger, I've been studying these skylands for a long time now. My notes are back in my room, but I'm sure I could work a path that would enable us to ride the majority of the way." Before he answered she added, "There would be plenty of opportunities to rest, and you did say you were remiss in your flying. This would be a good chance to accomplish several things. You would be able to get to Reenat quickly, save money, and get some more exercise in as well."

"I'll consider it for a bit, but you never know, I may yet find a caravan also keen to go."

"I've been on the road. All that dust!" she squawked. "I had to spend so much time preening. No thanks. I'd rather fly and leave the road for the groundlings."

Tipp refrained from sharing his recent experience with caravans, instead saying, "I won't make any promises. I'll still need to ask." He tapped the satchel with research from Niaarin's rooms. "Moving the rest of my luggage will be a task."

"Okay then. I'll head for my room to see what I can come up with while you make your inquiries. If you can't get a caravan, then you can join me skyland-hopping. I travel light so can help carry some of your stuff, but the majority will more than likely have to be sent up by road."

"And what if I manage to secure passage?"

"You won't." She sounded sure.

"Ah yes, but if I do, then you will agree to come too. It could prove to be a valuable experience for thee, as much as the flying would be for me." *'What am I implying?'* he thought, *'Do I really hate flying?'*

"Hah. You're on, but I'll have to leave you now to get my notes. Where will we meet?"

"How about the Heart of Gold? My treat."

"I'll see you around noon then," Biell called out the last as she wheeled away for the north sector.

Tipp watched her effortless glide for a moment, before looking down for the roof of the building where his room was located, where he could land to drop off Niaarin's notes. Then he would make a few inquiries about travelling north. He had to admit if only to himself, it seemed unlikely anything would be available in the short term. Afterwards, he would seek a meeting with Jade to let her know the outcome from his searching of the palace.

Within an hour after landing and securing the spell-notes in his rooms with both mundane and simple magical precautions, Tipp worked his way through the streets in fresh clothes. He had heard the news the city was now under the direct control of the military, more so now than ever before, and any ships fit to sail, as well as most wagons, had been commandeered for emergency and security reasons. The city was in a very vulnerable situation at the moment, if not from the land, then from the sea. Pirates still made the occasional foray into towns at night, and Delta, with all this turmoil and no navy, might appear too nice a target.

It was obvious he had no other option than to consider Biell's suggestion. What irked him the most, considering his sedentary lifestyle, was that he wasn't shocked by her proposal in the first place. A few days ago he would have laughed at her. Shaking his head at the vagaries life threw across his path he continued threading his way through the ever-crowded streets to meet with Jade, hoping she wouldn't take the news of Leonie's disappearance too hard.

He spied a familiar bulk shuffling through the crowd. "Brother Lemnon," he called out. The priest looked around in surprise, his bald pate glistening with sweat as the avian hopped up beside him.

"Well met, friend bard. If you perchance have some news, your timing is of great benefit. The guard captain, Levan Macreedy, has called for the judiciary. I was just on my way there. Perhaps we can discuss it en route?"

"I'd be glad to speak, but I'm also off to a meet. Let me know where to go, for it isn't something to be discussed on the street."

"In truth, I still need to call in at my temple first. The meeting is at the Great Hall of Unification, behind the large dais where we met in the plaza. How about I meet with you there?"

"Very well, I shall be there at the table as soon as I am able."

Bowing briefly to each other, the men separated, heading for their destinations.

———

Entering the tavern unobtrusively from the rear, Jade saw the bard standing in a corner by a window with a bowl of ale in his hands. She had to admit he cut a striking figure with the sunlight glinting off his lustrous feathers. Instructing one of the girls to let him know of her arrival, she made her way to her usual booth along the back wall.

By the time the bard was seated next to her in a discreet booth, she had a glass of wine for herself and another bowl for him.

"Jade, good of you to come at a run."

"I saw you watching out the window. Any trouble I should expect?"

"Simply observing," he assured her. "Just being circumspect."

"I take it then you've found something to tell me?"

"I found the dead mage, but nothing of Leonie." He showed her the gold amulet in his pocket. "This should give her position with much precision."

"You found it! Where is she?"

"No. This gold one is more for a *ceremonial* event; though the other was silver – it was far more potent."

"So, what happened to her?" the thief master asked, eyeing the medallion with keen interest.

"I'm sure she visited the mage in the palace. There are signs of esoteric traps and malice. There's no other trace of her anywhere near. I thought it best to report to you here."

"What does that mean? I can see from your face there's more. What is it?"

"Leonie's body was not found, not in the palace nor on the ground. That powerful magic was unleashed is beyond doubt. If Leonie was the target, what was it about? Grigorid is alive no more, but not by Leonie's paw." He let that sink in. "There is evidence of another, possibly Coundar, but why he was there is a wonder."

"I'm not surprised. There was rumour of an alliance." Jade tapped the table with her fingers, thinking. "She mentioned the young girl to me. I went to find her, but she's missing too. Her parents are frantic."

"This little visit is becoming epic." The bard shook his head. "And all because a book of prophetic—"

"No offence bard, but I don't give a damn about your prophecy. My ideals lie solely with what I can see, touch and take. I want Leonie, or failing that, to know what's become of her!" She became aware her raised voice got the attention of a few patrons as well as the staff. Jade signed to the staff that all was fine. "Sorry, bard. I haven't slept all night and I'm probably not dealing with this well."

"Nonsense, under the circumstances I too—"

"With all due respect, you don't know the half of it. She was no apprentice; she was like family." At Tipp's surprised look, she explained further. "We've been together since she was just a lost kitten on the street. I thought we had drifted apart for a time, but when she came back from her last trip, we finally spoke about what happened years ago."

"All people change, even best friends. It's nothing strange." Tipp offered.

"It was more than that."

"Oh well, even so, the same goes for lovers too. Many a relation—"

"Not like that!" Jade almost blushed. "I saved her life once when she was a kitten." The woman looked down at her nearly empty glass. She gestured for another refill for both before continuing.

"I was much younger then, much more naïve. Can you believe I was in the Royal Guard many years ago? The night the temple burned?" She paused to take a drink then told him about that night. "I couldn't continue in the guard after that. Not after the fire. Something snapped inside. Since then I've been with Leonie in the Takers. I thought we'd be inseparable."

She stood up unsteadily, falling against him briefly when he stood up. "I'm going to change if I can. I feel she's also changed. If it's within my power, I swear on every god, I'll not rest until I find her." Her voice was drowned out by the resounding crash of thunder from outside. Glass from shattered windows blew inwards, shards covered the floor.

The force threw Tipp back. He landed heavily on his side.

Before anyone could react, it was followed by another peal. Then another. It took a moment, but after the initial shock wore off, Tipp patted his vest and groped frantically through his pockets.

"Where is my torc?" He looked at Jade, his eyes bulging.

She was holding onto the table. A dull glow surrounded her and her hair was standing on end. Jade was very pale, more out of fright than injury, and though she didn't move, her eyes followed him as he slowly stood and approached.

The roll of thunder faded away, as did the glow around Jade. Her hair gradually fell limp to her shoulders. Transfixed by some unknowable force, she staggered sideways and clutched at the bard as she was about to fall.

"Are you queasy? Take it easy."

She nodded mutely at him, her colour coming back.

"Where's my torc?" he repeated with urgency.

Jade removed the torc from a fold in her tunic. "A habit of mine." She shrugged. "I was going to give it back." The runes glowed like fire, but the torc was icy to touch. "That's weird."

Tipp took it from her and examined it. "Do you know what you've done?" He helped her back into the chair after putting the chain around his neck.

"Not enough." Jade picked up the remainder of her wine and downed it in one gulp. "Enlighten me," she managed to croak.

Tipp quickly went to the door and looked out.

The city was as quiet as a tomb. Any priests in sight were on their knees in silent prayer. People in the street cowered in corners in fear and confusion. The sky was clear of clouds. The portion of the harbour that could be seen was motionless. Smooth as glass, as if even the tides had been quelled.

Slowly, people began to move about again, looking around in bewilderment as they headed off. They spoke to each other, but in hushed tones, making glances towards the sky every few paces.

"What happened?" Jade asked again quietly behind him.

"While you may have forsaken prophecy, prophecy has not forsaken you." His ruffled feathers showed his apprehension.

"You're speaking in riddles, bard."

He took her by the arm and went back inside and sat her down at the table.

"Prophecy foretold of this city's existence. Unusual things have occurred since my appearance – the use of great power not encountered for forty decades, and several new skylands have been made." He walked back and forth, from the rear of the room to the front as he spoke. "A codex missing for several hundred years, turns up in the paws of the one I was to see," he squawked. "The moons! An eclipsing of both, and to all deities, you make an oath!"

"I meant every word of it too!" Jade growled into another glass of wine.

"That is indeed evident, and it received acknowledgment." Tipp continued to pace the room, avoiding the glass splinters.

"I've said things like that before," Jade argued. "Nothing like this happened. What makes this time so different?"

"You were holding my torc," he said.

Again, she gave him a blank look.

"Even I'm hazy on the full story, so I can't expect you to know," Tipp answered. "What I do know is this: the torcs were made centuries ago when the Age of Powers was at its height. We bards stayed neutral; we refused to fight. Now we search the world, chasing every clue," he added. "We travel around as storytellers, to learn what is and isn't true."

"Should you be telling me this?" she asked.

"No, but even the best, when put to the test, can say their bit and not give a shit." Tipp sat down opposite her, stuck his beak in his bowl of wine and pulled a long drink before continuing.

They remained seated, mulling over what each other had revealed.

"So, you're saying my vow was acknowledged by the gods?"

Tipp nodded.

"And this power is in your torc?"

Again, the nod.

"And, let me get this straight, you *gave* one to Leonie?"

"A good idea of mine at the time." He leant back in his chair, wiping his eyes wearily.

"Uh-huh. Been there, done that. Another thing, I thought there were supposed to be eight gods?"

The bard's head nodded. "Us too, same as you."

"But there were nine claps of thunder."

"It is a wonder to ponder," he said quietly. His bowl was now empty, but he politely declined another offer of a refill. He looked around the now empty tavern. "I was expecting to meet a friend for lunch, but that won't be happening is my hunch."

Jade rolled her blue eyes. "I guess you want me to play messenger again for you?"

"No. I'll leave a message with the barkeep. You go and rest, it's for the best. I'll let you know if I hear any more, though I have an inkling you will hear of it before." He stood up and bowed to her.

"Always. And thank you again. If you get the chance, say hello to Macreedy for me." Jade sat back with a sigh.

As soon as Tipp left a message and coin with the Heart's barkeep, he moved towards the door, turning for a final look towards the mistress of the Thieves Guild. She had a look of deep concentration on her face. He stepped out into the daylight, striding out through the now sparsely populated street in the direction of the plaza.

———

"Too late for the date," Tipp chirped, seeing the other members of the judiciary vacating the hall. He spied a familiar bulk shuffling through the crowd. "Brother Lemnon," he squawked.

The priest looked around in surprise, his bald pate glistening with sweat as the avian hopped up beside him. "Well met, friend bard. If you perchance have some news, your timing is of great benefit. I was late myself. Perhaps we can discuss it on the way to Macreedy's office?"

The portly monk led the bard to the guard captain's office in the nearby garrison.

After brief introductions, Tipp recounted all he knew in great detail, showing him the remains of the High Priest's pouch with the Woorin motif on each side.

"This is his pouch, to that I will vouch."

Levan pursed his lips while he considered this information. "So, it would seem the mage and Coundar are dead. I will need to send some of my people up there. If your suspicions about a trap are true, your friend more than likely came to grief at the business-end of this spell. Then again, she was resourceful enough to evade the hunters; we may never be sure." He took a deep breath before continuing. "Though I only saw her briefly, she did a fine thing saving the young girl the other night. Not many would agree. Which reminds me, I should send out some men to find young Sussah to verify the whole story. I'm sorry your visit here ended sadly for you, bard. I'd like to assist you in your travels back to Reenat, but our resources are stretched."

The pair left the garrison, pausing in the plaza to take in the view of the new waterfront.

Vessels of all shapes and sizes thronged the harbour, collecting the flotsam blocking the canals while people searched for bodies. The palace had settled at a height of roughly a thousand feet above the city, Fleet and Admiralty slightly higher. All were slowly bobbing and revolving with the air currents.

Tipp noticed the group of brown-robed figures gathered on the new headland where the southern sector of Portside once stood. "I sense they are using power."

"We are attempting to retain the palace within the city. The wind or some other force is making it drift away. I'm sure Lord Zander would be most aggrieved to find his royal residence making its way towards the Central Ranges."

"Not keen for a broken chateau on a plateau?" Tipp chuckled.

"What are your plans now?" Lemnon asked. "From the looks

of it, sailing won't be an option for a while. More dusty trails for you, then?"

Tipp chirped a greeting as Biell swooped down to join them, grinning at Lemnon's look. "Please let me acquaint, before you faint." He introduced Biell to the Earther monk.

"Biell has suggested we skyland-hop to Reenat," Tipp continued. "With favourable weather and everything to plan, I could be home quicker than by caravan."

"Heaven forbid! You flying?"

"A novelty for me, I think you're implying. Under the circumstances, I'll take my chances."

"Amen to that, Brother," Lemnon nodded.

# 10

# A WAYWARD SPELL

Time stopped. Darkness surrounded Leonie – too dark to see a memory. A girl's fading scream lingered in her ears. The cold was everywhere and everything – the bile threatening to erupt froze in her gullet. About the only benefit was when the numbness set in; all pain went away. It felt like her limbs were no longer attached. She felt nothing; no pain, no movement, no sense of anything at all.

*Is this death?*

A strong gust picked up dust and grit, hurling it across the small, rock-strewn glade, adding to the accumulation at the base of the ridge. Boulders, some cracked open like dropped eggs, were in abundance. Dried leaves swirled within the eddies.

Leonie groaned as feeling returned; her limbs quivered with the effort of moving. The breeze ruffled her fur, exposing skin to the cold abrasive wind.

Through blurred vision, she perceived sunlight when it should be the dark of night. *Maybe I've been out all night ... but where am I now?* She shivered, realising she was in shadow. Crawling into the sunshine, she felt the warmth begin its magic. Leonie moved gingerly. Her leg refused to cooperate, making her task much harder. As she dragged herself further into the meagre warmth, the ground beneath her paws felt strange; not the hard texture she expected. She was no longer on a balcony.

Looking down, she saw her paw was wrapped up in a piece of ripped linen. Soft material, much like one would make a dress out of.

*Sussah! Where is she?*

Ignoring the aches, Leonie forced herself to a sitting position, noticing her surroundings for the first time. Immediately in front of her were piles of rock. Small spiny shrubs somehow managed to cling to the hard surface, their roots spreading out like a paw with far too many fingers. To see any further she had to stand. Bracing herself against the nearest boulder, she pushed herself into an upright position.

"Sussah!" The wind snatched her croaking away. Her throat was so dry. She needed to moisten it, but there was no water.


Sussah's scream was cut short when she hit the ground, the breath knocked out of her. She lay there sprawled and stunned. Her lungs refused to work and panic began to grip her mind. It seemed an endless time before she managed to heave in her first gasp. The panic settled, and she calmed enough to take stock of her situation.

A moment ago, she was a hundred feet in the air trying desperately to reach a trellis, then time froze as a cloak of total darkness engulfed her. Confused by the sudden change, she caught her breath as realisation penetrated her stupor. Squinting through bleary eyes, she saw the bluest of skies. And there was a vast sound. It surrounded her, pulsated through her, filling her head. The best she could think of was the sound of waves in a raging tempest.

When she was a little girl she'd cowered on a bridge between Diamond and Portside during a storm. The hissing and roaring as the waves rushed past sounded much like this. But there was no storm in sight now, just endless clear blue sky.

She wasn't sure, but it looked like the ground she'd landed

on stopped about an arm's length away. Sussah rolled over and edged forward carefully. Gravel shifted underneath her, causing her to slide. Flinging her hand out in panic, she struck something solid. Instinctively latching onto the vine, she ignored the twinge of pain from her palm and fingers as the rough bark bit in. Her momentum stopped. And for a second, so did her heart. Out of the corner of her eye, she glimpsed what was over the edge.

Nothing.

The shock was too much. She screamed for all she was worth.


Leonie heard the shriek, recognising it instantly, and the terror it conveyed. "Sussah! Where are you?"

There was no response. "Can she even hear me?" she wondered.

The scream sounded as if coming from behind, but it was tricky to judge with the buffeting wind. By degrees, she turned and clambered over the boulders, driven by Sussah's need.

Topping the last rock, Leonie gasped with delight at the sight. She was on the edge of a skyland, thousands of feet above a huge expanse of empty land. She'd seen similar sights before; from the days when she was flying with Slana, and later when she had visited a skyland with Feiron and Phil as they returned to Delta. Stunning as it was, Leonie turned away, mistaking where the scream came from. Then she heard the sobbing. It was unmistakably in front of her. Noticing the cracks all across the ground, reminiscent of the last skyland she had ridden, she realised the edges were unstable. A few chips of rock broke off at her slightest touch, she dragged herself to the edge and looked down.

"Hi." Leonie smiled to cover her concern when she drew closer. "Nice view you found."

"Get me away from here!" Sussah shrieked.

Sussah was on a narrow ledge – another few feet and she would have plummeted off the skyland.

"I'm here. Don't move!" Leonie reached for the dial of the

harness. "Slistorf's balls!" she swore. The crystal was cracked, rendering it useless.

"Don't leave me!" Sussah's voice became shrill.

"I'll be right back." Leonie hobbled away, searching frantically. She had found many dead branches, but they had crumpled with rot; this one was a recent break and decay hadn't set in.

"Try this." She lowered the cumbersome branch down. "There are some knots and branch stubs. Try to use it as a ladder."

"I can't!"

"You'll have to. I've got a damaged paw and leg. I can't do any more to help, so you'll be spending the night there if you don't." All she heard in response was crying and mumbling. "Put that anger to some good use. It's not too far."

"Says you." Sussah was almost halfway up. From time to time her foot slipped. She learnt quickly to test the foothold first.

When within reach, Leonie ignored her pain and did what she could to help, but it was awkward. The two of them lay there, nursing their bruises and catching their breath. Trying to make sense of what happened.

"See. Easy."

Sussah got up with a groan. "I need to pee."

"Just stay away from the edge." Leonie fought back a chuckle as Sussah scrambled around the rocky area for some privacy. Her smile disappeared when she heard another scream. "What now?" she growled softly. With pain lancing through her body, she did her best to get to Sussah quickly, but the girl came stumbling back, her face ashen. She didn't say anything, just pointed.

Whatever it was lay out of sight behind a large, thorny bush. Leonie hobbled around, seeing the remains of a body draped over a rock. Everything below his abdomen was missing, internal organs spilled onto the blood-soaked dirt.

Caught off guard, Leonie leant against a weathered tree trunk and threw up. She turned, after a final cough and wiped the bile from her lips. She limped to the nearest boulder to compose herself. After a few minutes, she stood and approached the remains, intrigued at the precise severing of his body, like that of a giant guillotine. His garments – or what was left of them – were of a high quality and in good condition. *Good enough for bandages.*

Reaching down, she removed the remnants of his cloak and shirt, tearing a length of the cloth and used it to remove his medallion and his rings, popping each into her pouch one at a time, careful not to touch any of them, and made her way back to Sussah.

They caught each other's eye, silently coming to the same decision; time to move from this place. Sussah got up shakily and followed as Leonie moved further inland.

Before too long, Leonie called a halt. They stood at the base of a large stone building, now in ruins. Most of the roof had collapsed. Judging by the amount of plant growth now in abundance among the fallen timber and rubble, this happened decades ago, if not longer.

The sky became a darker blue and grey clouds gathered on the horizon to the south-east. The moons appeared, two pale discs resembling icy-blue eyes staring from the heavens.

"The sun will be down soon, and it'll get much colder. It might even rain," Leonie commented.

"I've never felt so cold." Sussah shivered. "Where are we?" She wrapped her arms around her thin shoulders as the breeze stiffened, her ripped clothing providing little protection.

"I'm not sure. My guess is we're far to the north-west. Maybe even on the far side of Shak'aran."

"Why do you think we're so far from Delta?"

Leonie looked to the moons. "We can talk about that later. Let's get inside and start a fire to get you warm. I reckon the wood's dry enough to burn. I'm sure we'll see things differently once we're comfortable."

One at a time, they made their way through the warped doorway as the first drops of wind-driven rain splattered the dust. Inside was a mess of debris fallen from the floors above. In a back corner, they managed to clear an area big enough for them both. It was about as far as they could get from the windy openings.

Sussah offered to collect wood. "How do we start a fire?" she asked, dumping a handful in a small pile.

"Very carefully." Leonie concentrated, and soon a small glow appeared within her palm. Ever so gently, she placed the ball of flame on top of the kindling. The flames readily took hold of the dry wood and within moments, cheery warmth grudgingly spread out.

"How did you do that?" Sussah started to feed the flames larger pieces of wood. "Are you a powershaper too?" When there was no reply, she turned to Leonie. "What's wrong?" Sussah cried out in alarm.

Leonie opened her eyes, slowly shook her head. "Just tired. It's been a long, arduous day." She wriggled to get more comfortable and failed.

As she rested, her thoughts cleared, she considered what had happened in Niaarin's rooms. Never had she been so befuddled and could only assume there was some sort of enchantment. Even now, a short period after the event, a lot of the detail remained vague. Lost in thought, she stared into the flames. Her stomach growled, reminding her that she hadn't eaten a decent meal for over a day. But she was too tired and sore to worry about it. At least now there was some warmth.

"Who was that back there?" Sussah prodded the fire with a stick.

Shaken from her reverie, Leonie took a few breaths before she realises what Sussah meant. She sat up more. "Coundar, I think, High Priest to the Temple to Woorin."

"Did you know him?"

"I knew *of* him and had seen him around from time to time. But no, we never met." She briefly wondered why the High Priest of Woorin would be consorting with the priestess of Eternix. "He was taller last time I saw him."

The shock of it all jolted the young girl. She turned away and started to weep. In the confined space, the best Leonie could do was reach over and lay a comforting paw on her shoulder.

"You were going to tell me about the moons," Sussah said between sobs, "and where we are."

Leonie sighed, thinking. "The last I remember, when we were back in Delta, Luminor and Luxor were almost overhead when they eclipsed. The moons are now further south, which means we're further north. Since it's now dusk here and was the middle of the night back in Delta, we must be further west."

Concentrating on Leonie's explanation, Sussah stopped crying and moved closer to the fire. Sussah wiped hair back from her eyes. "I saw mountains before when I was over the edge; do you think they're the Central Ranges?"

"No. They didn't look right." Leonie took the time to examine her own wounds.

"What do you mean?"

"They aren't big enough, and there's no snow on the peaks. Even the ranges in the southern parts of Athglenn had snow on the highest peaks. None of them looked anything like the mountains I've seen. The Central Ranges are vast; these would be mere foothills in comparison."

Water started to drip from the floor above, causing them to rearrange their positions.

"How are you feeling now?" Leonie asked.

"Awful. Sore and thirsty, though it looks as though I should be asking you. You have far more injuries than me. Did you get them when you helped me, or from the hunt? Or would you rather forget about it?"

"As if I could forget. No, these were just friendly reminders from one of the guards last night when they caught me—"

"It's all my fault!" Sussah started crying again. "You should've stayed away. I'm so sorry. Everything would have been alright, I suppose." Tears rolled down her dusty cheek. "I would've gotten over it—"

"No. You'd never get over it, trust me on that." Leonie turned abruptly to face her. "The one who did this to me, he would've done it anyway; he was that type of guy. The guards that attacked you would've only come back for more, or attacked another girl. Unfortunately, it isn't something you'll forget in a hurry."

Sussah looked outside, away from her intense gaze. "Thank you."

"Did they ... *hurt* you?"

"Hurt?" Sussah wiped her face. "Oh." She blushed. "Not in *that* way. Slapped and roughed up. It could have been much worse though. Thank you."

Leonie nodded. "True. I'm glad I got there in time. Sorry it wasn't sooner." She tilted her head back under the dripping water and let the water run into her mouth, after several gulps, she turned back to the girl.

"Cup your hands to catch some water. After all that's happened, it'd be silly to die of thirst when there's a raging storm outside."

Sussah did as suggested. The cold water ran down her arm. She took small sips from her hand. "Leonie ..." she started, staring into the fire and not meeting Leonie's eyes. "Why'd you push me off the balcony?"

"Ah." Leonie eased her legs out with a sigh. "That I should apologise for. My mind was all muddled from an arcane trap. It must've been some illusion. I could've sworn you were Niaarin. She was the one I was after. I didn't know it was you until too late, but why were *you* there?"

"The mage wanted to meet us and talk about the hunt, to apologise and clear up the details. Since you survived, the gods must have deemed you innocent."

"I doubt she'd apologise, and I don't need any *gods* to determine my innocence or not. But there *were* a couple of details to clear up. Us!"

"Us? What do you mean? I didn't kill anyone!"

"Not for that. For simply being part of it. I heard the guards talking back in the dungeon and her son later confirmed it; Niaarin despises half-castes of any sort. This was her excuse to get rid of one more, me, getting richer and being popular all at the same time."

"It worked! My da's tavern was very busy, that night when the priests came to escort me to the palace. Everyone was so excited about the Hun– Sorry." She realised that was the wrong thing to say. "But why me? I didn't even know her."

"She somehow found out you were the victim; a potential witness. Niaarin must've thought you'd turn up and defend me." Leonie declined to mention the fact she hadn't. "If you had spoken up, her credibility and that of the guard would've dropped."

"But you survived! It wouldn't matter if I said anything. The gods decreed your innocence!"

"Ha. Some people may believe that, but she wasn't going to let me live. The hunt was staged as a ploy to get rid of me; she'd arranged for my death already. I managed to escape with the help of a friend." She hoped Jade managed to make it out alright.

"But Niaarin said she was expecting you to arrive any minute," Sussah pointed out. "So why have me join her to meet you?"

"She knew I was coming?" Leonie thought for a moment. "Her son, Phellicks, sent a message before he died. When did you arrive at the palace?" She carefully removed the disc from her pouch. "Recognise this?" Sussah took the disc before Leonie remembered what touching could do, but nothing happened. *Drained.*

"It was dark. After sundown. I think my wine was drugged," Sussah explained. "I was only awake for a short while before you arrived." She looked at the torc with the firelight. "The mage had one of these. Every now and then she touched it. I don't think she knew I saw."

"You were picked up *before* I escaped, proving she was going to get rid of you anyway."

Sussah covered her mouth with the back of her hand.

"Makes you mad doesn't it, having people out to kill you for no reason? My survival wasn't from any *divine intervention,*" she continued. "I reckon Niaarin was behind all those other mysterious deaths. She wasn't going to let *me* live, so why should I let *her*? That's why I wanted her dead."

"Did you kill her son too?"

"I didn't know Phellicks was her son until later, but yeah. He died."

Leonie eased a cramp out of her leg. She looked over to ask if it was the Woorin priests that collected her, but the girl had dropped off to sleep. Tossing more wood on the fire, Leonie tried to get comfortable. She removed the harness and studied the cracked crystal. A brief attempt to charge it proved futile. Growling softly, she reinserted the crystal and placed the harness on the floor. Within moments she too fell into an exhausted sleep.

———

In the aftermath of the eclipse, the ruins of the city became visible in the bright moonlight. Evlin returned to the temple with a look of complete and utter frustration on her pallid face. She had not been summoned. There was no need. Her master would soon know, if not already, the outcome of tonight's activities. There was no way her failure could be kept a secret. Once again, the enemy escaped death by her hands.

Evlin easily scaled the walls of the damaged temple and made her way to the lower levels.

"I've failed you, master." Those detestable words passed the assassin's lips as she found herself grovelling at the slippered feet of the High Priest.

Tirruk reclined on a lounge in the Receiving Room of the temple contemplating the outcome of the last few days' work. He too was frustrated at the apparent misfortune to thwart his plans. If he were a superstitious man, it would seem as though fate worked against him.

"I have not sensed our elusive prey entering the realm, which means either she isn't dead or is somehow hidden from me. It may be this new spell worked, though not the way our foolish mage planned – she drew too much power. I will ponder this conundrum. You," he regarded the slight woman before him, "are of little use to me here. If you sense this half-rrell, I will know of it. Maybe then I will have need of you."

Before Evlin could voice a response, she found herself in a dark and musty cavern. It took several moments for her eyes to adjust, but she knew immediately she had been returned to the realm of the dead; punishment for her failure. For how long she didn't know.

The caverns of purgatory seemed colder and darker than before. Having briefly tasted the despair and desolation in store for everyone when they died, it was all the incentive she needed to avoid a return. Her only hope had been to do her new master's bidding to his complete satisfaction so he'd find her irreplaceable.

All was going fine, up until her failure.

Evlin had traced the Enemy's movements successfully, but always a step behind. The Enemy evaded death yet again by disappearing. It wasn't *her* fault the troublesome mage cast the spell and sent the half-rrell to oblivion.

She hadn't planned on returning here. Unfortunately, the decision was not hers to make and never would be.

Niaarin was dead, Evlin had no doubt, having witnessed the results of the wayward spell. To avoid further wrath from her new master, Evlin would use what time she had to locate the mage before she was either accepted or denied by her goddess, Eternix.

Evlin reached into her pouch and withdrew the amulet found among the desiccated remains of the hapless mage. She recognised it for what it was, but not realising how useful it would become, until now.

The amulet would lead her to Niaarin, who could then tell her where the Enemy had gone. And anywhere the Enemy went, Evlin would find a way to follow. Somehow.

Only then could she continue with her real goal, to return the

Enemy to her master so he could put her to the question. Afterwards, she'd be Evlin's to play with. She sat on a rock and meditated, stroking the tail around her neck with one hand, holding the medallion with the other.

Niaarin was the key. If the mage were in purgatory, there would be nowhere for her to hide. Evlin smiled with confidence and began scrying.

## 11

## SKYLAND

Leonie awoke. Every joint ached. Groaning in pain with any movement, she turned to see if she had woken Sussah. The girl wasn't there. Using the wall, she gingerly stood and limped out of the shelter. The sun was shining and the sky crystal clear.

"Sussah," she called.

"Over here."

Leonie turned to the voice. The girl was about thirty paces away, walking back to the ruins, carrying something in her arms. What she could see of the skyland looked pristine in the morning light, seemingly washed clean by the rain. The grass and leaves on the trees dazzled with reflected light.

Sussah walked up the path of the ruined house. "I found these over there." She shrugged her shoulder, trying to point. Several wrinkled apples dropped to the ground.

Leonie bent down to pick one up and regretted it. Every muscle protested and it took her a painful minute to straighten up.

Sussah dropped the rest of the apples on the grass and helped Leonie. "There's a pretty pond over there, filled to the brim from last night's rain. And more ruins." She was bursting with excitement. "Oh. And good morning."

Leonie hated her for that moment. *No one should be that chirpy.* She found a section of garden wall stable enough to sit on without fear of collapsing.

Sussah collected a few of the fallen apples and brought them closer.

Leonie took one and bit into it. It was a bit bitter but manageable. She finished it and picked another. "Better not get too carried away with these," she advised. "Too many will probably make us sick." She stood and surveyed the area, turning around gingerly. Yesterday, she was too tired; her mind still vague. Today, she ached all over but felt clearer of mind. "Well done though, for finding these."

Sussah smiled. "It isn't much."

Leonie tossed the apple core over her shoulder. She needed to move and loosen up cramped muscles. "You mentioned a pond? I need a drink."

Sussah skipped away. Leonie followed at a more sedate pace, using her claw to remove apple skin caught in her teeth.

To her right was the nearest edge of the skyland; their arrival point – and where the remains of Coundar lay among the boulders. In front of her was an expanse of open ground with patches of brown grass. Most of it had reverted to the wild, tough weeds and brambles establishing their own territory. Tall shrubs, maybe an ancient hedge, blocked the view beyond. Turning left, she could see a rise littered with boulders.

Though in disrepair, it was evident the area had once been a manicured parkland. Broken or toppled statues were in abundance, surrounded by remnants of stone walls. Cracked paving crisscrossed what would have been ornamental flower beds. In the centre of all this was a double circular archway, situated on a raised section in the middle of a faded mosaic-tiled area. The pond Sussah mentioned was beside it. The elaborate circular arch was translucent, indicating its crystalline structure.

"Why'd anyone put something like that there? It looks too … important."

"I've never seen crystal shaped like that before. I didn't know it could be."

They walked to the edge. The pond still contained water even though there were cracks in the tiles. She knelt down, brushed leaves away and scooped up some to drink. The water was cool and refreshing.

"This must have looked wonderful in full bloom." Sussah turned around to take in the whole parkland.

Leonie only grunted in response. Sussah looked at her. Leonie had walked around the archway, staring intently towards the centre.

"Are you alright?" she asked.

"What do you see?" Leonie asked abruptly.

Puzzled, Sussah glanced at the archway in bewilderment. "Umm. The trees beyond, and part of a wall … I think. What else would there be?"

"Now come over this way."

Sussah shook her head. "What difference would that make?" She walked to where Leonie stood a few paces away.

"Now look," Leonie pointed.

Sussah gasped. Looking at the opening from an angle gave her a clear view of the opposite side. "It's different!"

"You see now?"

"Yes! But what is it?"

"More to the point – *where is it?*"

"What do you mean?" Sussah asked.

"I think it leads to another place."

"Is it magical? Will it take us back to Delta?" Sussah gawped at it, slack-jawed.

"That's not Delta. Power's involved if it's what I think it is; a portal to another world." She wondered why there was no aura; or why she couldn't see it.

Sussah bit her lip again, turning to her. "Another world?"

Leonie sat down on a patch of grass. Sussah joined her. Both kept staring at the archway.

"Sages say we didn't come from this world; that we all came from somewhere else," Leonie continued.

"All of us? Where from?"

"No one knows where exactly, nor which world the portals go to. The glins'ool have a world, as do the rrell, seleth, hroltahgs, vorien, illios and humans."

"I've got a world too?" she squealed.

"It would seem so. A portal to each. A native creature that lived here before us was a l'ith … something. A big bug, like a giant ant."

"I've never seen one."

"And you'll want to hope you never do. I have. It was huge; not as long as a wyvern but just as heavy."

"Now I know you're joking."

"Why?" Leonie asked.

"Wyverns. Dragons. They don't exist. I heard those stories in da's tavern every other night. Just stories told by drunks to other drunks."

"Yet you'll believe a portal will take us to another world?"

"But that's all magic." Sussah rolled her eyes. "And *everyone* knows magic is real. You do it yourself!"

"Hss. I used to think wyverns were a myth too. Maybe you'll see differently one day."

Sussah shuddered. "I hope not. If the stories are true, then they're nasty, vile beasts."

"Like I said. Wait until you see one. You might be very surprised."

"You believe in them?" Sussah tried to hide her giggle.

"They're fun to ride once you get the hang of it." Leonie sighed, missing her time with them.

They fell silent for a time. Leonie got up and picked up a piece of cracked paving. "Could you stand by the edge there." She pointed to the opposite side of the area.

Sussah did as asked, looking puzzled. "Why?"

"Can you see me?" Leonie called out instead.

Sussah squinted, shading her eyes against the sun. "Yes," she shouted back.

"Hss. I can't see you, just a blurry landscape. I'm going to throw something. Tell me if you see it land." Leonie tossed the tile through the portal. It sailed through the centre of the arch.

"I didn't see anything come through," Sussah called out. "Does that mean it works?"

"I think so."

"Can I try?" Sussah jogged around enthusiastically.

"Why not. Reckon you'll be able to hit it?"

Sussah poked her tongue out and searched for a tile to throw. It glanced off the top edge and went through.

From Leonie's angle, the tile was there, then vanished. She was sure she didn't blink or lose sight of it.

"What do we do with it?" Sussah asked when Leonie came around.

"*We* won't do anything. When we return to Delta, I'll talk to some people I know. No doubt a scholar will be able to work something out. Maybe find out where it goes." She put her palm on part of it. The crystal did have a very subtle vibration.

"But how *do* we get back to Delta?" Sussah asked, eyes downcast.

"Of course, your parents will be worried. Anyone else?"

"Well ... there is a boy ..."

"Aha. We'll think of something." She had no idea what to do but didn't want Sussah to get upset. "Maybe Niaarin will come looking, to gloat over her handiwork. I'm sure she's none too pleased with having half a priest on her floor." The widening of Sussah's eyes showed that didn't work.

"Only joking." Time for a distraction she decided. "But, before we start worrying about that, let's explore this place and try to find better shelter. I doubt anyone's been here for hundreds of years." Picking a direction they hadn't been, she walked off, Sussah by her side, listening intently as Leonie told her the little she knew about the skylands.

"There could be treasure here," Sussah enthused.

"You never know. If that *is* a portal – and *if* the rumours are true – then we could be standing in Dromas."

"Dromas?"

"You've heard of the Vale of Dromas?"

"Only a bit."

"They say around four hundred years ago there was a war among the powershapers. And the city was destroyed. They also reckon these portals were all there."

"And these skylands were part of Dromas?"

"It's what they reckon." Leonie shrugged.

"So, there *could* be ancient treasure here!"

"There just might be at that." Leonie smiled at the girl's enthusiasm.

"You never told me how you started the fire," Sussah reminded her.

"I have this ring." She slid it off to show her. "I just activate it. Anyone could do it."

"It isn't much to look at." She peered at it closely. "How long has it been cracked?"

"Cracked?" Leonie took it back and carefully studied it. She hadn't taken much notice of it at all. *Had it always been there?* It was true; the ring had a small but definite split. *Then how did I cast the fireball?*

She sat down on a log to rest her leg and think. Dredging Styx's last words from the dark recesses of her mind. *'You must learn to trust yourself implicitly – there is absolutely nothing – NOTHING – you cannot accomplish if you have the right attitude. You have to put your mind to it. It is that simple.'* Leonie rolled the ring in her fingers. *Could it be?*

"Are you okay?" Sussah knelt by her side in concern. "Have the apples made you sick?"

"No. Not sick." She popped the ring in her pouch. With a deep breath, she conjured a small flame in her palm. "Not sick at all."

"Is that *you* doing that?" Sussah's eyes lit up.

Leonie nodded, stunned.

"You *are* a powershaper!" Sussah jumped with glee. "I've never known one before. Now I do!"

"Creating a small flame doesn't make me a powershaper."

"It does to me. I bet you can do lots more." It would seem nothing was going to convince Sussah otherwise. "Can you fly? Can you go invisible?"

Instead of instantly laughing, Leonie considered her harness with its cracked crystal. *When did the crystal crack? How long …?* With a thought, the flame dwindled. "It can't be this easy," she muttered. She took her harness off, just to be sure, and placed it on the ground. Thinking of rising, she rose off the ground.

"See!" Sussah jumped up and down. "I knew it."

"Well, you knew before I did." Again, Styx's words *'there is absolutely nothing …'* She tried moving sideways just by thought. It worked! She practised going back and forth. Slowly, Leonie started to fly around to test what she could do. After a short period, immense fatigue came over her. She landed swiftly and inelegantly with her injured leg, slumping to the soft grass, exhausted. Drained.

The young girl came running over, not with concern but sheer joy, babbling incoherently with her excitement.

"Enough," Leonie put her paws up. Sussah helped her to stand. They wandered back to collect the harness, then returned to the building to rest.


Later in the afternoon, they worked their way through a thick grove of trees. Those on the edge were worse for wear, but further in, where years of accumulated leaves had made soft, thick compost, the smaller trees looked healthier. In here, the wind died down. Leonie heard the burbling of birds in the thick growth, out of sight.

Through the middle of the grove was another stone wall covered in moss. As Leonie climbed it, the bard's torc flopped out from her blouse. She had completely forgotten about it.

"That's beautiful? Did you …" Sussah stopped.

Leonie laughed, handing it to her. "No, I didn't *steal* this one, if that's what you were going to say." They sat down on the soft moss. "A glins'ool bard gave it to me yesterday before the hunt. He said he'd be able to track me with it. I don't reckon he counted on me being here, though."

"You don't think he'll find us?" Sussah turned it in her small hands, fingers running over the runes.

"Even if he could, it'd take weeks for him to get here. You keep it for a while."

"Can I?"

"If it starts vibrating, let me know."

"I promise." Sussah put it around her neck immediately.

After they left the trees, they found more ruins, but in better condition than the one where they'd spent their first night.

"This must be closer to the middle; the buildings here are in better condition," Leonie said. "The edge is unstable, but the ground here's more solid."

The front room of the first building was large. The marble floor was covered in remnants of a large rug which fell apart at a touch. The room even had a fireplace.

"At least we have a proper roof." Sussah looked at the ceiling where a faded mural of long-legged birds in flight could just be seen. She started to walk up the stone stairway on the west wall, but Leonie called her back.

The young girl came down reluctantly. "There are other rooms up there. I thought we were looking for treasure."

Leonie looked around them. "My guess is everything's rotten or fallen apart. Anything up there will be in bad condition, if not worse. There's a risk of falling onto the stone floor."

Sussah pouted.

They found a cellar, but whatever had been stored there had long ago deteriorated into hard lumps. A courtyard out back may have enclosed a vegetable patch. It had gone wild, but they dug up a few tubers which looked vaguely familiar.

Among other utensils, a thick pot lay upended in a kitchen corner. It was in reasonably good condition to use and after gathering water from the pond and wood, Leonie set to make a weak stew.

Sussah eyed it dubiously before wandering off to poke through the rubble, stepping into the next room for more.

"Don't go too far," Leonie cautioned.

"I won't," the girl answered.

The pot bubbled away merrily, and as Leonie stuck more wood in the fire, she heard a loud splintering, followed by a scream.

Dropping the faggot, Leonie loped to the door. At first glance, the room looked empty, but then Leonie spotted a pair of legs sticking through the ceiling.

Bounding up the stairs, Leonie stopped at the top. Several paces along a passage she saw Sussah buried in the floor up to her torso.

"I didn't go far." Sussah forced a smile.

Leonie slowly shook her head from side to side, relieved she wasn't injured. "I should leave you there. Maybe you'll learn something." She turned to go.

"Don't go!" the girl pleaded. "I'm sorry."

Leonie stopped and sighed. She was about to step off the stonework but paused. Although more agile, she was heavier than the girl. If they were both on the same section of floor, maybe they'd both fall through. She concentrated, mustering the smallest amount of power into a thought.

Sussah rose slowly and moved a few feet towards her before Leonie had to stop, energy depleted, but the danger was over. The floorboards creaked but held steady as the girl tiptoed to the stairway.

"Did you hurt yourself?"

Sussah shook her head hugging her. "Thank you. For everything."

Uncomfortable with hugs, Leonie's exhausted reply sounded more like a grunt.

Together they made their way down the stairs.

"I told you not go up there," Leonie reproved. "What'd you think you were doing?"

"Just looking," Sussah replied defensively.

Leonie held her tongue, then started to laugh.

"What's so funny?" Sussah's face went red.

"Now I know how Jade felt. She was my boss." *And friend.* Leonie sniffed. "I think dinner's burning. You better save it," Leonie said, limping down the stairs. "I'm too slow."

**12**

---

## REALM OF THE DEAD

Evlin's lifeless eyes took no joy in her surroundings.

Born lowly and friendless, she discovered great enjoyment in the taking of life at an early age. The bewildered and confused look on their faces amused her. The feeling that if a god created life, then how great was she to be able to undo a god's work, thrilled her as no other drug could. She took no delight however when her target, a mere half-breed street thief, turned the tables and took her life instead.

She wondered absently if the look on own her face when she had died was any different to *her* victims.

The landscape of purgatory was a desolate, barren wasteland; a dark, viscous fluid bubbled in the stagnant pools dotting the landscape. The dry, brittle crunching of gravel underneath her shoes turned out to be skulls and bones. *How many of them are the dead I have dispatched?* In some cases, she sank knee-deep in what she initially thought to be solid ground but turned out to be pockets of partially decomposing and bloated bodies. Not all of them were completely immobile; some lingering force kept these lost souls seeking something. Redemption?

*Not for me.* The thought of these poor bastards, lost and forlorn in this land of limbo and seeking forgiveness, made the grin on her face reveal the depth of the cuts on her lacerated throat. On a whim, she unsheathed her dagger and plunged it into the ribcage of a withering form so decayed she had difficulty deciding if it was man or woman. As suspected, no *force* of any description flowed into her. She wiped the dagger on her sleeve and stepped on the body as she pushed herself forward.

Dull and listless as she was, she had a task. Evlin had no idea of how long she wandered this desolation. While the dull light above sometimes rippled slowly with slight variations in shade and hue, no sun or moon shone here. No demarcation of night or day. No time.

Her goal, to drop the bleeding corpse of the Enemy at her master's feet. The Enemy that thwarted her every move. The Enemy that killed her colleagues. The Enemy that killed *her!* The task Evlin demanded of herself now was straightforward in concept; locate the mage, Niaarin Grigorid.

This mage was responsible for the disappearance of the Enemy by the use of magic. Niaarin's wayward powershaping sent the Enemy to a place even her master could not locate. But, if the mage sent her, then she must know where she sent her to. Find the mage, and she would find the Enemy. Bring the Enemy to her master, and receive her bounty. The reward she craved, to be removed from purgatory, to serve her master in the way she knew best; killing.

Once again, Evlin retrieved the amulet she had found on the mage's desiccated remains back in the palace. She held it in both hands and concentrated. Her sensing had diminished in strength here, but some sensing ability was better than none. Holding the amulet should increase her ability, at least regarding the whereabouts of this mage.

There was the faintest of vibrations. It was so minimal, she almost missed it. Evlin concentrated as intensely as only the dead could. There it was. She swivelled slowly left and right to gain a better direction. To the left increased the vibration marginally. With more purpose in her slothful stride, she moved in that direction, holding the amulet like a divining rod. The moment the vibration weakened, she stopped to check her bearings before moving off again.

A glow on the horizon caught her attention. This was new. In the distance, more shambling corpses could be seen. Slow as she was, Evlin was able to pass these dead easily enough, laughing as she pushed them over. They were all heading in the same direction. The closer to the glow, the more bodies there were. She realised this must be one of the gates to their heaven. If this was where Niaarin was, then this could only be the gateway for the devotees of Eternix.

Soon, the intensity of the glow was sufficient to create shadows. At this distance, it was hard to accurately determine its size, but from the silhouettes in front, seemed to be taller than three bodies and double that in width.

Evlin had to start shoving through the dead crowd as they converged on this avenue of escape. The amulet's vibration was now distinct and she started looking at each person carefully. If the memory of what the mage was wearing when she died was correct, Evlin kept an eye out for a tall, thin feline form in silky blue robes.

Finally, Evlin spotted her; there weren't many power-shapers here. She surged through the pack of dead and seized the mage by the arm, turning her around. There was minimal resistance and the mage shuffled in whatever direction Evlin pointed but if she let go, the corpse would slowly turn back towards the gate.

They stopped by a gnarled tree trunk. The mage's body slowly staggered in an arc trying to head back towards the gate until Evlin dragged her back and pushed her up against the trunk. Doing what came naturally to her, she drew the dagger, held the mage's paw and skewered it to the wood.

Try as she might, she could discover nothing from the dead mage. Talking was pointless, the mage's eyes stared blankly at the gate. Evlin had no mind-reading abilities, thinking perhaps the dagger's power would assist in some way, but no.

She decided to appease her frustration with a bit of torture, but that quickly proved tedious, and the dead felt no pain. Evlin was a better killer than interrogator. When she pulled the dagger out, the mage immediately stumbled forward to the gate. If it were possible, Evlin's despair grew. Not only had she failed in her initial task – to kill the Enemy – her only path to finding Leonie was standing here in front of her. So close, yet the knowledge was lost in her dead mind.

"I am so enjoying this new position," the voice behind her said. "Seeing such despair … is heartening."

Slow to react, Evlin turned to face the voice. "Master?" she managed to croak.

"Finally, you have made a minor success. It is so astounding to see how the right amount of incentive can drive one to triumph." Tirruk stepped past Evlin and laid both hands on the mage's brow.

Evlin watched on as her master muttered an incantation; a slow droning sound, much like the constant wind that scoured this forsaken landscape. The mage writhed under his grip. Her slender arm reached out, not to fight, but extending her fingers imploringly towards the gateway.

Absorbed by her new master's actions, Evlin became aware of the shaft of light emanating from the gate at the last moment. Slow to react, she stumbled toward her master to shoulder him away thinking it was an attack on his person. She fell through him. The light continued forward and engulfed the limp mage. The dagger pulled free and dropped to the ground. Niaarin Grigorid's lifeless body drifted above the teeming dead and disappeared into the glow of the gateway.

Tirruk's incorporeal form turned, studying the assassin curiously. "The mage is of no further use. I managed to glean the information from her before her returning."

"You know the whereabouts of the Enemy?" Evlin was startled into speaking. "Please master, send me to do your bidding. Let me redeem myself to you and Lord Opsyss," she begged, the sound of her voice dry and raspy to her ears.

Tirruk looked down on her, almost benignly. "Poor, poor Evlin. Haven't you failed enough? You failed your Jart'lekk master; you failed your previous Opsyss master several times." He shook his head slowly, surveying the bleakness around him. "Perhaps I am soft, but if Lothas, in his vast wisdom, deemed you worthy of an extra chance, maybe I should heed his example. Perhaps I could consider permitting you one last opportunity." Tirruk turned and started striding away. "Perhaps …"

Cruel and vindictive as she had become in her hard and unforgiving existence, Evlin's resolve left her as he departed. She dropped to her knees and whimpered in utter dejection.

"It was pointless to try and save me from that shaft of god-light." He put his hand out. "But I *am* truly touched by your loyalty."

Evlin looked up. Without hesitation, she took it, laying her cold, rancid hand in his.

"Come. Let's return to the other side. For your loyalty, I feel a slight reprieve is in order until Our Lord deigns to share His knowledge with us ."

## 13

# FLYING VISITORS

THE NEXT DAY WAS BRIGHT AND SUNNY IF A BIT COOL; LEONIE suggested a walk around the skyland to see how big it actually was. She felt her condition had improved enough to remove the bandages from her thigh, and she could use her paw without pain.

Trying to keep the edge in view, they walked around the perimeter. Most of the flourishing plants were in the centre, leaving struggling, stunted growth on the outskirts. There were low rolling hills and scattered boulders, and again the terrain was more broken towards the outside.

Standing at the front of the skyland, Leonie gazed down. Below, a vast plain stretched to the western horizon. The height didn't bother her, but she realised the previous skyland had been much higher. She was a few paces back, wary of the deceptive ground. She watched, fascinated at how the horizon changed, realising that as they moved north, the skyland rotated slowly. If she stood there long enough, the front would over time become the rear.

Sussah sat in the long grass, well back from the edge, still too wary to get closer.

Snacking on the remainder of the apples, they came across

half a stone tower teetering on the edge, the other portion was missing completely. How the whole thing hadn't toppled yet was anyone's guess. By mid-afternoon, they recognised their current shelter.

Crossing the old garden, Leonie spotted specks in the distance, too blurry for any detail. She stopped to watch until the image became more defined.

Sussah squinted, but couldn't see anything. "What is it?" she asked. "Birds?"

"I'm not sure if big birds fly like that?"

"Like what?"

"In a diamond shape. Quick. Let's get the fire going. They're glins'ool!" She bolted across the open area and darted nimbly through the grove where she lost sight of them.

A few heartbeats later, she had the fire in the hearth building up. She threw some of the carpet remnants on it, and anything else she could find. "Keep an eye on them," she called out as Sussah panted through the door.

"I can hardly see them." Sussah squinted.

"Keep this going then." Leonie ran out the door, searching the sky. She glanced to the collapsed chimney, relieved to see the smoke building up.

*Where are they?* Within moments she spied them. There didn't appear to be any change in their flight path. "Over here!" she yelled. She knew it was completely useless. No way would her voice be heard over such a distance, but it was borne more from frustration than common sense. With little thought, she instigated a fireball to flare into the sky.

She stumbled with immediate fatigue but continued to watch as the specks diminished, blinking back tears of futility, wiping her eyes before Sussah saw, not wanting to aggravate the situation.

Leonie heard coughing and turned to see smoke issuing from the windows of the ruins. *Now what?* Jogging to the doorway, she peered inside through the smoky haze.

"You okay?"

"I think I put too much on."

In her rush, Sussah had thrown more refuse in the hearth than it could bear. The ruined chimney couldn't cope and smoke started to fill the room. There wasn't much they could do about it other than making sure everything else was clear of the hungry flames. After they separated the unburnt material from the fire, they stumbled outside, coughing, to sit in the grass while the smoke cleared. Sussah sat, drawing her legs up to her chest and wrapping her arms around them.

"Hey, it's alright," she coughed. "It'll burn itself out soon enough. Lucky it's a stone floor, otherwise we'd need to find another shelter—" She spun at a noise behind her, jumping out of her skin when she saw the gathered group of glins'ool. "Slistorf's balls!"

"Well met. I am Talon Gruy si Ferik, of the Nest of Snarr, at your service." He turned and introduced his companions – ten in all, two of them females.

All had dark grey feathers, wearing hard leather breastplates. Each carried several long, thin javelins in a case strapped to the centre of their backs as well as a bow. Weird sacks, attached by sturdy leather braiding, hung down from wide belts.

Annoyed, and a touch embarrassed for letting them sneak up, Leonie introduced herself and Sussah, already forgetting most of the strange avian names, but she was curious to see the female avians, Sera and Wyth.

At a nod from their Talon, two soared into the air while another pair stepped inside the ruins. They had a strange gait, making them look awkward on the ground.

"My people will ensure everything is alright."

"I saw you. We tried to get your attention with the smoke." Leonie pointed.

"A sound plan, though your methods may need revising, but it worked," he chuckled. "You have extraordinary eyesight," he said to Leonie. "Shall we sit and share food?"

"That would be very welcome."

As the rest of the wing unpacked to prepare an assortment of unfamiliar foods, the leader looked to both of them. "This, of course, leads me to my next question; how you came to be in this remote place without wings?"

As they tried the food, Leonie explained, in part, how a vengeful rrell mage sent them here by some spell. She omitted to mention the hunt or the fact she was out to kill the mage herself. She wasn't sure what Gruy thought, though clearly from the wrinkling of his brow he had doubts. He remained silent, just nodding until she finished. "And you Miss? Did this mage, despise you too?"

"I don't know." Sussah looked down, the wing with their bright yellow eyes double-blinking at her. "I saw what happened to Leonie. Niaarin didn't want me to say anything against her or her guards."

Leonie coughed, choking on a slice of nuts and seeds. "I'm alright." She waved at the faces turning to her. "I just remembered something. Show them the torc, Su."

The young girl quickly pulled the chain free from her blanket coat, handing the amulet to Gruy. All the wing gathered around, craning long necks to see. Their quiet talk in their language sounded similar to the burbling of the birds Leonie heard in the grove. She suppressed a smile. "A friend of mine, a visiting bard from Reenat, gave it to me, knowing the mage was out to get me. He also suggested if I needed help, that would get it."

Gruy silently turned the torc over in his hands.

The wing cleaned up after the food was eaten, securing everything efficiently in their sacks. They moved a discrete distance away from their Talon, accompanied by Leonie and Sussah, quietly answering the girl's questions about their home and what they were doing in the area. They'd had word of l'ith-namagri sightings.

"It was fortunate we arrived. A small tribe of nomads were under threat. We assisted in fighting the creatures off and helped with the wounded. But we couldn't bring ourselves to help with their dead," Wyth said.

"We glins'ool cremate the deceased, to allow our spirits to

return to the Great Sky," Sera explained. "Walkers do not share this belief, insisting on *burying* their dead in the ground!" She shook her head.

"Where are we, exactly?" Leonie asked. "I don't recognise any of the landmarks below. It's only a hunch, but I think we are on the west side of Shak'aran."

"Your hunch is correct." Wyth nodded. "This sky-island is currently above the realm of Fisbane. While I have heard of Reenat, in Athglenn, I am not familiar with Delta."

They looked up when Gruy came over. He looked troubled; the deeper creases around his eyes and beak made him look older.

"We must be on our way, to report back to the nest of what has occurred with the recent battle. We will leave food. I admit finding what you say difficult to believe – even though I cannot furnish a plausible reason for your presence. If I was rude, I'd say you weren't telling the entire truth.

"This, however, is familiar to me." He raised the torc. "We had a travelling bard in the area three moons ago. We can get word to him, and in turn through his nest-friend to this bard of Reenat. It could take many weeks though."

Sussah looked as though she was about to burst into tears.

He handed Leonie the torc. She sat quietly, waiting for what was to come.

Gruy continued in softer tones. "The torc tells me all I need to know. This makes you *bardfriend,* and therefore a friend of all nests. As soon as we return to our nest, I'll organise help to get you off this skyland."

"Yes please," Sussah piped up.

"The view here is spectacular," Leonie said. "But the accommodation is a bit bland."

Gruy shook his head, bemused. "You are a strange one, Leonie, but these are strange times. Then it's decided. I'll leave you with a wingman to keep you safe, and help will arrive within a few sunrises."

"We'll stay, if it pleases you, Talon," Sera said. Wyth nodded at her side.

He inclined his head, clacking his beak. They nodded in reply and went to collect extra food parcels from a couple of their fellow wingmen.

"I have left you with two of our most gifted flyers. I'm sorry for not being able to help more. But before I go, I must know the name of this bard?"

"Tipp. Tipp nul Chor Tukk." *Slistorf's whiskers! How did I remember that?* "From Reenat Bardic Council."

"Truly? I have heard of him! I will get a message to him as soon as I can. We have telepaths back at the nest."

"Didn't you say you would get word to another bard and use *his* contacts?"

"But Chor Tukk is not just *any* bard." He bowed in farewell and turned to leave.

"Wait, you can't go yet. I almost forgot. There's something else you need to see. Something important to everyone! Follow me."

Clucking in annoyance, the Talon motioned her to lead on.

She hurried off as fast as her leg would permit, but it was improving. Sussah and a couple of avians followed. The others, seeing the difficulty with pushing through the trees, decided to fly overhead, re-joining by the pond.

"Do your scholars think we all come from other worlds?" Leonie asked.

Gruy fluttered his wings. "It's a theory, though where the rumours started I know not."

Most of the avians nodded in agreement.

"Ah. A sceptic I see. I felt the same – until I saw this." She picked up several pieces of cracked paving while asking the wing to move around the pond. "Don't take your eyes off these." She held one up. "Tell me what you see." She nonchalantly tossed it into the centre of the archway. From their squawks, she knew some had witnessed the disappearance. They moved around while Leonie tossed several more through. After a while, all witnessed the pavers vanish.

Questions burst forth in a rush. Leonie held her paws up as Gruy stepped closer. "I know little more than you." She touched on her conversation with Feiron over a month ago. It wasn't much, and it was plain to see they wanted more. "You might want to let your scholars know this."

The Talon nodded, staring at the archway.

"You're wondering where it goes," she said to him without question.

"That is true. All this time and I thought it was hatchling stories."

"You and me both. So, tell me, do you believe in wyverns?"


Three days ago, the wing had left. Wyth and Sera, the two remaining avian warriors, were good company, showing them what sort of wild berries and roots to eat or avoid, and regaling them with stories of Fisbane and life in the nest.

The *nest* was a term every glins'ool referred to for their home. It was, in essence, a community where everyone had a role. Everyone was provided for and there was no violence and rarely any serious crime.

At sunrise, the two avians went off with Sussah to look at the archway again. They went every day, fascinated by it.

Leonie stayed behind, grumbling about her restless sleep. There was the increasing ache in her bowels, and the wind howled constantly; sometimes louder or from a different direction, but it was always there in the background. The whooshing through small gaps in the roof and walls created whistling noises; depending on direction and force, the pitch changed. Sometimes it came through the damaged chimney, blowing ash and embers everywhere.

The tone of the wind changed. It reminded Leonie of the big, hollowed reeds the river-men back in Delta used as musical instruments; a deep, resonating drone they played non-stop by breathing through their nose and blowing through their mouths at the same time. Rolling over, she shook her head in a futile effort to get rid of the noise.

The sound of the wind increased. Now the air throbbed, coming through the gaps in the door. "Stomach-aches I can deal with, but this noise is giving me the shits!" she whinged to herself, chuckling at the irony. She stood and stretched to ease the cramping before trying to shut the door more firmly. It refused to close properly. She looked down and saw leaves and twigs in the jamb, so opened it fully to remove the debris.

Outside, something from a nightmare landed on the cracked paving. Leonie had seen it before – way down in the southern ranges, and the night Evlin attacked her. It was a brief glimpse, but you'd never forget a hideous sight like that. *Does that mean Evlin is here?*

The droning had stopped and she realised it had been the beating wings that made the loud buzz. She watched the multi-legged creature. Its head moved side to side. The long antennae on top were wiggling back and forth – much like she'd seen insects do.

Her mind tickled as it turned multifaceted eyes towards the house. *It is using psionics.* The clacking of the mandibles added incentive. As it lurched in her direction, she slammed the door shut and jumped back. The wall shuddered with the force of the l'ith's impact; the door flew in, broken off its rusty hinges.

The bug's head was too big for the doorway, but by the way it was ramming it, it would be through shortly. Leonie bolted into the kitchen, looking for something. Anything.

She spied the pot over the cook fire. She grabbed the handle and hauled it off. The l'ith was part way through. The doorway was a ruin; stone bricks and mortar littered the area, and dust made swirls across the floor, blown by the wind.

Leonie bounded in, flinging the contents at the creature's massive head. The remainder of the wall collapsed as the l'ith reared back with more force than Leonie had ever seen. Its screeching cut through her nerves. She clamped paws over her ears, but her mind felt it too.

It was only a slight reprieve. The creature leapt forward with nothing to hinder it now. Leonie sped back to the kitchen and leapt out of the broken window, leaving the l'ith to bludgeon its way through the building. She ran around the ancient courtyard wall, scampered across the lawn and ducked into the grove.

Behind her, the house collapsed with a thunderous crash. She stopped, hidden behind a thicket and turned to watch, quickly reciting a children's poem in her head to block thoughts.

The rubble moved. Old roofing beams snapped like twigs as the beast reared up and clambered over the top. From where she was, she could still see one antenna moving, the other looked shorter. It slowly covered the area from front to back as if searching for some sign of her. She realised it must have sensed her trail with its antennae, for it followed the path she'd just taken.

Leonie didn't wait any longer. She ducked and weaved as fast as she could through the tangle of trees hoping to lose it, and maybe gain time. Then she heard the droning again. "Slistorf's balls!" she hissed.

Ahead, she saw the two avians and Sussah. They were looking her way with bows in hand.

"L'ith," she screamed as she burst forth from the scrub.

The warrior women soared into the air with an explosion of wings.

"Su, come here!"

White-faced, the girl sprinted to Leonie, her sandalled feet pumping over the damp grass.

"Stay in among the trees. The close confines might be our only protection."

They both looked up from the scant cover of the trees. Wyth and Sera had split up and fired arrows at the l'ith. Every shaft hit, but nothing seemed to affect it greatly. The avians dodged and wove around the bug; what they lacked in brute force they made up with agility. If it wasn't for the dire circumstances, Leonie would have thought they were dancing.

The l'ith began to slow, but the avians' reactions were also growing weary. The droning changed pitch. The bug descended erratically, crashing to the ground in the middle of the wood.

With a whoosh of air and feathers, Wyth and Sera landed awkwardly by the edge of the trees. Both sat heavily, wings loosely pulled in, chests heaving in exhaustion; their gasping breath sounding like whistles. With quivers empty, they clipped the bows onto their breastplates.

"It still lives," Sera warned when Leonie and Sussah emerged. They could all hear the sound of the branches cracking from deep in the grove as the creature thrashed. "But we slowed it down."

"You did better than anyone I know. Certainly better than me, cowering in the trees."

"You'd be dead by now otherwise, as would Sussah. Talon Gruy would be most displeased with us."

"So would we." Leonie was at a loss. The bug was a creature she couldn't even hope to contend with.

"It comes," Sera stated as the thrashing grew louder. "It's almost done. We have few weapons left. I hope it suffices." She hefted one of her three javelins. "You two should move away. We can fly if need be, but you don't have that luxury."

"I've got to do *something*," Leonie argued. "I can't leave you with all the fun."

"If the Talon says we are to protect you, then that's what we'll do. Don't make this any harder for us."

With a final splintering of wood, the l'ith came into view, dragging several broken limbs through the scrub. Green ichor seeped from several cracks in its shell.

Simultaneously Wyth and Sera hurled their javelins, but the low angle caused the points to slide off the tough shell. Reaching for another, they stepped back, Leonie and Sussah moving with them.

With a cry, Wyth fell back, stumbling on the uneven ground

and debris. They heard the crack as she hit the ground. She rolled in pain, clutching her arm.

Sera threw her javelin while Leonie and Sussah darted in to help get Wyth off the ground.

"My arm," Wyth groaned.

Looking over her shoulder, Leonie tried to find a place to go. It was all open ground for a good distance, then the boulders. The bug would have difficulty, but so would they.

"Su, take Wyth that way. Sera and I will keep it distracted."

Leonie took the last javelin out of Wyth's quiver and moved with Sera to the right, yelling and waving their arms to attract the l'ith.

The l'ith tried to rear up, but its hind legs refused to cooperate. Instantly, Sera let fly with her javelin, but again, the hard carapace deflected the weapon. The l'ith hissed and screeched at them, clacking its mandibles menacingly.

"At least you got its attention," Leonie pointed out as it turned to them.

"Yes, but unfortunately, that was my last weapon."

"Here, take this. I'd probably miss anyway. If I get it to turn, you reckon you'd get it between those sections?"

"It would seem to be the weak spot."

When Leonie sprinted to the side yelling and waving, the bug continued after the avian. She searched for rocks, anything to hurl. Nothing. Reluctantly, but desperate, she conjured a small fireball at its eyes. The left side of the head flashed when the flame hit.

As it turned towards the new threat, Sera darted in and hurled the last javelin with all her might, sinking it into the softer joint.

The l'ith spun faster than anticipated, catching Sera unprepared. Awkward on the ground at the best of times, the avian stumbled back, her rear claw catching on a rock. She twisted and saved herself from injury, but struggled to stand up again.

Leonie sprinted in and cast another fireball; it was weaker, only damaging two of its front legs and blackening the carapace.

It stumbled, but lived, crawling closer to the fallen glins'ool. Feeling fatigued, Leonie had to think of another way to stop this monster.

She grabbed the javelin which had wedged in the joint. She jerked it back and forth, working it in deeper. The bug twisted in pain. Leonie held on grimly, or risk being crushed underfoot.

Using the javelin as a pivot, Leonie lurched onto the back and used its wings and joints as paw holds. She then reefed the javelin out and crawled to the neck. Here she stood and quickly placing the javelin behind the neck joint, drove it in with all her weight. She clung for her life as the l'ith spun around and hooked a claw onto Sera's leg.

Sera's scream pierced the air.

Every moment she got, Leonie sawed the javelin, goring the monster's internal organs until it collapsed. She was still working it deeper when she heard her name being called. In a daze, Leonie looked around. Wyth was kneeling by Sera's body.

"Leonie. It's dead!" Sussah yelled.

Leonie looked down at herself. She was covered in green and yellow ichor. The l'ith had collapsed and lay unmoving beneath her. Shaking like a leaf, Leonie's legs sagged. Still covered in slime, she slid off the l'ith and stumbled to where Wyth was kneeling by Sera.

"I tried," Leonie wept, collapsing to the grass. "I tried." She couldn't recall ever seeing so much blood.

"And you did well. Sera lives thanks to you," Wyth wept with joy.

"Sera's alive?" Leonie crawled closer.

"She has lost much blood, and may not be able to walk unaided, but she is breathing."

Leonie wiped her eyes, which seemed to be stinging. "I'm … glad."

"You are a powershaper?"

Leonie shook her head.

"Yes, she is," Sussah said. "She can create fireballs and she can fly—"

"Su," Leonie shook her head. "Look at me. I'm as weak as a kitten. We nearly died."

"But we didn't," Wyth pointed out. "You saved Sera, you saved me, and most of all, you saved Sussah. You should be proud."

Leonie chuckled. "In all honesty, I'm just damn tired." And she fainted.

When Leonie woke up, water and food had been placed nearby. She had also been wiped down, but there was still enough of the l'ith muck on her to stink. No one was in sight, but she heard them just beyond the trees. She ate the food quickly and headed to bathe in the pond, giving the trio a quick wave and looking forward to being clean again.

Turning, she saw the three of them strolling to the pond. She climbed out and wiped herself down as best she could as they approached, surprised at how refreshed she felt. She wondered if it had something to do with the proximity to the portal; it was the only area where she sensed power.

Sera was limping, using a broken branch as a walking stick to hobble around. Her wound was wrapped with lengths of Coundar's old cloak. Wyth's arm needed attention, but no one had the skill to set it properly. They had made a sling from Coundar's shirt to restrain it. "Good to see what I scavenged from the priest came in handy." Leonie grinned. "Good job.

"We found another shelter." Sussah explained how they kept busy while she recovered. "And we found as many arrows and javelins as we could."

Wyth bowed slightly. "I am sorry we did not move you to a more comfortable area to rest, but with our injuries, it was going to be difficult."

"I've been in worse places, believe me." Leonie brushed off their apology. "I should thank you for the food."

"Good to see you up and about. I owe you so much for saving my life," Sera hobbled over and placed her hand on

Leonie's shoulder. "And to think *we* were supposed to be protecting *you*."

"I promise I won't tell your boss."

They slowly started to make their way to the new shelter.

"It would be unusual for a l'ith to fly alone?" Leonie asked. She was looking at the horizon.

"It is unusual," Sera agreed.

"Maybe it was a scout," Wyth offered, following Leonie's gaze.

"Is it the wing returning?" Sussah asked, watching.

"More l'ith!" Leonie hissed recognising their formation.

"I count … eight," Wyth said.

"We had enough trouble with one. We can't hope to kill all of them."

"We'll die defending you." Wyth unhitched her bow. Sera did the same.

"I'd rather not die at all if it's all the same to you," Leonie said.

"There's nowhere to hide. Better to go down in combat than cowering," Wyth vowed.

"Can you still fly at all?" Leonie asked both of the glins'ool warriors.

"With difficulty," Wyth replied. Sera nodded.

"What about gliding?" Sussah suggested. "Is that easier?"

"It is irrelevant," Wyth declared. "We are unable to carry you, and we will not be leaving you, so it is pointless to think about it. We should be looking for a defensive position. Perhaps another old house." Wyth looked to the woods and the old buildings beyond.

"I don't want to sound defeatist, but we haven't got a chance," Leonie stated. "Those ruins will collapse on us."

"Can't you still cast your fireballs?" Sera queried.

"I have no idea for how long. If it's like before, I'll collapse after a few, and it will take more than a few to kill all of them." Leonie wracked her mind for something to help. *It was impossible.* Death would arrive shortly. She looked around, furious that it would end like this. "I will not be bug-food—" She saw the arch. *The portal!*

"What would you be doing if we weren't here?" Leonie quickly asked.

"Again, irrelevant. You *are* here."

"But, *if* we weren't?"

"There would be no reason for us to stay—" Sera replied.

"That's what I thought. Sussah, back to the portal." The girl looked at her, dumbfounded. "The gateway!" Leonie pointed. "We can use it to escape."

"You said we don't know where it goes," she wailed as she stumbled back in fright.

"But we do know what'll happen if we stay, and I will not be responsible for the death of any brave friends." The droning of the l'ith grew louder. "Go, girl!" She turned to Wyth and Sera, not bothering to see if Sussah moved. "We're leaving. So are you."

Wyth helped Sera as they followed. "Our Talon—"

"Isn't here," Leonie pointed out. "You were ordered to defend us. If we go, then you don't have to. Or, you can come if you want, but you have your nest …"

Wyth and Sera shared a glance, warbling urgently to each other.

"We will see you safely through the portal, then we will depart. The wing should not be too long now. We can easily evade these l'ith once we are in the air."

Leonie nodded. "I wish it didn't have to be this way." She quickly clasped their arms in farewell.

"It is what it is," Wyth said, always pragmatic.

They walked to the portal but stopped at the threshold to look back.

"Goodbye, nest-friends," Sera waved.

"May the wind sustain you both," Leonie called back. "Thank you for everything."

With a last quick wave, Leonie and Sussah turned to the archway, staring at the blurred image beyond. Sussah grabbed

Leonie's paw. On the spur of the moment, Leonie removed the bard's torc and placed it on the step of the portal. "I'll explain later," she said to Sussah.

They hesitated, then stepped through.

———

Evlin, intent on her prey, responded to the summons immediately. She had had her fill of force, sufficient to regenerate all her injuries and capabilities. The last few kills were just to pass the time. She moved silently through the shadowed alleys of Delta.

"My young Evlin. Our Lord has deigned to pass on His knowledge."

"What is it, master? Where is she?" She bowed at the feet of this young priest, not much older than herself, his shaved head revealing too few tattoos.

"As I suspected, there are many, many other worlds out there. It would appear our mage has managed to somehow link our world with another. I don't believe this was her intent. No one is capable of transferring someone from one world to another."

"Yet she did."

"True, but she died for her foolishness. In some unknown manner, she devised a spell, intentional or not, that directly tapped into her own god's power. A remarkable achievement, even for an accident."

"Where is this 'other' world?"

"From here, there's no way known." He looked out from the balcony overlooking the great plaza. "But from Realm, there are doorways to everywhere. One just needs to know where to look."

"I am ready, master." Evlin bowed her head.

"Very good."

A familiar stench assailed her. When she raised her head the barren wasteland surrounded her.

"As before, you will have a vast area to cover with even less information to go on."

"I will do whatever is required."

"I have no doubt, however, *this* should result in a faster resolution." He stepped away from her, raised both hands and spoke words of power. The voice emanating from his lips was too deep to be human. From the roiling clouds came a huge winged creature. "It will be far more useful than your l'ith."

The green wyvern landed without a sound. His horned head swivelled around to glare at them as the long, barbed tail curled around clawed feet. Clearly, he was larger than the wyverns encountered over Delta. The amber eyes were deep-set under bony ridges and the elongated snout had a beard of tendrils thicker than her wrist.

Although dead, Evlin stumbled back. She felt an immediate rage, both at herself showing fear, and this creature for causing it.

*What is your god's bidding, priest?*

*Simply to transport our servant here to undertake her task. What she needs to do is of no concern to you.*

*This is my final task?*

*By doing this, your transcendence to the elemental plane will be complete and permanent.* Tirruk turned to the assassin. "He has all the normal attributes of wyverns, so you will be able to communicate with him to some extent."

"I'm no telepath."

"True. You'll have to voice your thoughts."

She took a step forward. "If you fail me, I will dine on wyvern steak."

The wyvern reared up, balancing on its hind legs and tail. The wyvern's roar made the ground rumble.

"Ha!" Tirruk chortled. "You two suit each other. A fine partnership if ever I saw one. So then, to get to this other world, great strength and cunning are required, hence Our Lord's summoning of this magnificent creature. Noldor will need to fly you through the gateway of Eternix. This in itself is highly unusual – the realms of other deities are generally inviolable – but in this case, Lord Opsyss has imbued him with His power. It won't last long but will suffice to get you through. Take heed. Do not land at all or touch anything within the realm of Eternix; her power will take everything you have. Neither of you will return. Near the centre of her realm is the exit. A rift in the sky. What lies beyond is hidden from me, but I suggest you hang on tight."

"Master, why the Eternix realm though? I thought all roads lead to Realm? When those from this other world die, do they not come here too?"

"You are correct, but it seems the efforts of our foolish mage not only transported our target to another world, but also to another time. If you arrived at this world directly, it would be the wrong time. Navigating this rift is extremely devious. The words of power I spoke earlier were channelled directly from Our Lord. He has the information needed to arrive successfully."

"I will—"

"Do not make promises you cannot keep. Know this though; another failure and it will be your last. Go now."

Evlin strode purposefully towards the green wyvern. No words needed to be said. He lowered his neck for her to mount. There was no saddle but a lateral ridge of spines where the neck, torso and wings joined. She was barely seated when the wyvern raised his wings high and, at the same instant he slapped them down, his massive legs propelled them into the dreary sky. She wasn't sure if his ear-shattering roar was his elation to be flying again, or in frustration that he hadn't dislodged her.

# PART II

---

# EARTH

## 14

# STRANGERS IN STRANGER LANDS

THE TWO WOMEN FELL FORWARD ONTO THE DRY, HARD DIRT.

"Ow!" Sussah cried in pain as she stumbled to her hands and knees. Dust immediately rose, causing her to cough and sneeze.

Leonie suppressed a hiss when she hit, rolling to the side to lessen the impact. She lay on her back, groaning and panting. Her eyes squinted shut from the glaring sun. It didn't take long before her glossy, black fur matted with sweat.

It was several minutes before either of them was in a state to consider moving.

Using a boulder to lean on, Leonie slowly stood up. She shaded her eyes with her paw and took a long look at the surrounding area. Behind them, the portal they just fell through was near the edge of a cliff. The faint shimmering slowly dissipated.

They were at one end of a huge valley. Mountains all along the horizon dwindled into the distance. The crag they were on rose from a long ridge, forming the other end of the valley. There wasn't a lot of room to move around.

"How are you feeling?" Leonie asked, her voice shaky.

"Not too good," Sussah croaked, her throat dry from coughing and the choking dust. "That trip then … I felt frozen. It seemed much longer than the first trip." Sussah edged back from the cliff. "Why is it always cliffs?" she moaned.

"Me too. I reckon we travelled a lot further this time."

Sussah joined Leonie by the boulder. "I'm confused."

"We are in another world now."

"We are?"

"Yes." She nodded. "The sun's the wrong colour."

"What do you mean the wrong colour?" Sussah squinted up the sun directly above them, which only brought more tears to her eyes. "What colour should it be? It looks alright to me." She started sneezing.

"It's too yellow. The sun on Yarnik is a bit duller and more orange. It's so much brighter here. And hotter; the air smells weird." Leonie stepped over to the portal to examine it closely. She ran her paws along one of the sides. In size, shape and texture it was identical to the one on the skyland, but looking at it through both sides, she could see the landscape beyond. There was no shimmer or blurred image, and no vibration.

"I think it's broken," Leonie said flatly. "Or it works only one way." She picked up one of the broken tiles they had thrown through from the skyland.

"We can't go back?" Sussah joined her and tossed a rock. It soared through and over the cliff. "Will those monsters come through?"

"The l'ith? If Wyth and Sera flew away, I doubt they'd pay any attention to it."

"You don't know that," Sussah wailed. "You're just guessing."

"It's a good guess." Leonie put her paw on her shoulder. "L'ith don't think like us, but if it makes you feel better, perhaps we should move away."

"To where? How do we get down? I can't climb that."

They both peered over the edge of the pinnacle. It was at least as high as the balcony from the palace. Leonie could climb it easily enough but had to admit Sussah would be hard-pressed.

"Perhaps I could fly you down."

"You can do that here?"

Leonie shrugged, looking dubious. It would have been easier with the harness. "Give me a minute." She concentrated like she would have if she were going to use the fire ring, but this time thought about flying; raising herself off the ground. After a few seconds, her paws lifted off the dirt. She thought about moving sideways, towards the nearest edge, turning so she was now facing that direction.

On the precipice, she slowed and turned around to face the rock face. "I'm going to practise descending. If I feel tired, I'll grab the wall and rest, then return."

Sussah nodded silently, mouth down-turned and a crease on her forehead.

"Don't worry." Leonie began her descent. She felt fine and gained confidence quickly. Other than not having the harness, it felt exactly the same. She estimated she was halfway down before she was satisfied. She considered increasing her altitude, and she slowly reversed her direction. Within a few minutes, she was back beside Sussah, who hugged her fiercely.

"I was so worried."

"Not as worried as me."

"Were you really?" Su asked nervously.

"No." She smiled. "I feel fine."

"You flew much longer this time. You got very tired before."

"I don't think there was much power to draw from the skyland."

"Then how did the portal work?" Sussah asked.

"Pretty well, if you ask me." Leonie chuckled. "Maybe it was all that remained; maybe it was all the skyland had left? I only found out how to use the power a couple of days ago. I've no idea how world-to-world gateways work."

Sussah had another question on her lips. Leonie beat her to it. "Are you ready to go?"

Hesitantly, the young girl nodded.

"Climb onto my back and wrap your arms – not too tight!

And your ankles around my legs." Leonie waited until she had settled. "Here we go."

Leonie repeated the process as before, more nervous now because of the extra weight. "You okay?" she asked.

"So far. Your fur tickles."

"Can't be helped. Just don't sneeze over me."

The cliff face passed steadily as they descended. Leonie concentrated on her breathing, flying and relaxing. She did wonder how long she could have been doing this without the harness. Was it all down to the hroltahg training? Did something happen in the spell?

It was a relief to finally feel the dirt under her paws, as much as it was getting Sussah off her back. Moving around to the side, there was a marginal strip of shade. They both sat where they could.

Leonie took a moment to rest, staring out at the desolate area in which they had been thrown.

"That's like the picture in the palace!" Sussah exclaimed, pointing.

"What picture?" Leonie looked at the landscape.

"Niaarin's dining room had a huge tapestry. It looked like this." She waved her arms about. "It felt weird just looking at it." She shivered. "Didn't you see it?"

"I was a bit preoccupied," Leonie said.

"Those mountains, and those plains." Sussah pointed. "Maybe they're slightly different, but the colour and texture are the same." Sweat ran down her dusty face, leaving trails on her skin.

"I have no answers, other than I doubt very much Niaarin – or anyone from Yarnik – has been here before."

"But you said each race had its own world."

"I said it was what the sages believed, and it's also what is written in prophecy." She sighed. "Similar information from different sources tends to make one believe it. But what I did say was our people came from different worlds – not you or me. Our ancestors, hundreds of years ago." *And Dianah and Brendon.*

In the short time since her arrival, the oppressive heat was already starting to affect her. Her furred body was not conditioned to this constant dry heat. She looked towards the nearby mountains. "We're going to have to seriously think about moving to some shade and finding some water. This sun is going to burn you very quickly." Their little strip of shade had already gone.

Sussah glanced down at herself. Her tunic was torn; her arms legs were scratched and bruised.

"Let's head for those hills," Leonie suggested. "There might be a ravine to get some shade. There might even be some trees. Besides, it's the only exit out of this valley." She spent a few moments searching for the best path over the rough terrain. "You know, I think there's an easier way," she chuckled to Sussah shaking her head. "Climb onto my back again."

"Flying again?"

Leonie shrugged. "May as well see what I can do. I've no idea how long I can keep it up, and we could be walking for hours. I won't go high or fast." As they flew across the strange landscape, Leonie tried a few things. Firstly, she went horizontal; this allowed Sussah to lie instead of hanging onto her neck. Thinking back to when Sussah fell through the floor, she imagined Sussah floating; not to get her to fly, but to remove her weight. Sussah still had to hang on though.

"This is wonderful," she said ecstatically.

"Good. Quiet. I need to concentrate."

The sun relentlessly beat down on them. The land below was rugged in all directions.

The silence stretched. Leonie slowed as they neared a slightly flat area. "I need to rest," she panted. Finding a small patch of shade, they sat. It wasn't any cooler, but they were out of burning sunlight. Leonie tried to relax, beating off a pending headache. *We'll need water soon.*

"Looks like we've been heading east," Leonie spoke up. She pointed to the shadows. "See the angle? If we keep going at this pace we should be there soon. Maybe even find some water." She stood up and stretched to relieve some aches and pains.

Sussah screamed.

Leonie was alert instantly. Approaching from the other side of the clear area was the largest and ugliest dog she'd ever seen. It opened its mouth revealing lots of large fangs, and let out a horrendous howl. It was not only loud but felt like it pierced the soul.

Sussah shrieked again and started whimpering.

Leonie's headache came back with force. "Get behind me." She had to say it twice, then pulled her back. Sussah seemed transfixed.

As the hound approached cautiously, Leonie released a fireball, hitting the beast squarely in the mouth as it began to howl again. The sound stopped as the head exploded. Blown back into the rocks, the body dropped to the ground.

"Grab hold!" Leonie didn't need to repeat it this time.

Swiftly rising, she turned towards the shadowed ravine. Somewhere close behind, they heard more howling. It sent a shiver up her spine.

"Slistorf!"

―――――

Bern had been on the move for two days, taking advantage of the cooler weather. He loved being out here with no one around in any direction for hours. He had one last message delivery before he could get back home and relax until his next shift. Falling unconscious wasn't part of the plan.

When he recovered he shook his head slightly. Using the stump of a tree to get to his feet he looked around blearily, a mild buzzing deep in his head. Something weird had happened, and it had happened over to the west.

He slowed down as he approached the edge of the badlands. His senses guided him this way, but for what, he had no idea. He needed to concentrate, for this was a region of sandstone sitting on top of a vast cave system. Occasional earth tremors kept the terrain unstable. An unwary traveller could step onto a solid looking slab only for it to shift, sending him plummeting to the dark depths below. He followed as near as possible to the path taken the last time he was here but did not take any of it for granted.

It was at this time he heard the howling. "What now?" he muttered.

The sound echoed from down in the valley to his left but was far enough away to be of little effect on him. The scream afterwards, however, stopped him in his tracks. *What fool is down there*, he thought as he jogged as fast as the terrain would allow. Even though it was getting dark, he was able to sense when the terrain levelled out before the cliff edge. Bern skidded to a halt at the threshold.

About six metres below him was an old rockfall, slabs of rubble consisting mainly of sandstone and bits of shale. He concentrated on the strata of the scree. His experience told him that the underlying structure seemed to be more stable just below and to his right, whereas the greater bulk on the left side would give with his weight.

Bern gazed out into the ravine below. He picked up the image of two figures heading his way. While one was a young human girl, the other was a mutation he had not seen before, although she was distinctly female. Both appeared to be moving with some difficulty. About three hundred metres behind them was the forerunner of the howler pack. The animal was closing steadily and would reach the females very soon. They were fortunate to run into the gully. It prevented the howlers from cutting off their escape. Not that it made much difference in this case; they had nowhere else to go.

15
___

# WILDERS

As Bern watched their progress, they slowed down when the ground started to rise. Both females seemed to be near exhaustion. The older one, resembling an upright cat, was limping and the younger was also moving with difficulty. He quickly took off his backpack and utility belt, then without hesitation, stepped off the edge to the right and started jumping from boulder to boulder, making his way down swiftly.

Upon reaching the bottom he broke into as much of a sprint as he could muster. Another howl, much closer this time, echoed off the walls of the ravine. Bern wouldn't have made it this far as a runner if he froze every time he heard it, but his hackles rose all the same. As he neared, the young girl looked up, her haggard face freezing in shock at the sight of him. She stumbled, bringing her companion down in a cry of pain. It may have saved them, for that was when the howler leapt with a snarl; jaws wide and pale eyes flashing.

"Stay down!" he yelled to the women as he moved to intercept the creature.

It was a larger than average howler, about one-and-a-half metres long from slavering muzzle to tail tip and massing around one hundred and fifty kilos. Bern was two metres tall and weighed close to two hundred kilos.

They slammed together with a meaty thud.

Bern threw his hands up to catch it by the neck and snout, gripping it for all he was worth. This close to the creature, the biggest threat was its razor-sharp teeth. They fell thrashing to the ground. It was a struggle, but he managed to get on top and pound its head into the ground. The howler kicked with its hind legs, raking its claws down Bern's legs in its frenetic struggle to get away, almost succeeding at one point.

Bern ignored the pain and fought to keep the animal pinned. He had no doubt he'd die if he lost his grip. Bunching his muscles, he applied pressure to the beast's windpipe. He gagged at the stench and decided without a doubt the biggest threat with getting too close to a howler was its foetid breath.

Its struggles became more frantic, but with one last pathetic howl, the creature died in the dirt. Its fellow pack-members sent up a responding clamour when they sensed the death. They were getting close too.

Bern staggered to his feet, noting the two women standing among the rocks, watching intently. As he turned towards them, the taller one made a defensive stance. He hesitated for a second, seeing what appeared to be sharp claws. Aware of the blood trickling down his legs, he decided he had enough of claws for one day.

"That way, if you want to live." He pointed, breathing heavily.

The two females looked at each other for a moment, but moved in the direction indicated when another howl went up.

Bern followed, guarding the rear and trying to help where he could when they'd let him. As they finally reached the base of the slope, he moved in front and, with as much care that circumstance would allow, hauled them both up onto the boulder, repeating the process as they ascended to higher ground. They were about halfway up when the rest of the howler pack, some ranging from dark brown to tan, a few black, came into view.

Several stopped at the carcass to feed in a wild frenzy before moving on to join the others hungering for fresh targets.

Bern urged the women on and moved away to the area of looser rubble. He had no real psionic abilities but he knew the hounds did, so he sent thoughts of despair and fear. Luck was with him; the hounds headed his way. They had the taste of fresh blood in their mouths and were now in a slavering frenzy. As the pack started to climb, Bern rolled boulders down, partly to slow the hound's advance, but intending to create another slide. A couple of the hounds were struck glancing blows, making them scurry back, but the others dodged and continued, keen for the kill. At first, there didn't appear to be any great effect, then all of a sudden, the ground started to slide away.

He felt his feet slipping and desperately dove back, scrabbling for stable ground. Some of the pack managed to avoid the bulk of the falling rocks, but the majority were crushed or injured as the avalanche came upon them. A loud yelp to his left caused Bern to snap his head around. One of the hounds evaded the rockfall and approached the scree from a different angle. The furry woman hurled stones at it, striking it on the head most of the time. The young girl, higher up the cliff was doing the same but she was less accurate, forcing him to duck as he started making his way to safety. The beast scurried off to join the rest of the surviving howlers ravenously consuming the fallen.

At the top, the trio collapsed in exhaustion. They sprawled where they fell, gasping for breath. The young girl wept. The furry one dragged herself over and put an arm around her shoulders.

Bern reached over and picked up the belt he'd dropped earlier, removing one of the flasks. He winced as he stood up and staggered closer to the pair, carefully showing it to them. "I think you need to drink." To alleviate any suspicion, he sipped some and passed it on.

The furry one gave him a grateful look. "Thank you." She flashed a smile. The universal thanks.

As they drank Bern studied them. The younger girl had

slight cuts on her hands and feet as well as being badly sunburnt on her face, arms and legs, which were also scratched and bruised. She looked to be about sixteen years old.

The furry one had a limp and several cuts; she was simply exhausted. He reckoned she was older by the way she took charge, so confident. What he really wanted to know was who they were, where they were from and why they were out here. He did not recognise the feline, highly unusual considering he knew of everyone in the area by name if not by sight; the girl was indeed even more of a mystery. Maybe a lost citizen of one of the towers, whose aircraft crashed. Other than agtechs, he knew of no other citizen who would venture away from their safety – and she was far too young to be an agtech.

———

As parched as she was herself, Leonie gave the flask to Sussah who began to gulp it down greedily. "Easy Su." Leonie gently pulled it away. "Just a bit at a time or you'll be sick," she said before handing it back. Sussah sipped slower. Way before she had had enough Leonie reached for it again. "And not all of it either, we don't want to use it all at once."

"Water is not difficult to find if you know where to look." Their rescuer spoke to them in a deep voice, though it did not sound threatening. "My name is Bern."

Leonie turned back to him. "I'm Leonie, and this is Sussah," she said. He was a massive male who reminded her very much of Ro, except for the amount of hair, reminding her of Brendon. Her eyes widened in surprise at the sudden movement behind him.

Seeing her reaction, Bern spun.

Leonie jumped in front of him and raised her paw. The fireball hit the howler in the chest, blowing the bulk of it back over the cliff.

"How—" Bern stared.

Leonie fell to the ground.

"Leonie!" Sussah cried out limping to her.

Still dazed at what he just saw, Bern bent to collect Leonie in his arms.

"Come with me," he said to Sussah. He carried Leonie to a clear area out of the wind where there was soft sand. He laid Leonie down gently. "Stay with her, I'll be back shortly." Bern left his water flask and moved off into the twilight, back to the cliff.

Sussah tore a portion of her tunic then dampened it to wipe Leonie's brow and face. She then wrung it, allowing a few drops onto her lips.

"How is she?" Bern asked on his return, with his backpack and belt.

"She's very tired," Sussah replied, noticing his legs were lacerated and the thick hair was matted with blood. "You're injured too."

Bern shrugged. "You both look exhausted." He gave her a clean cloth from his pack. He looked to Leonie as Sussah accepted the cloth. "It will get cooler later. I'll start a fire … but perhaps not as quickly as your friend did."

When he left, Sussah used the cloth and continued dabbing Leonie's face.

Bern returned with an armload of wood. Grabbing some things from his pack, he had a cheery blaze going soon after. He sat down nearby and dabbed at his wounds with another cloth, then applied some salve. "Move closer to the fire and rest," he said to Sussah. "Those howlers won't be back. We'll be safe enough."

Sussah edged to the fire but remained close to Leonie.

Bern handed her a container. "For your sunburn." He strolled into the dark, leaving the pair to rest.

Sussah worked out how to twist the lid and found some whitish cream within. It felt lovely when she applied it to her arms and legs, and the pain dissipated quickly.

Leonie was still sound asleep.

Sussah curled up on the sand and was asleep almost instantly.

Bern reconnoitred the area around the camp. He knew the area well enough having camped here several times in the past. Going in widening circles, he entered the ravine. He could count roughly twelve howler bodies – what was left of them, including the charred one blown over the cliff. It had not been eaten and from his knowledge of howlers, that meant it had been the last one; any other howler would have eaten the remains. Still, he finalised his search, then set traps near the entrance to the campsite.

He trod on something smooth in the sand where Leonie had collapsed. It was a heavy disk attached to a silver chain. There was an inscription around the edge. Bern couldn't read well as it was, but it certainly was not a language he recognised. He marvelled at the workmanship, and that the surface was unmarked in any other way. Returning to the campsite, he placed it where Leonie would see it when she woke. On the opposite side of the fire, he too made himself comfortable and went to sleep.

———

Bern opened his eyes. Something disturbed his sleep, though what it was he couldn't pinpoint. He quickly looked about. The first thing he noticed was it was almost dawn. That was when he realised Leonie was not in sight, though the girl was still asleep.

He leapt up to go searching for her when she stepped out from behind a large boulder carrying one of the flasks.

Leonie stopped, looking startled for a moment. "Morning." She limped towards him.

"Yes, it is," he said. He walked over to her and helped her sit down. He noticed she was carrying a large orb he hadn't seen before.

"Are you hungry?"

"Famished," she answered.

He got the fire going again and hunted in his pack for utensils. Soon there was a pot of water for tea and strips of meat on a small griddle.

The aroma caused her mouth to water.

"It won't be long." He stood. "Nature calls," he excused himself, heading to the rocks.

"Oh." She quickly realised what he meant. "Can I suggest you pick a different area?"

"Not to worry. Plenty of rocks to choose from," Bern replied, moving in another direction.

As the pot began to boil she stirred in some of the tea leaves, thinking back to all the Tesakian Redleaf she'd shared with Feiron, wondering if that would ever happen again. While she was doing this, the sun peeked over the horizon. Looking up to the east, she was once again seeing the barren wasteland where she and Sussah almost died. The rim of the valley was only a short distance away. She hopped up awkwardly and limped over to the edge, but not too close. At the base of the rockfall were the remains of a torn and bloody carcass, evidence of yesterday's escape. As the sun rose, the darker shapes resolved into shredded carcasses.

"Gods I hate dogs!" she remarked to the silence.

"Do you have them where you're from too?"

Leonie almost went over the edge at his voice. Bern was behind her and grabbed her by the arm as she jumped in surprise, pulling her away from the precipice. It took her a moment to get her breath back before he would let her go, and even then, only when well away from the edge. She sat down gingerly.

"Sorry. I thought you were talking to me." He sat down beside her.

Leonie shook her head, not trusting herself to talk. She had obviously not recovered yet, a fact made clear simply by Bern getting so close without her hearing. He gave her the flask just as she was about to reach for it. Sitting back trying to relax, Leonie nodded her thanks and, despite the advice she had given to Sussah, drained it.

"And yes, we have both," she answered the question Bern asked earlier. "We have gods and dogs, and I haven't much use for either of them."

"There was a time, they say, when we had a god too, but religion and superstitious beliefs stopped centuries ago. One of our tutors spoke about it when I was much younger. She was a strange old bird."

"You've got glins'ool here too?" Leonie asked.

"Not that I've heard." Bern looked at her blankly. "You must have come a long way to get here."

"Would you believe me if I said we came from another world?"

"No, probably not, if I hadn't seen you blow-up that howler last night."

"Well, we are. Is that what you call those dogs?"

"Pretty self-explanatory. Their howl is said to petrify their prey." He nodded. "I better not burn your breakfast. I suspect you like it rare?"

"As long as it's not moving," she joked.

They walked back to the camp where Sussah was still asleep. Bern collected the tea and griddle and he and Leonie sat on the far side of the clearing.

"I found a medallion last night in the sand where you collapsed, but didn't see that round thing." He pointed.

While Leonie slowly chewed the meat strips, she let him examine the Nightsky Orb.

As Bern examined it with interest, Sussah awoke from her sleep. Leonie went over to bring her some food.

The young girl groaned as she sat up bleary-eyed. She looked around, confused momentarily. "It wasn't a bad dream then," she moaned. "I thought ... never mind. Can I smell food?"

"How are you feeling?" Leonie handed her the meat and her cup.

"I ache all over. I don't think there's a part of my body that's not feeling pain of some sort."

"I know how you feel," Leonie sympathised.

While Sussah started eating her share of breakfast, Leonie checked any injuries received last night with their escape, finding nasty blisters and scratches on her feet and legs, as well as severe sunburn on most of her exposed skin.

Bern appeared with more ointment to soothe the stinging of the burns. "Not sure if this will help much; your sunburn is very bad. I've added a few herbs in the tea. It will reduce the headaches we all have, and help replace some of the salts and fluids."

"What sort of world are we in now?" Sussah mumbled while chewing.

Bern looked at her, then at Leonie. "Is she okay?" he whispered. "I didn't see a head injury. It could be delirium, sometimes the heat can do that."

"Honestly, she's fine. At least, no head injuries, and no delirium." Leonie almost laughed. "I did say you wouldn't believe me."

Bern sat in the sand. "I recall a blast of fire too ... How did you do that?"

Refilling their cup, Leonie sat beside Sussah and tried to explain their origins and their arrival through the portal.

Bern nodded now and then. "Magic? They do magic there?"

"Magic, or powershaping ... yes. Here too, it seems."

"But how? What can you do?"

Leonie shrugged. "I can tell you what, but not the *how*."

"And she can fly!" Sussah added.

"Fly?" Bern looked between them, shaking his head slowly.

"Not like a bird," Leonie sighed, rising off the ground and moving back and forth.

Bern stood the moment Leonie lifted off the ground, wide-eyed. "Why were you stumbling last night if you can fly?"

"I can't do it continuously." She moved back to her sitting position. "I don't know my limitations yet. It's all new to me."

"And you, Sussah? Are you a magician too?"

"Me, a powershaper?" She laughed. "Not one bit."

"That's … all so fascinating. It's very hard to believe, but so is someone making fire out of nothing, or flying. Are you able to go back?"

"The portal we came through is no longer working," Leonie answered.

"Is it broken?"

"I think it's drained. It has no more power."

"Oh. Can it be … recharged?"

"It must, somehow. But I don't know. I also think it would need more than I could provide."

Bern thought about this, continuing his meal. "I'll tell you about here, but you might have been better off where you were. This place, this land, is not very good, but until you arrived, it was the only one I knew. Other people can tell you more but, until then, I'll gladly share with you what little I know."

They both nodded and sat back. Leonie started eating another slice of meat, with a side dish of his trail rations. Sussah screwed her face at the first taste, but she was hungry, and they both insisted she eat.

Bern poked the fire a bit and poured the herb tea before he began. "This country is Australia; the world is Earth. As you can see, it's desolate and barren, but it wasn't always like this. We've had wars and famine for the last couple of hundred years. Many people live in large towers, which is where I thought you came from, young lady."

"So that's where you live? In one of these towers?" Sussah queried, unsure if she would like to live like that.

"No. I live in a much smaller community here in the hills. There are lots of caves in this region."

"But why? You said the people live in these towers."

"*Most* of the people do. I bet in your world there are some who don't fit in, for whatever reason. Some free-spirits just go off on a tangent, not really belonging to any particular group. In my community, *we* are those free-spirits. But there is a price to pay for everything we do, every choice we make. In the towers – the sanctuary for humanity – life is so organised and controlled, that there is no *life*."

"So, what's the price for living out here?" Leonie asked in a serious voice. She knew quite a lot about not fitting in.

"Look around you. How much food and water do you see?"

Sussah swallowed the last of her meal. "You said all the available land was used to grow food."

"This land's not arable. The ground is contaminated by radiation. Only good for the tough, spikey scrub you see now, and an array of mutated forms of the native wildlife, like the howlers last night. We eat what we can get though." He offered the last strip of meat to Leonie.

"What's radiation?" Sussah stumbled with sounding the new word.

"Something like a poison left over from those wars. In sufficient quantities it could kill you, but in the amounts present today, it might only make you sick or babies a bit different, those that survive. That's our price. We've lived here all our lives, my father and his before him, we rarely get sick now that our bodies have adjusted to the conditions but the changes are still happening. Some changes are better than others. Most of us get on well enough though."

"Most?"

"There are some more affected by radiation than others. We do what we can for them, but it isn't pleasant, and thankfully, rarely long-lasting." He watched them silently. "I had been wondering how you two came to be with each other," he said, looking at Leonie. "I thought you were a wilder – a mutation – like me, and Sussah was from one of the towers. I couldn't work out why you were with each other. Tower people and wilders don't get on, and we certainly don't go walkabout together."

"So, the tower people are normal?" The young girl sipped the tea, screwing her face a little at its tartness. "Sorry, more like me than you?"

"Yes," Bern answered. "They are exactly like you, physically, but you aren't too worried about my looks or Leonie's. That's where you're different, in here." He pointed to his head. "You don't judge a person by their looks. In that, you are more like us."

Sussah blushed, taking another sip of the tart tea to cover her embarrassment. "Is this tea contaminated?" she asked.

"More than likely. Like the air you're breathing and the dust and sand surrounding us. But there are much worse areas than here. Where those howlers found you; there is a very bad area to the north-west. They seem to thrive in it." While they finished their breakfast, he got up and moved about to make preparations for departure. He stopped momentarily, looking to the west, sniffing the air.

"Anything wrong?" Leonie asked.

"Checking for storms. I know of an area where it'll be cooler and protected. It's a few hours walk from here. We can rest more comfortably there, and we'll be in Jenolan – where my people live – by tomorrow afternoon."

"It looks dry. Do you get much rain?"

"Rain?" He shook his head. "We only get sandstorms here."

They carefully cleaned up the area before leaving, covering the remnants of the fire with heaps of sand. Bern carried Sussah as her blistered feet caused her too much pain. Her slight weight was nothing to him.

By early afternoon, they arrived at the watering hole. It was within a deep chasm. Awkward to get to down the narrow path, but cool and shady. Bern topped up his water. Leonie and Sussah rested, still weary from the previous days' exertions. The peace and tranquillity was a blessing for everyone.

**16**

---

## JENOLAN

"Not far now," Bern said over his shoulder. Channelled by the narrow gully the wind howled around them, bringing with it choking, stinging sand. He was carrying Sussah, who had collapsed.

"You said that a while ago." Leonie walked behind him. She adjusted the scarf over Su's face to prevent the sand getting in her eyes and mouth.

"I was right then, and even more right now," Bern called back. "It's just at the end of this gully."

"I'll believe it when we get there," she muttered.

The small wilder community where Bern lived was nestled between craggy cliffs. The brunt of the storm was deflected, leaving the community in a cloud of dust and sand as it filtered down.

A young, slim woman met them as the group emerged from the ravine. Leonie saw her standing there; the thin shawl billowing about her in the breeze completely covered her, including her face. About a dozen other figures stood to the side of the small clearing. Most had coverings of some description to prevent the sand getting in their mouths, eyes and noses.

Bern stepped up to the young woman and introduced her.

"This fine lady is Rhiannon. She maintains what order she can here."

Leonie stared for a moment, under her veil the woman didn't have any eyes, only smooth skin from her cheeks to her forehead.

Rhiannon turned to greet the strangers. "Welcome to Jenolan." She stepped forward and placed an open palm over Sussah's forehead. "She is very badly dehydrated. Please take her to the medbay. Leonie, you should come with us too. You're not well either and your wounds will need attention."

"I did what I could," Bern said.

"You too," Rhiannon said. "I sense you're injured."

"I'll cope," he rumbled, but followed nonetheless, nodding to the surprised onlookers.

Leonie followed Rhiannon towards a cave entrance deep within the shadows of the looming cliffs, holding a paw to filter out the falling sand while looking curiously around the area. The community stretched in both directions along the ravine; lean-tos and shacks were propped up both sides, making the best use of the space available.

"This storm doesn't do it justice. Wait until tomorrow when it's bright and cheery," Rhiannon said as they entered the cave.

Leonie could only nod in reply, amazed by what she saw. There was the briefest moment of familiarity, but she shrugged it off, blaming her exhaustion.

The entrance was a naturally formed cave, but further in it had been cut with great skill. She could not see any chisel or tool marks. The interior was not bright but comfortably illuminated by a glowing moss along the ceiling and upper walls.

Once Sussah was settled inside on a bed, Rhiannon moved straight to a cabinet. "Bern, perhaps you should wait in the next chamber. I'll be with you shortly. Pull the curtains behind, would you? Thanks." She returned carrying some interesting looking containers on a metal tray.

Again, Leonie was amazed at the things she saw. She sat on a stool by the bed, her tail hanging over one edge of the cushioned seat, and picked up one of the containers. Not glass, she decided, but thin and clear. It was so lightweight, even with its contents of small, pale yellow discs. There were other containers, each with different coloured discs.

"We call them tabs or tablets," Rhiannon said. "Different coloured tabs have different chemicals – drugs – to help pain or promote recovery."

"You're a healer?" Sussah asked.

Leonie quickly put the container down and helped Sussah ease out of the remnants of her clothing. All of her exposed skin was an angry red colour. Her nose was peeling, and her lips dried and cracked.

"A healer of sorts, but I tend to wear many hats." Rhiannon unstoppered a long tube and squeezed out some green ointment and applied it liberally but gently to Sussah's lips.

Leonie frowned, unsure why headdress was important. She turned her head as the curtains parted briefly. A small, thin girl with very dark skin entered carrying a bowl of water and some towels. The young girl's eyes were wide at seeing Leonie. She didn't utter a word but smiled briefly. Leonie smiled back.

"Thank you, Jojo," Rhiannon said, then added. "Can you or Sid please run a bath for our new cat-friend?"

Silently, Jojo ran out.

Without pausing, Rhiannon continued as she bathed Sussah. "I can sense what the ailment is, and a good knowledge of the various medicines certainly helps. But there's so much I don't know. Your presence here is testament to that. One thing I do know, you also need attention."

"I'm all—"

*Nonsense girl! You're dead on your feet. I know it even if you don't!*

Leonie looked up in surprise. "You're a telepath!"

"Yes. My apologies. I do get quite upset when people don't look after themselves. They just make matters worse. No need to put on that bravado now. You're safe, and you can see Sussah's being cared for. You, my friend, will soon collapse in an exhausted heap. I hope you like baths."

Before Leonie could respond, the curtain parted and Jojo returned. Without uttering a word, the child took Leonie's paw and led her out. "I'll see you soon," she called back to Sussah.

They moved along the main passage, past several chambers similar to the first one. At the end, the passage turned and angled down.

In a cool chamber, a smooth trough had been gouged into a large boulder. Filled and emptied with simple plumbing, it was the most sumptuous bath Leonie had seen. Dropping her bloodied and torn clothing to the floor, she quickly used the steps and climbed in, sinking into bliss. For a moment, all her pain and weariness left her, but before she dozed off, she scrubbed herself clean. Apart from being gentle around her wounds, she vigorously removed the accumulated dust and grime of the last few days; the residual repellent from the harbour, the filth from the cells and the sewer as well as the caked blood and dried sweat. She realised she must have looked horrendous.

The effects of the last days finally took its toll. After her bath, she felt very lethargic and her mind was befuddled. Leonie was led through more tunnels to a chamber with a bed covered in cushions and sweet oblivion.

———

Leonie saw herself lying in bed asleep. She was back at the hroltahg inn at White Cliffs, swathed in bandages and recovering from her near-death experience. Styx, with his spikes, was at the side of the bed.

*Leonie, this is not a dream. I am not certain when, where, or even if you will see this memory. If you do it is because a prophecy – one of the oldest – has come into play. I have taken advantage of my new rogue status to do things previously unfathomable; in this case, to enhance your mind and abilities. You have my apologies for entering and modifying your mind, but you are destined to be the saviour of our races and as such, my resolve to ensure your survival is unyielding.*

*Do you recall the ease with which we communicated? I thought this very strange for a non-telepath but kept silent until I could fathom why. Your physical attributes were not the only aspect to benefit from your unique heritage. I believe Dianah's experiments included genes from illios and hroltahgs – it is the only explanation. This is partly why you heal so quickly, but also has affected your mental enhancement. I have assessed your potential, and quite frankly, it is stunning.*

*I am not sure if those words will impact you greatly. They should. You know we hroltahgs cannot lie. I can barely fathom what capabilities you may have, so I say this to you: trust in yourself and your talents completely. You have a talent for being a powershaper – use it; same with your telepathic abilities. Adhere to the training you've received, and anything you put your mind to will work.*

*I cannot emphasise that enough. Believe, and your true destiny – and ours – will be fulfilled.*

---

The elders of Jenolan sat around the glowing embers after the evening meal. All the youngsters were taken away to their beds or to study and a few of the community members lingered further back from the fire but still within earshot.

Clara stood to speak and everyone became quiet. "Rhiannon, we're concerned for our two visitors. Over the last couple of days we've all witnessed their dreams to some extent." Nodding heads from the circle indicated agreement. "In part, their world amazes us, and it terrifies us. All that hatred and violence—"

"Are you concerned our new friends will bring this violence here?"

"That is not our thought, though the feline one has a penchant for violence, albeit in self-defence. If *they* managed to get here, perhaps others will follow? We know not how they arrived. If it can happen to these two, it can happen to others."

"We have sent runners out to the area where they believe they arrived." Rhiannon shrugged. "Nothing has been found."

"All well and good, if they searched the right area. But

another fear though is for their safety in this world. This Yarnik appears to be low-tech, almost medieval. If there's no rad there, then our two visitors will be very susceptible to its effects. Maybe far more than even our new-born. For their own good, we need to get them *into* the tower."

"I also have thought this." Rhiannon considered these words. "Sussah will blend in quite easily if she can learn the tower ways quickly enough, and physically, she will have little problems. Leonie, on the other hand … surely she will be in more danger."

"Hazardous, for sure, but seeing her life back on her world, there will be little difference. She is adept at hiding."

"Do you all feel this way?"

*We do*, were the unanimous thoughts.

After a pause, Clara spoke again. "And … there is another matter?"

"I thought there might be. You believe something about them has been foreseen?"

"*You* are our seeress."

The corners of Rhiannon's mouth lifted in a faint smile. "So everyone keeps reminding me." She shook her head. "While I agree their arrival was unique, the prophecy pertains to an individual. '*From a distant land one of our kind will return. A pure one, to bring hope. With her will be a guardian to bring all the peoples together and to their true homes*'. A good heart she may have, but I cannot see Sussah being the 'one of our kind'."

"What about the other one, Leonie? Is she this guardian?"

"Perhaps. faithful and good-hearted. And she is not one of us."

"Is she not also mutated? How is she different?"

"If you've seen her dreams, you know there are other races out there. Alien or crossbreed yes; mutant, no."

———

*Good morning, Leonie.*

"Morning is it?" She sensed Rhiannon in the corridor. "Come in."

"Thank you. How are you feeling?" Rhiannon parted the curtains and entered.

Leonie was bent over, doing her stretches. "I thought you could tell already?"

"I like to hear it anyway."

"Surprisingly well. Perhaps a bit stiff. Seems like I've not done any stretching for ages, nor any climbing. I don't suppose there's any rooftops around here?"

"Rooftops, no. We have some interesting cliffs if you like. After breakfast, perhaps I could show you around Jenolan? I'll take you to them then."

"Sure. Being idle too long gets to me, and I do like to get an idea of where I'm staying – all the ins and outs."

"Do the clothes fit? They look good on you."

"This material is nicely woven, and smooth," Leonie said, running her paws down the front of the close-fitting shirt. "I thought it would be too tight, but it stretches so well."

"And the shorts?"

"Sorry, I had to cut a hole for my tail, but I don't see it hindering movement. The clothes are great, thank you."

They visited the dining area and had breakfast before starting the tour.

Further along the passage, past the chamber where Leonie had had her bath, Rhiannon led Leonie into the depths of the cavern. "You dreamt a lot while you rested. You and Sussah. In all those dreams, we glimpsed some marvellous things. Floating sky islands … magic … were those creatures dragons?"

"If you mean the large flying lizards, no. They're wyverns and telepathic too."

"How extraordinary. I've only ever read about them in old books on mythology. We have nothing like that here." The passageway descended, getting cooler, the ever-present glowing moss on the ceiling and walls shedding its eerie radiance. The smooth, sandy floor became wide, shallow steps. "This may not be the highlight of the tour, but I thought it prudent to show you that some mutations are not pleasant. Down here we have the less fortunate."

"Are they captives?"

"Oh no. These poor souls cannot abide the sunlight and need constant attention. This cavern we are about to enter is one of the largest in this group with easy access. Please, you should rub a bit of this under your nose." Rhiannon unstoppered a jar in a niche a few steps down.

Leonie screwed her face up the moment she smelt the strong, pungent odour. "This is needed?"

"It's far more preferable than what you will encounter. And don't lick it."

Reluctantly, and with watery eyes, Leonie smeared a line of the substance as instructed. They continued down the stairs. "Does this moss-light affect them?"

"No, just the sun. They prefer the cooler air." At the base of the stairs, the passage levelled and widened.

The scene was reminiscent of the caverns of White Cliffs, minus the crystal formations, the deadly fumes and the heavy gravity.

Leonie doubted she'd ever forget what she witnessed: so many deformed people; too many limbs, not enough limbs, most were without skin or hair. Many had sores and weeping wounds. They sat or lay on chairs or bunks; some lay on the floor or boulders or curled up on rocky ledges. As she passed nearby a thick, putrid odour assailed her nostrils despite the scented cream. She did all within her power not to throw up.

*Some think my blindness is a curse. In this job, I can only see it as a blessing. What I do see is their minds. Some may be insane, or having difficulty in even forming coherent thoughts, but there is no anger or evil in them. I see them for what they truly are – humans in dire need.*

Moving to the far side of the cavern, they stopped and looked back. "How many are there?" Leonie asked.

"We have thirty-three. We lose one a month on average."

Leonie's tail drooped as she shook her head. "I thought my

life was harsh." Further on, the cavern became more defined. She recognised the laser cuts same as the upper levels.

"Centuries ago, this was a bunker."

Leonie tilted her head in confusion with the unusual term.

"A refuge. A place where people could escape attacks," Rhiannon explained. "They could stay here for long periods. The air is recycled and filtered. Water is purified and stored in large tanks, and the food ... well, it is more a nutrient solution, but it is sufficient to sustain them."

The thick door to the bunker was partially embedded into the wall. Much larger, but she surmised it worked similarly to the one on the sanctum. "This door slides in and out?" She looked at the metal grooves in the ground.

"Yes. All the power to work this is held in batteries, charged by solar panels."

More words not known to Leonie, but Rhiannon was moving further in. A long, circular corridor led through a dozen large chambers; some with tables and chairs, some with double bunk-beds, some empty.

"I think these were storage rooms. Depleted over time, I imagine. We get some supplies from the agtechs. Not enough to survive long-term, but they all help. Like the food you and Sussah have been eating. Completely rad free."

"Don't you eat it too?"

"Only in emergencies, like when our crops fail." The seer led the way back to the surface.

Back in the warmth and sunlight, Leonie's mood picked up slightly. "I feel so bad for those below."

"It is a shame, yes. We do what we can to ease their burdens. Many of them undergo constant pain-relief medication. Luckily, we can manufacture the bulk of it here using essential oils from the garden and local vegetation."

———

Rhiannon moved quietly around the room and approached the young girl with a bowl of water and a towel.

Sussah gasped when the shawl parted, revealing Rhiannon's face briefly. "I'm so sorry," she said quickly, a quiver in her voice. The woman had no eyes, her smooth cheeks meeting her forehead almost seamlessly.

*You have nothing to be sorry about, Sussah. It is I who should have prepared you first.* "I forgot you were barely conscious when you arrived. While I may not have eyes, I can see more with my mind far better than many people can with all their senses."

Sussah nodded as she looked away. It would take a while getting used to looking at a face with … no face. She looked at her arms and lifted the covers to see her legs. In many areas, the skin was peeling and tender to touch. Some areas were tanned, and some still an angry red. Most of the bruising had gone.

"How are you feeling?" Rhiannon put the bowl down and reached for a jug on a tray by the bed.

"I'm still very sore, but much better."

"That's pleasing to hear. Please drink this." She passed a cup of water. "As you can see, our sun can be quite damaging to tender skin, and with no water, dehydration takes effect very quickly."

"How's Leonie?"

"She had a great need to rest too."

"That's something I thought I'd never hear; Leonie resting. She's amazing, and just keeps going."

"Yes. Her capabilities are extraordinary. But in this case, she pushed beyond what she could safely endure—"

"She's alright, isn't she?" Sussah winced when she started to sit up.

"Just move slowly. Yes, Leonie is fine. Just very exhausted, mentally and physically, but everyone has limitations. How long have you known her?"

"Um … how long have we been here now?"

"This is your third day."

"What!"

"Yes, you have lain here since you arrived, mildly medicated so you could rest. We have taken care of you both. Sometimes you dreamt. Sometimes you spoke, but at no time were you lucid or awake."

"Then I've known her for about eight days," Sussah said after taking this in.

"Only eight?"

"It's been horrible." Sussah started to weep. "We've had no time—"

"Be calm. You are safe, and can rest as much as you need."

"Can I see her?"

"Of course. I'll send for her and get you some other clothes. I won't be long."

———

Between her many visits to Sussah, and after the days of being inactive, Leonie needed to get out, stretch, see the sun and feel the breeze. She explored Jenolan from top to bottom the moment Rhiannon had assessed her as fit and well.

Jojo ran up to Leonie and tugged on her paw. She looked down and smiled. "And where are we off to, little one?"

The young girl just pointed and tugged.

"Okay then, lead on." She had an idea Rhiannon might be wanting to speak to her eventually. Jojo, while not her daughter, was always around the seeress' feet. Sure enough, they gained the main track which lead to the cliffs. Well-tended gardens lined each side of the track and their carers looked up and waved as the pair passed.

Leonie considered the terrain surrounding them, this cul-de-sac was a haven. Nestled within a large sandstone massif, erosion had created this niche. The community lived under large rocky overhangs, much like the cave where Rhiannon looked after the sick. When she'd asked about the number of caves and the smooth walls, she was told they used laser cutters. No one could explain to her what that was, but it seemed very effective.

The moment they arrived at the medbay Jojo let go of Leonie's paw and sped away.

*Good morning, Leonie.*

"Hey yourself. Everything alright?" Leonie rounded a corner to find Jenolan's healer putting a salve on young boy's third arm. She then wrapped it in some large leaves before sending him off.

"All is good, thank you. Still exploring Jenolan?"

"I finished that in a day. I was just in the gardens, as I'm sure you knew."

"Aren't they lovely? We've been so lucky to find this place," Rhiannon said as she washed her hands in a bowl.

"I've seen worse. Is Sussah about?"

"I think she's helping in the nursery. Could you pass me that towel?"

"No doubt where Jojo has rushed off to. So, there's our small-talk done." Leonie tossed the towel and grinned when Rhi caught it easily, sticking her tongue out in the process. "But I don't think you called me here for banter. Is something wrong?"

"Not wrong, no. Very strange, yes." Rhiannon leant back on the bench and faced her. "What can you tell me about Sussah?"

"In what way? I thought we covered everything."

"In all those dreams you both had—"

"You're reading our dreams again?"

"Not intentionally, but they were quite strong. If a person is yelling next to you, *not* hearing it is difficult. There was no ill-will or intent to invade your privacy."

"Okay. I'll try not to dream too loudly," Leonie huffed. "I guess I should be used to others being in my head. You were saying?"

"We glimpsed some marvellous things. Wyverns, floating sky islands and magic. But, some images remained dark. I sensed in both cases, what you've experienced was so traumatic your mind has blocked them. I certainly don't mean to pry into your secrets, but I believe something happened we don't know about. Something we should, hence why I asked about Su. Did she have a male friend?"

"A boyfriend? Yes." Leonie nodded.

"Maybe that's it, then."

Leonie paced the floor. "We did have some trouble, though."

"Did you know she's pregnant?" Rhiannon stated. "With twins."

"*Twins!*" Leonie hissed, stopping in her tracks. Her hackles rose and her tail flicked, but she had the wits to keep her voice down. "Surely you're mistaken?" she whispered in shock.

"What the body knows, I know. Your method of arrival, perhaps a side-effect of this spell, accelerated her body's normal rhythm." She waited for Leonie to come to terms with this.

"I ... when I found her, she had been assaulted. But she didn't tell me. Maybe she didn't know herself?"

"Probably. We need to decide what to do. Under normal circumstances I would know without any doubt. Childbirth is not unusual to us. This situation, however, is unique."

Leonie leant against the bench, to consider. "You want to know how she will take this news?"

"No, I doubt any of us could gauge that, especially with what she has endured or in the condition she's in. You have to understand something about the wilders; all of us here are from mutated stock, going back generations," she paused. "What we are afraid of is if Sussah has prolonged exposure to the rad we have here, she may become sick and her foetus may also develop abnormalities. Yourself included.

"You want us to ... go to the towers? Is that it?"

"Not *want*." Rhiannon reached out to clasp her paw. "We'd love for the both of you to stay. You came from another world! That in itself is astonishing, and you can do *magic*. If it were up to me, and we could assure your safety, and we have anti-rad tablets to help. You would both be very welcome here.

Rhiannon continued, "I will need to say quite clearly; the tower citizens will not tolerate you. If they see you or even suspect there's a wilder – a mutant – among them, they will not stop until you're gone or dead. You must limit your exposure at all costs. Those in the tower have lived there for many generations; always told that here, *outside*, is bad for them – and it can be – and we are dangerous. Like anyone in our situation, we merely want to survive. We have been on our own all this time."

"Bern mentioned something like that when we arrived."

"Sadly, it's all true. Sussah should get by with little difficulty, at least with appearances. You will be constantly in danger, but the dangers you face in there can be overcome; radiation poisoning is incurable. You will die out here. Although we can prolong it, it is inevitable."

Leonie took a deep breath and sighed, rubbing her face. "When do we leave?"

"The sooner the better for both of you. I'll need to contact the agtechs. They do infrequent drops of supplies."

"Why would they do that if they hate wilders so much? I've heard of them, but know little about them."

"Agtechs are different. They are conditioned to go outside to manage the vast crop fields around the towers. Because of that, they are subject to rad contamination. Not much, but enough. While they reside within the tower, they are separate from true citizens. They are considered crazy and unclean."

"But I still don't know why they need to come here."

"Once in a while, if there is a deformed baby born in the tower, or if a child develops abnormalities, they bring them here for us to care for, even those with minor oddities. Did you notice Jojo has six toes on each foot? Other than her being mute, she is perfectly fine, but it was enough. The agtechs provide the equipment and anything else they can; part of the payment for taking their mutant offspring."

"Surely they have better facilities in the tower?" she added, "No offence."

"It is true. They'd have far superior medical equipment and trained staff, but anyone found with a mutation is killed; they call it recyc. This is the sort of society you'll have to deal with."

"What's recyc?"

"Recycling … they use human remains for fertiliser, whatever they can make use of."

"That's barbaric! Even in my world we didn't do that. Surely they wouldn't kill babies?"

"Sadly, they have done, many times." Rhiannon walked up to Leonie, putting her hand on her shoulder. "Shall we go and see Sussah, now?"


Many tears were shed when Sussah heard the news, and about the need to go to the tower. It was all quite a shock to her. "Twins? I can't believe it! I even found a herbalist," Sussah wept. "She was supposed to prevent it!"

"Is this by the boyfriend you mentioned?" Leonie asked. "When was the last time you were together?"

Sussah wiped her face, thinking. "About two nights before you and I *met*. It was just the once, but I've known Rickard for a few months. He was so nice."

"Rhiannon says it will be twins and best for us to go to the towers. It'll be much safer."

"What about you?" Sussah sniffed. "Won't the tower be dangerous?"

"I'll be fine," Leonie said. "I always land on my paws. I'll be there for you."

# 17

# A FINAL CONFRONTATION

"At least we have something for our troubles tonight," Bern said.

"Will one wallaby be enough for dinner?" Leonie asked, looking at the strange creature balanced over his shoulder. They were returning to Jenolan after a couple of hours of hunting.

"It will do. Very little of it will go to waste, but more would have—"

A roar pierced the night. Several wilders, approaching to collect the wallaby for cooking, stopped in their tracks, staring up at the sky. Searching.

"Slistorf's balls!" Leonie's hackles rose and her tail lashed from side to side.

"I've not heard that sound before," Bern scanned the horizon.

"And you will wish you hadn't."

"You know what it is?"

"I do. It's a wyvern." She continued as Bern was about to ask questions. "Get everyone into that storage bunker. Do not open it until I get back."

"We can help—"

"Not with this, you can't! Until I know why it's here, no one is safe."

Bern stood there, dumbfounded.

"I will not have anyone risk their lives!" Leonie shook him, a rare time she genuinely felt fear. "This is something none of you can deal with. Go!" With that, she disappeared into the darkness, heading to where she last heard the noise. A dozen questions raced through her head as she worked her way through the maze of rocky formations.

A large, green wyvern circled over the area, reminding her of a hawk searching for prey. With a thought, Leonie rose rapidly and was soon flying above the creature.

Below her, her worst nightmare came true as she recognised the black-clad assassin.

Evlin's head was tilted, looking down; she had her arms out, palms down and fingers splayed.

*I am aware of your presence. You must be Leonie. This Evlin creature will not cease talking about you.*

Leonie clutched her head, suppressing a moan, trying to retain her altitude. "Undead have no thoughts," she gasped.

*Some do.* This time the impact of the thought was much gentler. *Perhaps I am not truly undead.*

"You're helping her?" Leonie barely uttered the words.

*Indirectly. A simple task I have to fulfil.*

"To kill me?" She moved closer, matching speed.

*That is not my task, only hers.*

Leonie sighed with relief. She had little chance of defeating a wyvern.

Evlin looked up, a startled look on her pallid face at seeing the half-breed hovering above.

Leonie noted the assassin's sluggishness and her deteriorating appearance. The gashes where her throat had been torn open were quite distinct. She took in a deep breath and flicked her paw.

The fireball hit Evlin in the chest, knocking her off the wyvern's back. She fell the forty metres, crashing into the netting over the garden, disappearing in the foliage.

Leonie descended and prepared another fireball, moving closer.

Evlin's attack took her completely by surprise.

As the twin blade pierced Leonie's shoulder, the fireball blew up in their faces. The resulting blast sent them sprawling in opposite directions across the small, sandy area.

Blinking the grit from her eyes, Leonie tried to focus through the intense pain; her arms and chest were scorched from the heat. Her whiskers had burnt off, and she could smell her singed fur and flesh.

"I'm still alive?" Half her body ached. Still dazed, she tried to roll over and stand up. She couldn't move her neck. Her left arm moved sluggishly, the vision in her left eye began to blur. Even her tail hung listless. She turned her watery eyes to the crumpled body of the assassin a few paces away lying motionless, but with wisps of smoke rising from her blackened body.

Amazed and relieved she was still able to do anything, Leonie reached over and pulled the dirk from her shoulder with her right paw. There was no glow to the twin blades. She brought it closer to her good eye to examine it closely.

*Her god's power has faded somewhat these past weeks,* the wyvern informed her.

"Weeks?" Leonie mumbled.

*We arrived over another continent and flew across a vast ocean to get here. It has taken its toll. There are no people for her to regain the necessary energies to sustain her, but much of the land itself has a peculiar energy which helps. Strange that it is stronger to the north of here.* There was a pause; a mental sigh. *She will recover now that she is back on land.*

"Why aren't you helping her?" She hoped her words made sense.

The wyvern snorted. *I am merely transport. That is all my compulsion requires of me. She is quite insane.*

"You aren't beholden to do her bidding?"

*An oversight of the inexperienced priest. I suspect he took me for a mere animal.*

Leonie spied movement near the cave entrance.

"Jojo? Get back inside. Stay away!" Leonie motioned frantically to the young girl.

An unearthly scream sent a chill through her. Startled, Leonie dropped the dirk into the sand. Awkwardly, the body of the assassin convulsed once and sat upright like a puppet, turning to look.

"You always spoil my fun." Evlin shook her boney fists in frustration, staggering to her feet. "I will gut your friends after I've finished playin' with you. Not even through time or distant worlds can you thwart my master's will. Finally, time to die."

"I've heard it before. How many times do I have to kill you?"

"I am beyond your reach. You can do nothin' to me." Evlin advanced.

"Then you won't mind if I try," Leonie retorted. "I'll try not to enjoy it too much."

As the assassin stumbled closer, Leonie realised Evlin was in worse condition than herself; her tattered clothing now burnt rags, and white hair mostly gone; the pallid flesh hanging off exposed bone. Leonie tried to sidestep, but her left leg failed her. Both blundered into the rock wall and fell to the ground.

Evlin crawled to her feet again.

Leonie struggled to a standing position. "Stop." She flicked her paw.

The assassin flew backwards a few paces.

"Why continue with this?" Leonie pleaded. "Can't you see it's pointless? Your god's power has dwindled. You will only fail again."

Relentlessly, Evlin came at her again. This time Leonie caught her arm and twisted it behind her back. Despite the struggles, she pushed Evlin's face down into the sand and pulled her other arm behind. Hampered with the use of only one good arm, Leonie had to kneel on Evlin's back to keep her down.

"You will die at my hands." The assassin struggled weakly, but relentlessly. "It is your destiny."

"Sorry to disappoint you, but my destiny has already been mapped out, and you don't feature in it." Leonie turned to see the young girl still standing near the cave. "Jojo! If you're not going inside, make yourself useful; fetch something to bind her?"

The young girl sprinted back into the cave, reappearing moments later. What she held in her small hands was completely alien to Leonie. Sensing her confusion, Jojo approached. She looped something around the wrists of the feebly struggling assassin, threaded one end through the other and pulled it tight. There was a scratching sound as the band tightened around the wrists.

"Thank you." Leonie rose, stepping back to see what Evlin would do. "Can you get Bern, Rhiannon and the elders, please?" she said to Jojo. "They need to see this."

Evlin struggled against her bindings.

"Give it up, would you? I don't know how long you've been an assassin, but I've been a bitch most of my life, so you've been outmatched by experience."

Noldor's head hovered over them both, angled to glance down with his amber eyes.

"Is that lizard talkin' to you? Noldor, kill her!" Evlin screeched. She pushed herself against a boulder, using it to stand.

"Noldor?" Leonie muttered, vaguely remembering hearing the name before. "You're Noldor?" She stared up at him. "Dorn misses you," she blurted.

*Dorn? You know of her?* Noldor cocked his head to one side, one huge eye focused on her. *How is this so?*

"We are good friends; her and her twins, Slana and Faldo."

*Twins?* Ponderously, Noldor's head moved back as he sat on his haunches. *When was this?*

"About a month ago, in the Central Ranges. I stayed for a while and rode with them. She has only praise for you. Philbert will be disappointed he didn't save you."

*My demise is not the fault of his.*

Evlin stomped her foot. "What are you doin', lizard? You're not here to chat. Eat her. I command it!" She staggered forward.

"So—" Leonie sidestepped as the assassin lurched past. "So, if you're strong enough now to quell the power of a god, are you capable of dealing with her?"

The tip of Noldor's tail swung around and lightly clipped the fuming assassin, cart-wheeling her into the rocks, where she landed awkwardly and became wedged.

*It would seem I am.*

Leonie could have sworn he grinned. She turned at a new sound.

Bern, Rhiannon, and many other wilders wandered out of the cave, hesitating at the sight of the huge wyvern, and looking uncertainly at the wriggling body among the boulders.

"You will pay for this, you stupid creature!" Evlin screamed. "Just you wait when you face the wrath of your Lord and Master!"

With Jojo pulling them by the hands, Bern and Rhiannon hesitantly approached.

"I should see to those burns." Rhiannon moved closer. "Is that blood on your shoulder?"

"It can wait." She nodded. "This is Noldor … a wyvern from my world. And a friend."

The wyvern inclined his head. *Greetings.*

Leonie noticed them glancing at the rocks. "And that's Evlin. She's an assassin; she's also been dead for well over a month. She tried to kill me, but I killed her instead. She's tried to kill me several times since then. This is, thankfully, her last."

"How is it she is dead, yet moving?" Bern asked, bewildered.

"Damn gods." Leonie shrugged. "I told you they were a nuisance. Luckily, they have no power here, otherwise I'd be dead now, and she'd have no hesitation in killing all of you."

*What would you like me to do with her?* Noldor asked.

Leonie picked up the twin-bladed dirk again to study. "You said earlier there is no power in the oceans?"

*Correct.*

"And she'd revive if she remained on land?" Leonie confirmed.

*To some extent, I believe so.*

"Would you consider dropping her in the ocean then? A long way away, and the deeper the better."

*I will do this.* There was little hesitation in his response. *It will be a relief to be rid of her.*

"What will happen to you?"

The great wyvern head tilted. *I am uncertain. While a god's power initiated my resurrection, there is a form of energy in some areas that appears to maintain it – the same as it would assist Evlin's recovery. If it fades sufficiently, we'd return to the dead.*

"Are you saying this energy would prevent that? Keep you here?"

*Time will tell.*

"Bern, could you help me?" Leonie limped towards Evlin.

Bern caught up with her. "You've injured your leg. Again."

Rhiannon was right beside him. "Leonie, you've done enough."

"I'm not finished yet," she protested.

"You will all die for this!" Evlin screeched, rolling on the ground.

*Allow me.* Noldor's taloned foot wrapped around the assassin, muffling her cursing. *She is quite uncouth for a young lady-human.*

"I don't know how I can repay you," Leonie called to Noldor.

Beating his wings, Noldor rose in a great swirl of sand. *For your friendship with my daughter, it is a debt already paid. Give my regards to Dorn, if you see her again.*

"A promise I will gladly make." She would do this for him, though the likelihood of that happening was extremely remote. As she was being led back to the cave, she smashed the twin-bladed dagger on the rocks. The blades snapped off at the hilt. "Is there somewhere we can permanently dispose of this?"

"We have a plasma incinerator," Bern replied. He picked her up, seeing she was limping painfully.

"And that will burn it?" she asked, unsure of his words, and knowing it would be pointless to refuse his assistance twice in one night.

"It'll break it down to slag and its molecules."

"What did he say, Rhi?" Leonie looked over her shoulder.

The seeress laughed. "He said 'yes'."

## 18

# AGTECHS' ARRIVAL

A strange buzzing sound and the increasing volume of voices disrupted Leonie's stretching routine. She stepped outside of the sparsely furnished grotto set aside for visitors, joining several other wilders who were also heading towards the noise. She spied Rhiannon on the edge of the clearing in front of the main cave.

"Ah, Leonie. Here are our visitors."

The humming dissipated by the time Leonie walked to the healer's side. Her jaw dropped at what she saw. In front of the small wilder gathering, a man and woman in body-fitting one-piece clothing stepped off weird-looking machines. Some wilders waved or called out greetings as children ran among them all.

"Maz. Lerry. Thank you for returning so promptly."

"You rarely contact at all, so we knew something was up." The woman hung her goggles over the handle of one of the machines and gave the seer a quick hug, but her eyes strayed to Leonie. "Who have we here?"

"Leonie, I'd like you to meet Maz and her partner, Lerry."

Leonie dragged her gaze away from the machines and nodded with a smile, her tail swaying from side to side.

"G'day." They both inclined their heads. "We've not seen you before. You must have come a long way?" Lerry placed his goggles on the padded seat.

"You could say that, yes."

The agtechs shared a glance. Maz turned to Rhiannon. "So then, you mentioned an urgent request?"

"Yes, please. Come into the shade and we'll have a cool drink. There is someone else we'd like you to meet. You'll need to sit down for this."

———

"Smuggling this young lady into the towers can be done, though with some difficulty," Lerry explained. "Her pregnancy is the issue. TowerGov is very strict on population control. But why on earth Leonie? Isn't she one of you?" He turned to Leonie briefly. "No offence."

The group were sitting on various chairs in Rhiannon's quarters, further down the main corridor from the medical unit. Sussah insisted on joining them, eager to meet the agtechs.

"Leonie's not from around here. While you may think she looks like a wilder, she is natural born and just as likely to succumb to rad sickness as Sussah."

Leonie kept silent and sipped her juice, choosing not to reveal details about being the culmination of genetic experiments.

"I don't understand." Lerry shook his head. Maz shrugged at his look.

Rhiannon indicated for Leonie and Su to take over the conversation.

The dust on the agtechs' faces could not hide their looks of disbelief when they heard their incredible story.

"I understand your disbelief of another world, but I can prove the magic to you." Leonie put out her palm and conjured a small flame. She then made it rise and move around the room.

Even Sussah squealed with delight. "You've been practising!"

Next, Leonie raised Maz and Lerry and moved them to

different chairs. "Don't ask me how." She shrugged, fending off their questions once they got over their surprise. "I can't explain it, but on Yarnik, where I come from, many people can do this, and a whole lot more."

"If I may, I can perhaps show you what I've seen in her mind? It might be sufficient to convince you."

Maz nodded straight away.

"Will it hurt?" Lerry asked.

"Idiot." Maz punched him lightly in the arm.

"Not in the slightest." Rhiannon put a palm on each of their heads and concentrated. "Relax."

From the incredulous looks on their faces, it appeared they were stunned, if not convinced by the images the seer was showing them. After their experience, many questions ensued. Leonie and Su tried to answer as much as they could.

"How come you're speaking our language? If people in another country speak different languages, how can it be possible those on another planet speak it?"

"Our language is only used in and around Delta, the city we're from. It's the language of the rulers of our city. I hear other travellers speaking another language, not totally different, but not the same."

"We did see something looking like large birds, upright lizards and a large grey ball. Are they all intelligent? They can all think and communicate for themselves?"

"Oh yes. The glins'ool – that's the birds – have another language of their own. As do the seleth, the reptiles. They have their own communities, religion and language." Leonie described the six other races on Shak'aran.

"And that grey ball creature?"

"They are called hroltahgs, or rollos. They're from a high-gravity world and were the ones that made the grav-harness. Rollos are purely telepathic."

The agtechs sat there, mulling this over, confusion and disbelief still on their faces.

"How about we stop for dinner, and rest?" Rhiannon

suggested. "We can continue this in the morning with fresh minds."

———

"Our first course of action is to get you both safely to Outpost 7," Lerry stated over breakfast. "It's out-dated, but the basic amenities are still there and at least you're protected from rad. We can share some of our supplies and bring more out later. The more difficult part is getting ID for you," Lerry said to Sussah. "We'll have to arrange a form of marriage—"

"Marriage?" Sussah looked dismayed. "Who to?"

"Perhaps partner contract would be a better term?" Maz suggested. "It won't be something on a physical level," Maz explained calmly. "A joining of convenience. There is no way you'll be allowed a child as a single parent. There are severe penalties for those who don't abide by the rules, though this is rare."

"Leonie is going to be … impossible to get in. The best we can do at the moment is Outpost 7." Lerry shrugged. "You in the tower would be your death."

"How long would I need to stay there?" Leonie asked.

Lerry paced the floor. "Rhi has told you what it's like inside the towers?"

"She has." Leonie nodded. "But I was hunted in my city too—"

"This is different," Lerry said, exasperated. "Honestly, I would if I could. Even the outpost has its risks; other agtechs go there too. Maybe not often, but several times a year."

"A year!"

"If we bring medicine, maybe you can stay here in Jenolan? At least you won't be alone."

"I need to be with Sussah."

"Why? I mean I understand you are friends, but why *with* her?"

"I have to look after her. It's … prophecy." Leonie couldn't believe she uttered those words.

"Prophecy?" Lerry looked perplexed. "Superstition?"

"Like you thought magic was?" Leonie argued. "Look, I know what you're saying. You can't get me inside. I will get in myself. Can I get to see a map? I'll need to know where Sussah is, and find a place for me to hide as close as I can."

"Tell you what. We'll take you to Outpost 7. There are comps there with gigabytes of data. Maybe you can learn enough about the towers – either to convince you how dangerous it is – or how to prevent your immediate death."

"I have no idea what you said, but if you have a plan, good."

They remained silent, digesting what was said.

"I need to stretch my legs," Leonie stated.


Leonie was looking curiously at the flying machines and heard the footsteps behind her. "Is this how we're travelling to this outpost?"

"Yes. These are mag-bikes." Lerry said. He and Maz wandered outside to adjust the bikes to accommodate passengers. "They fly by repelling the magnetic field. Don't ask me the finer details, not my field of knowledge. Maz?"

Maz stared blankly for a second before replying. "The exotic metal, named *jotnarium*, found in one of the meteorites that hit Earth in 2030, has unique properties. When energised by a specific frequency at a specific voltage, the repulsion field is generated. More power will increase repulsion." She paused. "Was that enough?"

"Yep. Like I said. Repels the magnetic field." Lerry turned to Leonie, who was looking sideways at Maz. "Maz has an implant. She can access any declassified information on TowerNet."

"She has a plant?" Sussah asked, joining them.

"Implant." Maz turned her head and revealed a small, rectangular cavity covered by a flap of synth-skin. "I use it mainly for updates on crop, weather and nutrient information. But as Lerry said, if it's on the net, I can access it."

Sussah grimaced. "Did it hurt?"

"Not really." Maz smiled. "I used pain-nullifying drugs."

"Is that like tabs or medication? It was something Rhi spoke about before."

"Yes. But injected; a needle in the skin."

"Hop on." Lerry turned to Leonie.

Leonie looked at the seat. It had a vague similarity to the saddle Phil used, but no stirrups. "How long to get to the outpost?"

"If we went flat-chat, about two hours." At Leonie's blank look, he added, "Flat-chat is full speed. But we'll take it easy and get there in about four."

Lerry showed her how the bike worked; twisting this part of the handle to go faster or slower; this lever determined the height, and how to steer.

"When will we be leaving?"

"We'll have to leave today. Maz and I can't stay too long from the tower. If anyone gets curious, they'll come out and look. We don't want that kind of scrutiny."

"And then what will we do?" Sussah asked as the three women strolled out of the cave.

"We'll get to the outpost late this afternoon, and check-in by the comlink; tell them we had some problem, and head in as soon as we can."

Lerry continued, "You and Leonie will make yourselves at home … and learn as much as you can about the tower. Once you're safe and comfortable, Maz and I will return and start working on a way to get you in."

---

"Funnily enough, I haven't much to pack," Leonie said sarcastically. She strode over to her bed, slid out the storage box from underneath, and tipped out her scant possessions: some more clothes provided by the gracious community, the torc and the necklace.

Rhiannon tilted her head for a moment. "May I examine those?"

"Sure." She held them out for Rhiannon. Even blind, she gently took one from Leonie's paw.

"I can feel something, very faint. What are they for?"

"This amulet belonged to the High Priest of one of the religious sects. Any power it had is gone now."

"You can tell?"

Leonie nodded. "Because our paws aren't burning."

"And this one?"

"The Nightsky Orb ... all that's left from my last *job*."

"This also feels ... very strange. Any idea what it is for? Surely not merely ornamental?"

"Only in theory. Jade told me it was a device that showed all the constellations of Yarnik, used for astrology."

"Astrology? Interesting." Rhiannon examined it. She rotated the orb, then cupped it in both hands, took a deep breath, then was utterly still; frozen in place.

Leonie stood up and moved closer, unsure what was happening. "Rhi?" She reached out and was enveloped completely in the night sky. In shock, she released Rhi's arm. The vision vanished. Leonie touched her again; this time she didn't flinch.

There was no horizon. All around her, above and below and in every direction, there was only sky. Night sky. Yarnik's night sky. She blinked back a tear as she looked around in awe. She could feel the young woman's arm, but she was a vague shape and Leonie could see right through her like a mist. "Where are we? Where are you?"

*I'm here. We are still in Jenolan.*

"But—"

*You're right though; this device is fascinating. I think it's like one of those planetariums used in the old days to teach people about our constellations. Do you recognise any of it?*

"Yeah. Some. We call that one the Key." Leonie traced her finger along a set of stars. "And that one there's the Lock."

The stars vanished, and the cavern reappeared.

"That was amazing." She turned to Rhiannon. "I never thought I'd see them again."

With a sigh, Rhiannon sat back, sweating. "Well. That was surprisingly tiring."

Leonie quickly stepped over to the table and poured a glass of water. "Here." She handed it to the young woman.

"You try." Rhi returned the orb, swapping it for the glass.

"Me? I wouldn't know where to start." She looked at the orb closely.

Rhiannon nodded, sipping from her glass. "You must know you have some psionic ability." *When we communicate telepathically, I glean a sense of power and control there.*

"Did you see it in my dreams?"

"A bit, but dreams are disjointed. And you had quite a few."

"You saw the time when I was almost killed in the caverns?"

"I did, and that … hroltahg saved you. He was your trainer?"

"I had several, including a wyvern, but I guess you could call Styx my mentor."

"Consider this another lesson then, and I can be your new mentor." The seeress put her glass down. "Take it in your paws, add a bit of energy – power – to it, and concentrate; think of what you just saw with me. Like when you fly; you know what you want to do, so the concentration is easy. This will be no different, except it takes a lot of energy."

Frowning, Leonie clasped the orb in the same way the seeress had done and focused. She felt a drawing of power then she plummeted into night. It lasted a second. The moment it worked, she was so surprised, she lost concentration and snapped back to the here and now.

Rhiannon finished her drink. *A born natural.*

**19**

---

## OUTPOST 7

IT WAS A LONG CLIMB TO THE TOP OF THE SMALL MOUNTAIN RANGE.
By late afternoon, as the departing sun's rays turned the high
clouds crimson, the party stopped on a ridge. From north to
south, the horizon was a distant, blue shimmer. Dominating this
view, a large grey block stuck up into the sky. Even though they
had been told about the tower, Leonie and Sussah were stunned
at the sheer size of it.

"The base of Blue Mountains Tower is five hundred metres
square; it rises to two thousand metres. The total population is
currently one million. How many people in your city on your
world, Su?" Maz asked over her shoulder.

"I don't know," Sussah replied. "My father ran a tavern and I
didn't get out much."

"I heard one of our sages talking about it," Leonie offered. "If
I remember correctly, about five thousand, but it's only a small
city; Reenat is much larger, but it's a capital city."

"We have a population of two hundred of your Delta in this
tower alone," Lerry said, briefly seeing Sussah's sceptical looks
when he looked across. "There are over a thousand of these
towers around the world, some are larger. The total population

of the planet is almost two billion. A long time ago, it was almost four times that much, and we lived on the land then."

"Was that before the sea levels rose?" Sussah asked.

"Yes. How did you know about that?"

"Bern told us when we first arrived. And that there were wars and famine, and most of the population died."

"He's right. You'll need to learn all that before we get you into the tower. There's a lot to take in, but we have a few tricks to get the knowledge in."

"And that tower is still half-an-hour away?" Leonie studied it.

"If we went there directly, yes," Lerry said. "But as you can see, the terrain is rugged. Much of the area has been terraced to make as much use of the land as possible."

"There's a lot of scrub between us and the tower, but the last twenty kilometres are the crops. Other crop fields stretch further north and south." Maz pointed out the hazy green smudge stretching around the tower base, extending left and right along the horizon for as far as the eye could see. "We supplement our food supplies with a lot of seafood, mostly fish and seaweed. If it wasn't for the seaweed, many would starve. The fish stock is growing, but it's a slow process. You can glimpse the ocean on the horizon; that blue smudge. You've seen an ocean before?"

"Our home was around a harbour," Sussah answered.

"Why is the tower so dark?" Leonie asked. "Don't they have windows?"

"Most of those windows are solar panels to convert to electrical power. There might be some windows in the highest levels, but most are covered. No one wants to see out," Lerry replied.

"Why?" Sussah asked. "The view must be lovely."

"Too much to explain here. How about we continue this at the outpost?" Lerry suggested. "There's a storm brewing." He pointed to the southern horizon.

There was a rudimentary path to follow to the lowlands, narrow and winding. Most of the vegetation in the immediate area – when there was any – was the same scraggy plants they'd seen most of the day; the only difference with the lowland vegetation was a darker shade.

"There's a slightly higher moisture content in this area, and the soil is marginally better, hence the lusher growth," Lerry said. "And the crops are all irrigated."

"And Outpost 7?" Leonie asked.

"Is further south and east of us. We'll be there in about twenty minutes … assuming we don't get hit by the storm."

They continued east before turning south along another ridge. Leonie tapped Lerry on the shoulder when they reached the flat.

"Can you stop for a moment?" she called out. "I'd like to try something." As the mag-bike slowed Maz, with Sussah on the back, pulled up beside them.

"What's wrong?" Maz asked when Leonie dismounted.

"You know I can do magic," she said. "I thought this might be an opportune moment to put my capabilities to the test, while it's safer, with people to help if I crash."

"You want to do it here? Now?" Lerry asked, uncertain.

"You're going to fly, aren't you!" Sussah squealed with excitement.

"You can do that?" Maz asked. "Not just move things?"

"She is a powershaper," Sussah said proudly. "She carried me most of the way when we first arrived. And killed a howler."

"Yes," Leonie answered Maz. "When I arrived, we were both exhausted, injured and confused. I didn't know what my real capabilities were; I still don't. This way, I can see if I can match your bike. If I get tired, then I'll know how far and how long I can go."

"This will be interesting." Lerry nodded.

"So then, if you guys continue, I'll see what I can do. Start slowly at first, and I'll try to build up speed."

"What happens if you get too tired? Will you crash?"

"If I kept going until I was exhausted, then yes, but I'm *hoping* I'll notice long before that happens. Ready?"

With a nod, Lerry started moving, with Maz on one side and

Leonie on the other. They gradually accelerated to a reasonable speed, and as Leonie sped up, matched her speed.

Leonie loved the feeling of flying but missed Slana underneath her. After a few minutes, her confidence growing, she pushed herself faster. If anyone asked her, she couldn't explain, she simply willed herself. When Lerry cruised up beside her, she gave the thumbs up and went faster again.

The dark cloud on the horizon was getting bigger by the minute. Even now she could see branches flying in the huge churning column of dust.

The outpost garage doors started to rise at their approach. They cruised inside as swirling dust blotted out the sun. When they dismounted, everyone brushed the dust and twigs from their hair and clothing. Both agtechs shook their heads in astonishment when they approached Leonie.

"I've never seen anything like it!" Maz exclaimed. "We were going at almost two hundred kilometres an hour."

"I felt I could go faster, but my eyes were getting blurry. That dust didn't help."

"That was amazing!" Sussah said.

"I've seen people with jetpacks fly around, but they are slower and much noisier. And," Lerry continued, "you've never done that before?"

"Back home, I had a device I used that allowed me to go up and down, but no other direction." Leonie told them about her introduction with the grav-harness as they grabbed their gear and made their way into the domed building.

"Where's this harness now?"

"I left it on the skyland just before we travelled here. The crystal was broken. It was too heavy to wear if it had no purpose."

"We'll have to find a set of goggles for your eyes," Lerry suggested. "Anyway, I think we'll need to hear much more about your world, and you ours. But, welcome to Outpost 7. Maz, can you show them around? I'll charge the bikes and grab our gear."

"Let's find you a room each so you can clean up, and then we'll show you around properly," Maz said, cheerily. As she spoke, the storm outside intensified. Every now and then, they heard thumps and scrapes as debris flew against the building.

"It's one of the reasons these buildings are domes – so all that crap glances off the walls, and not through them," Lerry called out.

Maz ushered them down a long corridor then turned at a curved wall into another corridor; this one followed the curve of the wall. Several doors were located on the right side. While some things were familiar, like the benchtops, beds and some utensils used in Jenolan, so many things were alien.

"There are two rooms here, each one with an ensuite." At their uncertain looks, she explained as she walked in. "Bathrooms adjoining your bedrooms. Here are your beds, bedding in these cupboards, and here is the bathroom I mentioned; shower, washbasin and toilet. There is another one next to this. Lerry and I have a similar room, but further along."

A bit of instruction was required for the showers and toilet. "When you're refreshed, turn right in the corridor, then first left. The centre of the dome is the galley and dining area." Maz left them to rest and clean up after the long day's travel.

"I have to say, plumbing is wonderful!" Leonie said later. Sussah nodded her agreement. Lerry and Maz laughed at her comment.

"You're going to think I'm crazy, but I've seen something like this in Delta." She rubbed her paw on the floor, still amazed at the texture.

"You're kidding? Where?"

"Under the palace, there was a place known as the sanctum. It looked like … I don't know, like a flying craft of some sort?" She shrugged. "It had a bed in it called a medicomp, and soft chairs which moulded to your shape." She looked around at the workbenches. "And these buttons too. Our sages believe we are all from other worlds. I even read a book on prophecy, which said the three people who ruled Delta were from another world. I thought it was crap, but now I'm thinking there are too many similarities to dismiss it entirely."

"Surely that's impossible?" He continued at Leonie's shake of the head. "The floor is poly-resin; there's no way something like this could be on your world. We haven't been able to leave the solar system, let alone travelling to other worlds." Lerry shook his head in frustration. "I don't know about prophecy, but what I can say is this – I didn't believe in magic until I met you.

"Clearly there is some explanation, but greater minds than mine will be needed to answer it; that means we will never get an answer because to get an answer – other than theory and guesses – those 'greater minds' would need to see you, your world and your magic. None of this can happen. Sad but true."

"How about I get the dinner going?" Maz suggested breaking the tension.

"I'll help," Sussah offered. Soon the sound of pots and crockery came from the galley, with the occasional squeal.

"Want to walk around?" Lerry offered, ending the silence.

The living area was to the rear half of the central dome, the central hub included the lounge, galley and dining area. The front section – called the 'con' – housed the control room where all the field equipment was monitored as well as the main computer.

"This scanner shows a twenty-kilometre radius. This outpost is ours to use as this area is our allocation for management. It's mostly automated, but with all the terracing, sometimes the pumps shut down, or the droids get stuck."

"Droids?" Leonie asked.

"Robots – programmable automated machines that do the bulk of the work."

"No one else will come to repair it?"

"No. Most agtechs tend to do their own repairs as it is. Unless there's an emergency, like a massive storm, no one should come. If, however it does happen, this alarm will start chiming," he pointed. "I'll show where you and Sussah can go if that ever happens. It's very rare for anyone else to interfere."

The outpost also had two smaller bubbles, one on each side. They had entered through the garage, and the other bubble was a workshop and storage. After Lerry showed her the various tools and machinery used in crop production, he showed her where the water was stored, and the purification system.

"Rare as it is, we can purify rainwater from any contaminants as well as grey water, and black water, but that would normally go to the crops. But most of our water comes from the sea via the tower, where they desalinate it."

Leonie cringed at the explanation of grey and black water. "You drink this grey water?" she sounded appalled.

"Drink and shower. You didn't notice, did you?" he chuckled. "Seriously, no, the grey and black water are only used on the crops, but our purification system is excellent and has built-in safeguards. If it ever went faulty, the bulk of our people would suffer and die from diarrhoea, cholera, dysentery, and typhoid."

"You mean they'd get sick," Leonie guessed at the strange words.

"Yep. This just goes to show there's a whole lot more to get accustomed to and to make things harder, not only will you need to learn about tower life, you need to learn general knowledge about Earth; its basic history, and geography. Especially Sussah, she's the one that will need it the most for day-to-day living."

"How can either of us possibly learn so much, so quickly?" Sussah asked later after dinner. "It all sounds too hard!" She dropped into a lounge.

"Well, there is a way. Easier and faster, but, well, a bit more involved and painful," Maz offered.

"I don't think I like the sound of that." The young girl looked worried.

"What would that easier way be?" Leonie asked for her.

"Wet-wiring." Maz pointed to the implant at the base of her

skull. "It's a neural interface, developed to transfer information into the brain. It is, without doubt, the optimal way to learn anything."

Sussah paled, looking squeamish. "What's the other way?"

"Studying, reading lots. It would take years to learn it all sufficiently," Lerry said.

"Years?"

"Well, if you wanted to socialise, meet people you'd need to." Lerry shrugged. "I guess, if you remained in your quarters and no one knew you at all, you could get away with it."

"I don't think I like either option." Sussah grabbed a cushion and held it tightly. "And I can barely read," she mumbled.

"However," Lerry continued, "I wasn't serious about being a hermit; with your pregnancy, you'll need medical attention, and with the 'Joining Ceremony', again, you'd need to meet a few officials."

"So, you're saying the only way she can survive in the tower is to learn everything, and that's best achieved with wet-wiring?" Leonie asked.

"Regrettably, yes," Maz added, "and then there's the chip."

"Do I need it?" Sussah asked, rubbing the back of her neck and pursing her lips.

"Everyone is chipped from infancy," Maz stated. "It is who you are; without it, you're a nobody, and a nobody has few if any rights."

"Can we use the medicomp to do that?" Leonie sat beside Sussah to comfort the frightened girl.

"Certainly. It's easier than the implant, but we still need to get one."

"If you reprogram it, why not simply program it so Sussah has been a Blue Mountains Tower girl from birth?"

"Well, other than what's on the chip, there will be no other records of her anywhere – and hacking into the database and installing a completely new persona is virtually impossible, certainly far beyond our skillset. Having her from another tower, one that has had major disruption covers that as well as the other things I mentioned; accent, tan etc. The good part is, the chip goes in the arm. A simple injection, and with a local anaesthetic you'll barely feel a thing."

"Can I get an implant?" Leonie asked.

"No way." Lerry stated. "Not too difficult to arrange for anyone else, but you would never get the chance. Reported and detained is the least you could expect, maybe experimented or dissected, but more than likely you'd be terminated the moment they saw you."

"I could learn to do it," Maz suggested.

Lerry looked to Maz. "What? Are you serious?"

"Getting it done after Sussah moves into the tower is dangerous for the reasons I said before. I can get the download. Let's face it, other than hands-on experience, most medics get their initial knowledge from medical downloads. We have a medicomp here."

"Isn't this equipment outdated," Lerry argued.

"It's fine, and if Harrond's work schedule allows, he can assist. He can download it too."

"It's too risky. That sort of download is for authorised medical personnel only."

"As risky as forging papers for Sussah, or arranging the Joining Ceremony to permit the birth of her twins? Everything we've done for the wilders over the last ten years has been a risk. This is no more or less risk to us; the real risk is for Leonie."

Leonie and Sussah watched this exchange.

"Who is Harrond?" Leonie asked.

"Our son," Maz answered. "He's helping out east for a few days. You'll meet him next time we're scheduled this way."

"You can practise on me," Leonie stated. "If it works, then you'll gain the experience to do an awesome job on Sussah."

The two agtechs looked at her; Maz was smiling, but Lerry kept shaking his head.

"These things are designed for humans," Lerry argued. "It might not be a match for your brain. We don't know what could happen if things go wrong."

"Then don't go wrong," Leonie said, matter-of-factly. "Look, I've had a lot of training with the mind. Do you have telepaths in the tower?" After they shook their heads she continued, "I've spent some time with Rhiannon, but I've had a lot more training with some very powerful telepaths back at home. I reckon my mind is strong enough, and I can handle the pain. Also, one of my – attributes – is I can heal very quickly."

"More magic?"

Leonie shook her head. "No, you could say this is a ... hereditary trait."

**20**

---

# KNOWLEDGE GAINED

It was another week before the agtechs returned, this time bringing their son, Harrond.

He looked curiously at Leonie when they were introduced and smiled shyly when he met Sussah.

Once equipment and stores were transferred from their ATV, Harrond and Maz took Leonie and Sussah into the medbay to briefly go through the procedure, and answering any questions. They spent the rest of the day getting acquainted.

The following morning Lerry ushered Leonie into the medbay.

There was a bed-like platform in the middle, supported by a thick, round pillar. One end of the bed had various mechanical arms, some quite robust, others extremely delicate which were folded whilst out of use. A couple of monitors emerged from the ceiling, lowering to head-height.

She looked curiously at what Maz and Harrond were wearing. The robes weren't too dissimilar to what she'd seen Rhiannon wear, but she hadn't seen the masks covering their nose and mouth before, nor the face shields.

"There you are. Thought you might have done a runner," Harrond quipped.

"Sorry if our appearances startled you," Maz said. "It's a precautionary procedure for hygiene." She helped Leonie onto the bed.

Leonie had to suppress a shudder. "Give me a moment." The last time she was on one of these was when Dianah was finishing her research. She hadn't told anyone about that night.

"Take your time to relax." From a container, Maz removed the implant. It was a small, rod about the size of the first joint of a thumb. At one end she could see hundreds of fine hairs, filaments; the other end was punctured with as many small holes.

"It doesn't look too bad," Leonie remarked.

"I won't get too technical, but these filaments will adhere to various parts of the brain, depending on the type of stimulus it's programmed for. The brain has many pathways to control and regulate every part of the body, as well as allowing our thoughts, memories, cognitive abilities ... sorry. I'm getting carried away." She chuckled. "It is an amazing biological computer."

"Are you ready?"

"As ready as I'll ever be." Leonie lay down on the medicomp.

Harrond showed her a set of large, opaque goggles with an adjustable strap to secure it at the back of the head, leaving the work area clear for the operation.

"These VR goggles will subliminally activate all the receptors of your brain with sound and images," he explained. "You'll see rapid images and flashing lights, and with these headphones, you'll hear a range of tones to stimulate your audio processing. Sight and sound are just very small sections of the electromagnetic spectrum."

"Harrond, you're confusing the poor girl. Leonie, once this is done, you can learn all you want about science, then you'll have a better idea what he's is blathering about." Maz helped her don the goggles for correct placement. "Earbuds would be better, but they're not made for your ears." There was a slight adjustment until it was comfortable.

"Now, you'll need to lie on your front," Harrond said a bit louder. "The bed will form-fit to your– for comfort." He guided her arm into the medidoc; a stubby cylinder on the side of the bed, with several tubes and glowing readouts. Once in position, he activated the device.

Leonie felt a slight pressure and vibration as the interior inflated, conforming to fit her arm firmly but comfortably.

"This will check your heart-rate, blood pressure etc … it also pinpoints your veins for the injections. We'll give you a mild sedative to relax you, and nullify any pain." He showed her two vials, one amber, and one with the slightest hint of blue. "The relaxant will clear your mind of extraneous thoughts, allowing your brain to be more receptive to the additions."

"As long as it's safe." Leonie's voice was muffled as her head was down onto a doughnut-shaped cushion.

"Almost half the tower population has some sort of implant. You'll be fine." Harrond gave her a thumbs up.

Maz held her paw. "I was there when they gave Harrond his. I wouldn't do this if I thought it was dangerous to you or anyone. Are you comfortable?" Maz continued after Leonie nodded. "Harrond will activate the medidoc. In a moment you might feel a slight sting as it sets a cannula – this is how the stimulant and pain-killer is injected."

Leonie felt a tiny sting in her right forearm. In moments she felt the numbing sensation spread through her body. After a short period the goggles activated and she heard deep, throbbing sounds through the earphones.

"The images and lights will go through a set sequence to stimulate every function of your brain, whether it be for memory, movement, audio or visual perception, senses like touch, taste or smell … everything."

Leonie tried to make sense of every image, but they flashed for barely a second and moved on to another image. Sometimes it was a picture, sometimes she couldn't make it out at all.

"Don't try to concentrate at all," she heard Maz say calmly. "Just keep your eyes open, and relax."

*Relax?* Leonie's last coherent thought. *What's that …*

• • •

Sussah and Lerry were waiting nearby. Lerry was calm, sipping on his coffee, but Sussah looked agitated.

"I shouldn't be worried, she's been through much worse," Sussah said, though she did start biting her nails.

Lerry put his hand on her shoulder. "Even with the slightest bit of truth to all the stories you've told me, she's tough. Maz and Harrond will be meticulous and thorough. They won't take chances. Agtechs wouldn't survive long out here if we weren't careful."

They both waited as Maz and Harrond donned thin surgical gloves and checked all their equipment again. Leonie was face down and unmoving on the bed. Sussah couldn't recall ever seeing her so still. With various settings of the bed, her head was tilted down, exposing the back of the neck.

"Do you want to stay, or I can teach you how to ride the bike if you like."

"That would be great, but I'd rather be here for her. How long will this take?"

"About an hour," Harrond said. "It takes a minute for the sedative to kick-in then we need to wait for the brain receptors to be fully stimulated before the filaments can attach."

During the operation, Lerry clarified what was happening when Sussah asked.

Maz shaved a section of fur to expose bare skin, before swabbing it with disinfectant. Harrond assisted with exchanging the various implements. From time to time he turned briefly to reassure Sussah.

Time dragged for the anxious young girl as she watched on. At first, nothing seemed to be happening, then once the vid-screen lit up with a schematic of Leonie's brain, everyone crowded around to look at it.

"I've not seen anything like it!" Maz said looking at one of the overhead monitors. "Does that look like a highly-active brain to you, or what?"

"What's wrong?" Sussah asked, her voice quavering.

"Nothing in the slightest. See this here?" Harrond pointed to a growing bright green area. "The colour shows us where her brain is being stimulated, the intensity indicates how stimulated it is."

"It's very bright. Is that a good thing?"

"The brighter it is, the higher the chance of the filaments adhering firmly," Harrond answered. "I've not seen anything that bright before."

"Surely that isn't the stimulant alone," Maz said in awe.

"She did say she's had powerful telepaths training her, perhaps that's why?"

"What does it mean?" Sussah asked, fidgeting.

"She has an astounding brain," Harrond answered. "The research I downloaded in preparation for this showed many different images of stimulated brains, depicting the neural pathways – how the brain communicates, what makes a thought become an action – and in all those images, you'd see an intricate web, the colour depending on the type of stimulus, and the brightness indicating the strength. You can barely make out a pathway in Leonie's images because there are so many with extreme intensity telling us there much more activity than anyone could expect."

"What it means," Maz interjected, "is that this operation will be very successful."

Getting back to work, they applied the goop.

"The nanites in the gel will either promote integration between the new filaments and the parts of the brain where needed, or even promote new pathways."

Once the op was complete, Maz and Harrond removed the VR goggles, medidoc and all tubing before heading to their rooms to change.

"How is she?" Sussah stood next to the bed, holding Leonie's paw.

"All indications say she's fine. The relaxant will wear off

shortly, and she'll be able to move properly," Harrond said on his return.

Even as he spoke, Leonie gripped Sussah's hand.

"She's awake!" The girl exclaimed.

Slowly, Leonie rolled over onto a sitting position.

Sussah hugged her immediately.

"Ok. Ok. Nobody died." Leonie didn't object to Sussah's embrace. "Looks like you were more worried than me."

"How do you feel?"

"I have a headache," she complained. "Did it go well?" She tentatively touched the area of the implant, feeling the padded bandage.

"You're still breathing, aren't you?" Harrond smiled. "The op went well. There was nothing to cause any concern, but true success can only be gauged when you download data correctly. You have a remarkable brain."

"Thanks, you sweet-talkers know how to pay compliments, but it's not me you should be impressing."

Sussah blushed and stepped back. "When can she download anything?"

"Maybe in a couple of days, even tomorrow. Let everything settle down inside first."

"What were these goggles like?" Sussah picked them up and put them on her face.

"Weird, and fascinating. When I did manage to make out an image, even for a second, it looked real enough to touch." After a few minutes she felt confident enough to move around. "What's that?" Leonie saw a small box on the other table.

"Ah. Something you might find handy," Lerry suggested. "Consider it a prize for surviving." He handed it to her.

Sussah moved closer to see. Inside was a device looking like a bangle.

Maz smiled at her confused look. "It's an activity monitor. You put it on your wrist and it shows you things like your health, and heart-rate and blood-pressure."

"Why would I need this?" Leonie asked as she took it out to examine closely.

"Dad tells me you can fly? Is that true?" He continued at her nod, "That's ... fascinating!" Harrond showed her how to activate it. "This also has a GPS function; it can track distance and speed. This will tell you how fast and for how long you fly."

"Ah. That *would* be handy." She agreed, putting it on.

"And I would be very interested to see you fly! But after you're healed, of course," Harrond said.

"Definitely the next time you're here. Thank you both." She put her arm out to show Sussah. "Ok, let's eat, I'm hungry after all that." She started walking out, following Harrond.

"Have you got a minute, Su?" Maz asked.

"A minute?"

"Sorry, a term we use when I'd like to grab your attention for a little while."

"Oh, sure."

"If you don't mind, we should probably give you a check-up."

Sussah blushed. "Now?"

"What's up, Su?" Leonie asked from the door.

"Maz says I need to undergo a check-up." She sounded worried.

"Ok. I'll stay here with you. Food will have to wait."

Sussah reached out and held her paw.

"It's simple really," Maz said. "We'll slip your arm through the medidoc for heart-rate and blood-pressure like we did for Leonie." When Sussah hesitated, she added, "You won't need any injections. No needles."

From a storage box recently brought over from the tower, Maz retrieved a small pad and plugged it in under the bed, then grabbed a jar of translucent gel.

"This gel provides a lubricated surface for the pads, and better connection," she explained. "If you slide your blouse up, I'll put some on."

"You've done this before?" Sussah asked, unsure.

"No, but have had it done many times, as does every other woman who is pregnant." Maz chuckled. "It's a new experience for you, but when I finish, you'll wonder what all the fuss was about. This should also be done regularly to check development." Maz pulled down one of the overhead monitors so Sussah and Leonie could watch.

Leonie failed at hiding her grin at Sussah's face when the squishy gel was rubbed over her abdomen. "Glad it's you and not me. It would take me a week of scrubbing to get it out of my fur."

Maz picked up the pad. "Keep still for a few minutes, and this will be over and done with."

Sussah flinched when the pad first touched. "Sorry. It's cold."

All eyes were on the monitor as Maz manipulated the pad, describing the various organs, but they could only make out different shades of grey until she zeroed in on her target.

"They're so tiny," Sussah said in a hushed tone staring at the little shapes.

"They are, yes, but much larger than what they should be at this stage. Rhiannon said this was about your fourth week, but that can't be right."

"Why not?" Sussah asked, gripping Leonie's paw more firmly.

"These foetuses are about double the size of what they should be."

"Did Rhiannon tell you any details of how we arrived here?" Leonie asked.

Maz nodded. "She did say you came through a gateway."

"Something like that. She suggested it may have had some effect in speeding this up," Leonie said.

"Is it bad?" Sussah asked, concern tinging her voice.

"Bad? No, not at all. Not health-wise at least," she hesitated. "And tomorrow, before we head back to the tower, we'll insert your implant and chip."

"I'll stay with you," Leonie assured her. "It isn't so bad, and you need to do this."

# 21

# THE PLAN

IN THE SECOND WEEK AFTER SUSSAH RECEIVED HER IMPLANT, LERRY, Maz and Harrond returned with some supplies and more data crystals.

"So, here's what we've been able to organise," Lerry said as they sat down for lunch. "Sussah, even with downloads, you'll not have any experience with life in a tower, and more specifically, everything that pertains to Blue Mountains Tower; knowledge is one thing, but learned experience is something different. Further, you have a bit of an accent, and slightly different way of saying things, as does Leonie." He paused while he dished out the fruit salad. "Several months ago there were riots in LA Towers 1-3 between the citizens and the wilders – they have far greater numbers over there. There were blackouts and widespread contamination. Over seventy-thousand died or are missing. We will make it your agtech parents were casualties. Coming from overseas will also cover any lapses or differences in dialogue or confusion about our tower, and it will also explain your tan. You might not think much of it, but tower citizens, never having experienced true sunlight, are very pale-skinned."

Maz took over while Lerry ate. "On a more personal basis, it will also be a convenient excuse for your pregnancy. Until everything settles, and the contamination has been cleaned, survivors from LA1-3 had been spread out to many towers around the world, wherever they could find places. As you were *orphaned* you were sent to Atherton Tower, way up in Far North Queensland. They are a small tower with not much space; they could take individuals, but not many family units.

"We also chose Atherton Tower because Harrond visited there a couple of months ago for his Uni studies. This conveniently ties in with you." She turned to Sussah. "You met while he was on a course and were immediately attracted to each other. Sorry to sound so clinical.

"With your current stage of pregnancy, it can be assumed you were pregnant before you and Harrond met. The tower would terminate the pregnancy rather than let one go full term to a single individual. If it is ok with you, Sussah, Harrond has volunteered to partner with you."

Both looked away, their cheeks flushing slightly.

Leonie ate some food to hide her grin.

"There is a slight problem though," Lerry said.

"Isn't there always?" Leonie rolled her eyes. "What is it?"

"We need to get Sussah on the train from the north before it arrives in Blue Mountains Tower. As she isn't on the tower registry, she can't just appear out of nowhere. While most citizens can fly in, it is rare for agtechs or refugees. The train would be more appropriate."

"And we can't just smuggle her in via the agtech entrance?"

"Believe it or not, because our entrances have direct access to outside the security is far greater than at the train terminal. Our tower trusts the security of the other towers more than its own people."

Harrond stood to start clearing the table.

"In the supplies we brought, there are some agtech basics, as well as data on LA Towers 1-3, a bit on Atherton Tower, and news reports of the rioting."

"When will all this come together? When can we expect Sussah to leave?"

"We hope to have everything ready in a couple more weeks, a month at most."

"The sooner the better, before her pregnancy gets too pronounced. What about the train?"

"We'll need to check the timetable and somehow come up with getting her onto a train travelling at 300kms an hour."

"How much is all this costing?"

Lerry and Maz looked at her.

"In my world, rarely anything is free – unless someone takes it. You don't strike me as the taking type, so, is this putting a burden on you? If so, I want to know, so we can pay you back somehow."

"There's no repayment needed."

"That isn't what I asked. What is this costing you?" she repeated. "Forging documents, hacking into software must have a price? Surely it's dangerous."

"Either way, it's irrelevant."

"Fine." Leonie scowled. "When I get in the tower, I will make sure you're compensated, somehow." She held her paw up to fend off any discussion. "In the meantime, I'm going to analyse any train data I can find. See if I can come up with some way to help. So far, all of you have been doing the work."

"Are you familiar enough with the comp?"

"I've had nothing much else to do for the last few weeks. I've managed to learn enough with that implant to work it." Leonie grabbed a banana and sauntered off to the control room.

———

Leonie slumped in the chair, joining them for breakfast.

"Is it that bad?" Lerry passed her a bowl.

"The train travels more than 460kms an hour. Thanks to the GPS tracker, I've clocked my max speed at 226kms an hour, and I'll be slower carrying Su."

"With 240kms an hour difference, getting on board sounds impossible," Lerry noted.

"When it's in motion, yes, but if we access the tube maintenance hatch closest to the tower, I can chase after the train and we can get Sussah on board once the train is at the terminal."

"Okay, so we'll need to wait until the train has come to a complete halt before getting in. Su will catch-up with Harrond on the train, grab her luggage and ticket and leave from the other side."

"One flaw, there is a platform on both sides; one for departures only, the other side is for arrivals only with check-points at each." Harrond poured everyone glasses of juice. "And there will be people on both platforms."

"Frack it!" Leonie cursed.

Maz laughed. "You've been watching some vids too, I see."

"Just trying to help Sussah blend in. Did I say it correctly?"

"Yes, but best not to use it too much, or in polite company."

"Only by myself, or with you guys then, cool."

"So, the train dilemma …"

"I'm thinking. If we can't get onto the train while it is in motion, and can't get into the train at the station … I guess we'll have to stop it beforehand. What would cause the train to stop mid-way?" Leonie asked.

Lerry considered for a moment. "Damage to the maglev track, obstruction in the tube, power failure …"

"And I'm guessing there are redundancies for all that?"

"For the power, yes." Lerry nodded. "But maybe not so much for the blockage or track damage."

"Because, it being in a sealed tunnel, that sort of thing would be unlikely." She paused considering. On the overhead monitor, running daily with news happening within the tower and the world, there was a weather update. "What about a storm?"

"That's why it is totally enclosed, for protection and safety," Maz said. "Rarely is there a storm large enough to cause too much concern within the tube."

"But, when you look at all our *limited* options, it is probably the most feasible. If, say, an access hatch came loose during a storm, then debris would get inside – not enough to damage the train, but enough to stop it until the track is cleared perhaps?"

Lerry and Maz gave it a thought and nodded.

"It's a matter of timing then," Leonie continued, "having a storm hit in an area before the train's arrival, and us being nearby to take advantage. Are these weather-maps accurate?"

"Accurate enough, there's a storm or two every week or so, some larger, some smaller." Maz nodded.

"Good. The storm doesn't have to be in-progress; it just has to be between the train schedule. Bern told me these storms can flare up and dissipate any time. Can they determine something like that?"

"Not accurately. We might hear about it as a newsflash, not as a forecast because they're unpredictable," Maz said.

"Even better. It won't need a strong storm; if a loose hatch just happened to let in some debris and obstruct the track enough to stop but not cause damage, that would be fortunate."

"And Harrond will still need to be on the train?" Lerry asked.

"I think it would be good to have someone on the inside, to assist if need be. We'll need to access two tunnel hatches then. The one closest to the tower is where the debris will blow in, and the next hatch is where Su and I will enter, chase the train and she can board it when it stops."

"Depending on how busy it is, we might need a distraction, to get the passengers away from your entry point." Lerry continued after her nod. "Then we'll see what we can do at our end."

———

There was a flash and the lights flickered and dimmed. Thrown back into the wall with a thump, Leonie lay there motionless for a moment before regaining her breath and awareness.

"What are you doing?" Sussah came running into the room.

"Experimenting," Leonie growled, picking herself up from

the floor when the tingling stopped. "I have to do something while the agtechs are away."

"With what? How?"

"It was pounded into my head before we left Yarnik, I could do anything if I put my mind to it. I know how to make fireballs, and I can fly. These were things I did with tools; I learnt fire by using a ring, and the flying – or levitating – with a harness. It turns out, once my mind knows how to do it, I don't need a tool to do it. So I'm getting as much data and understanding as I can to do other things." She staggered to the chair to rest, her heart racing.

"What *things* are you learning this time, other than new ways to get bruises?"

"I was watching an old vid last night. It was a fictional entertainment called a movie. So I thought if I put my mind to it, could I do it for real?" She clenched and unclenched her paws, waiting for the tingling to go. "It's given me ideas anyway."

"It looks like it's too dangerous."

"Probably. But you know how much you learn by doing nothing?"

"Nothing?" Sussah guessed.

"Correct, so I'm doing something."

"And what is the something this time?"

"Electricity."

"That's crazy! There's warning signs on nearly everything."

"Exactly the reason why I think it's worth learning; if they use it a lot, then maybe I'll try too." Leonie went back to the electrodes she had hooked up on the desk. "But maybe I'll try a lower setting." She adjusted the dial.

"Well I'm not going to stand around and watch you kill yourself."

"I'm recording it too." Leonie pointed to the mini-drone. "But yeah, I'd rather not have an audience next time I'm thrown across the room."

Sussah walked off in a huff.

Leonie hissed quietly. After this bit of experimenting, she'd get outside and take her flying; being stuck inside had gotten to both of them.

Hoping the charge was low enough, she touched the electrode with the back of her paw, feeling a slight jolt. She forced her paw to maintain contact and tried to understand what it was doing. Other studies included information on batteries, and how they stored electricity. She thought this was similar to charging the crystal she used for the harness.

Leonie pulled her paw away as it had gone numb. Again. After a few breaths, she brought her paw close to the electrodes, but not touching. Like she had done with the crystal, she concentrated to draw the electricity. It was a tricky thing; when she drew in power, it was everywhere, but the electricity seemed to fluctuate.

With a headache growing from the concentrating, Leonie was starting to pant before a spark jumped between the electrode and her claws. Encouraged, her fatigue forgotten, she willed more and was soon rewarded with a small web of charge arcing across the gap.

When she pulled her paw away, the arcing stopped. She then tried one more thing; with only a slight curling of her fingers she imagined sparks between her claws. Her vision dimmed. She blacked-out.

She woke up on the floor. Slowly climbing into her chair, Leonie waited a few minutes for the room to stop spinning before she checked her recording, zooming in on her curled fingers. Sure enough, just for a second, she saw the arcs between her claws before she collapsed. Leonie replayed it a few times before she was satisfied, turned off the equipment and sought food. Then after a rest, she took Su flying.

———

A few days later, when the agtechs returned for their scheduled visit, Leonie laid out her plan. "I think this is probably the best way for me to get into the tower," Leonie told the agtechs that evening, pointing to the schematic of the terminal on level 30.

"You want to go in.through the terminal?" Lerry asked.

"Yep. There are some large ventilation and maintenance shafts in and around the area. It's one of the least occupied areas when there's no scheduled train and separates the agtech zone from the upper levels."

"Maybe. It depends. The industrial zone runs 24-hours a day; commercial trains and passenger trains run to different timetables."

"Okay. We better make sure we get all schedules then."

"How will you do this? There may be more drones or security in the area; recent news from other towers report the stirring of mutant-haters has flared up."

"Mutant-haters?" Sussah asked.

"It happens every few years," Harrond answered. "A bunch of fanatics get riled up about something and blame it on the wilders."

"It shouldn't be an issue once Su's safely onboard. If I climb on top of the train and hang on somehow, I can fly into one of the ventilation shafts straight away, depending on how much clearance there is," Leonie said. "If I'm quick enough, perhaps no one will see."

"From memory, the ceiling is about six metres higher," Lerry considered. "It will be risky."

"Isn't everything? How about I stay in the tube until everyone departs?"

"There's still the vids. They have motion detectors."

"I'll have to be quicker then," she mused. "I'll work something out."

22

## CHASING TRAINS

The tailwind of the storm was still prevalent, gusting blasts of air made progress difficult, threatening to blow them over.

"Can't this wait?" Sussah's voice was muffled under the scarf. She kept her goggles on to keep the sand out of her eyes.

Leonie shouted over the tumult, checking her watch. "The train will be here in half-an-hour, and we still need to get the door open, get the debris inside, and then go back to the other entry." She staggered up the incline to where the door was located. "After this, we have a bit of leeway, but then it's a tight schedule with supply trains for the industrial section. And who knows when another storm will hit. Now's the best time."

The large construct stretched as far as the eye could see to the north. To the south, she could see the gentle incline where it entered into the tower on level 30, the junction between the upper levels and the agtechs.

The tube exterior, worn and scarred by the ravages of time and exposure to the severe elements, was covered in a web of cracks, and the base piled with sand and dead vegetation. The hatch itself, showing signs of rust, was a slab of metal with the tell-tale signs of many years of maintenance.

Leonie pulled a tube of grease from a pocket and liberally

applied it to the hinges, saving some for the next door they needed to open. Swearing at how the gunk squished into her fur, she wiped the remnants on the wall as best she could.

"I already hate this plan!" she growled. Moving to the dirt-encrusted alpha-numeric pad that controlled the lock mechanism, she compared it to the small amount of info she could find; it was a simple four-digit code. There were too many possible combinations to attempt.

"Can you blast it?" Sussah came up behind her.

"I could." Leonie nodded. "But when the techs come to check it out, it won't look like anything natural occurred; we want natural."

"Punch in 0000," Sussah suggested. "It's the default code for everything in the outpost."

"Ha!" Leonie scoffed. "What sort of security is that?"

Sussah shrugged. "Tick-tock." She pointed to the watch.

Leonie swore, stabbing 0000. Nothing happened. "See!"

"Better blast it then, before I go into labour."

Shaking her head before she said anything they'd both regret, she idly punched in 1234.

The door released.

Sussah chuckled.

Leonie had to smile too. She pulled the door open with an effort and checked inside, noting the light-fitting in the centre of the ceiling. The air was cool and musty. "Time to get dirty."

Together, they tossed in some rocks and what scrubby branches they could find, and lots of sand; nothing too big that a reasonable storm couldn't pick up.

Leonie stuck her head in to survey their work. "I reckon that's enough, we don't want to disable it, just get it to stop for a few minutes." She then concentrated and waved her arm; sweeping the area with a gust of air to make it look as authentic as possible.

"You're getting better," Sussah observed.

"Thanks. I've had plenty of time to practice. Now we've got to get to the other door and wait for the train. Hop on." Leonie lifted a set of goggles hanging around her neck to her eyes; something Lerry brought over in his last visit.

Sussah put her goggles on and then hooked herself onto the belt they'd made to prevent her from falling, and held her shoulder. "Ready," she said.

Leonie rose and cruised a few metres off the ground. They spotted a pack of howlers in the distance. She heard the distant howls but left them behind as they sped on, following the tube until they reached the next door, twenty kilometres away. The storm had moved on to the south, so the air was back to normal; dry dustiness underlaid by a subtle scent from the gnarly vegetation, and something dead.

"Ten minutes to go." Leonie checked the time when they landed. "You want to open the door this time?"

"Me?" Sussah asked.

"Why not? 1234." She gave her the tube of grease, with a smile. "Off you go."

Once the lock mechanism released, it took both of them to pull the door open.

"Three minutes to go," Leonie warned. "Once it passes, we'll go in and fly to catch up. Then it's up to Harrond to get the rear door open."

Sussah nodded, hovering near the open doorway, waiting in anticipation to see something move so fast. "I think it's coming!" The end of her scarf flapped and billowed lazily over her shoulder.

Leonie could feel the air pressure building as the train sped along the tube; the stale, cooler air with an unusual odour wafted out the door.

A blast of air punched out the door. Instinctively, Leonie adjusted her stance to prevent being blown off-balance, and put her paws up against Sussah's back to stop her from being blown back. Through the door, they glimpsed the massive machine whiz past in a white blur.

As quick as it came, it went; the vacuum in its wake sucked Sussah through the door before Leonie could react.

"Frack!" Leonie leapt inside after her. She saw Su sprawled on the narrow floor of the tube. "Sussah!" There was no response. Leonie jumped down into the trough between the wall and the central guide rail.

She shook her gently. "Sussah, can you hear me?"

There was a murmured response. Slowly she shuffled around so she could straighten her legs and sit up with Leonie's help.

"Ow," she whimpered, putting her hand to her face.

"No rush, we should have plenty of time," Leonie soothed. "Anything else hurt?"

Sussah winced. "My hands and knees, and my back."

"When you're ready, I'll help you up, see how it goes." She unclipped a flask from her belt and twisted the lid. "Drink this."

In small sips, Sussah drank some water.

"Let's have a look at you?" Leonie gently pulled Sussah's hand away, finding a lump on her forehead and grazing on the left cheek. "That's going to bruise."

"Is it bad?" Sussah handed the flask back.

"Nah. A couple of minutes on the medicomp should fix it. Can you stand? See how the knees are."

With help, Sussah stood, pulling a face as she straightened her legs. With the aid of the light through the open door, she examined her clothes, streaked with dust and grime.

"I'll see if it can be brushed off," Leonie said and began gently flicking the trouser legs while Su brushed her sleeves.

"Not too good, but it can't be helped." Leonie stood up. "We have a train to catch if you're ready."

"At least I don't have to walk." She hobbled around in the cramped space between the wall and the central maglev rail and hooked on to Leonie's belt.

"Here we go. Goggles on."

They cruised in the centre of the tube, above the guide rail, accelerating slowly. Leonie checked her tracker; 175kms an hour. After about five minutes she began to slow, wondering why she couldn't see the train in the distance. By the time they came across the previously open hatch, she knew something wasn't right.

"Where is it?" Sussah's voice was in her ear.

Almost stopping, she could see a small amount of the debris they tossed in earlier, but there was only a minute amount.

"I reckon the blast of air in front of it must have blown the crap away – at least enough to not hinder the train's progress."

"So now what?" Sussah asked, concern touching her voice.

Leonie shrugged. "Let's see what's up ahead."

They sped off. Soon, the tube began to ascend as it neared the terminal. Still, the train was nowhere in sight.

"–where are you?" Leonie faintly heard Harrond over her comlink. She slowed and pulled the mike closer. "The damn train didn't stop."

"I know. What are we going to do now?" he asked.

They could see the platform about fifty metres ahead.

"I'm– wait a minute." Leonie stopped and lowered to the ground at a noise behind her. She turned around.

"What—" Sussah was about to ask.

"Shhh." Leonie pointed. Back along the tunnel something resembling a mag-bike, only much larger, lowered onto the central rail from a recessed door in the roof of the tube. Four maintenance technicians stepped out from another side door and climbed on board. They sped off back along the tube.

"I reckon they're going to do a clean up. Maybe we can get inside through their door?"

"But what about Harrond?"

"Harrond?" Leonie called on her mike.

"Yes?"

"Change of plan. We'll get in via a maintenance access point. We'll make it up as we go along."

"What about registering Su?" Harrond asked.

"It isn't going to happen, at least not straight away," Leonie growled.

"She needs—" Harrond started.

"One impossible thing at a time, thanks. Go to your parents' apartment. Lerry might have an idea. I'll contact you later." She turned the mike off. "Hear all that?" she asked Sussah, still clipped behind her.

"Yes," Sussah replied. "I'm worried though. I thought I'd mention it."

"Just another conundrum looking for an answer." Leonie approached the side access door. There was a standard keypad. Sussah unclipped when they stopped.

Leonie tapped 1234. "I didn't think this one would be so easy." She then tried 0000. No effect. "Move back a bit," she directed Sussah. "Whatever you do, don't touch me."

Leonie put her palm on the pad and concentrated. Like the previous times she'd tried something relatively new, it took a few moments before what she was doing felt right. The moment she felt the tingling surge in her paw there was a zap and flash of blue light. The pad smouldered, and there was a faint click. She leant against the door, making an effort before it swung in to reveal a lit corridor. Grey tiled floor and walls stretched in both directions. Unlike the rising tube, the floor was level. Other than the faint sound of air ventilation, it was deserted. She stepped in, followed by Sussah. Leonie pushed the door closed, but it didn't lock.

"Your eyes glow when you get charged up," Sussah observed.

"You say the nicest things."

"Which way now?"

Leonie recalled the map schematics for the terminal area, trying to find a way down to level seventeen. "This way. Stay behind me." Leonie hated this corridor; it was far too clean and bright, with absolutely nowhere to hide. "There's something called an elevator. It has a shaft going down to the lower levels."

They passed several identical doors. There was some faint talking from one of them.

"Shhh," Leonie warned as they crept passed.

"Doesn't elevate mean go up?" Su whispered.

Leonie nodded, continuing to listen ahead.

"Why call something that goes down elevator, and not ... decliner?" Su muttered.

"At the moment, I don't care. It's up ahead, around the corner."

At the junction, she stopped.

Sussah bumped into her. "Sorry," she whispered.

Hearing nothing, Leonie risked a glance. The corridor, a T-intersection, went left and right. A few paces to the right was the elevator. The area was clear, though there was the hubbub of voices and machinery further to their left.

Leonie crept around the corner to the doors. This was a different door to the others in that it slid into both sides of the wall. There was only a single, round button in a panel on the wall. Shrugging, Leonie touched it. Other than lighting up, nothing happened. She pushed it again, but the doors remained closed. Then she heard a faint whirring coming from behind the smooth doors.

"Something's happening," she whispered. Then she heard voices getting louder behind her. A glance to the side showed the empty corridor, but not for long as the voices got louder.

There was a chime, and the doors slid apart. The small room, only a couple of paces wide in either direction, was empty. They stepped in. Nothing happened.

"This is too cramped for my liking," Leonie growled. She saw a series of buttons on one side of the door. She pushed seventeen. Moments later the doors slid closed and the floor dropped from under them.

Sussah squealed and Leonie put her paws out for a second. She hit the red stop button in a brief panic. The room stopped abruptly.

"Was that supposed to happen?" Sussah asked, concerned.

"I think so, but it feels too cramped. I don't like it. We've nowhere to go, and anyone could walk through those doors in an instant." She examined the floor and ceiling, seeing a small hatch above. Rising, she pushed, then pushed with more force. The hatch snapped open, flipping up and making a loud bang.

She fell up with her exertion. The shaft continued up for about ten metres. There was one door above, and one partially obscured by the elevator.

A beeping sounded from the button-panel.

"What's that?" Sussah asked.

"A beeping sound," Leonie called down.

"I know that!" Sussah complained.

"It's not as if I've had a vast amount of experience, you know," Leonie retorted.

The beeping stopped. There was some hidden clicking and the elevator continued its descent.

"Here, climb up." Leonie reached down and grabbed Sussah by the wrist. She lifted her through and kicked the hatch closed.

"Now what?" Sussah looked worried at the dark walls speeding past. She looked up and squealed.

"You're going to have to stop doing that," Leonie hissed in annoyance. "Clip on."

"Sorry," Su mumbled, stepping behind Leonie.

The elevator slowed, then stopped. They heard the doors slide open and then voices as people got on. The elevator descended once again. The mechanism for the elevator was similar to a train, except the guide rail was vertical, and one on each side.

"It smells like the tube. Any idea what floor we're on?"

"None."

Soon the elevator stopped. The doors opened and closed, and the voices dissipated. It remained in place.

"I have an idea though. Hang on again." She flew to the top of the shaft, where the last door was. "We got on the twenty-ninth floor."

"I thought it was thirty?"

"Thirty was the floor of the terminal. Remember, the tube angled up, but that maintenance corridor was level, so we got on the elevator at a floor lower."

"Oh. I didn't think of that."

"Also, the buttons went from one to thirty. This was the

door above us when we stopped." Leonie pointed. "So if we count the doors as we descend, we'll know what floor seventeen is."

"Couldn't we meet Harrond on floor thirty instead."

"Harrond?" Leonie called into the mike. She waited. "I think he's out of range, or the walls are too thick. He's expecting us at Maz's so better stick to the plan."

"This is a plan, is it?"

"Yep, it is now. Down we go. You count too."

"One, two, three …"

"Backwards, dopey."

"Twenty-seven, twenty-six …" she counted.

Shortly, they were back on top of the elevator.

"Looks like it stopped on the seventeenth floor after all," Leonie shrugged. "Harrond?" she spoke into the microphone.

"Leonie? Where are you? How's Sussah?" She heard Harrond in her earpiece.

"Sussah is ok, a bit of a limp and bruising – she can explain later. I reckon we're on top of the elevator on your floor."

"Which one? There are several."

Leonie considered the question, trying to picture the layout. "We caught the elevator from the maintenance section somewhere below the north side of the terminal."

There was a pause. "Wait there, Lerry is coming. He knows the area better than me."

After another few moments, they heard Lerry. "Did I hear you say you were *on* the elevator, not in?

"Correct. Too easy for anyone to get on and see us," Leonie explained.

"That's okay. Good. Stay there, and when I'm in I'll call again."

They heard the elevator door slide open and close. The elevator dropped several floors. Sussah clamped her mouth before she squealed in fright again.

"Thirteenth floor," she whispered when they stopped.

Leonie nodded, finger to her lips for silence while they

waited. She reached around and unclipped Sussah, and sat down.

As Sussah, sat down, the elevator rose swiftly. She sat hard, stifling a groan.

When it stopped, the doors opened.

"I think I'm in the right one," Lerry said in her earbuds.

"Tap on the ceiling," Leonie suggested. They heard the tapping straight away. "Wonderful." She pulled the hatch up and saw Lerry below, looking up, relief on his face.

"Down you go, Su." Leonie helped Sussah down as Lerry grabbed her around the waist and set her on the floor.

They looked up expectantly.

"This is where we part company for now," Leonie answered their looks.

"What?" Sussah looked up in surprise.

"It's not as if I can just go wandering about, you know. This is your life now. It might take a while, but I'll contact you once I've found a hiding place. All part of *the plan*, remember."

"I know!" Sussah lamented. "I … it was a shock."

"Can't be helped. Take care of her, Lerry. Give my regards to Maz and Harrond."

"Consider it done. We'll help where we can." He nodded.

"I know, and thanks. Sussah, bye for now." She waved before closing the hatch.

23

———

# YEAR 2332

IT TOOK SEVERAL UNCOMFORTABLE WEEKS OF SCRAMBLING THROUGH the ducting and maintenance passageways crisscrossing each level, mapping each nook and cranny, looking for and finding a suitable bolt-hole close to Su's.

Leonie was in a world of her own. She was unique to this planet. Her new environment, the hundreds of maintenance tunnels, air-ducts and bolt-holes; elevators and service areas were hers to roam relatively freely.

She learnt quickly from experience what constituted a threat, and what was safe. Maintenance bots – small, multi-limbed machines – completely ignored her as they followed the grid-lines embedded in the floors.

She followed one along its programmed routine until it eventually returned to its charging bay; a workshop rarely used by humans except when conducting repairs. She found all manner of tools, their functions unknown until she conducted research.

Food was an issue at first, and there were a few narrow escapes when searching food-halls for left-overs.

In due time she came upon a wider section of ducting. One of the more detailed schematics indicated it to be a junction box, though it was large enough to be a small room. Six ducts led into it, one in each wall, including floor and ceiling, ideal for any rapid escape if required. The one small, square door to access the junction was stuck tight. When she managed to locate its position on the other side, it had been built over, whether by mistake or design she had no idea, but it served her purpose – no uninvited guests.

Surprised by some of the piles of refuse she came across in her ever-widening travels, she gradually made the room more homely. Most of her furnishings were rugs or the many cushions she found, and when she deciphered the tool functions, she put in some shelving to get other items off the floor.

Over time, she explored and mapped what she could around the agtech zones. She knew three ways of getting to Sussah's, found two more possible bolt-holes if the need arose, and located where Lerry and Maz lived and where they worked in the huge agtech workshop on level 2 when not outside. The entire twenty-eighth floor was for shopping and recreational use. Scrounging around there in the quiet hours also provided food and useful items.

Level 1 was full of the machines used to sow and harvest the thousands of hectares of crop fields. Most of the machines were automated, but at various times they required servicing or updating. She enjoyed this area the most; it was such a massive space with few personnel, and a myriad hiding places if needed. The majority of the levels between 2 and 28 were for accommodation which meant too many people and little seclusion.

Other than outside, level 1 was an area large enough where she could exercise, practice some powershaping, her flying, and any new idea that came to mind. She also started to practice multi-tasking. It was harder than it looked, trying to concentrate on several things at the same time. She theorised her abilities to fly and create fire became easier because she had been doing them much longer. The electricity was a new thing and producing a flame in one hand and electrical sparks in the other tired her quickly.

After a particularly tiring session, she had settled down for a nap in a massive harvester when she heard a man screaming in pain. Jolted out of her reverie, she cautiously explored the area. Following the groans, she saw a mechanic wedged under one of the smaller machines.

"Lerry, Maz, are you on?" she spoke into the mike as she crawled closer. No one else was in sight. By the time she reached him, the man had lost consciousness. Taking several deep breaths, she concentrated to lift the machine.

"Can you hear me, Lerry?" she groaned, sweating under the telekinetic strain. Her nose started to bleed and her head throbbed, but there was the slightest hint of movement. Feeling encouraged, she forced it up another few centimetres. It wasn't much, but enough to drag the man out by the feet.

"Maz here, Leonie. What's up?"

She slumped, her breath labouring. "Seriously injured man … east wing … level one. Was pinned under a harvester."

"Was? I'll be there with a medic. Any idea of injuries?"

With her head spinning, Leonie tried to look at him. The front of his overalls was red and blood dribbled from his mouth. "He's unconscious, with chest or maybe abdominal injuries, blood all over his front, and his mouth."

"Shit! Got it."

Slowly her vision steadied, as did her throbbing head. The man was still breathing, but it was shallow. Distantly, she could hear a siren getting louder. Using the next machine as support she pulled herself upright. Moving towards the back, Leonie looked for a hiding place.

"Can you tell me what bay? Look for markings on the floor."

Leonie glanced down, then bent to her paws and knees to look under the machine. "Near bay seventy-eight."

"Twenty seconds." Maz added in a softer tone, "Don't be there."

Leonie took the cue and staggered away from the approaching sirens, using the machines as cover. She didn't stop until she had five machines between them, then climbed into the cabin and ducked low. The sirens stopped.

She could hear indistinct voices, both from below and her earbuds.

"How the hell did you get him out from under that?" she heard Maz whisper. "It's six-and-a-half tonnes."

"Would you believe with a lot of difficulty." Leonie found a rag in a small door compartment and wiped her bleeding nose on it. "Besides, it was barely a few inches."

"It was enough. Are these other drops of blood yours?"

"Probably. Is that bad? I have a nose bleed." Leonie relaxed in the chair. She could see the distant flashing light through the cabin windows of the other machines.

"There's always an investigation with these workplace accidents. I'll sort it."

"When everyone goes, I'll head off."

"You're still down here?" Maz asked.

"Nearby. Too tired to get home, but I'll be fine in a few minutes."

"Ok," Maz spoke softly. "We're going. Take care. Well done, you saved his life."

"All in a day's work." As she looked on, the flashing lights moved away rapidly. She'd give it a couple of minutes before she headed home.

———

"Good day Ms Carter. I hope I'm not intruding, but I'd like a few moments of your time, if I may?"

"Oh, please come in," Sussah said. "I hope everything is alright." She escorted the doctor into the lounge room, trying to hide her nervousness. "Can I get you a drink?"

"No thank you. I'm fine." The smile the man gave didn't reach his eyes. "Everything is very good. In fact, the results from recent tests are astounding. So astounding, I wouldn't believe them if I hadn't conducted them myself."

"What do you mean?" Sussah struggled to keep her voice normal, but inside, her stomach churned. "Please, have a seat."

"Thank you." He sat down on the edge of an armchair before continuing. "Everyone knows from childhood nearly every centimetre of this planet has been poisoned by radiation after the wars, some areas more than others. For generations, every living soul has suffered exposure to it in some form. Looking at the records, not even before the wars, did anyone have less radiation than you. What's more remarkable is there's hardly a trace. Can you explain that at all?"

"No, but isn't that good news?"

"Both yes and no. It raises questions. You see, I'm a scientist. When I come across an anomaly, I delve deeply to try to find some understanding. Have you any idea what I've managed to learn, from going through your records?"

Sussah dared not speak, managing to swallow and shake her head.

"Can you tell me anything about your labour?" he asked.

"I … not much really. There were … complications." The sad memory burned in her mind. She had lost consciousness during the traumatic event. It was hours later they told her only one child survived, the other had died and been removed immediately, then a nurse put David in her arms to establish the mother-son bond. He was so small and fragile. She wept for the joy of her new son and the loss of the one she'd never know. No one would talk to her about it, encouraging her to appreciate and love what she had.

"Are you okay, Ms Carter?"

Broken from her brief reverie, Sussah realised she was still standing at the open door. "Oh. Sorry. I …"

"Never mind. I can see it's upsetting, understandable considering the circumstances." He paused for a moment. "The records indicate you're a refugee from LA3, sent to Atherton Tower where you met Harrond, and then moved down here when he offered to partner with you to allow the birth."

"Yes, that's right. It was a very confusing and trying time," she replied.

"Oh, I believe it would be. Can you furnish me with the father's name?"

"I can. Rickard Fletcher." The name of her boyfriend back in Delta. "He died in the earthquake."

"That is unfortunate." He nodded, making notes on his tablet. "Ms Carter, it's like this; I don't know where you really came from, but it wasn't LA3 – while there are no records to confirm either way, you would have far more radiation in you than us. The LA towers were quite close to a blast site, in fact, most of North America became a blast site. There is also no clear record that you existed before 2330, nor can we find any refugees by that name, except on some substandard report."

"It was a traumatic and chaotic episode." Sussah hoped he thought her nervousness was simply emotion from the tragedy. "I'm surprised there are any records at all remaining."

The doctor nodded, then continued. "A suspicious person might think there was some criminality at work; some forgery being done. I'd also be inclined to believe Harrond and more than likely his parents, this Maz and Lerry Carter," he read from his notes, "were somehow involved. I believe they're well-regarded, dedicated and experienced. They wouldn't have the ability to forge these documents themselves, but, hypothetically speaking, there must be people that do this sort of thing.

"Imagine the disruption caused if this were revealed, not to mention the ill-will towards anyone involved, even towards you and your son, David. Forging TowerGov documents is a serious crime, as is illegal entry into the tower, unregulated conception, and chip-fraud."

Dr Felton got up and paced the room. "Mind you, that's academic. I'm in a unique position you see, being the only one who has put all this information together. The only thing of real interest to me is you both have so little radiation. This is why we are having this chat, and not you and the authorities. Perhaps we can come to an arrangement to benefit both of us?"

"Assuming anything you say is remotely correct, I don't think there would be a choice."

"Of course my dear, there is always a choice. The colonies on the moon are always keen for dedicated, experienced and well-regarded agtechs. More than likely, however, they would be used in the pit mines out near the badlands – such terrible conditions, and radiation sludge everywhere. The living conditions are so harsh, and there are so many fatal accidents. And of course, the various orbitals will snap-up a young, attractive lady such as yourself. I'm not sure of your skills – it's a lonely existence for the men who work there – I'm sure some appropriate use would be found. Most of the orbitals are correction centres, supervised, of course, but with mostly criminals inhabitants; I'm sure you'd fit right in. They don't do well with toddlers though.

"It would be sad for David not to know his real mother. The good news is, many of the Elite would pay very handsomely to have such a promising child to call their own. Luckily though, I have little love for money, but so much more for my research. So, you see, you have plenty of choices."

"And your silence would require me to do what, exactly?"

"If you willingly comply with my request, I propose to compensate you both and bring you into the upper levels of the tower as a citizen. You will be housed comfortably with full access to your son and allotted an allowance and a choice of occupation, including training, and a new identity, with a bona fide chip and proper papers.

"Your DNA is ideal for my new research; the same with David. We can't have such a spectacular gift left to the vagaries of the agtech community. I can easily make all this go away. You will, however, need to say goodbye to Harrond and this life."

"New identity? Why would I need that?"

"We can't have someone else stumbling over this and then arresting you. That would jeopardise my research."

"Can't Harrond come with us?" Tears ran down her cheeks and she started to sniffle.

"He would not fit in. Harrond is a product of his trade and upbringing. He would not cope with being a citizen, furthermore, citizens would not accept him. From the earliest years, everyone is educated to ensure they conform to a prescribed thought regime. Outside is not good for us. We can't have over a million residents all pining for the great outdoors, so it is ensured they remain comfortable and compliant with the idea of living indoors. The thought of going outside is abhorrent to us. It's the reverse for agtechs; we want them to go outside, so their education and upbringing is different."

He paused while she wiped her eyes with her sleeve. "Please understand, this is not a personal attack on you and your family. I'm a devoted scientist, and you and your son provide a unique potential. With your help, and it *is* your help I seek, we could do wonders for humanity."

"Can I see Harrond before I go?"

"Of course. I wouldn't dream of dragging you away like that. I will give you a week to get yourself prepared, and to say your goodbyes."

---

"Can he do that?" Leonie asked, livid.

"I don't know, but I don't want Harrond, Maz or Lerry going to the mines. That would be horrible for them!" Sussah wiped a tear.

Harrond sat beside her and held her hand.

Lerry was pacing the small living area. "I trust our contacts, but with the threat of the mines – who knows what they'll do?"

"Will this Dr Felton actually go through with it? He said it wasn't what he wanted."

"But he was clear he was after David and me," Sussah said. "It might not be what he wants to do, but don't they train scientists to be clinical and methodical, not emotional? Maybe he would think little, if anything, about sending us all away to get his research."

"I'll get to the bottom of this," Leonie promised.

"Don't make things worse," Sussah argued softly.

"Worse? This doctor is taking you away from your home and family. How can it get worse?"

Sussah wiped her tears. "Getting them imprisoned in the badlands, or the moon colonies is worse."

The agtechs nodded in agreement.

"Fair point," Leonie replied, controlling her breathing. "Well, I'm going to check him out anyway. I'll be careful. If they cut off communication between you all, I can deliver messages."

"Will they do that?" Sussah asked.

"More than likely," Lerry stated. "It'll be monitored at the least."

"I hate goodbyes," Leonie growled. "I'll leave you to it." She walked over to Sussah. "We will get through this, one way or the other." She gave her a quick hug, then turned to the others. "And I'll see you guys around. Call me if there's anything you need."

"Oh, Leonie," Lerry said, "I don't know if it's you – probably unless there's someone else in the ducting – there is talk about noises behind the walls."

"Okay, I'd better be more careful, but some of the ducting is so narrow. Thanks." She climbed up into the air duct and Harrond closed the vent behind her.


With the pending separation, it was a rough few days for the Carters. Leonie avoided the worst of it, spending her time scouring the workshop computer to find access to Dr Stefan Felton and his work. The most she could find was a link and address to a company called Genlabs. More data could only be accessed by providing personal details, so she entered Sussah's details considering she was a bona fide patient.

Genlabs had several addresses, R&D, Administration, and Logistics; each on different levels, but all fairly high up. The site informed the reader about the board members, a brief history of achievements, and current projects. Apart from various medical studies, genetics was what stood out to her.

Not since the confrontation with Dianah and Brendon did her

heart beat so hard in her chest when she read that. Little more pertinent data could be found. Leonie hissed in frustration, not that she was expecting detailed information of research. Now she had a goal to strive for; look into GenLabs, their work and Dr Stefan Felton specifically.

# 24

## SEEKING SUSSAH

After a week, Sussah and David's forced relocation went ahead. Leonie visited Harrond to get information, but he had no idea where they had been moved to.

"The agency hardly answer my calls, and when they do, no one can tell me anything." He ran his fingers through his unkempt hair, looking tired from lack of sleep. "Lerry and Maz have had the same response."

"That's just shit. I'll look into it and let you guys know. Take care." Leonie climbed back through the venting, surprised how much Harrond was affected by Sussah's departure. She thought the new-found attachment surprising – but encouraging – considering they were both thrown into this situation without warning.

As she discovered before, retrieving information to do with the upper levels by computer – anything that wasn't within the agtech zone – proved difficult. She needed to be physically in the upper levels with a terminal. If the routines up there were similar, she'd have to do her searching in the downtime of that level. To reduce the overall power consumption needed to run the tower, the upper levels, containing the vast majority of the populace, were divided into blue, red, and green zones. Each zone had its own routine; nine hours of shift work, with fifteen hours of downtime. Her best bet would be to search a zone when it was deep into its downtime.

Leonie put two water-flasks and protein bars in her pack and headed up to the next zone – red. The most direct way of getting higher was via the elevator shafts. Each shaft had an access between the levels, secured, alarmed and hardly used. She was now familiar enough with the simple alarm system and had accumulated enough skill to work out how to undo the locks. *Just like back in Delta.*

She found the ducts in the higher levels to be larger, providing more airflow to the much larger spaces. The layout was quite similar too, except for the centre of the tower, which was reserved for a huge, open-air atrium. Leonie discovered this while cutting across the centre of the green zone. The ducting she was travelling though stopped at a large grille. She estimated the gap between this grille and the other side to be around two hundred metres, and from the ground floor, the atrium height looked about three times that, indicating 120 floors per zone, with many walkways spanning the gap every fifth-floor.

Having to work around the perimeter slowed progress, but finally she located a maintenance workshop. The security and monitoring was a fairly standard, low-key set-up, taking a few minutes to deactivate before getting to work on the computer.

There was no *Sussah, Su,* or even *S Carter* anywhere in any of the zones. Leonie swore. This was going to be far more complicated than she first thought; she hadn't considered a name change. Leonie hoped they kept her first initial at least; she narrowed down all the entries with 'S' as the first initial regardless of the surname, discounting any paired names; leaving her five-hundred-and-forty-seven possibilities over the three zones! On a whim, she also searched for *David, Dave* or *D*, and cross-referenced with the 'S' results; narrowing it down to seventeen, including some paired, which she had discounted earlier.

The time was 16:43. Green zone had fifteen minutes more before their downtime commenced, and the blue zone had just started. Leonie activated the vid, ensuring this monitor's camera and identifier was off; she didn't want the possibility of someone seeing her or checking the caller location. She started working on the list.

It became a tedious task; she'd key the number and the moment it was answered she'd see or hear the person at the other end. Grown males answering eliminated that address, same with anyone not looking or sounding like Su. After several hours, she halved the possibilities; some didn't answer and some had their vids off; none had a male child answer.

Leonie stood up and walked about, stretching and snacking and checked the time. Red zone was still a few hours away from their shift change. Not risking a technician stumbling across her, she cleaned up the area and climbed back through the ducting to snooze, then moved to the green zone in their downtime to complete her calls from another workshop higher up.

It took her over a week to finally trace Sussah. She was now known as 'Susan Osbourne', living at B63NE/4B. The address indicated Su was now on the 63rd floor of the blue zone in the North-East sector, apartment 4B.

After the initial call, full of tears and smiles, a time for a reunion was made; all Leonie had to do now was work out how to get there safely. She learnt David was allowed to stay overnight every 5th day, coordinated with Su's new job as a customer service officer in the GenLabs office conveniently nearby. Leonie promised to visit on one of those days. He was being schooled thirty levels higher, but because he lived in a dormitory with other boys and constantly monitored, it wasn't a great idea to visit there.

Afterwards, Leonie called in with the agtechs, relaying all the news. Even knowing the address, restrictions between the agtech zone and the zones above still prevented direct contact. Leonie took it upon herself to keep both groups updated regularly.

Now came the search for another suitable habitat for herself;

not too difficult considering the similar layouts. Some of her personal belongings – amazing what people threw out – she hauled up, but much of it she dropped in the garbage chute for recycling.

Once the removal was over, daily life settled to the regular foray to accumulate food stocks. Leonie discovered life for the citizens in the green, red and blue zones was much more refined than that of the agtechs. A wide area immediately around the atrium was designated as shopping malls and rec-zones, with the accommodation beyond. It was all far more elaborate than what the agtechs were provided with, and she started to despise these citizens who had a relatively safe and easy life because of the risks and efforts of others.

———

Leonie lay on her bed, concentrating as she held the orb. In moments the Yarnik night sky surrounded her. She was getting far more adept with the orb, and the regular exercises helped strengthen her mind, and she never tired of looking at the stars she longed for.

Reminiscing about Jade, Styx and Feiron; wondering if he had joined Phil and the wyverns and flown to Tesak, a ridiculous idea entered her thoughts.

She hadn't been clearheaded when they arrived through the portal, due to her injuries and distress from the l'ith attack, and the shock of being on a new world. The portal on the skyland had power, but this one was dead on their arrival. Was the power used in their transit the reason it discharged? She now wondered if, with her new-found talents, she could charge it like she charged crystals and batteries?

Her watch showed 06:20, the blue section of the tower was mid-way through its downtime; nice and quiet. Grabbing her backpack, she filled it with the nutri-bars and medicines she'd stored over the last weeks. *It's time I visited Jenolan again anyway.*

From her new abode, Leonie descended to the 60th floor of

the blue level and navigated the ducting to the outer wall. Every 10th floor had several large air intakes to filter, decontaminate, and provide the large volumes of air to be circulated. Using one of the technician security passes in her pocket, she accessed the maintenance door, climbed over the filtration units, and squeezed between the large mesh screens. She had done this several times over the years, but from the agtech zone; it was by far the most direct way out, and the designers patently hadn't considered anyone infiltrating the tower, especially at over one-and-a-half-thousand metres.

She enjoyed this time of day; although warmer outside even at dawn, the sunrise was always a beautiful sight. *Far better than four grey walls every day.*

With the patchwork of terraced gardens zipping past, the uneventful trip to Jenolan became regular. She tried to get out once a month, and the longer flights increased her endurance. Zigzagging along the many ravines and valleys, she arrived in Jenolan a couple of hours later.

Jojo immediately came running up and gave her a hug when she landed.

"Hey there, little one," Leonie laughed. "So nice to see you again too. Where's Rhi?"

Rolling her eyes, Jojo pointed to the cave.

"Of course she is." Hand in hand they wandered in to see the seeress as several wilders looked up from their duties and waved.


"I really don't think you should do this alone, Leonie," Rhi said, concern touching her voice. They were sitting in the seer's room trying a new flavoured drink recently concocted by the wilders.

"Would you be able to pick up my thoughts, if I called for help?" Leonie pulled a face at the tartness of the drink.

"Possibly, but chances are howlers could sense you too. Why not use this instead?" Rhi put her cup down and reached for a comlink on a nearby shelf.

"I didn't know you had them." Leonie laughed, shrugging.

"We aren't backward here. There's a comhub in another chamber. Each of our communities has one."

"You have more communities?"

"Oh yes, we have four others: Northcliff, Burraga, Kanangra and Westridge, which has the most wilders. Why do you think we have runners? The radios are used for emergencies only since the tower could pick up the signal."

"I had no idea. So, only if needed. Got it." Leonie drained her cup. "I reckon this needs to be a bit sweeter." She stood up and refilled her water bottle before donning her backpack. "I should be back by tomorrow evening. I'd like you to consider something else too."

"Jenolan's always here to help where we can."

"No, not Jenolan. You. I've come to the inevitable realisation my mind is different than most. I'd like you to teach me what you can about telepathy."

Rhiannon nodded slowly. "I was wondering if you'd think of that."

"You did?"

"Of course. It occurred to me when you were dreaming, and that day when you first activated the orb. You shouldn't have been able to do that, not unless you had a talent."

"Why didn't you say anything?"

"I was only sure the day you left, and I wanted you to come to the conclusion too. This had to be your idea, not at someone else's suggestion."

"Ok then. We'll talk more tomorrow night. I'd better go if I'm going to find the portal before nightfall."

Rhiannon walked outside with her. "Take care, and thank you for the extra medical supplies."

Some of the wilders gathered, watching in amazement and waving as she flew away.

·  ·  ·

Watching the terrain below, it amazed her she and Sussah had managed to do what they did; it was so rugged and uninviting, broken in all directions with sharp rocky crags, erosion and land-slides, and deep ravines littered with boulders.

She was in a good mood when the familiar rocky pinnacle appeared in the distance. After her morning flight to Jenolan, Leonie's trip to the portal was not as bad as she expected, and the sun was only touching the western horizon now.

The portal hadn't changed since she last saw it three years ago. There was no shimmer, and the rocks she tossed through from either direction landed in the dirt. She took a long drink from her water bottle and rested, relaxing … concentrating. Her idea was to try and charge it like she had done previously with the crystal, the fire ring and batteries.

She placed both paws on the structure and willed energy into it, gathering what she could from the terrain around her. It felt different to the power she absorbed at home; *wild* came to mind. If power on Yarnik was smooth and soft, this was hard and rough, but it was still power. *And no one else here can use it.*

Leonie stopped her idle thoughts and concentrated on the task and lost track of time. The sun had set and it was fully dark when she stopped, exhausted. Too tired to do much else, she curled up in a ball and fell asleep instantly.


The sun was up and blazing away by the time she awoke. Her head ached incredibly. She fetched her water bottle and two snack bars from her pack, then dozed again. A couple of hours later, she managed to stand and examine the portal.

If she had accomplished anything yesterday, other than draining her energy, she couldn't see it.

"I reckon you're a lot bigger than a crystal," she muttered, tossing another rock through it. Expecting nothing; the rock clat-tered over the edge, then hit the boulders below. Moments later, there was a howl.

Stepping carefully towards the precipice, she surveyed the

valley floor. Three howlers were moving towards the base of the rocky spire. She retrieved her pack, sat on the edge, legs dangling down and ate two more bars watching them as she rested.

Her little project had failed. It was going to take far more energy than she could provide to power a portal that spanned the incomprehensible distance between two worlds. In the back of her mind she knew it, but had to give it a try. There was no point in continuing; she'd only exhaust herself again and be stuck here another day with little more to show for it than headaches and exhaustion. Finishing the last of her water and securing her backpack, she dropped over the precipice to return to Jenolan.

# 25

# EXPANDING THE MIND

One week of headaches. One week of frustration. One week of arguments.

Eventually everyone calmed down, and progress was made.

*Are you going to talk to me before you go?* Rhiannon asked.

*Perhaps.* Leonie finished towelling after her bath.

*Join me for lunch?*

*Okay.* She dressed and made her way to the dining area.

"All refreshed now?" Rhiannon said as Leonie strolled into the room. "Nothing like a long, hot bath to ease the soul and mind."

"Maybe all your training should be done in the bath from now on." Leonie sat and selected some of the sliced vegetables and salad. Some were raw, some were cooked, all were delicious. All she had been able to eat in the tower were mostly leftover scraps and protein bars.

"That would be awkward, and all too revealing." Rhiannon smiled.

"Says the woman who can see into everyone's mind."

"Only when invited, or for health reasons," Rhi answered. "Congratulations on your progress."

"Is that it then?"

"It's a good beginning. Whatever was done to your mind back on your world has made things so much easier. It takes years for much younger minds to get to where you are now."

"What's next ?"

"Practise. Continue with the exercises I taught. You have everything you need to go much further; the door is open, all you have to do is step through. Where you go is up to you. The powers of the mind are not limited to mind-reading. You know from when you cast magic – which is very much connected to the mind – most of your capabilities are dependent on will; it is much more than mind-reading."

"Is it?" Leonie thought back to the times with Styx. "Telekinesis?" she guessed.

"Very good, but why limit yourself? Take your fireballs for instance or your flying. These are things you have experienced, and find easy to do."

"I've been mucking about with electricity recently. What about teleportation? I read about it. I think that was how Su and I got here."

"Who knows? If someone created a spell to do it, then I can only guess it's a matter of time before someone else does it. If it can be imagined, there is a chance it can be accomplished, especially if it's a known technology."

"Styx, my trainer back on Shak'aran said the same thing. How did you get into this?"

"My mother and uncle both had quite strong minds. My uncle had studied a lot of history, some of it forbidden in the towers because it was against the doctrine TowerGov was trying to instil."

"He was from the towers?"

"Yes, when my auntie died, he had nothing left to keep him there, and with the tower discouraging free-thinking, he smuggled himself out."

"And now?"

"Passed away years ago, but everything he taught me is still in my mind. He might be gone physically, but there's always a presence."

"Perhaps I can find some of the data he read."

"I doubt it. The tower destroyed most of those books. He had this belief; centuries ago, long before technology appeared, we were far more spiritual, more connected to the land, the earth. Magic existed because we believed in it, but as technology advanced we lost our connection, or belief, and finally, our ability. We rely solely on technology to get things done now."

"And this magic, you mean powers of the mind? Or fireballs and flying?"

"If you can't find the books or information to study, you'll need to come up with that answer. It's called experience."

After farewelling the wilders, Leonie headed back to the tower, thinking of the best way to put her new skills to good use. She could read minds when close, but from a distance would take more practice, and it was difficult for her to get close enough to anyone in the tower.

As she topped the escarpment, her attention was drawn to the south by a low cloud of dust. At first she thought it was kicked up by the wind, but she realised the cause was a group of people. *Wilders?* She turned to fly closer, wondering what wilders were doing so close to a tower and where they'd come from.

The aircraft took her by surprise. As it shot past, she wondered if the pilot had seen her. There was no way she could out-fly it; while her speed and endurance had improved, the speed of this thing surpassed anything she could do. *Definitely faster than the train.* She angled sharply down towards thick scrub, landing roughly among the foliage.

"Idiot! That was too close," she muttered as the pilot banked. "No doubt he's reported this to the tower." Leonie berated herself for not paying attention to what she was doing.

The jet circled once, then resumed its course towards the

wilders. She heard a loud, rattling sound from the jet. The group scattered and disappeared in the bush.

While the jet repeated this manoeuvre several times, another noise grew louder. From the tower, she saw three other mag-craft emitting a faint buzz like the mag-bikes but stronger, two flew towards the same area, and one in her direction. When the first two landed, several figures jumped out of each craft.

If there were wilders in danger, Leonie felt she had to help. She waited to see what the lone mag-craft would do.

When it passed overhead, she stayed low and scurried south at an angle, dodging between the vegetation and hiding when the mag-craft circled her way. It started to hover around fifty metres up, slowly rotating as if scanning the area. She decided to wait it out, until the mag-craft left.

The cracking of a branch sounded behind her. Looking over her shoulder, she saw a pack of black howlers sneaking up to her position. It was clear they knew of her location, but if she fire-balled them or took off, the pilot would see her.

Leonie counted eight hounds. "Too many to fight!" she growled. "Frack this." She burst out of the bushes, heading to the south, low and fast. The howling faded quickly as she picked up speed, but the pilot must have spotted her and changed direction to intercept. *No point trying to avoid it now.* She waved. A loud, staccato noise came from it; the ground below her peppered with spouts of dirt; the same noise she heard from the jet.

"Bugger this!" she hissed. Darting to the side, she flew towards it. Her speed and altitude dropped slightly as she created a fireball. The wind promptly whisked it away, dissipating as it fell to the ground. As she watched it in surprise, the shooting started again.

Leonie evaded by soaring straight up, devising another attack. *It's all electrical.* Summoning a charge, she pivoted and sent a bolt to the pursuing craft. There was no explosion. After a brief spark, it simply dropped like a rock to the ground, crumpling on impact. A couple of soldiers emerged; the first rolled out as if pushed and the one behind staggered for a few metres before collapsing, unmoving. There was no other movement, nor could she sense life.

Another burst of gunfire from the south snapped her attention back to the plight of the wilders. She changed direction, swiftly, trying to think how best to assist. Stopping the mag-craft from shooting was one thing, but over a dozen soldiers were strafing the scrub. She soared up for a better view of the area and regretted it. From her vantage point, she witnessed the bloodbath. Leonie counted nineteen wilder bodies. Some adult, some small enough to be children.

*Defenceless and unarmed, gunned down like vermin!*

She picked up thoughts of terror and hate, intensified by the situation. The soldiers were too spread out to attack without alerting others and risking her coming under fire.

*I don't have to attack all of you at once* she realised, looking down at the nearest soldier.

She manipulated his memories so he was still seeing mutants everywhere. He turned and started firing indiscriminately at the others. There was a couple of seconds of confusion. The other soldiers returned the fire. Four soldiers were down, including the initial victim. Leonie chose another. Within 30 seconds, all were down; blood seeping into the soil. *Probably not the training Rhiannon had in mind.*

Frantically, Leonie searched for any wilder survivors.

"Hello?" she called. "I can help you." There was no response. She, repeated it, both verbally and telepathically, flying in ever-widening circles, hoping to cover all areas with her eyes and her mind. Some belongings were found as if this group was moving from one location to another. "But why, and from where?" she pondered while quickly going through their scattered belongings to see if there were any names or something to identify the owner. All she found was a crumpled photo with some names scribbled on the back, dated 2330.

Tears came unbidden and she dropped to her knees, barely feeling the gravel as she hit, and cried for the cruel and unnecessary waste of life. She covered her face with her paws and cried for her part; not only the death she wrought – the taking of lives – but the hatred and vengeance she felt while doing it. *How am I any better?*

She staggered to her feet, deciding she had to move before more soldiers arrived.

Reluctant to leave them to be food for howlers or other scavengers, Leonie gently gathered the wilder bodies to make a pyre. She did the same for the soldiers, though not as gently, heaping them into the mag-craft and igniting it.

As she collected one of the weapons to examine, the jet reappeared from the south. She quickly ducked low against the nearest craft. Diverting the smoke to screen her escape, Leonie slung the weapon over her shoulder and slowly moved away from the area undetected, the trail of smoke curling overhead. The jet circled, then headed north.

"No doubt more will be arriving soon enough." She briefly considered resting at Outpost 7, but when she saw it half an hour later, there was a vehicle parked nearby. She didn't think Lerry and Maz were scheduled to be out here, so she cautiously flew on to the tower, wondering why someone else was there.

Several more craft appeared from the tower, as well as ground vehicles, all but one heading to the south. One ground vehicle drove to the first mag-craft she had zapped.

Leonie decided the risk was too high to attempt approaching the tower. She wearily turned west to head back to Jenolan. She remained very low, not looking forward to reporting the tragic news. On her way, she speculated on how the wilders were seen in the first place.

# 26

# THE RETURN

Pausing on the edge of the escarpment, Leonie watched the tower for a while, still weary even after two days resting in Jenolan. No one knew the southern wilders but would send the runners around to make inquiries and pass on the news.

Below her lay the skeleton of the first downed craft and the two dark shapes of the others lay to the south. The tower was about thirty kilometres away and there was no unusual activity visible. She opted for a safer route, flying a low, circuitous route to the north-east and gradually curving around towards the tower as she paralleled the tube. Two mag-craft emerged, they descended quickly, heading unerringly in her direction.

"Shit!" Again she briefly wondered how they had become so alert.

She spun around and dashed to the access hatch she'd passed a few minutes earlier. The craft were zooming in.

Her landing was hard. *That needs practice!* She rolled to a stop, clambered up the slope, punched in 1234 and pulled hard on the handle. At first, there was resistance. Even with her will, the hatch barely creaked open, and she was thankful she and Sussah had greased it three years ago.

The high-pitched buzzing from the approaching craft indicated the pilot was braking hard, almost standing it on its tail to reduce its forward motion.

As the sound screamed in her flattened ears, the mag-craft started to land, kicking up clouds of dust. The other craft shot past and spun around. A rapid-fire noise burst from the craft on the ground. The walls and door pinged loudly. Chips of mortar and sparks from the metal erupted around her. She hissed at the sharp stings she felt on her arms and shoulders. The soldiers swarmed out as she leapt inside, struggling to pull the door behind her.

Finally, it closed with a clang. Quickly punching the code, she heard the lock click. Taking a moment to catch her breath and concentrate, she placed her paw on the panel and summoned a small charge. There was a flash of blue light followed by an acrid smell. The lights on the ceiling flickered.

Shortly after she heard banging on the other side of the hatch.

"Just in time!" she gasped. Pivoting, she quickly headed towards the terminal.

After about ten kilometres, she felt the air thicken around her. Glancing over her shoulder, a distant light approached.

"Slistorf!" Leonie accelerated. Her only hope was getting close enough to the terminal so the train slowed on its approach. Apart from the central guide rail, the channels on each side were narrow. *No cover and nowhere to hide there!* The distance between the tube walls and the train was unclear. Becoming a smear along the tunnel wall was not something she relished.

Leonie willed herself faster until her head throbbed. Her tracker glowed 315kph. The train was closing the distance. *It has to be slowing soon!* She raced on, forcing greater speed. 332kph! *Still nowhere near fast enough.*

At long last she saw the distant light ahead for the terminal. Checking where the train was, she estimated the distance widening. *Finally, faster than the train.* She hoped she had time to get in through the maintenance door.

Slowing abruptly, she landed hard on the top of the guide

rail, dropped into the channel and zapped the panel immediately. Her fur started to ruffle with the approaching wall of air.

*This is going to be close!* She could see the lights out of the corner of her eye.

The door was stiff. She pushed against it.

It reefed open.

She fell through, seeing four armed guards as she rolled onto the floor, the one who pulled on the door also on the ground. In shock, she leapt back into the tube instinctively before any of them could react.

The air was packed with light, wind and noise. Leonie flashed to the roof and turned her head sideways, flattening herself into the recessed maintenance door on the ceiling. The train, slightly flatter on top than expected, passed. *Ah. Because of those light fittings,* she realised. The smooth metal surface rushed by at a whisker's distance. It had slowed down considerably now as the head carriage entered the terminal. It saved her life and gave her time to think about her predicament.

There were four armed men at the door, now alert to her presence, and without a doubt many others on the platforms or on their way. More than likely, the soldiers had forced the other tube access door by now. Staying here would be suicide; heading back would be suicide; going to the terminal would be exceedingly bad. There was virtually no escape with her first two options – her against several armed guards; fireballing them would simply pinpoint her location to everyone. The third option was a well-lit, larger space with many more eyes and cameras. Possibly an avenue of escape, but very likely to be seen. The whole tower would be in an uproar if a wilder was known to be in their presence. *They're really pissed about something.*

Time was quickly running out. She made a frantic decision. As the tail of the train glided past, she skimmed along the roof in its wake, scraping her back and shoulders at times, until she was again above the train. What she had glimpsed on the top of the carriage as it passed provided a slightly less insanely suicidal option, but she had to get to it before the train fully entered the terminal.

Encompassed within the streamlined skin of the train's roof were the cooling units. It needed airflow. She noticed dark recesses before and after each unit. As the last carriage crossed the threshold of the tube, she lay flat in the depression and kept as still as possible, hoping the curve of the train would provide sufficient cover for anyone trying to spot her from the platform. The warmer, stale air from the unit exhaust washed over her.

As she lay there, waiting for the yell, her paranoia led to other anxious thoughts; *Drones and sensors.* She dare not risk moving at all for fear the movement registered somewhere. She willed herself to be small, to blend into the dark recess, to be still, to be cool, to relax!

"Mutant seen in the tube ..." she heard, and similar outbursts. There was more shouting, sounding more like orders than alarm. Numerous heavy boots ran by on both sides.

Leonie listened, trying to discern what was going on. There was a series of hisses from the right side of the train. *Doors.* More voices – male and female, frightened and confused – not military. *Passengers disembarking.*

From the corner of her eye, she saw a drone pass overhead.

The voices dwindled. More orders. Boots stomped on the train. *The terminal had been cleared and now they're checking carriages?* Boots behind her and voices echoing in the tunnel. *Meeting up with the other guards?*

The boots on the train stopped. Another drone whirred overhead. While she waited, she tried to listen with her mind, blocking the sting from her back and shoulders scraping along the concrete surface.

At first, it was static noise; lots of faint whispers all bunched together making no sense. She'd felt snippets, words, *wilders ... cat ... mutants ... incursion ... tube ...* but no full sentence, no solidly constructed pattern of thought. Like the static noise she sometimes heard on the comlink. Her head began to throb after a few minutes. She stopped; the flight and race through the tube had stretched her limits. Her time was best spent relaxing to conserve energy.

If she could out-wait them, they might think she either died or managed to get down the tunnel. When the train left, she'd hop off, and work out another plan which didn't involve confronting dozens of armed guards.

Leonie studied the ceiling without moving more than her eyes. There were shadows, but not dark enough to hide in; rows of lights; she counted five security cameras, and the various drones flitting about. *Why haven't they detected me?*

There was something there, some connection.

Time dragged on. Boots came and went as did the voices and orders, strangely muffled now. The train powered down, making a slight jolt as it settled on the guide rail and silencing the noise from the cooling units. Then the ever-present sound of the main ventilation fans cut out. *They're shutting the air down?*

The drones she could see moved to the sides and hovered. *Waiting?*

With no background sound, she strained her ears to pick up any orders, but only heard muffled words, like they were wearing masks. *Gas masks? That's why they cut power to the air!*

Stopping the train indicated how seriously they were taking this, and were being thorough. In time, she was certain they'd find her. *Should have just fireballed the jet first time.*

She couldn't do that here, now … not a fireball.

Leonie concentrated, soaking in energy to try an idea; to shut down everything at the same time. The one time she did it was by accident. She had been experimenting with electricity but sneezed at a crucial point. Now she had to do it with purpose; her life depended on it.

She kept absorbing. Her tongue went numb and her teeth tingled. The nearest lights flickered, and a drone fell. The sound of it clattering to the hard surface surprised her. She released the contained energy in an electromagnetic pulse, spreading across both platforms instantly.

Anything carrying a charge sparked and stopped; more

drones crashed, the security cameras stopped, the lights crackled and dimmed. For a few heartbeats, there was complete darkness. With all fans and air-purifiers shut down, the silence of the terminal was profound. Before long, the panic started; muffled shouting and general chaos spewed from the terminal floor.

*If only I had the energy to move.*

The last time there was a blackout it took a few minutes before any power returned; she could only assume they would be quicker in this important area. Forcing herself to sit up, she blinked away the spots. Thirty guards on the platform moved about with arms flailing in front of them. When a pair touched each other, it started a blind, panic-laden brawl.

With a deep, shuddering breath, she rolled off the roof, taking advantage of both the chaos and darkness. As she moved, her wounds stung; it felt like they peeled off the metal surface, leaving little doubt in her mind there'd be traces of her blood as evidence if they chose to look. She lowered herself to the platform, barely staggering between the guards, heading to the tube and the maintenance hatch, manned by two guards.

A shot rang out from the terminal, the muzzle flash lighting up the immediate area. This set off a few more panic shots until orders were screamed to be heard. It was enough to distract the guards. Leonie slipped by and quickly padded to the elevator.

Cries and calls of "Mutants are attacking!" from panicked people carried all along the corridor. At the elevator, she slipped her claws between the doors and willed them open. It was an effort, but it was wide enough for her to slither through. The lift was far below.

With effort, she flew the short distance to the top of the shaft. The alarm system was still off, but she by-passed it anyway in the off chance the power returned sooner than expected. Lifting the hatch, she climbed through, secured it and navigated to the massive, central elevator shafts.

According to her schematics, there were dozens of elevator shafts around the tower, getting larger further towards the centre. The four main shafts, the most structurally sound areas, went from the foundations all the way to the top, each one housing twelve large lifts.

She checked the time; 19:36 meant green and red zones were in their downtime and blue would be well into their shift. Her new abode was still over four hundred floors higher.

Too tired to fly up through each zone, she waited within the vent until a rising elevator stopped nearby. She then quickly jumped to it and rode it up as high as it went, leap-frogging to other ascending elevators if and when they passed. If the lift stopped on a floor and remained there, empty and silent, she quickly opened the hatch, popped down to push the highest button then climbed out as it continued its ascent.

She repeated this process through the green zone until she reached her floor in the blue zone. From the shaft, she crawled through the ducting and wearily made her way back to her hide-out. Slumping onto the pile of old cushions she used as a bed, she dropped into a deep, exhausted sleep.

———

Even with four hundred and twenty floors and two zones between them, Leonie remained hyper-vigilant for several days to ensure no one followed her or discovered her enclosure.

She considered this was probably the first time a wilder – *a mutant* – had entered the tower.

Many news reports on the vid revealed expanding searches and security. She had to come up with a plan to end the violence, stop the searches, and remove any chance of discovery. After the effort in finding and securing her convenient little niche, she was reluctant to abandon it quickly.

A group calling themselves 'RAM' – *Rage Against Mutants* – started making waves, with factions in all three zones. According to records, the group had been growing on and off for several years, and throughout many other towers; low-key disturbances were the norm. After further searching, she found a report regarding mutants on the move due to harsh, dry conditions. This was also not an unknown occurrence, though when and where was difficult to gauge. *And that explains the higher level alertness and increased patrols.*

The recent incident outside and now at the terminal gave the group more impetus, more motivation, more recruits. Although quick to deter any large gatherings, security was stretched, and they couldn't anticipate what a few small, motivated groups might do.

With the citizens on edge, anyone or anything considered not-quite-right was suspect. Things started to get ugly. Two days ago, a man fell to his death from a balcony under suspicious circumstances; the only offending feature was a birthmark.

Feeling partly responsible for the growing erratic behaviour, she considered a plan to quell the panic.

———

Limiting her scouting to night only, it had taken a few days to locate the howler pack. Once she spotted a black one roughly her size, she lifted it out of the pack and stunned it, bringing it back to the tower as a final stage for her scheme. The pack followed, howling in her wake, but lost interest quickly when she climbed to several thousand metres.

She barely gave them a second thought, other than thinking how different her arrival here with Sussah would have been, knowing what she knew now.

On the south side of the tower – a side she rarely used – Leonie entered the air vent near the south-eastern corner, red zone level 10, dragging the howler inside. The timing was beneficial, as the zone was also in downtime for another hour, but most inhabitants would be awake. She closed the outer vent and proceeded to the ducts leading down, lowering the creature to level 5. She positioned it in a maintenance corridor and waited in the air duct, having made certain earlier doors at either end were closed.

After a while the howler stirred, slowly regaining conscious-ness. The growling and sniffing started, then the scratching at the smooth floor and walls. It padded back and forth perhaps in search of its pack or a way out of the alien enclosure. When it passed underneath her, she gave it a little jolt. It growled louder, then sensing her, let out a howl.

Although immune to its effects, the sound irritated her ears due to the confines. If her plan came to fruition, she'd stir up enough panic to get the security in here while keeping the citi-zens safe. Then security would find the animal and kill it, reduce the mounting tensions, and she could continue to live in relative peace and quiet.

When the howler stopped howling she gave it a tingle. A commotion further along the corridor suggested the soldiers had finally arrived.

The howler turned to face the noise.

When the door burst open there was yelling and some panicked screaming, followed by gunfire. Lots of it. The explo-sion surprised her.

Leonie saw chunks of flesh and gore splatter the small section of the floor in view. She quickly rose out of the ducting at the next level and, once her ears recovered, listened in. The howling had stopped and frenzied yelling and orders were given. *I'll get better info via the vid reports later.*

"Let that be an end to it!" Leonie hoped she could now get some sleep.

# 27

# YEAR 2340

Over the past eight years, Leonie had put her thief-skills and knowledge of the workings of each tower system to good use; her survival depended on it. Access between the levels became easier once she knew how to by-pass a few locks and sensors – and being able to fly. It was because of this knowledge she was able to finally get the information she wanted on Stefan Felton. The aching head and restless nights were worth it in the end.

For months, she'd ridden on top of the elevators nearest the GenLabs' facilities, using telepathy to scan the minds of the occupants. After very brief skims of surface thoughts to see who it was and if they had anything to offer, she'd move on to the next occupant; the next lift. Eventually, she found a secretary who had Dr Stefan's itinerary in her head. With that, Leonie knew when and where the doctor would be.

At the appointed time and place, the doctor arrived. It was too easy for her to peek at his open mind. There was a lot of information she didn't completely understand, but it looked like he was researching and … *making people*; identical people! She saw an image of several copies of the same woman, and quite a few different people, all with replicas. She vaguely recalled the word *cloning* in one of the data cubes and would need to go through the medical ones again to make sense of what she was sensing on her return.

Leonie decided she'd have to do further reading to understand exactly what was being done, whether it was legal, and whether it gave her any leverage to treat Sussah and David better, maybe even get them back with Harrond. At the very least, destroy all records of Lerry and Maz's efforts to organise Sussah's tower arrival.

———

*'How the mighty fall. Good evening viewers, breaking news. Doctor Stefan Felton has been arrested for unsanctified human cloning operations.'*

The vid showed a tall, thin man being frog-marched down a corridor into a lift.

*'It is unclear how long Felton had been allegedly carrying on these illegal activities. His company GenLabs has had its assets frozen and the offices have had all comp-data seized for further investigation and analysis. It is our understanding the sister company HelixR – the makers of the ReJuv wonder-drug – is not involved in any way. Stay tuned. We will keep you posted as the story develops.'*

"Well, that's just shit!" Leonie threw the remains of her nutri-bar at the screen. She had better go and see Sussah.

Over time, and with patience, Leonie modified the retaining screws, so they could be removed from either side and added spring-hinges, making the vent self-closing. For the past three years, she arrived as normal; sensing Sussah's presence without scanning her mind, and then sending a brief *'I'm at the door'* message to her. She would wait a few minutes, and after checking the corridor was clear, lithely drop to the floor and dart to the unlocked door.

The only difference with this visit was sensing the turmoil in her friend's mind.

"What have you done?" Sussah asked the moment Leonie closed the door.

"I didn't do it," Leonie said immediately.

"I got this handed to me in the office!" Sussah shoved the tablet into her paws.

Leonie read the e-doc displayed, with the TowerGov logo and looking seriously official.

*'Ms Osbourne, with the recent arrest and internment of Doctor Stefan Felton, the Council hereby inform you the special privileges accorded to yourself and your son, David Osbourne, by GenLabs Corporation, are now null and void.*

*Due to your single-parent status, in ten days of the issue date of this notice, access to your son will be reduced to one day in twenty. With successful completion of the entrance exam, he will come under the guidance of the Council and be enrolled in Tower University – fees paid for by the Council. As GenLabs Corporation has now been deregistered, your position is no longer viable. An agent will contact you shortly with employment options suited to your knowledge and experience.'*

"I didn't do this!" Leonie repeated. Her tail and ears drooped at the distressing news. "I've no idea how this came about."

"You were going to look into him for what he did to Lerry, Maz and Harrond! To *us!*"

"That was three years ago. We were all angry." *I still am.*

"And you found out what he was doing?"

Leonie nodded. "Yes, I found out about the illegal cloning last month, but I didn't tell anyone. I didn't even know what he was doing *was* illegal until I read up about it."

Sussah wept. "Now I can't see David for two more weeks. I have to change jobs and I have to move *again.*"

"That's shit! What can I do to help?"

"Help? I think you've done enough *helping*, thank you!" She fled to her room, slamming the door.

"Su," Leonie called through the door. "I did not do this!" The door was locked, and there was no answer, just the crying.

Leonie left. *Now to find who leaked the information and ruined my friend's life. Again!*

———

Try as she might, Sussah had been uncontactable for the last three weeks. The contact number had been deregistered, and there had been no update or information on the move, which should have been at least five days ago. No new numbers or names had been listed on the register, no 'S Osbourne'.

"I better visit David," she decided in a huff. "See how this affected him. He should have joined Tower University by now."

Now that she had a worthwhile reason, she looked forward to the challenge of getting into the white zone.

In earlier explorations, Leonie discovered there were no access hatches in the lift shafts. All maintenance corridors with access had heavy security: cameras, heat and movement detectors everywhere. An EMP could knock out any or all of it, but too many occurrences would arouse suspicion.

Other than flying in from outside, she discovered there were only two internal methods of gaining access to the Elite section. Four restricted lifts – used only by Elite personnel – one housed within each of the main elevator shafts, were completely sealed units. No access hatches, and no air-vents of adequate size. The schematics indicated a door on every tenth floor, and in her previous reconnaissance, each of those doors was heavily monitored and in busy areas; far too open for her to make an appearance.

The other access was the express lifts, which also travelled from every tenth floor of the lower levels to the air transport hub on the top floor; there were no stops in the Elite zone itself. These appeared to be the most straightforward method of getting where she wanted to be, and as only a very small percentage of citizens travelled inter-tower by air, or even to the orbitals, the risk of being seen was minimised.

Once on an express lift, getting into the white zone was moderately easy, but with fewer people accommodated and far better equipment, there were few maintenance corridors to use, and the ducting was generally narrower.

From her experience, some excursions could take days, and it was prudent to bring a pawful of protein bars and waterpac as standard. She loved her waterpac; a simple bladder slipped on to her pack with a small hose she could clip to her front and sip whenever thirsty.

Leonie hadn't seen David since the last time he stayed with Sussah for a night; a reward for acing his final year of school studies early. His previous school had dormitories; her research of his new institution indicated each student now had individual apartments. From within the ducting, she scanned the minds nearby – most of them young adults – looking for any reference or indication of David. There were some very confusing visions and thoughts – mostly to do with hormones – but finally she found him. Thankfully, she sensed he was alone.

*David, this is Leonie. Can we chat?* To his credit, he didn't flinch at the mind contact.

"You can visit. Are you far?"

*I'm in the air vent next to your room, I think. Are you monitored?*

"No. We all have privacy now." David got up and from his desk drawer, brought out something and removed the grille in moments.

"Hello, Leonie. It's nice to see you again." He stepped back.

Leonie contorted to squeeze out of the tight opening. "Hey, little man. I wasn't sure if I'd find you. It has been a while; almost half a year isn't it?" She noticed he was wearing a one-piece jumpsuit with coloured flashes on the sleeves and the Tower University logo on his left chest pocket.

"148 days, 17 hours, 35 minutes, give or take a few seconds."

"Yep, about right." She was amazed at his accuracy. "Can I just use your bathroom, and wipe myself down? It was a bit dusty in there."

"Sure." David pointed to the door.

The ensuite was basic, with a toilet, cupboard, mirror and shower. "That's better!" she said when she emerged, brushing the tip of her tail while glancing around the room. The small unit was sparsely furnished; a single bed, desk and chair as well as an armchair. "What's been happening with you? Have you had a chance to speak to your mum lately?"

"Last week. I was able to give her a brief vid."

"That's great. I'm sure she was relieved to hear from you. How are you liking the new school?"

"Do you know what a university is?" He continued after she shrugged. "It's the highest level of education."

"Aren't you a bit young to be doing higher education?"

"I've done everything I needed to do in junior school in a few years. Now I'm the youngest in my class," he said proudly.

"How old are they normally?"

"Some are sixteen, but the average is eighteen."

"And how old are you now, nine?"

"Nine years, six months and four days. I'm not sure of my exact time of birth."

"What are you learning?"

"Computer Science and Applied Robotronics." David showed her the pile of data cubes and sketches.

"That's a mouthful. Is that one subject?"

"It's a double degree. That's what the arm colours indicate." He pointed to each arm; one orange, and one gold. "Each discipline has its own colour code. I'll look at another subject in a couple of years. Maybe Experimental and Theoretical Physics."

"And a degree is a good thing? Like an award?"

"Yep, a qualification, but it isn't so much the award in itself, it's about what I learn, and do afterwards."

"And what do you think you can do?"

"Invent new things, make what we've got more efficient in operation or design, anything I put my mind to." He shrugged.

"I'm with you." She tousled his hair. "If you're determined to do it, your mind will make it possible, regardless of the obstacles thrown at you. I learnt that the hard way."

"You've got a degree?" he asked.

"Me? No," She laughed. "Can you keep a secret?"

He nodded solemnly.

"My studies were more of a *metaphysical* nature." She levitated, floating half a metre off the carpet. She chuckled at the look of amazement on his face.

"Wow!" He bent down and waved his hands under her paws.

"You like that?" She then created a small flame on one paw and then arching electricity on the other.

"How can you do that?"

"Have you heard of *magic*?"

"We're told it is a myth, like religion. Superstitions from centuries ago."

"Well, not everything they say is true. I see it as using the mind to control natural forces, much as your technology also uses natural forces. The results are generally the same; the application is different."

"I'll say." He nodded, wide-eyed.

"One has to study those forces first though, to understand what they are and how they can interact. However, magic can only work through absolute belief, and pushing your mind to its limits."

"What can you do?"

"When I started years ago, it was fire and flying, so I learnt everything I could about heat and what causes it, what stops it, and air, wind and how birds and aircraft fly."

"So you somehow create a low pressure above you and high pressure below?"

"Something like that. Then when I found out about electricity, I studied that. It still hurts a bit, but I got used to it. Now, after years of practice, I can create a small flame, a fireball, or just warm things up; flying and levitating – that's how I get around the tower ducts and vents – I'd get sore knees if I crawled everywhere. And with electricity, I can create small sparks, shock for defence, lightning bolts and electromagnetic bursts."

"Was that you five years ago? At the terminal?"

"You know about that?"

"Sure. It was on the vid."

"You would have only been four years old." Her ears pricked up in surprise.

He shrugged. "I remember everything I see, hear, smell, taste or touch."

"That's … impressive. This has to be a secret – my magic. No one else can know."

"I promise." He nodded. "Does mum know?"

"She does." Leonie landed, absorbing the energy from the fire and sparks. "As do the rest of the family."

"She hasn't spoken about you for a while. Is there something wrong? I thought you were friends."

"We're still friends, she just needs time to get over the … new situation."

"You mean her change in work, accommodation, and me being sent here?"

Again Leonie nodded. "Not something you need to worry about though. You're being treated ok, aren't you?"

"I am, but I *do* worry. This is all because of what happened to Dr Felton from GenLabs, isn't it?"

"It could be … or they just wanted to give you the best education because you're so smart."

"They will benefit from me regardless, but what happened to mum is my fault."

"You can't blame yourself." She took his hand in her paws. "When I was your age I was angry and blamed myself when things didn't work out, but I was wrong. GenLabs did the wrong thing and got caught. It happens, but unfortunately there are victims."

"Especially when someone leaks those *bad things* to the authorities."

Leonie stopped breathing in surprise. "What bad things?"

"I found about his cloning R&D. That's illegal and unethical." David flopped in a chair. "I was angry. Dr Felton took us away from Uncle Lerry, Auntie Maz and Harrond, and stopped us from seeing or talking to them."

"How did you find out?" Leonie noticed he didn't say father.

"I used the computer and hacked into his database."

"You can do that?"

"Sure," he said. "Most kids know how to use computers, some more, some less."

"Well, that answers that. Your mum reckons I did it."

"That's silly. I'll tell her it was me next time we talk."

"David, you will do no such thing! Things are hard enough for you both as it is. None of you needs this crap to get worse. If you told her, she'd be embarrassed and upset about accusing me, and be irritated at you."

"But if she's blaming you, then *I'll* feel worse."

"Well … don't," she huffed. "You've told me; now I know. I'll take responsibility and remove the burden from you."

"It's not right!"

"David, you're still young." She got down on her knees and hugged him as he was getting upset. "You will see soon enough, sadly, there are many things that aren't right in the world. Some we can change, some we can't. Survival is knowing which one is which."

"Maybe, when I get smarter, I can fix everything?"

"I have no doubt." She smiled. "By the way, do you have a new contact for your mother? Since her move, I can't locate her."

"They gave me her new contact yesterday," he said, sending her a quick e-note.

She checked her wrist-com when it arrived. "That's wonderful and saves me a long time searching. I better go, but it has been great to see you. Don't forget our secret."

"Don't forget, I never forget anything. Ever." He smiled and waved. "Bye, Leonie. Thank you for visiting."

"Any time."

Leonie negotiated her return trip, amazed at how David was progressing and at his maturity. She checked the time: 23:48. Time to sleep. She'd organise a visit to Sussah in the morning and give her the update on David.

# 28

## SEND IN THE CLONES

Sussah opened the door with a huge smile on her face. "Leonie! How did you find me?"

"David. He's a great kid. I went to visit him a couple of days ago." Leonie stepped in and followed Su, looking around the new quarters. "I reckon his place is bigger than yours. Where are you working now—"

"Oh!" Sussah wailed, suddenly reaching for the remote. "This is terrible."

Leonie turned to see what had upset her so much.

On the vid-screen a reporter announced the death of a prominent citizen.

*'… I repeat, it is with great shock and sorrow we bring you news of the incident in Blue Zone earlier today. Tragically, Ivana Zodaich, Miss Oceania four years in a row, and partner to Nicholai Zodaich, fell to her death today.'*

The image flicked to drone footage from multiple views of the fall, cutting the feed seconds before impact. There was no doubt of it being a tall, slim woman with long, black hair.

*'Ms Zodaich died on impact with the fall of over 350 metres. TowerPol also states Mr Redmond Collins also plummeted to his death during a scuffle with a bodyguard. Viewers are warned of the graphic*

*footage. Mr Collins hit numerous walkways in his fall. It is alleged Mr Collins pushed the supermodel off the seventy-first-floor balcony in an unprovoked attack.*

*'In an inexplicable twist, the bodies landed within the Central Zoo precinct on level one. While zoo attendants rushed to cordon off the lion enclosure where the body of Ms Zodaich landed, the remains of Collins splashed into the nearby aquarium. There was little chance of his remains being recovered before the numerous sharks and other fish were netted into separate areas, however authorities believe there will be enough evidence on the walkways to examine his remains.*

*'The bodyguard of Ms Zodaich also fell. He landed on the seventieth walkway, five metres below. He is currently undergoing emergency surgery with serious head, shoulder, and back injuries.'*

Drone footage showed two men scuffling, then toppling over a railing. A snap to a different angle showed the bodyguard land central to the walkway, while the other male figure hit the railing, cartwheeling as it fell to hit three other walkways before a large splash from the aquarium. The water turned a shade of red before the footage was cut.

*'We will give you a full report as further information comes to hand.'*

"She was so beautiful," Sussah wept, muting the vid again.

"Any innocent death is a damn tragedy. The name sounds familiar though."

"Hello? Miss Oceania four times in a row," Sussah said. "You must have heard of her. Over sixty-million fans around the Pacific rim."

"Maybe. I don't watch the same vids you do. No, I know the name from somewhere else. Maybe a vid-cast, maybe from someone's head. That's going to shit me now."

"Her murder?" Sussah was about to get up, but then the vid went to a special report showing highlights of the last four Miss Oceania contests; she sat back down.

"No, the name," Leonie watched the silent vid for a minute whilst wracking her brain for the origin of the name. Ivana was certainly attractive; fine figure, tall and slim, jet-black hair and startling green eyes. "Certainly going to be a lot of very sad men."

"That lady is so stunning," Sussah agreed and resumed her trip to the kitchenette to make coffee.

"Have you a new job yet?" Leonie asked, changing the subject.

"Coincidentally, I'm now training to be an animal attendant at the Central Zoo." She pointed to the vid. "I hope it will be much quieter by the time I finish training."

"Is that a good thing for you? The zoo job?"

"I hated the last job, sitting at a desk all day and being polite to arseholes, not that I had much of a choice. It kept me close to David, that was the best part about it. I've always liked animals though."

"Now I know why you like having me around," Leonie quipped.

"I didn't mean—"

"I'm joking." Leonie smiled. "How long will the training last?"

"When they moved me to GenLabs, they upgraded my implant, now training is much quicker. It should take half a day for the full course."

"I'm happy if you're happy."

"The upgrade is so much better. It would be great if you had one too." Su came over with two steaming mugs.

"I see very little chance of that ever happening, and I'm in no rush. I've got enough to worry about as it is." Leonie accepted her coffee, putting it on the table to cool.

"I'm sorry for the way I treated you. I was stupid and angry – but angry at the wrong person. I think back on everything you've done for me, you even left your own world and stuck by me. How could I ever think you'd do anything to put any of us in danger?" Sussah sat beside her and reached for a hug.

"Don't worry about it." Leonie hugged back. Not ever being used to hugs before, her years of isolation only increased the discomfort. She patted Su on the shoulder. "It's okay," she soothed when Sussah was shaking in her grief. "We all say stupid things when angry. Do you know who told the authorities yet?" she changed the subject.

"No, no. I don't care." Su sniffled and wiped her nose. "He got what he deserved. And to be honest, while David's absence is painful, I'm in a better headspace now, and I'm sure David can only be doing far better than what I could provide." She took a sip from her mug, idly watching the silent vid.

"That's crap. You're a great mother. David, he is one smart lad. I think he'd excel regardless of where he was educated."

"That sounds like my son." Sussah almost spat her coffee. "Oh, I just remembered; did you know Ivana's partner, Nicholai Zodaich is the last of Blue Mountains Tower's founders, and not only part of the Elite, but he is also the highest-ranking member of TowerGov. I met him once."

"Ah yes. Still … not sure where I came across the name. It'll come eventually." She sipped her coffee.

The silence grew. The vid went through the news cycle, repeating the highlights. The footage of the recent tragedy showed again, sometimes with a slightly different angle of view from the many drones or vids from distraught fans.

"Can we repeat that bit?" Leonie sat up.

"Yes. Which part?"

"The bodyguard and Collins fighting."

"Sure." Su used the controller to review the vid.

"I know that guy. I just didn't know his name."

"Who, the bodyguard?"

"No, Collins." Leonie moved closer to the vid. "Pause there."

Su looked at the screen. "Who is he? He's damn fine too."

"He was, and he was one of Dr Stefan Felton's personal staff."

———

Leonie was in high spirits. Catching up with Sussah was a great relief, not realising how much she missed her. She was in such a good mood, she decided to share the mood with Lerry, Maz and Harrond. It was early evening outside, so they should be home now, *Probably about to have dinner.*

She tried Harrond's first as she had direct access through the vent. She opened it and stuck her head out.

The unit was completely dark, silent and colder than she remembered. "That's strange," she muttered. There was normally some appliance standby-light on. Leonie scanned the area, but there was no indication of anyone home, just faint blurs on the periphery from surrounding apartments.

She slid out, landing silently on the floor and padded around. Not only was nobody home, but there was also no furniture. Leonie had a bad feeling about this. She was going to dial Lerry and Maz, but the vid had no connection. She called from her wrist-com, hoping the thickness in walls wasn't enough to block the signal. There was a disconnected signal – just a soft, continuous tone.

Zipping back through the venting, she sped to Lerry and Maz's, high spirits forgotten. It was trickier getting to their unit as direct vent access wasn't possible. The corridor was clear, so she dropped down to the floor and padded quickly to their door. She couldn't hear anything, nor sense their presence. She knocked, nervous about standing in the passage for too long. When no one answered, she zapped the lock and stepped inside, closing the door behind her. The unit was the same as Harrond's; empty, cold and silent.

"Shit. Shit. Shit." Her bad feeling only got worse. "Maybe they simply moved. Got promoted, perhaps a different job," she guessed. Opening the door and slipping into the corridor, she was halfway back to the vent when there was a scream behind her. She spun around to see the woman collapse. "Frack it!"

Leonie didn't wait. She bolted to the nearby vent and slammed it closed behind her as she heard doors open and running footsteps getting closer. "Idiot!" she berated herself as she hastened through the vents, bumping into the sides when turning too fast.

She stopped, bracing herself against a wall and tried to relax, slowing her breathing, then continued at a more sedate pace. In her current state of mind, she headed for her old home, not risking flying up four hundred floors.

Unsurprisingly, other than a bit of dust nothing had changed. She had a drink from her waterpac and snacked on the protein bars she always had in her backpack as she contemplated the situation. The last time she had contact with Maz was over a month ago. She hated herself for being slack.

The best-case scenario would be a promotion or training for different tasks, but to have all moving at the same time was unusual. The worst-case scenario involved the tower authorities. With all three disappearing so close after Felton's arrest, it was too coincidental.

Leonie cautiously approached the TowerPol precinct. While the air-ducts were still safe, this area – understandably – was highly secure. These air-ducts were at floor level, with the vents below knee height. She hated it. Ceiling vents were out of people's reach, but any fool could open these vents if they felt a need. Nearing the main area, she remained ultra-quiet. Now to relax and scan minds.

*Where are the agtechs, Lerry and Maz Carter?*

It took hours, but even her patience was wearing thin. With so much activity, it wasn't as if everyone knew of every arrest being made. It did occur to her that, with so much indoctrination and programming, the amount of discontent was unexpected. If there was a bonus to her spending so much time here it was the interesting data about the inner workings of the tower, including codes for security doors, but nothing specific about Lerry, Maz or Harrond.

She started having doubts whether there was another precinct to go to when she noted a change in activity. Checking her watch, she realised it was a change of shift.

*Where are the agtechs, Lerry and Maz Carter?*

She kept sending it out the phrase and scanning, waiting for a spark of recognition. Their confused reactions were no longer humorous.

*'They were imprisoned a week ago.'* It was such a shock, she almost sat up. The officer with the knowledge of their whereabouts also supplied a vague memory of the layout when he had been there years ago as a young officer.

*Finally.* With relief and a throbbing headache, Leonie slipped away.

Time was of the essence. Her friends had already been there for over a week; she was sure every day was a trauma to them. Now she knew where to start looking, she hoped it wouldn't take too long to work out exactly where the Carters were, and how to get them out.

"I'm just glad it isn't high-security," she muttered, going over the schematics on the industrial sector, all twelve levels of it directly below the tower. *If only I had paid more attention when I was mucking around in the level one machine shop.*

She considered many potential threats and compared them to the assets available. Even low security, there'd be movement and heat sensors, probably facial recognition as well as codes for access.

On the plus side, if it was during downtime, she'd have the element of surprise – *Who breaks into a prison?* – a vast machine and tool shop at her disposal, and of course, her powershaping abilities. Her mind flicked back to a conversation with Styx during her training – *'…anyone with all these abilities could be virtually unstoppable …'*

It didn't look good. With inadequate vents, she'd be exposed too much, and easily spotted. "Assuming security aren't all dumb and blind," she muttered. She could adjust her body temp to fool the heat sensors, but was not confident with the cameras or movement sensors, and it was too much to hope there'd be no suspicion of all the power failures.

*There has to be another way.* Leonie went back over the schematics. There were many plans, from engineering and architectural aspects, down to basic maintenance vents and electrical plans. The one thing most of the towers had in common were the elevator shafts, but as these led to heavily monitored corridors she ruled them out.

"There has to be something here! What am I missing?" Leonie growled, rubbing her face in frustration, deciding to have a break to regain concentration.

She nipped out to the nearest food hall before the next shift started and quickly filled her pack with a mixture of tubs and nutri-bars as well as replenishing her water supply. She ate and drank and relaxed for a while before bringing her fresh eyes and mind back to the task.

Resuming her search, she scrolled through more maps. They were generally identical to all the others, which is why she overlooked them, but different agencies sometimes highlighted different details, as in this case.

She combed through the dozens of drawings before finally finding one with a larger scale of the area in question. Within the structure of the lift shaft, there was a large vertical pipe labelled garbage disposal. *I don't like the sound of that.* The more she looked into it, the more it became the obvious, if least desirable, choice.

# 29

# THE ESCAPE

IT WAS A GOOD TIME TO LEAVE THE AGTECH ZONE. AFTER HER STUPID slip-up when leaving Lerry's apartment, patrols had stepped up their searching of the area, and more and more rumours about feral infestations spread. Again, riots had to be quashed, some ruthlessly.

Leonie thought it was a worry that a single mutant appearance could flare up so quickly with such violent consequences. She was no psychologist, but surely that behaviour indicated a massive amount of dissatisfaction in the community.

Leaving the concerns of the agtech zone for another time, Leonie started her descent of the garbage disposal chute, but after a minute, had to retreat. The stench was overpowering. Searching the waste disposal area, she found some gas masks, reminding her of the mask Styx gave her in White Cliffs. Once one was adjusted to fit, she grabbed three others and returned to the chute. As she opened it, a load of refuse fell past her.

It was probably her imagination, but even after checking the mask fit, the chute still reeked. She hurried down the shaft. At the base was the fresh pile of garbage, waiting for workers to sift and disperse the contents for the relevant treatment. Exiting the chute, it took her a moment to get her bearings. Unlike the higher levels where all pipes and maintenance works were out of sight, this area was the opposite; dank, dark and filthy. She rose to the dark ceiling and took advantage of the chaotic infrastructure, making her way along the exposed pipework.

Below, she saw two large creatures – *mutant rats!* – scurry between bins of some bubbling, putrid concoction that reminded her of the muddy swamp near Qelay. Leonie grimaced and moved on. At the end of this large area, an opening led into recyc. The only demarcation was the large plastic curtains. She was glad she could slip through the top, most of the lower part it was grimy and stained.

"I should've grabbed gloves," she cursed. "Maybe even overalls."

Moving through recyc, it was notably cleaner. There were large, shiny metal vats along one wall almost reaching to the ceiling, with a multitude of pipes, pumps and gauges. It occurred to her, the ceiling pipes she was following from the food processing section each ended at these vats. Spying movement, she stopped and hid. Two human-like droids carried drums, passing behind the vats.

A conveyor belt disappeared into the base of one of the vats. It was moving slowly, and several stripped bodies, laid out in a line head to toe came into view. The sudden realisation of recyc and bodies adjacent to the food processing plant didn't sit well with her. She shook her head and moved on quickly.

At the far end, she made her way down a stairwell to the bottom, where the prison section took up the lower three floors on the east side. A stray thought from the sergeant she'd scanned earlier indicated prisoners worked in both recyc and the food processing plant. She hoped that meant normal shift-work hours, and the lack of any activity other than a few droids raised those hopes.

Leonie checked her watch: 23:43. The prison section was beyond the next door. Having a good look around, there were no monitors or alarms visible. "Not even a code-lock?" *Why would there be? There's nowhere to go from here.* She waited and reduced her body temperature as a precaution before proceeding, slowly opening the door.

The area was dimly lit, indicating it was sleep-time. Great for her, but not for their security. The corridor in front of her went left and right as well as straight ahead. To the right were the lifts, and even though they only opened to the various judicial precincts, she expected them to be heavily monitored. *An area best to be avoided.*

There were still no niceties like false ceilings here. She rose as high as she could and slunk through the shadows. Now, she had to start scanning to pick up thoughts.

Many thoughts were like incomprehensible whispers. *Inmates dreaming,* she guessed. When she picked up coherent thoughts of a sordid nature, it was a cell she could gladly remove from her memorised list.

Leonie came across a cell at the end of a row, with whispered talking coming from within. Scattered thoughts of a farming-nature.

*Lerry?* She waited for the thoughts to change. She wasn't disappointed. The moment he heard her he visualised her. Anyone else would have had no idea. She dropped lithely to the floor and zapped the lock. The door clicked.

Lerry pulled it ajar, and she stepped in, almost gagging at the stale sweat odour.

"How did you get in here?" Lerry asked in disbelief.

"Nice to see you too." She accepted his bearhug. Behind him stood Harrond, his smile from ear to ear. "Hey, Harrond," she grunted a greeting. "So." She squirmed politely out of Lerry's embrace. "Where's Maz?" She then saw the three other men sharing the cell. Her jaw dropped. They were identical to Redmond Collins, the murderer of Ivana the supermodel.

Lerry took a huge sigh. "She's in another cell, upstairs."

"What's wrong?" Harrond asked, seeing her stare.

"Who are these three?" she asked, eyes wide.

"Crazy isn't it, identical brothers! It's unheard of."

Leonie snapped back to concentrate. "Probably because

they're clones." The connection with Felton and Ivana Zodaich formed in her mind.

"Clones?" Harrond repeated.

"Yeah. Long story for another time." She was curious how long they'd been here, and why together with the agtechs.

"What's the plan?" Lerry asked.

"Lots of fresh air and sunshine, but I need to find Maz first. What do you know about the security?"

"It's all pretty rundown. Most inmates, especially the long-timers, have succumbed to their drugs; everyone's docile and compliant."

"Not you?"

"Not yet. We're technically still being processed. But given time, it'll happen."

"Okay. Nice. What about the clones?"

"They're going to be recycled in a day or two."

"Then they're coming with us. You all okay to get to the stairway?"

They nodded, as did the triplets.

She gave them the masks. "I was only counting on three of you."

"Why these?" Harrond grabbed his mask.

"You'll find out soon enough." She stuck her head out. The corridor was clear.

"Keep together. Let's go." She trotted out, looking over her shoulder quickly. Harrond brought up the rear, ushering the three Redmonds.

As quietly as they could, they jogged to the stairway, following her up to the next level.

"Okay. You know where the garbage chute is at the far end of food processing on the next level up?" She continued after their nods. "I'll start looking for Maz. You guys get to the chute and hide. There's a couple of droids about."

"They're basic models. No threat," Harrond told her.

"Good. I'll be as quick as I can."

"I'll come too," Lerry offered.

"You can't fly, and you're no telepath. Just keep this lot safe." She entered the level after a quick look and repeated the process as before. She checked her time: 23:50.

Part of her loved the ease of this; part of her was waiting for the trap.

She sensed more incoherent whispers, and she became aware of the subtle difference between female and male dreams. Many of these cells were empty.

It took longer to find Maz, as no one was thinking of crop fields or agtech-like thoughts. Leonie passed her cell twice, unknowingly. Turned out the thoughts of violence mixed with tending to cuts and bruises and, of all things – sex – were coming from the cool calm and collected agtech. Maz wasn't alone either.

*Maz?*

Immediately, like Lerry, the thoughts changed to visualising Leonie.

*I'm coming in.*

Opening the door, she stepped in, meeting Maz with open arms. It was pointless trying to avoid the hug.

For the second time in less than ten minutes, Leonie was dumbstruck. Two Ivana clones were sitting on the back bunk. Wearing the same prison garb as everyone else, but ripped and bloodied. She staggered against the wall, suddenly feeling warm and fuzzy as a wave of lust engulfed her.

"Better have this!" Maz smeared a foul-smelling paste under her nose.

"Argh! What is that? Something died last month." She reached up to wipe it off.

"Don't, otherwise we'll never get out of here," Maz chuckled. "Smelling salts. The guards like their ladies fully awake."

"Why are you laughing?" Leonie scowled at her. "What's so funny?" Her gaze wandered to the Ivana twins, the way they filled-out the prison suits ... *No woman should look that stunning.* "Shit! Can't they just wear sacks?"

"Poor Leonie. I know how you feel. Try being with them for a week!"

"What's happening? What's going on?"

"These goddesses you see before you are exuding pheromones. They're concubines for hire."

"Conc—"

"Escorts. Sex slaves for the Elite." Maz went over to them and finished cleaning a livid cut on one of the goddess's arms. "They're clones, of course."

"You know about them?" Leonie froze.

"There's no way they could be natural. Clones are the obvious answer."

"If only Lerry and Harrond had your wits," Leonie said.

"Where are they?" Maz asked calmly. "I assume you're here to free us?"

"If only I had your coolness!" Leonie fought the temptation to move closer.

Maz stood up. "I've been around long enough and seen enough to not get too fazed. You are a pleasant surprise though. But I've seen you in action. I know you wouldn't be here without a plan."

"I think I love you," she sighed.

"That's just probably the pheromones speaking." Maz laughed again.

Leonie shared a smile. "Lerry and Harrond should be waiting by the food processing garbage chute. If these pair are okay to move, we should go."

"Yes, but we're not leaving yet," Maz's reply was hard. "There's four more goddesses here."

"Four?" Leonie's mind worked furiously at how she was going to get twelve people out of here. "Where are they? What cell?"

Maz smiled left her face. "They're at the guardhouse."

"Why are … never mind. I think I know." Her tail lashed in agitation. "Where is it?"

Maz walked to the door, ushering the twins with her. They

hardly spoke but followed Maz's directions. "It's up the stairs. Shall we?"

Leonie had to admire her confidence. "Hey, this is my rescue." Shaking her head, she held her breath while squeezing between the twins and went out first, leading the way to the stairs.

Maz stifled a laugh.

"At the top, take our goddesses to the chute, I'll be back with the others shortly."

She watched Maz lead the Ivanas away before heading to the guardhouse. It was easy enough to find, with all the noise they were making.

Looking through the door, it revolted her. Her mind flashed back to Sussah in the alley–

*And look how that ended.*

All eyes were focused on the activity on the meal tables at the far side of the room – elegant legs, and hairy arses. Leonie looked around quickly. There were no other guards around. Body armour, clothes and weapons were stacked along the walls or on shelves.

She counted eight guards, four were busy and the others were cheering them on. No one noticed her stalking up behind them, eyes blazing with revulsion and power.

In quick succession, she stunned the four spectators. When their bodies collapsed, she roughly dragged the first guard off his Ivana, stunning him before he yelled.

The guard beside them saw it anyway and cried out.

Leonie lashed out with her claws, not wanting to stun him in case his Ivana copped the charge. The two other guards leapt or fell off their ladies in utter surprise. Before they reacted she zapped them until they were twitching on the ground.

Regardless of how she felt, there were four surprised and naked supermodels looking at her. *No clothes.* "Clothes, girls. Put your clothes on!" She desperately needed more of that foul-smelling gel. She tossed the jumpsuits to them then focused her attention out the door in the off-chance other guards turned up.

When she dared to look back, the four sisters were up and waiting, looking damn— "Ok. If you can move, follow me." She waited to see if they obeyed. They did. "A bit faster, if you please. Your sisters are waiting." She immediately regretted it. Jogging made them bounce.

*Argh.* Leonie zipped ahead to the corner, then across to the stairwell. Maz and Lerry were there waiting for her.

"Thought you might need a hand," Maz answered her look.

"I wasn't counting on twelve of you ..."

"Lerry has an idea if you can get us up to the machine shop."

"He has? Great. Take the Ivana sisters to the chute. I'll be back in a minute."

"Aren't you coming?" Lerry asked.

"I'll be with you shortly. There's something I *really* need to do."

"Let her go, Lerry. No time to argue." Maz winked at Leonie. "Give them hell!"

"Count on it.' Leonie spun and disappeared into the dimness.

Back at the guardhouse, the guards were stumbling around. Most were dressed, some were armed. One activated the alarm just as she flew in through the door.

She slammed the door behind her.

"Going somewhere, creeps?" Her eyes flared with power.


With bright lights now flickering on, and an audible alarm blaring throughout the complex, Leonie threw caution to the wind and sped towards the chute and the escapees.

"Leonie, you're glowing." Maz stood up from behind her cover. All the clones were sitting out of sight.

"You say the nicest things, or is that *your* pheromones talking now?"

"No. You *are* glowing!" she sniffed the air. "What's that smell?"

Leonie shrugged. "Depends, it could be ozone or singed fur."

She checked her body, there was a bit of singed fur and wisps of smoke from her smouldering clothes.

"Singed fur?" Harrond asked.

"It got very hot back there." She noticed a smear of gel under his nose; she smiled and turned. "Lerry, if I take you first, can you get your plan into action?" She saw gel under his nose too.

"Yep."

"Mask on." She turned to the others. "Can you shoot these if need be?"

"Oh yeah." Maz grabbed one of the weapons Leonie had slung over her shoulder. She checked it, then gave it to Harrond before grabbing the second weapon.

"Do you think the guards will be getting here soon," Harrond looked back towards the prison.

"I can assure you, those guards won't be, but there might be others."

"This one's for you, Lerry." She gave the big agtech a rifle. "You'll need to hang on tight." She donned her mask while he slung the weapon. She turned her back to him, indicating for him to wrap his arms over her shoulders. When he did so, she held his hands tightly, lifted off the ground, then angled into the chute. She hoped no garbage was on its way down.

"How are we going to get outside?" she asked when they arrived at the machine shop, glad the alarm from the prison didn't reach here. She lashed the hatch open for easier access. "You said the doors were heavily monitored."

"Getting out is easy enough. It's the getting *in* that's monitored, with the decontamination and all." He handed her the mask and readied the stun-rifle.

"Okay. Do what you need to do. I'll be back as soon as I can."

"Better bring Harrond next." He winked. "He's only human, and still partnered."

"So is Maz." She laughed at his look before disappearing down the chute.

. . .

All nine clones were finally marshalled into a corner of the waste disposal room. They were sitting quietly, chatting as if breaking out of prison was a non-event. Two of the Redmonds were treating the wounded Ivanas with a first-aid kit.

"Why aren't they all over each other?" Leonie was by a wash-basin, cleaning off the muck from the last trip when a pile of refuse showered them.

"Immunity, I guess," Maz answered. "Something in their genetic make-up to ignore the pheromones. I'm sure it would be chaos otherwise."

"I need no convincing of that." She checked her watch. Half-past midnight.

"I've got a set of overalls you wanted, and for that last female clone," Lerry said as he walked over with Harrond.

"Thanks."

"You want overalls?" Maz asked.

"It's going to be cold where I'm going. I need to concentrate." She noticed a shelf with over a dozen boxes along a wall. "Are those batteries?"

"Yes. U-pacs," Maz answered. "Universal powerpacs. Back-up power supplies for the mag-bikes and most small equipment. They're recharged here."

Leonie put that information to the back of her mind.

"Where do you think you're going to find cold around here?" Harrond asked her.

"Around six thousand metres up."

"What?" Harrond was incredulous. "Why?"

"Lately, there's been a jet making an appearance. I hope it doesn't, but with the alarm raised, I reckon there will be lots of attention out there." She hadn't told them about the wilder massacre. That was for later. "He shot at me a few weeks back, and he's damn fast too. If I can get above, and he's looking down, maybe I can drop him before he starts shooting at you."

"That would be good." Harrond nodded.

Maz took the other pair of overalls to the goddess in the filthy jumpsuit.

The last Ivana who was with Leonie when the trash hit wanted to pull her soiled clothes off as soon as they landed, but Leonie convinced her it was a very bad idea to be standing around naked.

"And are you ready?" Leonie pulled on her suit after cutting a slit for her tail. It was a snug fit but would keep her warmer.

"Yep." Lerry nodded. "I've got a mag-bike fully charged, and a service truck. Both transponders have been removed. It might be an uncomfortable ride in the back for them, but it won't be for long. I checked the schedule. Outpost 9 is vacant for the time being. I've also got a decoy vehicle all set. We're good to go."

"Where's 9 situated?"

"Further south. If no one is following, we can hide out there for a few days before heading to Jenolan. I'll send the decoy directly to the powerplant. It'll keep their attention for a little while."

"Smart move. I know it has to be done, but how do you feel about leaving all this behind? Will you cope?"

"Anything is better than prison. There was talk about sending us out to the badlands mine or even the colonies." The man looked away for the moment. "Jenolan is the best we could hope for. And I need to thank you for that."

"Crap. Sussah wouldn't give me peace otherwise. Besides, I told you years ago, I would repay you for your help with Su. This is it." She noticed Ivana had dressed. "We better make a move," she said before Lerry tried to thank her more. She went to the door to keep watch. "It's all clear."

The group quickly ran to the waiting vehicles. Harrond started the truck, Lerry mounted the bike and Maz gathered the clones to climb into the rear of the truck.

After activating the inner-door sequence from the bike, they moved through into the airlock. The outer doors were bigger and slower, and time seemed to drag as they waited for them to slide across. As they opened, swirls of dust billowed through the gap.

"Is that a good thing?" Leonie asked Lerry.

"Depends on how severe it is. A small storm we can cope

with, but if this is building up to a big one, we'll have a lot of trouble."

On the spur of the moment, Leonie sped back to the maintenance locker where she'd seen a rack of goggles. Drones appeared, flying in low and fast. She zapped them, but probably not before one sent a signal.

An energy pulse hit the machine beside her as she was returning. Leonie dropped to the floor for cover, briefly spotting a group of uniformed personnel near the elevator corridor. Hearing shouts and footsteps approaching, she sent a few fireballs their way to slow them down and returned to the outer door.

Maz had left the moment the door was wide enough, followed by the decoy van at full speed with lights blazing. As soon as it cleared the tower exit, the auto-drive turned it around to the east. She handed Lerry a pair of goggles, then threw the rest in the back of the truck. "Put these on," she yelled over the rising wind.

As the truck moved out, she turned and lobbed another fireball towards the last place she'd seen movement, then hit the emergency close button.

"Here we go. Time to be unstoppable," she muttered.

"What was that?"

"Nothing, just giving myself a pep talk."

"We'll need it." Lerry waved and sped off after Maz and the truck.

Once the door shut completely, Leonie fried the circuits, donned her goggles and escaped outside. "Hopefully that'll slow the ground crew down." She adjusted her goggles in the strong wind.

Outside, she accelerated up the outside of the tower, skimming a couple of metres off the wall to avoid the air intakes and exhausts. Proximity to the tower structure would help make her radar-invisible, or so she had read.

As she ascended, she kept an eye on the various landing pads. They were used by the many corporations, like HelixR and

GenLabs, to transport goods to other towers, but the storm had stopped all traffic.

She paused near the top of the tower, glancing south. She could barely spot anything with the clouds of dust. It had all been too easy. *Nothing's ever that easy.*

Lerry had estimated it would take forty minutes at maximum speed to get there, but this storm was going to slow them down a lot. The decoy truck should be halfway towards the power-plant. While it was too small to do much damage, if any, it would still be a nuisance.

Leonie continued her climb, skimming past the roof and its shuttle terminal until the altimeter on her watch read 6000 metres. Looking down, the square roof was still sizeable. She could see little else other than the tower roof. There was no sign of the bike or the truck with the dust from this height. Two flyers left the shuttle terminal towards the decoy. Several minutes later three more took off in different directions to scour the terrain. They all became vague in the storm.

She shivered in the cold, buffeting wind as she waited. *If only these coveralls were lined.*

It was so quiet up here, Leonie heard the jet first. It sounded much higher than she expected and further to the west. *Damn storm!* She zipped at maximum speed in that direction, trying to see it. What she saw first was the heat-signature of its exhaust, then made out the vague dark shape in front. She was sure she had seen it travel faster.

She put on a burst of speed and tried to calculate where the jet would be by the time her EMP would be ready. It was going to be a long way. Concentrating to draw in as much power as she could, Leonie hurled the ball of energy.

Suddenly, feeling delirious, she started falling, having drained her supply.

As she fell, the EMP burst was like an expanding blue sphere, full of tendrils of lighting. The jet barely hit it, only the briefest of sparks before its direction changed, as did its sound. Then she disappeared into the dust.

Leonie had always wondered what would happen in this predicament, but put it to the back of her mind, as she rarely flew this high. Now it was forefront to her thoughts.

Having seen old vids of people skydiving, she twisted her body to lay flat, arms out and paws flat, trying to create as much resistance as possible.

She tried to relax and draw power. Her altimeter ticked through the numbers, showing her a rapid rate of descent. *Crap!*

All too soon, the counter hit 2000, then 1500, 1000, 500. *Now!*

Throwing everything into it, she tried to slow her speed.

300 ...

200 …

150 …

100 …

She saw vegetation rushing up to her. She was still falling too fast.

**30**

---

# OUTPOST 9

HER AWAKENING WAS GREETED BY THE DAWN, DUST AND PAIN. A LOT of pain. Trying to sit up, her back spasmed. When she gasped, her breath gurgled, the dust making her cough even more. She went to wipe her chin, but her right arm refused to move, so she had to use her left paw.

Her paw came away red.

"Oh, that's just great," she growled. "Back injured, broken arm, and something wrong with my lungs." She coughed again, wiping her chin, then wiping her paw on her shirt.

The storm still raged around her. Other than the howling wind and hiss of the sand through the foliage, she couldn't hear anything else. Her fur rippled with the harsh wind. After a lot of blinking and wiping of her eyes, she managed to remove most of the dust. Leonie adjusted her goggles awkwardly.

With concentration, she slowly stood, using the power to minimise physical effort. Hit by a blinding headache, she slumped back to the ground.

Consciousness came and went. She tracked it by the changing angle of the sun through the billowing dust clouds. Her head throbbed. Her arm was numb. Dead. Any time she tried to move, stabbing pain in her back stopped her.

Every now and then, over the wind, she thought she heard a noise, like a mag-bike.

*Those idiots ... still searching for the agtechs? Useless in these conditions.*

The wind howled. *Why on mag-bikes?*

She raised her good arm. "Lerry?" she spoke into her comlink.

*"Leonie! Where are you?"*

"Here." She waved. *Idiot.* Even in her stupor, she knew her next action was stupid. She raised her arm and concentrated. Her head exploded in pain.

———

"She's coming to." She heard an unfamiliar voice. More noises of people approaching.

Leonie opened an eye. A goddess was leaning over her. *Ivana?*

"Okay. I've finally died and this is heaven."

"You nearly were. Another couple of hours and you would have bled out."

"I didn't see you there, Maz." She swivelled her head to see the concerned faces of the agtechs. "Hey you guys," she mumbled.

"Welcome to Outpost 9," Harrond said, relief in his voice.

"Which of you idiots came looking for me?"

"All three of us idiots," Lerry answered. "And we would have missed you if you didn't cast the fireball."

"I didn't know it worked."

"Almost blew me out of the truck," Harrond said.

"I guess I fainted." She lifted her head. Her right arm was in a cast, her chest was wrapped in bandages. "I'm numb."

"Relax. Just pain-killers. You were in a bad way."

"I've had worse." Leonie coughed. "What was it this time" She slowly took a breath. "I'm keeping a tally."

"Broken arm, fractured vertebrae, punctured lung and concussion, and a whole bunch of cuts and bruises."

"Pffft. The lung thing's new. That would explain the blood from the coughing?"

"It would."

"Why are you still here?"

"Clearly looking for you," Lerry replied.

"Is this place still safe?" Leonie asked.

"It's fine. Nothing is up in this storm," he said. "What happened?"

"Me being stupid."

"Besides that." Maz chuckled.

Leonie frowned, remembering. "I waited for that jet. It arrived, but much higher than before."

"Probably because of the storm," Lerry guessed.

"That's what I thought. Anyway, I got as close as I could, which wasn't much, and tried to EMP it from a distance. I used too much power, drained myself, and fell."

"Surely not from six thousand metres," Lerry stated.

"Not quite. I was dazed but conscious. I tried to draw as much power as I could while freefalling, and when I was about a hundred metres, slowed as much as I could. I think the slope and vegetation helped."

"Did you get the jet?"

"It sparked a bit and changed direction, but I don't know for certain. After I crashed I lost consciousness, and woke up this morning, but faded in and out."

"When you didn't return last night we started combing the area."

"Time to let the girl rest." Maz ushered everyone out.

"How long will this take?"

Maz turned back. "We'll have to see. At least another day, maybe two."

Leonie huffed. "Leave me if you have to."

"Okay then." Maz chuckled as she turned to leave. "I'll come to check on you in a couple of hours."

————

"We'll be here another day," Maz said as she checked Leonie's progress the following day.

"Seriously, I'm feeling fine." Leonie flexed her arm, feeling barely a twinge. Her chest felt great too; no pain with a deep breath.

"And you'll be feeling finer tomorrow," Maz retorted.

"We can't stay here. It's too risky."

"Let us worry about that."

"How's the storm?" Leonie changed the subject.

"Almost finished, from what Lerry says."

"Am I able to have something to eat and drink?"

"Of course. Anything in particular?"

"Whatever you've got."

"Back in a minute." Maz left the room.

Leonie immediately unplugged the medicomp and removed the sensors. She was zipping up the new jumpsuit by the time Maz returned.

"What do you think—"

"I'm much better, see?" Leonie made her claw-tips spark and rose off the ground. "I can take it from here. If the storm's passing, they'll be out looking for you. Haven't they got security bots for this sort of thing? I mean for bad weather? How many outposts in the area?"

"Five. They don't send the bots out alone."

"And it won't take them long to send a flyer out to any of them. Let's hope they don't start here first." Leonie stepped closer to Maz and gave her a quick hug. "I can't thank you enough, truly, but I'd hate to go through all this crap only for you to get caught."

Leonie was famished after almost two days on the medicomp. Intravenous fluids just didn't cut it. She raided the pantry for anything palatable, washed down with a couple of mugs of coffee.

Outpost 9 was almost identical to 7. The bunking arrangements were tricky – eight beds for twelve people – but Harrond and the Redmonds were okay on the floor. By morning the next day, all the vehicle batteries had recharged.

While she ate and drank, they stripped the place bare, including all food and medical supplies, for their trip to Jenolan. The clones worked alongside each other well. Intermittently Leonie caught herself staring. *I need more of that nose goo.*

Like a good mother, Maz had ensured the clones grabbed clean coveralls, water and covered any exposed areas with sunblock. "No telling what this sun will do to unconditioned clone skin," she said as she walked to the garage door. "While you boys do the heavy lifting, I'll warm up the truck."

The laser cannon took her in the central body mass, throwing her back along the corridor.

All hell broke loose. The clones panicked and screamed, running for cover. Moaning in grief, Lerry ran towards Maz, slumped against the wall. Another blast scorched the wall above his head. He dropped to the floor, his eyes never leaving Maz's body. Harrond stood and stared.

Leonie *willed* Lerry back as another shot hit the floor in front of him. "Stay back!" she growled, throwing a fireball out the door. She dashed to the entrance, quickly glancing out. The fire-damaged machine whirred erratically. She zapped it for good measure, silencing it. "Security bots. That one's down," she called.

She then bolted to the maintenance shed, feeling a headache coming on already. Blowing the door open, she sent an EMP into the room, then flew out straight after it.

The droid waiting by the entrance was smoking. She saw movement outside. *The controllers?* Closer to the window, she saw more movement among the vegetation.

She whirled around at the sound behind her.

Ashen faced, Lerry came through with a pulse rifle. "The

storm must've damaged the security sensors," he said. "What's out there?"

"I can't be sure. Maybe four or five armed guards."

"Incompetents, sending security bots then not knowing how to follow up."

"Well, now they know we're here. What's Harrond doing?"

"Guarding the other door."

"Is there any other way out?"

"Here and the garage, front door and windows," Lerry said.

"Too obvious, and there could be more bots out there." She looked around trying to form an idea. "Stay here and keep an eye out. And keep down." Leonie rested her paw on his shoulder. "I can't lose anyone else." She ran back into the dome, her mind still reeling.

Harrond was crouching behind a desk, watching the front door and main window. Glancing now and then at his mother's body, he wiped his face.

There was nothing she could say.

Leonie went to check the clones in the bedrooms. She walked through the kitchen area, blinking at the bright shaft of light through the roof. She stopped, looking up at the skylight. She levitated directly below. The window swung inwards silently, dumping a pile of sand onto the floor. Leonie coughed, then rose to look out.

All the dome's external doors were at the front. No one was paying attention to the rear as there was no exit there. Keeping low, she edged out and down the side. Using the dome as cover, she moved into the surrounding foliage and made a wide sweep around to the front and behind the guards. She counted eight concentrating on the front of the building.

As she had done years ago, she entered the nearest one's mind, convincing him his comrades were the enemy. Four went down before they realised the attack was coming from them. They returned fire, but not before another one went down.

Leonie fireballed the remaining two. A quick scan proved all were dead and no other guards were in the area.

"Harrond, I'm coming in," she called as she approached the front door, noticing the mounds of sand against both garage doors.

Both Harrond and Lerry were kneeling by Maz's body. Joining them, she placed her paws on each of their shoulders.

"They laser-cut through the roller doors," she said softly. "We had no idea." Leaving them to their grief, she went to fetch the clones. "Are any of you able to drive the truck?"

They all shook their heads. "We weren't assigned that function," one goddess replied.

*Even their voices are a turn-on.* Leonie hissed in her frustration. Wondering how the guards got here, she went back outside. Hidden behind the scrub were two ATVs. "Slower but quieter than a flyer, and probably better in the sandstorm."

After looking at the controls, she darted back inside. "I've taken out the guards. Can either of you drive an ATV? The garage door's blocked with sand. We can't use the truck."

Lerry nodded silently, still in grief at the loss of his life-partner.

"We'll take Maz with us," Leonie promised. "We won't leave her here ..." She walked towards Maz.

"No," Lerry spoke up. "I'll get her. Show Harrond where the ATVs are."

"Harrond, you're with me." She put her arms on his shoulders when he didn't respond. "If we don't go now, they'll get all of us."

"I want to kill them," he moaned in anguish.

"Next time, I promise I'll save you a few." She doubted he'd have the stomach for it. He was too nice a person. *What's that make me?*

With dead feet, Harrond plodded after her. She wished he would move faster, but decided anything she said would be pointless.

He showed her the basic controls as he drove the first one back. "I'll get the other one if you get the clones to load the supplies in the back," Leonie said. *Give him something to do.*

She flew to the second ATV and with only a few mishaps, managed to park it next to the other one, then collected all the guards' weapons. "Harrond, can you remove the GPS transponders?"

"On it," he replied, woodenly.

Maz was wrapped in a blanket and laid out on the office desk. From the maintenance room, Lerry found a shelf to use as a stretcher. While he lifted her, Leonie slid the shelf underneath. They both used straps to secure her body and carried her out to the vehicles. Leonie could have used her power but felt Lerry needed to do this himself.

"On the roof?"

Lerry nodded. They lifted and lashed the stretcher to straddle the racks.

With the last of the boxes stowed, there was nothing left to do. The clones climbed on as best they could.

Both agtechs took the wheel, each with a Redmond sharing the front seat. *Wise choice.* The remaining clones shared the back; two in the seats and two more in the tail.

"Lead on, I'll fly above and keep a lookout."

The vehicles moved off. As Leonie launched, she saw the transponders tossed on the ground. On a whim, she grabbed them and flew south-east at a low level for an hour and dumped them in a crevasse. She then flew back at a higher altitude, looking for the ATVs. To the far north, she spied several flyers far on the horizon.

Half-an-hour later, she saw the dust-trail ahead. Luckily, there was still a breeze to disperse it quickly.

It was a slow, bumpy ride for them, but they managed to get to Jenolan just after nightfall.

Leonie flew ahead to give Rhiannon notice and informed her of Maz's passing.

When the ATVs arrived, there were two lines of wilders holding torches, the flames lighting up the trail. As the vehicles passed, each of the wilders turned to walk behind the vehicles in pairs.

When the ATVs arrived in the clearing in front of the main cavern the rest of the community stood silently around them. They parted to allow the seer to come through.

"We're all so sorry for your loss. Maz was always energetic, bright and exuberant. She is already sorely missed," Rhiannon said, holding their hands and feeling woefully inadequate. "You are welcome in Jenolan."

Lerry and Harrond nodded. When they let go of her hand, they both hugged her, then moved around the vehicle and lowered the stretcher.

"If you would follow me?" Rhiannon asked.

The two men followed the seer into the cavern. Leonie followed them all to the area used as the sickbay. The agtechs lay the stretcher on the bed. "Would you care to have a wash and some refreshments? I sense you're both dehydrated. Leonie knows the way."

"Come on guys. Reckon we all need a drink." Silently they made their way to the dining area. There was a cooler, with water and some fresh vegetables, and half a loaf of bread. Lost in their thoughts, it was a sombre meal with little conversation.

Leonie excused herself and went to see Rhiannon, telling her in greater detail of their escape and how Maz was shot. The seer had cleansed the body and wrapped her in a blanket.

"They shouldn't have waited for me," Leonie wept. "If they left, Maz would still be alive."

"And most probably you'd be dead—"

"And I'd be fine with that!"

*There is no blame, only shared grief at the loss of a loved one and a good friend.*

"Where would you like her buried?" Leonie finally asked, wiping her eyes.

"We have an area set aside down past the gardens."

"I remember." Leonie nodded. "I'll be back shortly." As she walked out, she ran her hand gently across the body.

Outside, lit by torchlight, the clones were sitting to the side, surrounded by the wilders who had brought them food and water. Leonie chuckled drily. "I better let Rhiannon know about the potential pheromone problem."

Needing to be distracted, she worked out how to dig a hole with her magic and then spent time making sure it was long enough and deep enough. Wearily, she made her way back inside, had a quick wash, and looked for a bed.

As she passed the sickbay, she saw both Lerry and Harrond in chairs, asleep by Maz's side.

The following morning, they buried Maz.

Similar to the previous night, the wilder community made two lines. The agtechs walked between them in the wake of the floating stretcher. Behind the two men, Leonie controlled the stretcher. She walked beside Rhiannon who led the Jenolan elders. Once the procession passed, those forming the lines peeled off and followed.

Gathered around the gravesite, Rhiannon stood at one end, with Lerry and Harrond. Leonie, the clones and the elders stood on the opposite side to the rest of the wilder gathering.

"While many of us only knew Maz Carter briefly, she undoubtedly touched us all in some way. Some of you may never have said a word to her. Maz continued the responsibility of bringing the unwanted babes from the tower to live among us. Many of the young here and in the other communities owe their very existence to the risks she and her family took. Our community has only benefited from their efforts.

"Today, Maz will rest with our other family members. Let the energy and exuberance of the life she led be an inspiration to all wilders, her second family.

"To her life-partner Lerry Carter, and son Harrond, we solemnly regret her passing, but believe me when I say her life-force is not lost. She will remain with us, always, in our hearts, our memories and our minds."

· · ·

Leonie stayed a few days, catching up on the happenings over the years, but after a while made her departure.

"I will try to visit regularly." She hugged Lerry and Harrond in turn. "You guys look after each other. I'm—"

She turned away and saw Rhiannon waiting by the cavern entrance. "I can't thank you enough for taking them in."

"Think nothing of it. We might have to split the clones up, to share the food requirements, but we are more than happy to help where we can." *You know this.*

*I do, but I had to say it, nonetheless.*

*Until next time.*

The wilder community waved as she headed back to the tower.

"When will be the next time, though?" she asked herself.

# 31

# BRENDON, DIANAH & HELIXR

FOR YEARS, BRENDON CHURNED OVER THE NEWS OF HIS POSSIBLE birth in the tower. Rumours had been circulating all his life of how on rare occasions some babies in the tower had been smuggled out because of their genetic mutations.

It could have been as minor as an extra digit, or marking, webbed toes or fingers. In his case, his hair covering and marginally webbed fingers.

"I'm still human!" He shouted at the dusk, hurling another rock off the cliff. The tower was visible, a large, menacing blot on an otherwise picturesque landscape, its dark solar panels reflected the setting sun. He turned and stirred the campfire, building it up, sending sparks and embers swirling into the air.

The reports of wilders going missing over the last few years had become more regular. Some of the southern and northern communities were decimated, with survivors making the treacherous trip to Jenolan. Too many died, either through howlers, injuries, or simply not having the care needed to survive their disabilities.

He could change all that. He was certain of it, which is why he was here, now, with his large fire. The elders were all wrong, old and scared. Wilders were misunderstood. Those in the tower

– uneasy with anything different – reacted like anyone else, with fear. If he could show them there was nothing to fear, wilders would be accepted and then their ailments could be treated. Better care for all.

A flying craft approached. He would surrender to them. Show them he was peaceful.

Other than the death and destruction, there was one other aspect all survivors agreed on – all the missing wilders were telepaths. *Like me.* He was strong in his abilities, even his elders said so. If they wanted wilder telepaths, he would help them understand the ability better, so they could understand wilders better.

As the craft circled the campsite, he knelt showing empty hands.

*Time to go home.*

———

The arrest of her father devastated her. Dianah idolised him and his calculating and methodical approach to all things science. He confided in her as she grew older, helping him with some of his experiments and research.

Genetics was such a wonderful gift; to create a living being but without deformities, without congenital diseases or medical conditions. Pure, pristine and perfect.

Gone. They wiped every computer to do with GenLabs. Any evidence, even the remotest possibility of his research, was taken and destroyed.

But they overlooked his young daughter.

Maybe it was the fluffy rabbit ears she stuck on the protective cover of her tablet that swayed them, or maybe it was the docile 'I'm-too-young-and-stupid' look on her face when they ransacked the apartment? Maybe they were so over-confident and eager to make an example of him? More than likely, however, it was probably her telepathic suggestion to the investigating officers that she couldn't possibly be a threat or be hiding anything. Besides, the tablet didn't have enough memory to hold the terabytes of data required.

But it did have a password and a link to a secret storage unit on a geostationary satellite. Over the last couple of years since his incarceration, she had read his notes over and over and improved on his work. The one flaw she felt her father had was his desire to recreate what *was*, even if it was perfection.

For better or worse, humanity was evolving. Why not make what *will* be?

And that was the slogan of HelixR *'Making humanity better'*. Everyone thought it referred to the ReJuv drug HelixR made.

If only they knew the truth; that the enzyme used as the base for ReJuv was extracted from mutants. The one thing all citizens despised was the only thing keeping them disease-free and making longevity possible.

Once HelixR was cleared of any involvement with GenLabs – an obvious consideration, being a sister company – it was business as usual. It too had a sideline in genetics, but strictly for wildlife. It enhanced genetic research, made a small amount of wealth with those visiting the zoo, but it maintained a gene bank for the far future when humanity could walk the Earth again.

She drank her coffee over breakfast, and looked at her schedule for today, intrigued by a last-minute update regarding a new subject for testing. A *volunteer* subject.

---

Brendon groaned as feeling slowly returned to his extremities. His skin felt raw. He tried to open his eyes. *Too soon!* The glare of the light above him was too intense. He quickly realised he was tied down, unable to move anything except his head. His head throbbed mercilessly.

Over time the pain receded and his eyes adjusted somewhat to the glare. He squinted around the room. It was large, containing benches with shelves above them, and several tables much like the one he was tied to.

The ceiling was white. The walls were white, as were the furnishings. Craning his neck forward, he saw he was partially covered in a white sheet. Little round things with wires stuck to his skin. The only things not completely white were the machines on the nearest trolley. The wires led to these machines. The floor, as much as he could see of it, was also white.

He heard a whisper of noise from somewhere behind him, followed by the sound of approaching footsteps.

"Awake now, are we?" It was a female voice.

"Yes," he croaked.

"How are you feeling?" Her voice was close behind him now.

"Not too good," he replied as the owner of the voice came into view. "But I'm starting to feel better," he added after seeing her. She was wearing a white robe, some sort of mask and carrying a small device which she was studying now and then. With dark brown hair braided behind, green eyes and the finest looking skin, she was the most beautiful woman he had ever seen without a doubt; which didn't say much, he reflected wryly.

"Glad to hear it," she said, though there was no warmth to it. As cold and lifeless as the room.

"What's that smell?" He wrinkled his nose in distaste.

"That would be you. We bathed you. We don't want any bugs or filth in here. You're in a quarantine section until we know you're not carrying any contagion."

"Any what?"

"Disease ... germs."

"Uh-huh. My name is Brendon."

The woman turned to monitor some of the equipment.

"What tests do we have to do?" he asked after a while without a response.

She ran off a list of incomprehensible words.

"Will they take long?"

"That partly depends on you."

"What do I have to do? I want to help."

She turned from the blinking lights to look at him. "Yes. I had heard about that; you gave yourself up. Interesting. We need you to carry out psionic tasks, or mind-tricks, if you prefer," she said to his quizzical look. "To ascertain which specific part of the brain is activated. You can do these mind-tricks, can't you?"

"Yes. I said I could. That's why I came."

"Hmm. What can you do exactly?"

He thought about it for a bit. "I can move things, heat water, tell what people are thinking, communicate with others over a distance ..."

"How far?"

"I don't know. A few kilometres I guess. Not now, though. My head hurts too much." It was a half-truth.

"Can you read beyond these walls?"

Brendon concentrated. It was blank. "No. What happened to me?"

"Drake happened. He didn't think you would cooperate."

"But why? I said I wanted to help."

"Yes well, he's not an overly trusting type. Let's face it. We aren't on the best of terms with you mutants. No one in the towers likes ferals. You're an aberration to humanity. Some of us have our suspicions. Many would just prefer you all dead."

"What do you think?"

"Frankly, I agree with the suspicions. At this stage I see no reason to trust any of you. I've had no experience with *coopera-tive* ferals. I—"

"After the way you people treat us? Coming into our communities and dragging men, women and children away, killing those who try to defend themselves!"

"Perhaps the method may leave room for improvement."

Brendon heard the words, but the sentiment wasn't there.

The woman continued talking. "But that still doesn't explain why you're here to help." She remained silent for a while.

Then he felt a faint touch probe his mind briefly then withdraw.

"If you want to help so much, why are you holding back?" she asked.

"What? I'm not. I mean, I'm not doing it on purpose. It's just a natural response." He would have to start doing something quickly if he was going to get her trust. "I didn't know you people could do that. Look, I've dropped my walls already. If you want to come back in, you'll see that I'm telling the truth." Again he felt the slight touch of her mind on his. Now that he was prepared for it, he realised the probing wasn't light because of finesse. Far from it; she was very weak and unskilled with it.

This was good news as he had not dropped his walls entirely, only enough for her to see that he was telling the truth. Now that she was preoccupied, he used his skill to probe her thoughts. A skill Rhiannon had been teaching him.

The woman, Dianah, was keen on learning the secrets of telepathy in any form, and would stop at nothing to get it; she had a half-brother named Alexander; who owned something called Icon and it made him rich. She only got what she wanted when she used her telepathy to coerce someone; she was unhappy because of this, didn't anyone do things for her simply because they wanted to? That's how she got Alexander to help her, that's how she succeeded. Telepathy got her everything she wanted, everything she needed. He managed to get a glimpse of deeper details but he felt her withdraw from his mind, so he did likewise.

"Hmm." Dianah leaned on the table behind her, the effort of what she did already tiring her. "It would appear you believe what you're telling me. This was your idea?" She wiped a bead of perspiration off her brow.

"Yes. I have other friends who want to help too." He nodded. "I don't know how deep you went," he lied, fully aware she had only detected what he wanted her to see. "But, like some of my friends, I was born here. In this tower. We were cast out as babies because of our differences. We just want to come back. Maybe find our parents ... but mainly to be a part of this life."

"Preposterous. You would never fit in. Look at you."

"We thought if we helped you, you could help us. There's not much difference between me and you. My other friends are almost normal too."

"It's not that easy, and besides, what makes you think I can't get what I want with or without your help?"

"But can you? How far have you come with your tests? Not too far I imagine and I know why. What you want can't be taken, it has to be given freely. Sure, you can force them to show you tricks, but to learn how to do it, you need training. Someone has to be inside your head to guide you."

"And just who do you suppose will do that? You? I think not."

"You'll have to trust someone sometime." He had read a lot more when he probed her mind earlier. Memories of her youth. Of her father and mother. If he was to play a part in this, he had to get her trust, to convince her in some way he was genuine. "Your father was working on cloning humans. This was illegal by your TowerGov and when he was caught, was exiled to the colony on Mars. You managed to keep the research of his work. You continued with it, trying to isolate the psi-gene after his exile." *You see, I've already been in here. I could have done anything without you knowing ... I'm sorry I did it, but all I ask is for you to trust me. We can help each other.* Brendon let his mind withdraw.

She reeled back, eyes going wide, stunned by the power of his thoughts. Hurriedly drawing a small pistol from one of her lab-coat pockets, she tried to aim it at his head.

Anticipating a response like this, Brendon re-entered her mind the moment she moved. With an effort, he overlaid his will onto hers. Dianah's arm slowly bent until the gun was aimed at her head. The strain on her face was evidence of her struggle to fight back, but she had no control over her actions.

"As I said, you'll have to trust someone sometime." While still controlling her arm, he manipulated the locks restraining him. Each one made a soft click as they released. All she could do was stare wide-eyed as he slowly sat up.

The effort of the last few minutes had cost him dearly and he was sure he would pay for it soon. But not yet. Not now. With his head still throbbing and pain wracking his body he slid off the bench and stood up. As he walked over to her the sheet dropped to the floor.

*I will teach you everything I can. You know now, you need me as much as I need you.* "Can we work it out? Can we trust one another? Please?" He relaxed his hold.

Slowly, the weapon lowered. Dianah's hand shook as she replaced it in her pocket. Although nervous, a hint of a smile appeared on her pale face as she looked into his eyes. "I'm sure we can work something out."

"That's good ... to hear," he gasped, feeling both elated and very weak. "To begin with, could you release any other wilders you have captive? You won't be needing them ... anymore." Brendon fell unconscious to the floor.

"Perhaps," she said to his prone, naked form, tossing a sheet over him.

———

Brendon frowned in confusion for a moment before recalling where he was but noticed this was a vast improvement on the previous room. He wasn't tied down for a start. He had some sort of robe on. There was furniture scattered around the room and no instruments. The walls were a striking blue and there was some of that carpet stuff on the floor.

An interesting aroma wafted from a table nearby where he spied a tray of food and a jug of fluid. He hesitated at the strange food but decided if he was going to live in the tower, he had better get used to it, and considering what was available in Jenolan, it couldn't be any worse.

He was finishing the last of the dishes when Dianah entered the room. She was wearing an unusual head-piece. Brendon couldn't scan her mind at all.

"I apologise for this headwear. It's to provide security and privacy for my colleagues until they can trust you. They are almost in agreement to accept your assistance in our research. If you can prove to us that it's in our interests to keep you here, then we will help you adjust to life in the tower, but I should warn you that it will take a while and won't be easy."

Brendon considered this. "Prove? I overpowered your mind. I could have killed you, but I didn't. I volunteered to be here. What more do I need to do to convince you?"

"It's not me that needs convincing. While you have a stronger mind than mine, maybe you didn't kill me simply because there would be little chance you'd be able to escape? Maybe you *volunteered* because you were caught and were too scared to do anything else?" She put her palm up. "As I said, it isn't me you need to convince. The board needs something more. They are putting their necks and reputations on the line."

"So am I!"

"Pretty sure they think their necks are more important than yours."

"What do they want?"

"Since you're prepared to give up your wilder life ... are there any wilders like you with powerful minds? Who trained you?"

"I can't do that."

"That wasn't a no, so there *is* a trainer. If you truly do have family here, perhaps we can arrange something, but until then, I'm afraid much of what you ask won't be allowed." Dianah added, "You can stay here. We'll continue to feed and clothe you. However, we'll wait until you're fully recovered. There's no rush to start."

"I will start as soon as you can. I will do what needs to be done."

"Okay," Dianah said. "It'll take me a few days to organise a regimen of tests anyway." She noticed the empty tray. "Would you like anything else to eat or drink?"

"If I could have more of the same, that would be good."

"Good then. After that, I will show you how to use some of the gadgets in this room. This is where you'll live for a while.

One of the conditions my colleagues imposed was that the door was to be locked at all times, but," she continued as she saw he was about to protest, "once you've proven yourself to them, you will be given more access. And don't forget, some of the people here don't like your type in the slightest. It's also for your safety. I'm the only one able to get in."

# 32

## ZOO BUSINESS

"It's been six months, Bren. You've been extremely useful." She looked him over after his shower. "In more ways than one. Nice to see all the hair has stayed off. You look quite the man, now."

"I'm amazed by what the medicomp can do." He examined his fingers. There were no scars after the web removal.

"Sometimes, the medicomp simply needs a minor adjustment. Many other wilders could benefit, as you have."

"When can that happen?" he asked.

"You know when. The board won't wait any longer. I can only manipulate them for so long. If I lose their trust, we can say goodbye to all our plans, and I dare say, they'll remove you too."

Brendon pulled his pants on and sat down on the edge of the bed. His mind ticked over the ramifications of what he was about to do. Dianah had kept up her end, ensuring he was taken care of. The fact they were attracted to each other had benefits too. But, he undertook this risk for all wilders, not just for himself.

"Her name is Rhiannon. She is a strong telepath. If you promise to just take her, and not hurt or kill anyone else, I'll take you to her community, Jenolan."

"While I can't promise no one will get injured, I can promise all efforts to ensure everyone's safety will be made."

He didn't try to scan her to seek any deceit. No more scanning was a promise he had to make for this to be successful. He made it.

"You going to Jenolan is not an option either, but this is a huge step in that direction. Where's Jenolan located?"

"You know of the badlands?"

"The radiation pits. Yes." Dianah climbed off the bed and reached for her tablet.

He got distracted when her robe opened. "More of that later." She almost blushed, patting his hand away and brought up a detailed map of the area surrounding the tower.

"Jenolan is just under halfway, due west of here. There. See these three hills? There is a ravine along here. It's well camouflaged."

"It must be, to have evaded our detection for so long."

"Some of us might look grotesque, but there are well-developed brains. The tower has underestimated us."

———

"What is that stench?" Leonie's nose wrinkled at the noisome odour. She sat up and rubbed her nose as she looked through the foliage. "Nothing living could smell that bad," she complained.

This tree had the best view of the zoo, the climb kept her in shape, and it felt good to get her claws out and dig them into the bark after years of skulking around on plascrete and metal floors. Other than the machine floor in the agtechs' sector – which was too dangerous now they upgraded the security – it was the largest internal space she knew. The area went for almost a hundred metres in each direction, but it was six-hundred metres up, like a huge, vertical tunnel.

Leonie looked at the expanse of synthetic grass. *And eight years ago, a goddess fell half that distance to her gruesome death, landing there.*

Finding this area had been such a joyous occasion, she almost got eaten in her distraction. One thing she had to keep reminding herself, in the zoo she was not top of the food chain. Over time, many of the animals became accustomed to her comings and goings and her scent, but what really interested them were the treats she'd sometimes bring.

Her only regret was not finding this place sooner, instead of all those nights in the dull, grey vent junctions. The zoo was the ideal neighbourhood for her. It was only busy during the day, and even then, nowhere near as crowded as the rest of the tower during their shifts.

Leonie stealthily climbed down and crept through the foliage, flying over the higher electrified fences between enclosures. Every now and then, she paused and listened. A little bit of paranoia and lots of caution meant she'd not be on the menu.

She followed the smell, creeping closer to the tiger pit. "What are they feeding you guys?" On a large flat rock she saw the offending piece of rotten meat.

The six toes were still evident. "A wilder human foot!" She saw several other bones scattered around the area as well. While it had teeth-marks, the foot had been cleanly cut at the ankle. "Who's feeding wilders to the animals?"

A cold feeling came over her. Jenolan was the nearest wilder community she knew.

At first she considered burying it, but the smell would still attract attention. She considered other areas where it could be disposed of. "Recyc will have monitors to detect rad and other contaminants," she muttered. "I know. Sharks will eat anything."

Leonie rummaged through a nearby bin. No way was she going to get that smell on her paws. She found an empty food container just big enough so she could get a grip.

Wary of the tigers, still asleep with their fuzzy animal dreams, she quickly collected the foot and flew below the canopy of leaves, weaving through the trees to the aquarium. She rose over the wall and hovered, unrolling the foot and letting it fall into the dark waters with a splash.

"Poor sod." She worried there were wilders being used in some bloody research. "When will this shit end?"

Back on her tree after scrubbing her paws, she thought hard about who arranged the feed for the zoo animals. They were all cloned, with HelixR being the sole supplier. Nothing here happened without their approval, and it wasn't as if some random citizen would dispose of a wilder foot.

*Is it a coincidence they both do genetics?"*

She recalled some of her reading and news items after the arrest of Stefan Felton; GenLabs was a sister company to HelixR. Once all the cloning fiasco was over and done with, HelixR simply scrapped the GenLabs name and all assets were rehoused under the HelixR umbrella.

"HelixR it is then."

———

Not being one of the areas she frequented, mainly due to the higher security around these corporate R&D labs, Leonie's travels were cautious, scanning as much as she could before proceeding.

While there may not be night and day within the tower, they still stuck to a working/not-working regime. Regardless of what time it was outside, her best time to do any sneaking and exploring was that section's downtime. Sensors were easily tricked when she dropped her body temperature or slowly raised the ambient temperature of the area, but cameras were the bane of her existence. Luckily for her, no one considered putting cameras in an air-ducts here. *Yet.*

Looking at the small screen on her wrist-com, she was very close to the HelixR offices. She stopped and scanned again, picking up a couple of minds of late-night researchers. As she had done on previous occasions when seeking information, a quick insertion of a thought would stir their curiosity.

*Dead wilders?*

She sensed confusion before realising she used the wrong terminology.

*Dead mutants?* There was no luck with these two.

As she paused, a loud noise diverted her attention briefly. Moving towards the source, through a grille in the floor she saw she was above the loading dock; a mag-craft had returned.

While she waited to see what happened next she kept scanning, stifling a yawn. A short time later, four workmen came through a side door with a large crate on a trolley. She scanned inside. As expected, she detected a drugged animal. They boarded the back of the craft via a ramp; one man steering up front and the other three pushing. In a few minutes they re-emerged with the trolley only.

*Dead mutants?*

The men looked at each other. "What was that?" one asked his colleagues.

Nothing there either. Leonie slowly moved on. With nearly fifteen businesses to check, she still had a lot of area to cover. Already she was getting bored, which wasn't a good attitude to have as a spy.

A faint banging came to her attention. Intermittent, with no rhythm. Random. Sometimes a bit louder. It stopped for a while, then started again. Always curious – and it broke the monotony – she drifted in that direction.

Closer now, as it was clearly louder. She sent her mind out but hit a wall. Not a physical wall, a telepathic wall. "Now *that* is interesting," she mumbled. "Why would anyone in a society devoid of telepaths – shunning them due to being a *mutation* – even have one?"

Leonie worked her way around, squeezing through some very narrow sections to do so. It was uncomfortable, and she was sure she left some skin and fur behind, but the map did show access all around here. It was a relief to know she wasn't heading for a dead end.

Having done a complete circuit, it annoyed her to miss the vent. The banging continued. Leonie sighed and went around again, even slower. Finally, the air vent she missed was only a series of very small holes. There were lots of them, tiny perforations, but too tiny to see much, and there was no light.

Putting her paw over it and holding her breath, she thought she could feel the slightest bit of airflow. "That's not much." She squirmed closer. There was an extremely faint sense of someone. The thoughts were vague, incoherent. "Drugged?"

She put her face against it, still unable to make anything out. She sighed again, getting frustrated. Might as well give it a shot. *Where's Hagan?* Nothing. Vague thoughts continued.

She felt a cramp coming on. She wriggled, tensing and untensing muscles, there being no room to stretch. Leonie pushed back, as it was closer to the larger duct. Still, a telepathic shielded room made her wonder.

*Le ... o ... nie ...*

She froze. *Rhiannon?*

*H ... elp ...*

*What are you doing here? How?*

*H ... elp ...*

*I'm coming!* Leonie's eyes flared. "Bastards!" she hissed. In her agitated state, any discomfort was forgotten as she surged backwards, her mind churning. Back in the larger duct, she scrolled through her map. Knowing corporate security was a high priority, this would be nothing compared to the prison. Once any attempt at rescue was started, she would have very little time to do anything.

"Relax," she told herself. "How and why Rhiannon is here isn't a concern now. Plan!"

Leonie counted two sets of security doors to the loading dock and fifty metres of passages. A couple of EMPs to cancel the alarms, which in itself would bring attention, but it would also unlock anything in her path. She reviewed her plan, looking for alternatives. Burdened with an unconscious body, there was little leeway and no reasonable access to other levels. The best and only route available to her was the dock, which had three entrances; the security doors, the doors on the far side, and open air with over a thousand-metre drop.

She still didn't like it. The risk of Rhi getting injured was too high; there were too many things that could go wrong before they reached the loading dock.

*Where did that caged animal come from?* she wondered. More flipping through the images on the screen. She wished, not for the first time, the screen was bigger. A large section labelled dispatch seemed normal enough but next to it was Veterinary Clinic. And that meant animals. And they did clone animals here.

She purred with an idea. "Let's create a diversion."

Skimming through the ducts, she made it to the area in a few minutes. From what she could determine it was a less secure area too. She smelt them before seeing them. Who would have thought her time in the zoo, surrounded by the odour of animals, would be of benefit?

The lights were dimmed. One thing she noticed at the zoo, even cloned animals were always awake during normal daylight hours. Their circadian rhythms were instinctive and couldn't be fooled.

Her view of the area was limited, but by being patient and doing the rounds she counted six Tasmanian devils, eight kangaroos, and two cassowaries. There were also a pair of tigers, but from what she could read from their minds, they were drugged.

Quantity was better than quality in this instance.

Carefully forcing the vent open she turned it diagonally, pulled it inside the duct and peered out.

There was one camera in the corner. A carefully aimed zap took it out. At this hour, she doubted anyone would be rushing in to check on the animals. Silently descending, she padded across the floor. The animals were awake and wary, watching her, their senses as good if not better than hers.

The 'roos hopped about, agitated while the cassowaries just stared. The horrendous growling from the devils sent a shudder up her spine. Each cage was simply secured with a pin and a latch. She pulled the pins as she moved past and then trotted to the entrance doors, using a clipboard to wedge it open.

At the back of the room, she climbed onto the back crates before willing open the unlocked cage doors.

None of the animals made a move, too wary. Without wanting to hurt them, she gave them an encouraging zap. The kangaroos bounced around like maniacs. She waved her arms to frighten them in the right direction. The cassowaries looked more agitated than frightened. *Good.* When they eyed her, she sparked them gently. They too finally stalked out the door after the 'roos.

The little black growling fur-balls still sounded hideous, scurrying around in all directions. Her zaps just agitated them increasing the volume. "Out you go!" she lifted them one by one and floated them outside. Once the room was clear she scraped together an armload of the straw bedding and piled it outside. A quick flame got it going. She closed the door and nipped into the vent, skimming back to Rhiannon.

Finally, a distant alarm went off. Leonie waited a few minutes to see what would happen. She hoped, at the least, some of the security guards would head out. Her scans showed a few minds fading towards the commotion on the far side of the complex, but not everyone.

Lying next to the vent closest to the door to Rhiannon, she did the same thing as before; forcing the vent open, then bringing it inside and sliding it out of her way. The cameras in both corners got a zap before she slipped out.

The door to Rhiannon was solid and clad in a metal sheet. She zapped the lock, but the door remained tightly closed. Checking left and right that the corridor was still clear, she placed her paw where the lock mechanism should be and created an intense burst of heat and air. Her paw throbbed, but the blast was enough to buckle the door so she could then force it open.

Rhiannon was laying on a bunk, still in a dark-blue robe,

though dirty and blood-smeared.

"Hey Rhi," she called as she ran in. "Can you move?" *Can you move? It's Leonie.*

The seer was still comatose. "Sorry about this." Leonie picked her up over her shoulder and turned to the door. A quick check of the corridor and she glided to the junction and the security doors. This time her efforts to short circuit the lock worked.

Both cameras left and right got zapped. "Surely I'm bound to get some attention soon." The moment she uttered the words, the door halfway down opened as two guards stepped out. They turned directly to her, raising their weapons.

A solid blast of air lifted them off their feet, hurling them back into the wall.

Leonie glided warily closer. Her mind picked up four more inside, one was yelling into the com and the other three were moving swiftly to the door. She waited. The moment they appeared, she zapped all three, leant in over the falling bodies and zapped the fourth. There was no intent to kill anyone, just hoping they were stunned, but she wouldn't shed a tear either way.

Another set of security doors loomed ahead. Once unlocked, there was resistance when she pushed them open. The dock air pressure was greater to prevent the outside air entering. On the other side was the loading dock; she saw a few workmen, but their attention was on the single cassowary running at them. One man was on the ground, as was the other bird.

There was a noise behind her. She pivoted, seeing four guards raising their guns.

Something smashed into her shoulder, spinning her around in agony. It felt far worse than when she was shot with a crossbow bolt. Sprawling to the floor, she fell heavily while cushioning Rhiannon. Bullets peppered the doors, shattering the glass as they swung shut. Growling in pain and frustration at the blood dripping down her arm, she tore out of the dock area into the night. A man's scream got her attention. She glanced back, seeing him fall off the platform, the cassowary looking down from the edge.

She circled quickly and slowed his fall. Not realising how lethal those birds were, his death would be her fault. Back in the loading bay, she floated him into the back of the craft still sitting there. He buckled when his feet touched the floor. She then focused on the cassowary, stunning it with a zap.

The guards burst onto the dock, firing blindly into the night air. Without looking back, Leonie wrapped her one good arm tighter around Rhiannon and flew into the cool night sky. She dived to as low as she could safely go and made a beeline for Outpost 7. It was a gamble, but the only place she was familiar with, doubting she'd get as far as Jenolan in her condition.

Behind her, searchlights scoured the ground. Her left shoulder hurt like hell. She tried to dull the pain. Her arm, matted with blood, hung uselessly, the swaying in the slipstream bringing more pain. Twisting slightly to better support Rhiannon, Leonie quickly let go of her, grabbed her left paw, and hooked it into her belt.

With Rhi secure again, Leonie sped on towards Outpost 7 as the sun began to paint the sky. The approaching craft surprised her, but she was unsure if they were after her, or just on a flight. *Now? Going my way?* She landed among the swaying crops and lowered Rhiannon gently to the ground, crouched and waited.

The aircraft cruised past.

Sighing with relief, she studied her mentor. *Rhi, can you hear me?* There was no coherent response. No improvement. Raising the unconscious wilder to her shoulder, Leonie noticed the craft had started circling.

"Shit. It *had* been too easy." Once again, she lowered Rhiannon to the ground. Moving a few paces away, she concentrated. *And they're always full of armed soldiers!*

The craft slowed, and a powerful spotlight stabbed the night. They began sweeping the ground with it. As they were getting closer, she aimed and released a burst of energy. It faltered and the light flickered, but the flyer continued, now moving more in her direction.

"Frack!" She drew in more power. It was almost upon her before she felt she had enough energy to deal with it. The craft faltered and tilted. It started again, but there was a flash, then silence. The momentum carried the craft to where she and Rhiannon were hiding.

*Too damn close!* Raising her one good arm, she spent every erg of her remaining strength, barely shoving it to the side. The sound of the crash was deafening. She slumped to her knees in exhaustion. It could only have been a few seconds, but she heard cries of pain and swearing. She shook her head to wake up.

Two figures climbed out of the wreck. One stood up, holding his arm and peering into the gloom. The other fell, but when he regained his feet, was limping, using his weapon to support him. The cries of pain continued from the wreck.

Leonie kept still, doubting she'd have the power to deal with both of them. She was black; Rhiannon's garb was dark, they were surrounded by tall foliage and it was still mostly night. The soldier limped past, missing them by a couple of metres.

Rhiannon moaned.

The guard turned, hampered by his leg. As he brought his weapon to bear on the sound, Leonie rose silently and clawed his neck out with her one good arm. As he fell, she grabbed his gun, awkwardly shooting at the other soldier with one arm. He fell out of sight behind the craft. Leonie pushed through the foliage. She needed to confirm he was no longer a threat.

He was injured and surprised when she appeared above him, he raised an arm. Using the rifle butt, she clubbed him to unconsciousness.

She stumbled back to Rhiannon, hoping there was some improvement, but other than that one moan, there was no change. Too weak to fly and carry, she sat, cradling the weapon and relaxed. There were few moans now. Whether they had lost consciousness or the will to live she could only guess. As long as they were no threat she didn't really care.

"Get up, idiot! More will be here soon," she berated herself. Sunrise was imminent, and her only asset was darkness. She dropped the rifle. It was too awkward one-armed. She groaned to her feet and staggered to the soldier she had killed. He had a pistol in a holster. Cursing at the effort and time, she undid the belt and buckled it around her waist then checked the setting, dialling it down to stun.

Getting the seer onto her good shoulder with difficulty, she changed plans. Heading directly to Outpost 7 now would be stupid. Leonie staggered under the weight. "Too much protein girl," she growled in protest, pushing her way through the crops and moving south towards Outpost 9.

The sun blazed as it hit zenith. Back to the north several aircraft combed the general area between the downed craft and Outpost 7. Leonie continued plodding south, mixed with brief stints of flying.

She was nearing the southern outpost when a craft cruised overhead. She groaned, ducking low, waiting it out. The pitch changed. She lowered Rhi to the ground and tentatively floated off the ground to get a view. Outpost 9 was only a few hundred metres ahead. The soldiers fanned out doing a quick patrol of the perimeter while two went to the door. As she watched, four agtechs emerged.

There was a quick discussion and the two soldiers went inside. Ten minutes later they emerged, calling back the others. Once everyone mounted the craft, it took off. The agtechs returned inside.

"Damn it," she cursed. "It'd be too much to expect they were always vacant." Leonie's shoulder throbbed. The excruciating pain, exacerbating by carrying Rhiannon, now affected her whole left arm, neck and back. She had to get to the medicomp, agtechs or not. When the craft was out of sight, she got as far as the garage and put Rhiannon down in a strip of shade.

It had been almost ten years since she'd been this way …

almost a decade since Maz died. Little had changed on the outside, other than the doors being repaired. Inside the garage were two mag-bikes and a service van. She crept inside and slipped between the vehicles to the side door. It was unlocked. "Who would be breaking in?" she mumbled. Maybe her luck was changing.

Voices came from the galley. *Lunchtime, perhaps.*

Leonie spied the four agtechs around the table. Not wanting to injure them at all, she took a deep breath and concentrated, attempting her head clear. She gently entered their heads one by one and gave them a mind-tap, a subdued mind blast. Each one fell forward onto the table. A quick scan confirmed they were all unconscious and would wake up with nothing more than headaches. Bad ones.

Walking outside, she checked the area before retrieving Rhiannon. Back inside, she made the seer comfortable on one of the beds, then closed and locked all the external doors and activated the alarm system. Lastly, after tying the agtechs up, and locking them into a storage compartment, she checked the exterior scanners. Other than movement around the tower, there was nothing within fifty kilometres.

Since all the outposts were standardised, activating the medicomp was straight-forward. She was reluctant to go first, but she was weak with blood loss, her shoulder had been numb for hours, and her left arm refused to work.

Leonie set the time for an hour, climbed onto the bed and promptly fell asleep. When she woke, the wound had closed and she was able to wriggle her fingers. "Good enough for now." She swapped positions with Rhiannon. The seer wasn't injured, just hit with a powerful drug. The medicomp rectified that in just over half-an-hour.

"Leonie. I knew you'd come." Rhiannon sat up slowly.

"Hey, you." Leonie came over and unhooked the device. "That must be the seeress talking. I had no idea."

Rhiannon put her hand out, which Leonie held. "Your arm is injured."

"I can manage for the moment. I wanted to make sure you were okay. What happened?"

"Jenolan was raided. We were gassed. I don't know what happened after they drugged me." She hung her head.

"Never mind. As soon as we've eaten, I'm taking you home."

"I must get back to see what's left."

"And we will *after* you've eaten. We'll take a mag-bike, so we'll be quick."

They heard shouting and kicking from the back of the complex.

"You've got four men in a cupboard," Rhiannon observed.

"Four sore and angry men, yes. But not for much longer. Are you okay to stand up?"

"One way to find out. When I do, we will swap. I will keep watch, and you will complete your healing."

They compromised. Leonie would do another hour only. "I will heal soon enough." *But just one hour. You better eat.*

After the hour, Leonie unhooked the medicomp.

"Better now?" Rhiannon called.

"As if you need to ask," Leonie answered.

"Just being polite."

Leonie growled while she headed off to have a quick shower to remove the dried blood. She found an agtech jumpsuit to fit her and got one for Rhiannon. By the time she emerged, four agtechs were sitting docilely at the table.

"It's okay, Lee," Rhiannon said from the kitchen. "They're in a trance for the moment. I couldn't leave them in there, tied up."

"I wasn't going to leave them like that," Leonie said in her defence.

"Well, it's done now. I see you've changed outfits. Thinking of signing up?"

"Hardly. I suggest you do the same. Assuming they're looking for a dark, hairy mutant and a slim woman in dark robes, it can be our camouflage. I found a suit for you. I laid it out on the bed."

"I've always wanted a maid."

"Did you eat everything?" Leonie huffed. "Or do I have to check the bin for food scraps?"

*Yes, mother, I ate everything.* She laughed exiting the kitchen. "Wilders will rarely leave food."

"I'm going to grab supplies—"

"Done," Rhi called out from the other room. "Two backpacks; one full of protein bars and one full of medicine, and two water-packs."

"I'm impressed."

"It's not like I haven't lived around agtechs for thirty years or anything," Rhiannon returned.

"Fair enough. What about them?" Leonie looked at the agtechs, still staring blankly into space.

"They'll wake up about ten minutes after I leave."

"A nice trick. More training for me then."

"In time."

Leonie disconnected the mag-bike's GPS, stowed the packs and once Rhiannon mounted behind her, headed out. Keeping away from the tower area at all costs, Leonie guided the bike further south before turning west, taking a very large circuitous path, following the similar path to what Lerry and Harrond did with the ATVs. Rhiannon filled her in on what else she could recall of her abduction.

# 33

# REFUGEES

THEY ARRIVED IN JENOLAN AT DUSK. IT WAS VIRTUALLY DECIMATED, the gardens in ruins and burnt, as were most of the wilder dwellings. Leonie grounded the mag-bike near the cavern entrance.

*It's safe to come out,* Rhiannon called as she dismounted looking around at the devastation.

A dozen wilders emerged. Bern was among them. No words were said. The solemn group of survivors rushed forward in tears of joy, tears of grief, tears of relief.

Leonie stood to the side. Bern saw her and came over.

"There was no warning," he said. "They gassed the place. No quarter. Anything found was killed or destroyed. Burnt." He hung his head. "I was not here. I only returned a day ago."

"Lucky you weren't. We'll need you to lead them out of here."

"Rhi is their leader."

"She is their heart and soul. *You* are their guts and determination. Where would you take them?"

"Westridge," he said immediately. "It's further south and safer, but for how long, I cannot say." He looked at the group, and the ruins of his home. "We thought Jenolan was safe."

"I have an idea about that. Are there any elders left?"

"A few. Some injured and in the infirmary."

"I gather the coms are down too?"

"Everything they saw they destroyed." Bern nodded. "What are you up to?"

"I'd rather not say yet. I don't even know if it will work. What about Lerry and Harrond?"

"You've been absent too long. They moved to Westridge several years ago with the clones."

"That must be a relief about the clones. I'm surprised they moved away though … considering."

"They do come back regularly to visit Maz's grave, but Westridge needed the man-power and the extra mouths here would be a burden."

"Remind me, how far away is it?"

"At a guess, it is a bit more than seventy kilometres as the crow flies. As a runner, it's about two days."

"So, less than an hour on the bike. Good. Are your people able to move?"

He nodded. "Most, but some of the injured are serious."

"No medicomp then? We brought what medical supplies we could find."

"What happened out there?" Bern asked as he saw the seer disentangling herself from the group and walk their way.

"With Rhiannon?" She followed his look. "I found her in the tower – pure chance, I can assure you. We got away but had to hide, and we took the long way here. I'm sure no one followed or tracked us, but if they know of Jenolan, they will come looking. No one should be here when that happens, and they could come at any time. What about stretchers? If we made some, are there enough of you to carry those that can't walk?"

"I'm not sure. We'd have to look at what we've got."

"What are you two plotting?" Rhiannon came over to join them.

"Evacuation and revenge, but evacuation first."

"Yes. We can't stay here. And too many bad memories now."

"Bern was saying Westridge would be the safest."

Rhi nodded in agreement. "Difficult to get to, though."

"Difficult is better than dead, but we'll need to carry those too injured."

"The bunker is still locked. I don't know if they missed it, or didn't have time. It's still intact."

"What's in there again?" Leonie asked.

"Storage shelving, ration packs and seeds. We'll take what we can with us."

"And I'll grab anything left when I can."

Once Leonie spoke about her plans to the Jenolan elders, the seer decided to undergo contacting the other communities through her mind. Gathered inside, it took the efforts of the three other remaining elders to get enough strength to cover the distances. Even so, it was brief and arduous, but it saved a five-day round-trip by runner. Time was of the essence now.

While the elders rested, Rhiannon stood and stepped into the passage to speak to Leonie. "Although they understand the risks involved, they are reluctant to agree with your plan. The consensus is the wilders will not go to this Yarnik world of yours."

"What? Did they say why?" Leonie paced the floor.

"They believe the upheaval of the community from the only land they have known for generations is too much." She took a deep breath and continued. "They would rather take their chances, scatter and hide like they have done all their lives."

"And how has that worked for them?"

"They are still alive," Rhiannon answered.

Leonie looked down, shaking her head. "Not enough of them."

"How do we get to the portal?" Clara, one of the surviving elders, joined them. "Is there any way to prove what you say can be done?"

"It's very difficult to get to, it's on top of a spire of rock. Also,

I still need a way to recharge it. Over a decade ago I thought I could, but it wasn't enough. I'll need a much larger power supply. Even then, I'm not sure if it will work, but now I reckon it's our only option. I'll have to make it work."

"How will you use the batteries?" Bern asked from the entrance.

Leonie sighed. "You know when you plug a device into a battery charger?"

"Sure, but has this portal got a socket to plug into?"

"No. That's where I come in. I'll have to be the connector."

"Isn't that dangerous?" Clara asked.

"Probably, but there's only one way to find out."

"If you need batteries, I know where we can get some."

"Where?" Leonie asked.

"The bunker door," Rhiannon answered.

Bern nodded. "They are old, but fully charged."

"Better go and get them then," Leonie said.

"In the meantime," Rhiannon said. "We need to make preparations to evacuate."

"I agree," Clara said. "We need something to carry the injured and immobile, so the bunker's shelving will be our stretchers."

Rhi nodded. "Always practical. Good, can you see to that?"


Within two hours, Rhiannon, Clara and Bern had finalised the last of the evacuation plans. Every useful item, every bit of food was packed and bundled in old sheets and blankets. There was as much excitement of the prospect of going to a new, better home as there was sadness leaving their old home. The only home any of them knew.

Six batteries wrapped in the old camouflage netting from the gardens sat next to the mag-bike.

"This has been such a wonderful place for us." Rhiannon couldn't weep, but her sorrow leaked to everyone's mind. "I'm sorry." She pulled her emotions together.

"Nonsense." Clara embraced her. "We'll shed your tears for you. This something you cannot keep for yourself. You are our seer, our light and our soul. Release your burden, share your grief."

As when Rhiannon returned from her abduction, the wilders all gathered together and held each other. Everyone was in contact with another and by doing so, were in contact with their seer.

Leonie left them to their grief. It was not hers to share. This was for them and them alone. She walked through the Jenolan ruins, recalling her first days, climbing everything she could to explore what she thought was going to be her new home.

She came upon the graves. And found Jojo's.

Now she wept, remembering the mute, mischievous girl always one step away from trouble and three steps away from being caught. "You would've made a great thief," she whispered, tears matting her face and dripping off her whiskers. She heard footsteps behind her. With a deep breath and a wipe of her face, she turned to face Bern.

"Ready then?" she asked.

"As long as you are."

"I'm always ready." She started making her way back.

Bern silently fell into step with her.

Everyone was gathered in front of the main cave entrance, apprehensive about the journey ahead, and leaving the only home they knew. A few came over to her to thank her for her help and in bringing their seer back.

"No thanks required. Look after each other." Leonie smiled and nodded, not trusting herself to say much more.

"You be careful," Bern said to Leonie.

"Can't a girl have some fun?"

Shaking his head, Bern took the lead while Rhiannon stayed back. "We will be alright," she reassured her. "You have given us hope already, and it is more than we dared wish for." She hugged her. *Sorry physical contact makes you uncomfortable, but you've done so much.* The seer released her, then followed the last wilder into the shadows.

*Rhiannon, I will charge the portal and prove to the others that this is for the best,* Leonie sent.

*Ever since we met, I never doubted.*

———

Once everyone left, Leonie secured the netting to the back of the bike before mounting.

The trip was uneventful but much quicker than the last time she flew here. She grounded the bike, hopped and stretched briefly before unwrapping the batteries and moving them closer to the portal.

Leonie knelt between them. "This WILL work," she growled. *It has to!* Placing one paw on the battery and one on the portal structure, she focused on feeling the power within the battery, then drawing it, channelling it into the portal. *Just like when I was charging a crystal.*

Unlike crystal charging, which used far less power, she felt a tingling along her arms, breasts, shoulders and neck. *Not entirely discomforting.*

When the battery was flat, she sat back on her haunches and looked at her handiwork. At first, it looked like there was no difference, but when she glanced between the night sky and the portal, there was a subtle change. She grabbed another battery and then another as she repeated the process.

It was almost dawn when Leonie opened her eyes. Crusted with dried tears, or sweat, she rubbed them clear. Her head pounded, and she realised she had fainted. She fumbled in her pack for the water bottle and more protein bars and ate them with effort; all her movement felt like she was moving in thick mud, her jaw moving up and down, but not tasting the food. She slumped back against the portal in a stupor.

When her vision cleared and she was able to make sense of her surroundings, she sat upright in shock. The movement felt strangely abrasive in the suit. Fumbling at the front of it, she undid the zipper. Under her shirt, the fur on her chest and abdomen felt brittle. When she rubbed it, the fur crumbled leaving dark, bare skin. The same with her paws, shoulders and face.

"Well that's just shit!" she hissed loudly, brushing the fur from her paws. "Lucky I've no one here to impress," Leonie growled as she carefully stood. Her legs still had fur, even after rubbing. "I hope it grows back." The fur-free phenomenon spread across her upper body and arms.

She gingerly mounted the bike and strapped herself in as a wave of dizziness and nausea took hold. On instinct, she slapped the button which engaged the autopilot before slumping forward in the seat.

Everything was quiet and calm when Leonie woke. She looked around in bewilderment before she became aware of her whereabouts.

"Jenolan?" Leonie cursed, realising it had automatically returned to the last destination. She had trouble dismounting before she remembered she was strapped in. Digging into her pack for a drink, she walked slowly around the bike to get her blood flowing again and to remove nausea and the buzzing in her ears. Replacing the water, she fished out a nutri-bar, the buzzing grew more strident. Belatedly she realised it was an approaching flyer.

In a rush, she mounted the bike and sped down the ravine the wilders used hours ago. On the other side, she left it high on a ledge and scrambled back along the clifftop under cover.

The flyer had just landed in the central clearing. A group of six armed men disembarked quickly. Two went straight into the cavern, two headed down the ravine and two searched the garden area and beyond methodically. The pilot stayed behind, pulse rifle in hand protecting the flyer.

In five minutes, they were all back. She couldn't hear their voices clearly, but a quick scan satisfied her that they were convinced no one else was around, and the place had been evacuated. After their reports, the men sat back in the flyer in the shade.

Leonie noted they deferred to one man. She focused on him but found it strange she could read nothing from him, like he was shielded.

He strolled sedately towards the garden, casually tossing rocks whilst talking on his comlink. When he came across the graves, he paused and straddled one.

Briefly curious to his actions, she realised he was relieving himself over the graves. He was too far to make out anything more than a short, slim male with short dark hair.

Enraged, Leonie turned back to the relaxed men. One looked asleep. *Who's your boss?*

Drake was the name that came to her. She etched the name and associated image into her memory, hoping there would be a time when she'd meet him. As much as she wanted to, she was in no condition to do anything right then. If anything happened to these men, it would simply bring far more attention to the area.

"One day, Drake."

The man in question strolled back to the flyer and jumped in. Immediately it rose, spun and flew back towards the tower.

Once it was all clear, Leonie returned to the mag-bike and headed to Westridge to let them know the portal had been charged.

Less than an hour riding, she spied a familiar figure ahead and below waving to her.

"What are you doing here, Bern?" Leonie said when she grounded the bike.

"Rhiannon sensed you were in trouble and sent me back to find you." She saw his eyes taking in the lack of fur.

"That's nice, but I'm okay now."

"You don't look fine at all," he said.

"Well … I am on the inside. The fur will grow back." *I hope.*

"Are you sure—?"

"I said I was, so let that be the end of it. I had some trouble, but now I'm over it."

"What are you doing here then?" he asked.

Leonie wriggled in her suit as the brittle fur on her back tickled.

"The bike's autopilot took me back to Jenolan. While I was there a flyer arrived. Some men were checking it out, probably thinking Rhiannon would return there. They buggered off, and here we are."

"Did you manage to charge the portal?"

"I did, and it was worth every bit of it. I was going to Westridge to let them know, but now you're here, I've got another idea. Want to see my world?"

"Have you tested it?"

"No, but I have no doubts it will work. Hop on and I'll give you a lift. We can still get to Westridge by lunchtime." She saw him hesitate, looking at the machine dubiously. "Surely you've been on a mag-bike before?"

"Umm, no."

"Climb on, we'll get to the portal in no time." She edged forward to give more room on the seat.

"To be honest, running is fine." He grabbed his flask and took a drink.

"You'd rather run for hours than ride this for less than one?"

"Yep," he shouldered his pack, not looking at her.

She laughed. "You're scared."

"I am not."

"No?"

"No."

"Climb on then, otherwise I'll tell everyone."

"You wouldn't."

"Oh, I wouldn't get any enjoyment out of it. Lerry might have a chuckle. I know Rhi will."

"If I was less polite, there are names for people like you," he groused as he tentatively climbed on.

"You think I've never been called them?" She laughed again. "It's what I strive for every day."

"I'm starting to believe it."

"Hang on, big boy." Leonie powered the bike.

He hurriedly wrapped his arms around her, his tension evident.

"Not so tight," she gasped. "Relax."

"Sorry." Bern loosened his embrace.

"And, as *comforting* as it is, maybe a bit lower so I can concentrate on driving instead."

———

"There it is," Leonie said as she slowly grounded the mag-bike.

Bern climbed off, grimacing. He walked around awkwardly.

"You do get used to it," Leonie said as she spun around on the seat and dismounted in one fluid movement.

"I'll pass, thanks. My legs haven't ached like this even after my hardest day on the trails." Bern walked around to get the circulation going. "I don't think I'd be able to walk straight for a week."

"Wish I could say that," she mumbled. "Maybe you should stretch more," Leonie suggested louder.

"That looks amazing." Bern stared open-mouthed noticing the shimmer.

"You can see it?"

The wilder only nodded as he walked around it.

"I still reckon it will need more charging though. When Sussah and I first came through, I'm sure it was more intense." Looking down at the batteries, there was only the one remaining with a charge.

"Do you think it will work?" he asked.

Leonie tossed a rock through, it disappeared. "Yes!" She skipped about in joy for a few moments before she got serious again.

"Are you finished?" Bern laughed. "I've never seen anything like it."

"Of course you haven't. I'd be surprised if you did."

"I meant the dancing." His grin reached from ear to ear.

"Arsehole." She wrapped the spare battery in the net and secured it to the bike again. "I guess you'll be staying behind then?"

"What do you mean?"

"You heard the saying 'there's a whole world out there'?"

"Sure."

"Well, now you have another one." She mounted the bike. "I can get the proof myself, but a trusted wilder's word might sway them. Are you a trusted wilder?"

He looked dubiously at the bike.

"It'll be much quicker this time. You'll barely notice, but if you need more convincing, I just put 150kw through me. Surely you can risk a cramp."

"If you put it that way …" Bern clambered behind her, careful now to grab her waist.

Leonie powered up the bike and rose off the ground. "Fast or slow?"

She felt his shrug while flying the bike in a wide arc. "Fast it is then." With a deep breath, she accelerated, disappearing into the shimmer.

———

It was cold. There was a light rain and two beautiful moons, Luxor and Luminor shining their light between the heavy clouds.

Leonie ground the bike roughly as the effects of the transition took hold. Though not as bad as her first time, the trip was still cold and disorientating. "How are you feeling Bern?" she asked when confident she could speak. His grip around her waist was tight, but he was breathing in her ear.

"I'll need a minute," he mumbled over her shoulder. "I feel sick."

"Better turn your head away. I should have warned you."

He breathed heavily for a while. "It's passing. That was very uncomfortable."

"It's worth it." She climbed off. Not caring about the grass being wet, she lay down and rolled in it, getting her suit saturated. She didn't care. Real, living grass, not like the genetically engineered stuff in the zoo. It smelled fresh and alive!

Bern stood and took a deep breath, staring at his surroundings, especially the twin moons. He slowly climbed off the bike and knelt, running his hands through the blades of grass.

A little while later Leonie stood up and walked around, breathing in the crisp clean air, sinking her claws into the damp, fresh soil. Air she never thought she'd breathe again. She jogged over to the trees and clawed the bark, she sniffed the pungent odour of the leaves when she crushed and rubbed them.

She brought it over to Bern. "Welcome to my world." Leonie put the crushed leaves under his nose. "I thought it would be daylight." Leonie spied the torc she left twenty years earlier. She retrieved it, fond memories returning.

When she left, she had been drained of power. Leonie held the torc between her paws and concentrated. When she examined it a few minutes later, it glowed. *That's more like it!*

"Is that another medallion?"

"It is, sort of a calling card. I've just charged it."

"Meaning?"

"Meaning perhaps it will now be able to call." She placed it back to the side of the portal. "What do you think of my world so far?" she asked, walking back to the mag-bike.

"This is all ... astounding. I never would have thought it possible."

"Even after my magic show when we first met?" She chuckled. "I agree though, it would be hard to believe without seeing it. Speaking of which, shall we?"

"Where are we going now?" This time he mounted without hesitation.

"This is a sky-island. I'll take you to the edge."

They rode the mag-bike to the rim and hovered, looking out at the horizon. It was different than what she remembered, but she knew it had been wandering the skies of Shak'aran for two decades. It could be anywhere around the western seaboard.

What they could see below was a vast swathe of grasslands with a dark patch of woodland far to the south and mountains to the north, stretching northwest.

"If I'm right, the land below is Fisbane, which is on the far west side of the continent Shak'aran."

"And your hometown, Delta?"

"A few thousand kilometres southeast of here. Too far for this trip, or this bike." She rose fifty metres and moved the bike around the rim, circumnavigating the skyland pointing out the ruins. "One more thing to show you." She turned to where she'd battled the l'ith. The carapace remained where it died. A subtle odour of decay lingered still. "Ever see anything like this?"

He shook his head wordlessly and began walking around it. "This is huge, as big as a flyer. How did it die?" Bern touched it, feeling the hardness, and smooth texture of the shell.

"Gruesomely and slowly. A couple of fireballs and a javelin in its head finished it off."

"You did this?" he asked, astounded.

"I had help." She tapped the shell, listening to the hollowness.

The moons disappeared behind a thicker bank of clouds. Soon the rain started getting heavier, and the initial euphoria of being home wore off. She shivered as she started to feel the cold in her wet clothes. "Ever felt rain before?" she asked.

"I have not. It's water?"

She laughed. "Sorry for laughing. Yes, it's just water. Lovely as it is," she sighed, "we better go."

Bern grabbed a few small leafy branches off a tree and put

them into his satchel, as well as a few handfuls of the green grass.

The wet pair returned to the portal. Still shimmering, but a bit less than when they left Earth. They dismounted. Leonie brought the last battery closer.

"If I faint, don't stress. I'll be alright soon." Leonie knelt, made contact and began charging, doing it much slower so she could stop the moment she felt queasy. Eventually the shimmer intensified to her satisfaction. Once the battery was drained she took a deep breath and relaxed, sitting on the pond wall for a moment.

"How are you?" Bern asked.

"I'll live." She noticed he too was shivering. "Think you'll remember this place?"

"I could never forget any of this. I've never felt so wet or cold in my life!"

"You might have to get used to it."

Back on the bike and one last look around, they shot back through the portal.

34

-----------

# EVACUATION

"NOW TO WESTRIDGE," SHE MUTTERED. THE NIGHT WAS CLEAR WITH a bright moon.

She still felt weak in her powers, but her ranging mind picked up the Jenolan refugees ahead. *Hey, Rhiannon.*

*Leonie. You still out here?*

*Yes. I have good news, and Bern is with me.*

*Bern? On the mag-bike?*

Leonie laughed. *He's loving every minute of it.*

*Liar.* Rhiannon laughed. *How did it go?*

*It was a success. I'll be with you in a minute.*

"What happened to you?" Rhiannon asked even before she hopped off the mag-bike. The seer stepped closer and put her hand on Leonie's forehead.

Leonie felt the seer's senses examine her body.

"Didn't you know we moult?" Leonie joked as she waited for Bern to dismount. "It's the after-effects of the charging. A bit of fur loss, and I'm a bit weaker."

"I sensed your trouble, and it was far more than a bit of hair loss and weakness. And you are terribly weak even now."

"Well, as you can see, I'm still breathing, and would do it again if I had to." She turned to Bern. "Want to tell them?"

"I have something better." He fished the branches and grass out of the satchel and passed them around the gathering of the wilders.

In awe they sniffed and touched the leaves and grass, passing it around so everyone could share.

"Everything Leonie said was true. There *is* a whole new world. It's cold! And there's water falling from the sky!" He sounded like a boy in his enthusiasm. "So much green, it would put our gardens to shame." He told them about the skyland, and what he saw below. "I know how sceptical you will be when I say this – I would be too if I had not seen it – but I saw green grass stretching to the horizon. And a forest!"

Leonie watched in amusement at the refugees, enthralled by Bern's descriptions. "How are things with you? Everything okay here?" Leonie asked Rhiannon.

"We have one concern, a twisted knee from a fall, but we can manage," the seer replied.

"I know he'll be disappointed, but I can leave Bern here to help, and I'll take your injured to Westridge. Then I'll start a ferry-service, at least for those worse off."

"That would be a kind service. Thank you, Leonie." Rhiannon walked to the rear of the crowd to find the injured wilder. "This is Jarn."

"Hey, Jarn." Leonie smiled, helping her to the bike and onto the seat. To her credit, Jarn didn't balk once.

"Hey, Bern, can I have the evidence back now? I need it to convince the elders in Westridge."

Bern gathered the grass and branches and returned them to the satchel.

"I hope you don't mind if Jarn takes your place." Leonie punched him in the arm. "You might have to walk for a while."

"I'll try to manage." Bern smiled back.

"See you all again soon." She waved at the group as she soared to the south.

. . .

When she arrived in Westridge, Jarn was delivered into the waiting arms of the locals.

A tall woman strolled over. "You must be Leonie? I'm Lana."

"Pleased to meet you. Rhiannon and the refugees should arrive tomorrow, but I'm going to bring in the injur—"

"Leonie!" Lerry came striding up. "I thought I heard the bike." Harrond was close behind with a huge grin. "What happened to you?" Lerry asked trying to hide the stare.

"After-effects of charging the portal. It'll pass." Leonie beamed. "It's really good to see you both again."

"I'll let you all catch up." Lana smiled, making her departure.

"I'll talk to you soon, Lana," Leonie called out.

Even with all the hugging, seeing the agtechs again was cause for much rejoicing, there were several years of catching up to do. Westridge was also a much different layout from Jenolan but still built directly into a cliff face.

"Want the tour?" Lerry asked. "We can talk as we go."

"Later. Rhiannon and the rest are on their way. I'm ferrying in the injured."

"No, you look dead on your feet," Lerry spoke up. "We'll take over."

"Wait. What?" Leonie asked. "How?"

"Remember when we came here? We had two ATVs?" Lerry explained. "We still have them and because we don't use them much, the small solar chargers here have kept them topped up."

"That would be great."

"So, we will continue the ferry-servicing, and you can put your paws up for a change."

Lerry and Harrond jogged off to get the vehicles.

The wilders in the area moved back a few steps when the pair of agtechs cruised in a few minutes later. Leonie used the vid display to point out the trail the refugees were using.

"Easy. The same way we came," Lerry said looking over. He and Harrond coordinated with their screens.

"Before you go …" Leonie dug into the satchel, bringing out the branches and grass. "I've brought proof the portal works."

She smiled at the wide-eyed faces. Even the agtechs prolonged their departure to feel and smell the foliage.

"Okay," Lerry sighed. "We'll get this over and done with in no time and then you can tell us all about it." In their ATVs, the pair rose above the group and sped away.

A large flat rock to one side of the clearing served as a table. Leonie spread the grass and branches over it and stepped back. The wilders gathered around as the blades of grass passed from hand to hand so they could feel and smell it.

"What is it?" one asked.

"What is it? It's grass," Leonie replied.

"We've never seen grass before."

"Leonie, if it has no nutritional value and we have no animals to feed, no one here would ever have seen anything like it," Lana explained.

"Well," Leonie said. "There's a shitload of it where you're going." Then a thought came to her. "Do you know what rain is?" Her eyes saw many bewildering looks.

"We can't thank you enough for this hope you've brought to us," Lana said to her.

"You can thank me by surviving." She looked at them all. "Where you are going will be completely different, alien to you and much colder, but it's a far better place than what you have here. And no one will be hunting you down." She stepped back so other wilders could move in to feel the grass and branches.

"You're all okay with the evacuation?" she asked when Lana joined her.

"We are, but there are some not convinced it is as bad as you say."

"Did you speak with Rhiannon?"

"I did. We've never had any trouble before." She put her hand up as Leonie was about to speak. "But, even if Jenolan was closer to the tower, it *was* a great place and a shame to lose it. If the towers know of it because of an informant, none of us are safe."

"I wish it were otherwise. I'm surprised no one has come out yet. How many of you are there?"

"We have about a hundred here in Westridge, with a few small outlying family units. They are also preparing." She paused. "Maybe another forty."

"And there are the other communities as well?"

"Yes, Burraga, Northcliff and Kanangra. All are preparing, but whether they scatter across the land or use this portal of yours, I am uncertain."

"How did you get the word out? Runners couldn't cover the distance in time."

"Don't worry, Leonie, we didn't use the radios. No chance of a signal being picked up. As Rhiannon did, we mind-linked," Lana advised. "People are worried. Your evidence will convince many. Is that all there is?"

"I took Bern with me. I gather everyone knows him?"

"Many know him." Lana nodded in approval. "Everyone's heard of him."

"We can start as soon as I can get the portal here, which is another reason why I'm here, but it will have to wait until they return. I need their technical expert—" She stopped, staring past Lana.

She turned at her stare as a goddess strolled by. One of them had a distinctive bulge.

"She's pregnant?" Leonie asked in shock.

"Not all of them," Lana answered.

"How? I thought they were designed to *not* be pregnant."

"Rhiannon explained what they were. I can only guess nature finds a way."

Leonie couldn't take her eyes off the Ivanas and Redmonds. "I'm amazed the clones fit in here."

"The training program the elders devised worked well. Other telepaths here have been continuing with it, so they don't revert to their ... *old* ways."

"That could have been interesting." She accepted a plate

being passed down the line and found a seat. "And the pheromones?"

"Gone." Lana sat beside her. "Which many here are relieved to hear."

"I didn't think orgies would have been a good thing." She chuckled at the blush of some young men sitting at the table. "However, I reckon some will find it disappointing."

Less than an hour later, six more wilders arrived on the ATVs. They were taken inside. The agtechs launched for another trip.

With Lana and the wilders busy with the newcomers, Leonie was left alone. There was little for her to do and, feeling somewhat recharged, she decided sitting around was next to useless. She launched herself to chase after the agtechs.

The take-off was chaotic at best. Overwhelming tiredness took her by surprise. The last thing she saw was the cliff face approaching at speed.

———

Her surroundings were blurry, but there was a familiar smell.

She couldn't grasp where she was, and everything being fuzzy didn't help. Her head throbbed mercilessly and when she tried to move, couldn't.

Beyond her sight, she became aware of a nebulous sound. It got louder. Shapes of heads appeared around her, but they were dark, shadowy figures at best. They didn't appear threatening in any way with their distorted noises. They drifted off as darkness descended.

Leonie opened her eyes. This time her vision was much clearer. She tried to sit up but found it difficult, and her head ached. Looking down, her legs were strapped. One was in a cast, as was her left arm. *Again?* "What am I doing in Outpost 7?" she mumbled.

"Dad, she's coming around," she heard Harrond call out from the door.

Within moments, both agtechs were by her side.

"What happened?" she asked.

"Hey, Leonie. Take it easy. You're in Outpost 7."

"I know that. I'm not stupid," she said testily. "Why am I here?"

"Not stupid? Leonie, you flew into a cliff!"

She tried to think back. "I was having lunch … you dropped off some injured wilders … I was bored and wanted to help …"

"And you scared the hell out of everyone at Westridge when you suddenly lurched into the air and promptly smashed into the cliff and fell ten metres. You're lucky to be alive," Lerry said.

"You sure?" Leonie questioned. "I don't remember any of that."

"Maybe the concussion, fractured skull and broken arm and leg will convince you?" Lerry told her.

"We shouldn't— *you* shouldn't be here." Leonie tried to sit up "It's too dangerous." She slumped back into the pillow as darkness threatened again.

"You need to stop trying to be a hero. You almost killed yourself, and for what? Because you were *bored*?" Harrond chimed in.

"To me, boredom *is* death," Leonie retorted. "I was trying to help."

"And you have done more than anyone could think possible," Lerry said. "You *have* done the impossible, but it would appear even you have limitations. It's our turn to look after you."

"But it's too dangerous for you," Leonie repeated.

Lerry grabbed two chairs and sat beside her. "Not all agtechs are out to get us. We still have friends."

"How long have we been here?"

Lerry sat in the spare chair. "We got here four days ago, but that's irrelevant. No one is going anywhere until you are one hundred per cent recovered."

"Four!" Leonie heard Lerry's matter-of-fact tone. "Reckon I can have something to drink?"

"We can manage that." Lerry disappeared.

Harrond propped her up with another pillow, Leonie wriggled up to more of a sitting position.

"You had us worried," he said, running his fingers through his hair. "The good news is, your fur is back."

"I'm sorry for giving you a scare."

Lerry returned with a glass of water and some soup. "This was made earlier. I hope it's to your liking."

"Depends. Who made it?"

"He did," they both answered, pointing to each other.

Leonie accepted it with thanks. "I like teamwork. What's the prognosis?" she asked, tasting the soup. "Not bad."

"You don't have to sound so surprised," Harrond said.

"At least one more day on the medicomp." Lerry turned a monitor so Leonie could see it. "The bones are healing nicely, but you'll still need to take it easy for a while, just in case. The effects of the concussion are unknown. Only time will tell how your head is. Whether you can still do your magic or not remains to be seen."

"I'll be next to useless without it."

"No, then you will be normal, like the rest of us," Lerry said.

"Me being *normal* here is a death sentence," she growled. "How are the wilders?"

"They've survived out here for centuries. While what they're facing is serious, it isn't something they've not experienced before. They will cope for as long as they have to."

"Until the portal can be fully recharged," Leonie said.

"And as to that," Lerry continued firmly, "we will not be supporting any more crazy plans that put you in danger." He put his hand up, stopping Leonie. "Let me finish. Yes, the portal is amazing and is no doubt the best possible solution for the wilders' predicament – for all us – but if this is what happens to you with a small number of batteries, then we need another way."

"There is no other way," Leonie objected.

"You don't know that. But, if you're right, then it simply won't happen. No one is going to kill themselves over this. Not if we can help it," Lerry finished.

"But—"

"Even the wilders agree. They're all prepared to leave if it becomes possible, but not at your expense. Not at anyone's. Rhiannon and the elders are adamant."

Sinking into the soft pillows, Leonie listened to this news quietly. She didn't agree but lacked the strength to argue. She knew, deep in her soul, somehow a way had to be found. As reluctant as she had been to accept it even after all these years, her gut feeling told her there had to be a way; it was prophecy, and somehow she was involved.

"We'll let you rest more." Lerry stood up. "Get some sleep. You'll feel better once you're fully recovered."

When she slept, she dreamt of her time before her arrival – especially vivid in her mind was the last memory involving Styx.

*I cannot emphasise that enough. Believe, and your true destiny – and ours – will be fulfilled.*

And hroltahgs can't lie.

# 35

# REVELATIONS

THE NOISE AND MERRIMENT FROM THE PATRONS MADE THE MUSIC from the balcony barely audible.

All the Elite and half of TowerGov and partners were in attendance, as befitting the thirtieth birthday of the only son of the remaining Founders. Two hundred guests filled the banquet hall. Food brought in from all around the globe was artistically laid out along the ancient tables made of real oak.

At the head of the table, Alexander sat flanked on each side by his father, Nicholai Zodaich and step-mother, Veronica.

"Why a toga party?" Brendon asked, tipping his head close to Dianah's so she could hear.

"It *is* his birthday. Alexander has his whims. Besides, I like togas. They definitely have several advantages." Dianah winked with a cheeky grin, her hand brushing the skin of his thigh.

"What advantages?" he asked.

"Well, for starters, I'm sure you've noticed there is a lot of exposed flesh."

"I only noticed your exposed flesh." Brendon had to admit, he had never seen so much toned and oiled flesh. Everybody here was beautiful, the best bodies credits could buy, and a great advertisement for the ongoing benefits of ReJuv. Apart from halving your age, the wonder-drug regenerated the skin almost to the softness of a child.

Nearly everyone had a white sash draped over one shoulder, much like what he and Dianah wore. Some of the males had a kilt of some description, while others had longer robes. Some of the more modest women wore full-length sash wrap-arounds, but in many cases, the sashes became much shorter, see-through or both.

"I see your point. What other advantages?"

"In a minute." She turned to watch the gathering. "Let it get a bit busier, a bit rowdier."

"I don't know why you insisted we be here. It's not as if he gives a shit. He's just a manipulative little turd."

"It's not as if I could really decline the invite."

"Why not? Someone did." Brendon pointed to the empty chair opposite.

Dianah shrugged. "I have no doubt he's just late. But, this gives me a chance to show you off."

"I don't—" Brendon started.

"Besides," Dianah cut off his protest, "Al's my half-brother now. If you are nice, though, I have a surprise for you too."

"What is it?"

"A recent discovery that might be of interest to you."

"I know that look. You're up to something," he said.

Drinks were constantly being topped up, and as soon as a plate was empty, it was whisked away and replaced. Anyone who's *anyone* had been invited, and they all came. An invitation from the son of the last tower's founders did not get treated lightly.

"But right now, I feel it's a fantastic opportunity for another lesson in concentration and control."

"Here? Now?" Brendon looked uncomfortable.

"Oh yes." She smiled at his blushing. "I'm sure you'll feel the benefits soon enough."

"I—"

"*Your* subject today is ..." She considered as she dropped her fork on the floor. "Tell me what your research says about this mysterious *shadow* we've been hearing about in the tower. It's been keeping you away from me long enough." She bent to retrieve her cutlery, disappearing under the table.

"The shadow? As far as we can tell, it started about twenty years ago. There's very little confirmed, nothing definite, just rumours mostly."

*You know I can't hear you. Go on.*

*There have been minor power interruptions, noises in the air-ducts.*

*Where?* Dianah asked.

*In the agtech zone at first. A couple of years later, it moved much higher, into blue zone. It was sporadic, but the reports were consistent; a dark animal shape – so they said – more bumps and noises, some growling.*

*Drones went missing or broke, and corridor monitors kept malfunctioning. It was a pain in the arse for maintenance. Then it was all over the blue zone for several years. Remember that massive blackout at the train terminal? There was no hard evidence, several soldiers swore a large black animal resembling an upright cat entered the tube beforehand. Two months later, a black howler was found and killed in the air-vents on level thirty. Then in 2340, the sounds recommenced. It moved back up to the lower level of blue zone.*

*2340, the same year my father was arrested?* Dianah's thoughts cut in.

*And the same year Ivana Zodaich was murdered by Redmond Collins.*

*My mother's cloned servant.*

Brendon gasped. "You think it's linked?" he whispered in surprise, forgetting himself for a moment before continuing. *A clone killing a clone. Can that be considered murder?*

*When it's the documented partner, yes.*

*Shortly after, there was that incident in the prison where the clones escaped, no one knows where to other than outside. They say agtech prisoners helped, but again, a dark, flying animal was also present.*

Dianah paused. *These were the same agtechs arrested just after my father? Escaping with the clones? ... Go on.*

*Nothing much other than the same small noises and minor faults for ten years. Then I came on the scene.*

Dianah prompted. *Your seer was captured – then escaped the same week.*

Brendon continued. *And from all reports, taken by a flying feline animal. Power failures, blackouts, fires, but no dead guards and the creature saved one of your workers from falling two thousand metres.*

*So, an intelligent creature not always prone to violence, but with uncanny abilities?*

Brendon breathed deep. *You have uncanny abilities …*

*How sweet. We both have, now concentrate!*

He jumped when he felt the sharp tines of the fork against his thigh.

*Not much else after that. It's been very quiet.*

*Just like you have been. Well done.*

Her chair moved to the side. "Found it." Dianah emerged, brandishing her fork, looking flushed and her hair slightly dishevelled. "You agree now, toga parties have advantages?"

"No arguments from me." Brendon wiped the sheen off his brow and wriggled in his seat to get more comfortable.

"This little conversation has brought much to mind though; so many coincidental links." Dianah chose some of the delicacies from the offerings. "I've been involved with my research, and grieving for my father, I lost track."

"With well over a million people …"

"My turn, now you've stirred up some thoughts that correlate with things I should have seen earlier." She chewed a bit, pondering. "My father had evidence of those agtechs in the prison. They had smuggled a pregnant girl into the tower twenty years ago, but from where, no one knows. There are no records of a missing girl from any other tower, and there's no one with her name or description registered at the shuttle port or terminal."

"So, the agtechs smuggled her in with one of their crop machines?"

"Only logical conclusion." She shrugged. "But why would a

pregnant woman be out there with no documentation, and who was the real father?" She saw his inquiring look. "That's what the agtechs got done for – forging the documents for her, her undocumented pregnancy, even a partnership arrangement."

"You said she was pregnant?"

"And she had twin boys."

"Twins? But—"

"Unheard of nowadays, I know. Records show the second child was stillborn."

"Not adopted by the wilders then?"

"Nothing is on record, not that it would be, evidently."

"Some old wilders believe I was adopted." Brendon nodded. "Sympathetic agtechs take them out before they're recycled." He shook his head sadly. "What about the first child?"

"This is where it starts getting curious, and why my father had an interest in them. He arranged to have this pair – the girl and child – brought into the upper levels of the towers, threatening the arrest of the agtechs if she didn't comply."

"Why was he so interested?" Brendon asked.

"The only thing to interest my father to get involved would be genetics."

"But the agtechs were arrested anyway."

"Yes, but that wasn't my father's doing. He kept his word. I believe mother was the only one who knew. I wouldn't put it past her to lash out at them. She had to blame someone. She didn't take the aftermath well."

"What aftermath?"

"When father was taken, she lost a lot of social standing. Being an *Elite* was the centre of mother's existence. If there's a sordid affair or a party, she's there, like tonight."

They both looked to Veronica Zodaich, smiling and carrying on like a girl thirty years younger. Alex was sitting beside her with a smug look on his face, a circular wreath on his head.

"I don't think he knows that didn't end too well for Caesar?" Dianah smirked.

Alexander noticed their attention and raised his glass. They acknowledged the toast out of courtesy.

"I can't believe he's now your half-brother," Brendon forced a smile.

"You would be *very* surprised at the convolutions of some relationships inside the tower." Dianah had a wry grin on her face. "I can't believe mother partnered with Nicholai, or him with her for that matter."

"But it *was* a huge rise in social standing for her. She's now Prime Lady. When did this happen?"

She rolled her eyes. "After Ivana was murdered."

"Yes, but how long after? Don't you find it curious it was her servant that killed Ivana."

"You don't think it was a defect in the cloning like they reported?"

"Do you?"

Dianah looked again to her mother, this time with greater scrutiny. "I wouldn't put it past her. She definitely benefited."

"But still, she is your flesh and blood, and it's just a theory."

"It's funny, the two people I've never scanned were my parents. I might remedy that later. Not for retribution, but confirmation."

Brendon grabbed a napkin and scribbled on it then handed it to a waiter, whispering in his ear.

"Get ready to scan your mum," he said to Dianah, indicating with a nod of his head.

"What are you up to?" Dianah saw the waiter moving through the crowd and hand something to Veronica.

"Probably nothing or it could be everything. Whichever the case, you'll know the answers shortly. Now it's your turn to concentrate and remain calm."

Veronica dragged her attention from Fredricks, the merchant banker beside her, and took a sip of her wine whilst glancing at the note on the napkin. She almost spilled her drink in surprise, putting the glass down quickly looking around at the crowd. Her eyes lingered on several people before moving on.

Dianah looked casually ahead at the empty seat but scanned her mother's thoughts. The note simply said 'Who murdered Ivana Zodaich?'. Immediately she saw the image of a naked Redmond Collins sitting on a bed looking sweaty but anxious. The thoughts indicated that if he killed Ivana, word of him being a clone would never get out and she promised to look after him, make him a fully-documented human, as Nicholai had done for Ivana. She assured him Nicholai would sign his release of servitude.

The traumatic vid scenes started playing in her head, but Dianah lost connection. It was there, pure and simple. Her mother got Ivana killed! Her hands started shaking.

"Shit! Okay, it's going to be harder than I thought," Brendon whispered in her ear as he gently held her hand. "Concentrate, relax. Not here, not now. You need to act casual." He sent calming thoughts to her, thoughts of their lovemaking, of their shared times, anything good he could think of was shared. Finally, her hand stopped shaking, the tension dissolving.

"We need to act like we're enjoying ourselves," he said.

"Arsehole, did you have to do that now?"

"You didn't have to scan. Seriously though, who would have known? I'm sorry." He kissed her bare shoulder. "You ever scan Alex?"

Dianah breathed deeply and finished her glass in one gulp, signalling for more. "From the earliest days. If it wasn't for the convenient partnership of our parents, I'd have nothing to do with him. He is a spoilt, paranoid little shit. I think he got wind of my scanning and avoided me for a while."

"You're here now. Why the change?"

"He had a layer of some new metallic type mesh inserted under his scalp. He's shielded."

"Because of you?" Brendon asked.

"I hate to brag. He's paranoid. Eat up, you'll need your energy for later. And after your stunt, I am not going to be easy on you this time."

Brendon started eating his meal. "Do you have the name of

this smuggled agtech woman?" he asked between mouthfuls. "I doubt she was a wilder, but I might recognise it from Jenolan or the other wilder communities, even after twenty years."

"Sussah Carter," Dianah replied.

Brendon thought, swallowing. "Nope. Nothing. Was that the surname of the agtechs? No name beforehand?"

"Yes, Carter was their surname, and the name she entered the tower with." Dianah saw something beyond his view. She sat up. "Later, father changed her name when she moved to the upper levels. Oh, here comes David now."

They saw him stroll in, unperturbed even though he was way past the polite lateness stage. He found his seat opposite Brendon and Dianah, giving them a quick smile.

"No partner?" Dianah called out by way of greeting.

"I had to recharge her," David responded as a waiter filled his glass with red wine.

"You know, he's the same age as you?" Dianah looked to see if Alex had noticed David's late entry. He had, and he was livid if she read his glare, flushed cheeks and creased forehead correctly. She smiled.

"Is he?" Brendon glanced over at David. "I hardly know the guy. Like you and Alex, different circles."

"In your case, no circle. Why not scan him," Dianah suggested.

"I can't." Brendon took a long sip of his drink. "Is he shielded?"

"If he is, he has been for years. I've never been able to get inside his head."

"Huh." Brendon chewed some more food. "So, back to the woman's name."

"Father changed it to Susan Osbourne," Dianah replied.

"Susan Osbourne? You mean. David's mother?"

"Yep. DNA confirms it without a doubt. He also has the same ailment as you."

"I didn't know being charming and witty was an ailment?"

"Depends, but no. He also has a very unique version of progeria."

"Like me? So, he's sucking down ReJuv too? How rare is it?"

"This particular version? There are only two known cases."

"What are the odds of that. Him and me?"

"The odds are incalculable unless they were twins." She let that sit for a moment. "Brendon, meet your brother."

**36**

## HOW TO PLAN A PERFECT MURDER

THE ELEVATOR DOORS OPENED. ALEXANDER STOOD IN THE CORRIDOR, talking to a couple of people who he dismissed immediately when he saw Dianah and Brendon.

"How did you enjoy the party, sis?" Alexander asked as he strode in.

"I've had worse." Dianah pulled her toga up.

"Not being shy now, are we? Everyone's seen your breasts."

"Call me old-fashioned, but it just doesn't seem right to be flaunting them in front of *family*."

"Is that what we are? Family?"

"Only on paper."

"Will your toy-boy be part of the *family* too?"

"If there's a point, it would be great if you could get to it."

"I have a favour to ask. It's about a subject we've both been working on lately. Or, a *someone*, to be more precise."

"You, asking me for a favour? This should be good. No other sycophant to pester with your games?"

"It wouldn't go well for you to deny the son of the last Founder."

"See, Brendon, I told you he is such a manipulative little shit."

"David Osbourne," Alex said through gritted teeth.

Dianah looked surprised at the mention of the name. "Osbourne? Is this part of your vindictive paranoia? Just admit it; he's a far smarter and respected person than you could ever be, even if you lived to be a thousand years old."

Brendon stepped forward and picked Alexander bodily off the floor. "You know, Al, my advice is to catch another elevator." Brendon dropped him in the corridor.

"How's the cloning business going, sis?" they heard as the doors closed.

Dianah stabbed the door open button swiftly. "You mean the animal cloning?" she asked quietly.

Alex's malicious grin almost reached his ears. "You can call them *animals* if you want. Might be safer that way. We wouldn't want anyone to think you were conducting human cloning again. Imagine how it would look after your father was removed and imprisoned for the very same thing."

"I think this discussion should be continued in a more private area."

"I didn't think animal cloning was that secretive, but if you insist. Your place or mine?"

"Yours, otherwise I'd need to fumigate my apartment."

Alex chuckled quietly. "As if you haven't had reason to do it already."

Brendon's knuckles cracked as he tensed his fists.

"Let it go, Brendon. He's not worth it."


As she had been brought up as one of the Elite families, Dianah was used to the opulence. Brendon, on the other hand, tried hard not to gawk at everything.

Alexander chuckled then got to business. "Please sit. How quickly can a human clone become viable?"

Dianah sat next to Brendon on the plush lounge. "*Hypothetically* speaking, under the right circumstances, a clone can be activated within six months."

"No sooner?" Alexander brought over three glasses and a bottle of wine. He poured the drinks for each.

"Not really, depending on the age. A child, maybe four months, but a walking, talking adult, six is the best time. You want to be cloned? *Hypothetically.*" She looked around at the apartment.

"Don't worry." Alex noticed her interest. "I've dismissed the staff, and this place is secured. I want Osbourne cloned."

Diana stared in disbelief. "Osbourne? What on earth for? Is this part of your paranoia getting the better of you again?"

"He is, as you say, smarter and ... respected. Truth be told, he's too damn clever and too damn respected. Anyone that clean, I don't trust."

"And what are you intending to do with the clone? If there's two Davids, shit will hit the fan. If I go down, I'll be taking you with me, since we're family and all. How embarrassed will your father be about that?"

"He won't be concerned in the slightest, but I recall your mother didn't take it too well last time. I'm surprised you're not more concerned about her."

"I care as much about her feelings as you do about your father's. But that doesn't answer the question. What are your intentions?"

"I suspect you are aware of my ... methods."

"Sure. You blackmail and bribe your way into every nook and cranny in the tower. Why would you need me?"

"Because I can't find anything on him. Not one shred of dirt. No scandal. And now, he's up to something. Something I can't get my hands on. Some R&D project TowerGov has him working on."

Dianah looked to Brendon as she reached for her drink.

Alexander continued. "Since I need your help, I'll be open and honest. I can't stand Nicholai as much as I can't stand Osbourne. My sources inform me my father is about to disown me."

"Can a father disown a son?"

"He's the last Founder. He has enough influence to do whatever he wants."

"So if we're dragged into this, and it fails, he can remove all of us?"

"But, if he's not around, he will have no influence at all."

"Not *around*— You're going to kill him?"

"No. David is. Or, David's clone. That way, I get rid of father; get rid of David, and can take complete control."

"There is a problem, the real David."

"That will take work," Alex admitted. "But he's so secretive, no one will be aware if he goes missing. Then when the clone comes out, everything will fall into place."

"And that leaves my mother?"

"What about Veronica?"

"You think you're the only one who can hate a parent? What if I told you I'd like my mother gone as well?"

"You do?"

"She never loved my father, and, as it turns out, was only after the prestige … the social standing. When he was arrested she became a nobody. Maybe we can both benefit."

"As long as it gets me what I want." He drank his wine

"In a way, I think you and I are similar. Did you ever love your mother?" Dianah asked.

"Very much. She was too good for father. I was … since we're being honest, I was devastated when she was murdered."

"You do know your mother was a clone, don't you?"

"All lies!" Alexander jumped up, spilling his wine. "That was a cheap, fabricated lie to try to discredit my father."

Dianah took a deep breath. "How do you explain all the other clones, identical to her?" It seemed to her some of Alex's information was either missing or incorrect.

"Obviously, your father saw her beauty and used her DNA. My mother couldn't have been a clone because there's irrefutable proof Ivana gave birth to me."

"Fair enough." Dianah had the records of when the Ivana clones were created, and they were long before the real Ivana came on the scene, but she wasn't going to argue with a madman. "Do you know who killed her?"

"A defective clone, I heard."

"That defective clone was Redmond Collins, and Veronica's manservant."

"Why would she do that? What did my mother ever do to your mother?"

"Nothing, as far as I can tell. But within a few months of his arrest Ivana died, and a few months later, Veronica partnered your father."

"You're implying your mother killed mine just so she could partner my father?"

"And become Prime Lady, but no accounting for taste is there." Diana poured everyone more wine. "Why David though? If you've got your fingers in everything, why do you hate him so much? Just ignore him. Don't give him any credence or recognition."

"Wherever I look, he's had some input." Alex took a long drink. "Everything I've ever accomplished, he has wiped. I had the highest score in a dozen university subjects – he beat me. I finished my degree in record time – David did two. I had the largest and fastest increase in wealth in a month, in a quarter, in a year – he beat me on all. Every damn time I turn around, David is there doing something better. *And he's not even twenty!*"

"So, you're jealous of a better man," Brendon said. "Isn't that petty?"

"As if you are in a position to judge *me!*" Alex spat.

"Ok, boys, settle down otherwise nothing will be achieved. Alex, I'll do this simply because we both get something out of it. Since you're the master villain, how do you propose to do this?"

"There's one award he hasn't got yet, and I'm going to be the one to give it to him," Alex gloated. "I'm going to make him an Elite."

"An Elite? How? He needs six nominations."

"And I have six Elitists on the council to put his name forward."

"Then what? He becomes an Elite, how the hell does that serve our purposes?"

"Because then, we will know exactly when and where he will be. We'll substitute him with our clone. And both parents will be there to hand him the award."

"You want to suggest the clone kill them?"

"No. You see, I know your boyfriend has a trick or two up his sleeve, don't you, Brendon?" Alexander skewered him with a steely blue gaze.

Brendon swallowed. *How did he know?*

*I've no idea. Not from me.*

*Then you have a mole in your department.*

"Mind-chatting now, are we?" Alex laughed, looking to each of them. "If you want any part of this life, Brendon, this will be your one ticket in. This is the price, otherwise I can guarantee you won't last another week in here. We're *all* getting our hands dirty in this."

————

Later, back in Dianah's apartment, Brendon lay in bed. "You're going along with this?"

"To an extent. I have nothing against David personally, but if it goes according to plan, it could go well for all of us."

"How do you mean?" Brendon rolled over to face her.

"Apart from preventing Alexander's threat to kick you out? David is your twin brother. DNA proves that conclusively. With people in high places, you could receive similar entitlements."

"But I don't know him."

"Then maybe we should introduce you to each other."

"What, 'hey Dave this is Brendon, your twin from the mutant community'."

"Maybe not exactly like that. And of course, there is your mother to meet too."

Brendon looked dubious. "I don't know if I want to meet with her."

"Awkward yes, but why not? She didn't give you up. You were taken from her unconscious body. She has no idea and was told you were stillborn. My father didn't even know until later."

"Well, maybe not so much an introduction, but we can accidentally run into each other at the same gatherings. I could scan her, find out about her, maybe get to know her that way."

"That could work. I'm going to start the replication in the morning, see how things progress. No point getting too worked up if the cloning doesn't work." She sat up throwing back the sheet. "Now then, let's see if you have the energy to finish what I started at dinner."

———

Dianah's wrist-com chimed. She checked both ways to see if the corridor was clear before she answered.

"Alex?" she answered. "What can I do for you?" She shrugged at Brendon's curious look. "There's been no change to the schedule if that's what you're worried about," she spoke into the link.

"Great. I've managed to get Osbourne listed as an inductee to the Elite. You'll have everything ready to go in four months?"

"It's cutting it close."

"But it can be done?"

"Of course."

"Good." Alex clicked off.

"Arsehole," Dianah swore as she hit the lift button.

They only had to wait a moment before the lift opened. Several people started to move out. One of them had a familiar face.

"Oh, David," Dianah called, startled. "This is a surprise."

David nodded allowing the last person to depart before responding. "Dianah. You're looking well."

"As well as ReJuv can make me, but you'd know about that." She shook his hand but read nothing from him. "I don't think you've met my partner, Brendon."

"David," Brendon acknowledged, reaching out to shake his hand. "From what I hear from Dianah, I understand congratulations are in order for SciCorp's rapid success. What secret projects are you working on now?" he asked jokingly. The moment he touched skin to skin, Brendon was able to enter David's mind.

He felt like he was on a cliff overlooking an ocean of data. The man's mind stretched to the *beyond*. Never had he experienced a mind so … so vast. Responding to the question, a myriad images flashed in his mind; a spaceship with an unusual column at its centre, the moon jumped at him then disappeared, an impossible city, a modified control panel in a cockpit. He also felt sensations, and registered ideas and thoughts … *time-travel?* … too many impossibilities—

"Pleased to meet you too, Brendon," David replied. "Strange. I sense we have some connection, though we've never been introduced. As to secret projects, I have far too many to mention." David winked.

It had only taken an instant.

"Oops." Dianah waved her arm to prevent the lift doors closing.

"Oh, my apologies to delay you both." David stepped away from the lift entrance as other citizens approached. "I should let you go."

"No bother at all." Dianah turned as she stepped in. "We should do drinks one evening."

"Sounds good to me. Send me a wave," David called out nodding to the other passengers.

Dianah had to wait until they were back in her apartments before they could safely speak. "So, spill. What did you find?" Dianah asked the moment her suite doors closed and locked.

Brendon wiped his brow. "I … I've never felt a mind like it."

"How much could there possibly be in that second or two of handshaking."

"You would not believe me," Brendon said. "I need a drink. You'll need one too."

Dianah stared at him for a moment. "This had better be good. The suspense is killing me." She went to the bureau and selected a single malt whiskey and two tumblers.

Brendon finished his whiskey and poured another one before Dianah's glass touched her lips.

"You're starting to worry me," she said.

"Probably best if you hold my hand and scan me first. Seriously, there is too much to say in words."

After a pause, Dianah drank her whiskey then put the glass down.

"We better sit," he advised.

They moved to the sofa and sat beside each other.

"Ready?" He reached out and held her hand. "Scan me."

Diana took a tentative breath, both intrigued and concerned with what she would find.

She gasped. It was true! She would never have believed him if he had told her, and there was far too much to say in an evening.

"Was that an ancient city – pre-cataclysm?" she asked, incredulous.

"I can only guess. Nothing like that exists anywhere now, but it was Earth. The old-style buildings and cars."

"You don't think it was simply a vid he had seen?"

"I doubt it. Maybe you didn't sense it, but I could smell and *feel* it; dirty, humid and polluted. He had *been* there."

"Amazing." She poured two more drinks. "And that spaceship. What was that?"

Brendon studied the whiskey swirling in his glass. "On the outside it looked like most other space-yachts I've seen … but the changes on the inside? I have no idea." He sipped his drink, considering. "To have visited a city destroyed over two hundred years ago … I can only hazard guess he's done the impossible."

"What is it?"

Brendon looked at her. "He's made … a … a time-machine?"

# 37

# ASTROGATION

"You know mum, I can get people to take those things for you?"

"I can manage two bags, Davey," Sussah replied, bringing luggage from the bedroom. "It's not as if I've been hoarding anything. Besides, there's not enough room here." She looked up as if hearing a distant sound. "Leonie will be here in a minute. Want a coffee?" Su left the bags by the lounge and unlocked the front door before stepping into the kitchen and making a fresh pot.

"Why not?" He turned as the door opened. "Hey, Leonie."

Leonie quickly stepped inside, barely stopping the door slamming behind her. "That was close," she laughed. "I nearly gave your neighbour a heart attack. Hello, *Davey*," she chuckled. "How have you been? I hear you've moved up in the world."

"Moving up?" Sussah came over and wrapped her arms around him. "He's a wealthy businessman now."

"Hardly wealthy."

"When is a couple of million credits not wealthy?" she asked, walking back into the kitchenette.

"When everyone else has a billion or two."

"He's got a point, Su." Leonie rolled her violet eyes. "You can't go around comparing millionaires to billionaires."

"Well, I'm still proud. And he's earned it, unlike those other parasites born into it." Su placed two mugs of coffee on the bench then got one for herself.

"You've changed, Leonie," Sussah observed. "Your fur is different. Shorter. Do you moult?"

Leonie picked up her mug and looked at it. "I umm … had an accident. I've spent the last week in Outpost 7 on the medicomp."

"You did? Why? How?" Sussah came over concerned, sitting beside her. "What did you do this time?"

"Do we have to discuss this now?"

"Yes," both Sussah and David said.

"Bugger," she growled. "The good news is, I learnt how to charge the portal; the bad news is, too much takes all my fur off and I lose my powers temporarily. I thought I'd recovered and tried to fly, but crashed instead."

"Crashed?" Sussah asked. "How bad was it to go into a medicomp for a week?"

"I had concussion, a fractured skull and a broken arm and leg." Leonie sipped her coffee.

"I have a medicomp, if you ever need it," David offered.

"Knowing Leonie, she'll need it regularly," Sussah patted her paw.

"Thank you, David, and thank *you* for the vote of confidence," Leonie growled at Sussah. She then updated her on the agtechs, the clones and the evacuation of Jenolan.

"That's horrible!" Sussah cried, clearly upset. "I'm so sorry to hear about Jojo."

"Many died, but many more were saved. Now they're depending on me to charge the portal so they can all escape to Yarnik. It will be difficult, but better for them in the long run." She put her mug down. "Mind if I use the bathroom?" She stood, following Sussah.

•  •  •

"I can't get over how well you've done. How did you make it so big, so soon, David?" Leonie asked, on her return. "It seems like only a short time ago I was contorting out of your air vent."

"Your last personal visit was two-and-a-half years ago," David confirmed. "TowerGov contracts mostly," he continued as she sat down. "After thorough research, I advised improvements and efficiencies in manufacturing and design of eighty-per cent of their services and products. That proved successful and the TowerGov were so impressed they kept giving me something else." He sipped his coffee. "To our benefit, everything before was so inefficient."

"And the wealth?"

"TowerGov *does* tend to have a monopoly on quite a few things." David looked down, getting a slight blush to his cheeks. "I get a percentage of the profits on top of a retainer as a special consultant. They sell on the improvements to the other towers."

"And apparently it's working. Now you've started out on your own?"

"Yes. All my tuition debt has been repaid years ago, and I've been legal to do what I want after my eighteenth birthday."

"I've missed so many of your birthdays," Leonie apologised.

"We both did," Sussah added. "Now they can pay for it."

"Sounds fair," Leonie agreed. "Ok, spill. What's the business and what will you be doing?"

"The business is SciCorp, and I'll be doing much the same as I've been doing the last few years; improving efficiency in design and manufacture, but also my own thing in robotics, astrophysics and the occasional special R&D project," David replied, running off a checklist.

"Sounds impressive, and I still haven't got a clue of half of what you're doing, but I get you're busy. All your education's finished, I gather?"

"One is always learning, but yes, no more school."

"And enough is enough," Sussah said sitting down next to him. "Two Masters degrees in both science and engineering, and a doctorate in astrophysics."

"Mum—" David protested, clearly embarrassed.

"I'm impressed. Well done, seriously. A real rags-to-riches story." Leonie raised her mug to him.

"Thank you." He nodded, blushing even more.

Leonie swallowed her coffee. "Su, what does young David know of *our* past?"

"Nothing. I just didn't know if and when it would be safe." Sussah looked at David's surprised face. She smiled nervously.

"I agree." Leonie nodded.

"What do you mean?" David asked, looking from face to face in bewilderment.

"David, you've never flinched at my appearance," Leonie started. "What if I told you I wasn't a mutation – a wilder – that what you see is part of a genetic experiment?"

"I never had any concerns about your unusual appearance because you were a friend of mum's, but I thought all genetic experiments stopped when Felton was arrested? I've not heard anything about it." He finished his coffee. "I've only seen the vids on mutants, or wilders, but you do look far more in proportion and well-developed than a 'normal' mutant. You are certainly different, but don't look *defective* in any way."

"He says the nicest things." Leonie smiled at Sussah before continuing. "I was around long before Felton, and I can guarantee this has nothing to do with him in the slightest. Your mum can vouch for that too."

"Okay. I'm intrigued. What's this *big* conspiracy?"

"No conspiracy. Facts." Leonie took another long swig before putting her mug down. "You said you remember everything?"

"Yes, both the good and the bad. It really isn't a blessing." David put his mug down.

"I can imagine. That can't be easy. What if I showed you something extremely complex?" She pulled out the orb from under her shirt.

Sussah came over and looked at it. "I've always admired that."

"Are they diamonds?" David moved around the table to

examine the orb. "As mum has said, I've three degrees. How complex can it be?"

"Hold my shoulder, both of you. I'm really going to enjoy this."

They each put one hand on Leonie's shoulders.

"Why?" David asked, perplexed.

"Because, David, I'm going to bitch-slap that smugness into orbit."

Leonie took a deep breath, concentrated and activated the Nightsky Orb. Immediately, the apartment vanished, replaced by the mesmerising starscape.

Both David and Sussah gasped.

"You're welcome," Leonie muttered.

David's grip on Leonie's shoulder tightened momentarily as if he was about to fall. He stared at the complete sphere of stars.

"So, genius, let's see if the three degrees including a doctorate in astrophysics mean anything? I'll wait."

"Where is this?" He breathed the words in awe.

"This is home, David," Sussah wept.

"I don't understand. I don't recognise any of these stars, but it all looks so real! Amazing VR."

"It is real, and I guess you *could* still call it VR. What you're seeing is the sky around a different world – Yarnik — psionically inserted into this orb. I have no idea where or how far away these constellations are. As your mum says this is the night sky seen from our world – where your mother and I are from."

"I can't believe this." David stared, mesmerised. "You can't be serious. For this to be the stars visible from your world, it would be hundreds if not thousands of light-years away. Humanity hasn't even managed manned space-travel past Mars!"

"It's all true, David." Sussah reached out for his hand. "I was born in a city called Delta. My parents – your grandparents – owned a tavern by the docks. Leonie saved me, and a crazy magician lady sent us here."

"Would you be able to locate Yarnik with this?" Leonie asked.

"There's an astrogation comp on my ship, linked to the computer in my office."

"You're the expert. I barely know what that means."

"I see you have a data implant – where you download data," David noted.

"I do, yes." Leonie dropped the vision and relaxed. The apartment returned.

"This is the same thing, but in reverse. I can transfer data, upload straight into my computer. We should continue this in my suite where I can do it directly."

"What apartment is it? I'll see if I can get there. Those white zone air-ducts are very tight."

"SciCorp has a quarter of the floor. North-east corner."

"You're doing that well?" Leonie asked, turning.

"Some of the research and development projects need a large area." He nodded, quite chuffed from his grin. "And I have a private loading dock on the east side. But it *is* two-thousand-nine-hundred-and-eighty metres high."

"That's no problem, but your private dock makes access much easier. What about security monitors and staff?"

"There are a couple of trusted people, but everything is automated. The security is mine as well – much to the annoyance of Icon."

"Icon?"

"They're a security and surveillance group, trying to butt in. Their reputation isn't great, especially since it's run by Alexander Zodaich. We don't see eye-to-eye on ... anything. Besides, I'm not trusting anyone else with any of my work. Some of it's quite sensitive government-contracted research."

"But not sensitive enough to tell *me*?"

"Somehow, I doubt you'll be wanting to go to the authorities. Besides, you're family."

"I'm ..." Leonie looked away, getting misty-eyed. "So, when will I be okay to fly up to the loading dock?"

"How about this evening?" David suggested.

"I guess the sooner we get started, the better," Leonie agreed.

"Since mum's moving in, and it's secure, there's room for you too," he added. "You can both have each other's company on a more permanent basis. I'll probably be away a lot."

"You're sweet, and I can tell you air-ducts don't make a nice home, and neither do zoos." Leonie wiped her eyes. "We'll see. Seriously though, do you think you can find Yarnik?"

"With this knowledge, I am sure of it, given time."

"I'll see you guys tonight then." Leonie gave him a quick hug, totally out of character. "Better turn off security for three minutes at 19:00. That's when I'll be there."

After sunset, Leonie landed on the edge of the SciCorp loading dock. She liked the flyer parked to the side, much smaller and sleeker than other craft she'd seen.

David was inside, in the docking area to meet her. "It is fascinating to see you fly, unaided," he said as he walked out. "There has to be a way to study how you do it, all of it." He paused, thoughtful. "Good timing, though. 19:01:25."

"What's that?" she stared at an aura of energy, like a blanket, covering the entrance to the building.

Dave looked to where she was looking. "You can see it?"

Leonie glanced at David. "You mean you can't?"

"No, it's invisible – or supposed to be – a kinetic force field to keep the worst of the air and winds out." He turned to her, looking at her eyes closely. "The faster an object is, the more resistance it will meet."

"Is everything okay," she asked, uncomfortable at the scrutiny.

"You have amazing eyes."

"Why, thank you."

"Oh, no, I meant to see that field – but you do have lovely eyes too. I mean—" He stopped at Leonie's chuckle, sounding much like a purr.

"It's okay David. I know what you mean. It's one of the things I've always been able to do. Another part of my genetic make-up; seeing in the dark, and things others can't."

"Sorry. My people skills sometimes need work, but I'd like to examine your eyes sometime too, to see what wavelengths they can see."

"I think we can manage that." She turned and pointed to the field. "Your invention?"

"Yes. A work-in-progress. I'd like to see it's practical implications ... and waiting for the next big storm to see if it functions as designed."

"I have no doubt it will." Leonie examined the sleek flyer parked to one side of the docking area. It was a surprisingly dull grey, unlike all the other flyers she had seen pics of, roughly fifteen paces long and half that wide at the stubby wings. "Is this the ship you talked about, with the astro computer?"

"No, this is for local flying. My other ship is locked away. It's part of my next project. Would you like to have a tour? Dinner perhaps, or we can do the data upload."

"That would be great." She glanced around, impressed at the docking facilities. "Wow. A proper meal. A girl can't live on nutripacs and protein bars alone."

"That's what mum says." David led the way inside. "Can I get you to look into this scanner for a second?"

"Is this for my eyes?" she asked as she looked into the scanner as requested.

"No, security. I have a couple of security cameras installed." He tapped at the small keyboard. "They use facial recognition. And that's done. The cam will ignore you like it does mum."

"Speaking of which, where is she?" Leonie walked around, amazed at the interior layout. There was so much room. She liked the lines of the white plush furnishings, and the contrast with the blue rugs. The floor was wall to wall white tiles, and the walls light blue.

"Mum's having a bath, she should be nearly finished for dinner."

"I'm glad, but surprised she's here. For so long, she wanted to stay where she was. What made her change her mind?"

"Remember the part about a bath? Underhanded tactics, I confess. Unlimited hot water supply, a bathroom larger than her whole apartment, real food and no more having to scrape out animal stalls at the zoo."

"Your mum's had to bear the brunt of tower life for so long. She deserves this; you both do."

"I told you my boy would look after me," Sussah said as she entered wearing a pale blue robe.

"Mum, I'm nineteen and two hundred days. I'm hardly a *boy*."

"If I'm staying here, you'll have to let me be a mum for a while." She ruffled his hair. "You will always be *my boy*."

Leonie shared their laughter. It was good seeing Sussah happy – in her life, there hadn't been much of it.


SciCorp was fascinating in every way. In the highly-secured research and development section, robots of various shapes and sizes were dutifully carrying out assigned tasks; if it could be automated it was.

"And you did this all in a year?"

"Slightly over, but yes. Development-wise, the tower is stagnating as are so many of the towers around the globe. Innovation is rare these days. My theory is because everything within the tower is the same day-in, day-out there's nothing to stimulate the senses, no changing weather, no changing seasons. Mankind was never meant to be hiding in a box – regardless of whether that box is three billion cubic metres."

"Why hasn't anyone worked this out before?"

"I don't know. Maybe they have but didn't have the resources or willpower to do anything about it. And then, there are those in control who like the status quo; they like the power, especially when they *are* the power."

"Sounds a bit like Delta. Our rulers there like having control.

I found it very entertaining in thwarting it." She walked around, turning in a circle. "I think what you're doing here is excellent. A shame it's for the betterment of the tower though. From my experience, not many here deserve it."

"I'd like to think it won't be just for this tower. The thousand other towers have their problems, Blue Mountains Tower isn't the only one, I agree, but there are those with a far less authoritarian attitude."

"Going to change the world, one tower at a time?"

"I can but try."

"What's in there?" Leonie looked at another closed-off section.

"One of my special R&D projects. Maybe it's … a time-machine," he replied quietly.

"Oh. Okay. Don't tell us." Sussah laughed.

"I'll show it to you one day when it's ready," David chuckled. "Let's get this orb data started, then we can eat and relax." The young scientist took them into an immaculate office. "This is where I do most of my work."

"This is far too tidy to be a workplace."

He tapped his head. "Actually, in here would be more accurate." He strode over to a large, plush chair by the desk. There were three large monitors arranged in front of the chair for efficient viewing. "This is a little gadget of my design."

"You do office furniture design too. How quaint," Leonie said.

"Not quite." He laughed and pointed to the back of the chair. From the headrest a thick bunch of fibres went into the floor. "This is hardwired into the computer where I run the astrogation software. It's like your data implant but takes ten times the data at three times the speed. The new metal we found has some amazing applications."

"And you need that much data that quickly?" Leonie turned to Sussah. "You think he's showing off?"

"I'm sure of it."

"If it's any consolation, it does give me a headache from time to time. I'm sure I will have a big one later this evening too."

Leonie looked at the front of the plug, but instead of seeing dozens of pins or holes, it was a circular depression. "Is this it? It looks very different from what I've seen."

"It's an optical contact." He brushed the back of his hair up, exposing a convex circular bubble. "This fits snugly into the pod when I'm seated. Much more efficient."

"Let me guess, your design?"

"Third version of the prototype. So then, I'll take my seat and plug-in to the computer. Once that's done, you can show us to your star sky and I'll get to work."

"What exactly will you do?" Leonie asked.

"The computer has every known star, galaxy, nebulae, quasar ..." He stopped when their eyes glazed over. "Once it's uploaded, I'll cross-reference what you've got with what I've got. What I see, the computer will see, then it will start crunching numbers. When that starts, it's dinner time."

David checked a couple of controls and turned the device on before sitting. He wriggled his head slightly before placing a light strap across his forehead. Once in place, he tapped a button on his armrest console. There was a slight hum and a faint snick.

The lights went out, and the Earth version of the night sky appeared as a hologram above them. A holo-keyboard also appeared in front of him.

"It's not as dazzling as your light show, but as far as I'm aware, there's nothing like it on the planet. I'm ready."

Leonie lifted the orb from under her jumpsuit top. "Su, if you want to join in, hold my shoulder and relax." She then put a paw on David's shoulder whilst holding her orb in her other paw. "Here we go."

Instantly the room disappeared, replaced by the Yarnik night sky. David's fingers started dancing over the holo-keyboard.

"Is that the Lock? I forgot how beautiful it is," Su said, pointing to the constellation.

"And Key, too," Leonie replied. "I'm sorry I didn't share it more often with you."

The trio remained silent; Leonie and Sussah lost in the moment while David did whatever a genius does.

"Since I can't move much, can you slowly rotate it for me, Leonie?"

"Sure." *I think.* With only the slightest bit of concentration, the whole starry sky slowly rotated to the left. She started to be enthralled by it all …

"Leonie? Leonie?"

"Hss … sorry. Finished?"

"Almost, just one rotation with it rolling downwards now."

At a thought, the sky moved again. When the Lock and Key constellations reappeared in the starting position, he gave the all-clear.

"Done," he said but remained reclined, eyes now closed.

"All of it?" Leonie relaxed and the office reappeared. She checked the time. *Forty-six minutes.* Activating it for that long was tiring.

"All done, yes." He waved his hand. "Feel free to make yourself at home. Eat, drink, relax. I'll be with you in a minute."

Sussah wiped her eyes.

"Hey Su, show me where the bathroom is?"

"I'll need to freshen up as well."

By the time they both returned, David was already seated, so they moved to their chairs. Only in the vids had Leonie seen a table laid out so orderly. At a signal from David, droids brought out trays of food – nothing too excessive as there were only three of them, but many of the dishes were unknown to either of them. David relished in explaining each dish. "And I have a small aquaponics section as well, so most of this is home-grown," David said when they were all seated at the table.

"David, this is so wonderful," Sussah's eyes were moist again.

"I have to say, I'm impressed," Leonie added, pouring the wine. "Su just showed me some of the apartment. It is amazing."

"In a way, I have to thank *you* for inspiring me. I don't believe any of this would be possible."

"Me? What? How? Su," Leonie turned to her friend. "David's hit his head or something."

"I'm serious,' David said. "You're an inspiration. You do readily what was once – still – regarded as impossible. No one can create fire or lightning, or fly without any tools or devices of some sort, yet here you are. And today I find you are now both an enigma. Even with today's advances, mankind hasn't left the solar system, and here I am, sitting with two ladies from a completely different world."

"Where many people can do the magic," Leonie reminded.

"And if you can do it here, who else can?" David asked.

"Not me," Sussah admitted.

"You have to believe in it completely," Leonie told him. "It's all done with the mind. If you doubt, then it won't happen, but I'm no teacher. You'll have to go to my world to properly under-stand what I'm doing."

Sussah coughed, looking to Leonie meaningfully.

"So David, would you like to go to our world?" Leonie asked.

David swallowed. "It will take some time for the computer to—"

"I meant the way your mother and I came here."

"You— we can do this now?"

"I think you should tell him all there is to know about this portal, and how you recharge it," Sussah said.


Over dinner, Leonie and Sussah shared the details of their lives, the portal, their trip, and how it began with Niaarin the power-shaper back in Delta. Taking cues from each other, they both refrained from mentioning the assault in the alley on that fateful night.

"So, batteries are sufficient to charge it?" David asked.

"No. They're too limited for what we need. I know it can be

done and how to do it, but I believe how much power is needed to keep it going will be a great deal. More than I can do safely. If five solar batteries drain me so much, and that only moved a couple of people on a mag-bike, I can't imagine what would be required to move every wilder and their supplies."

"I do have several portable power sources at my disposal, only one would fit in this flyer though. A larger vehicle would be needed to get any other powerpacs out there."

"I can fly beside you if you need more room."

"I think it best you sit with us. After your recent *incident*, I'm not comfortable with you exerting yourself more than necessary. I'd also like to examine you on the medicomp at some stage later on."

Leonie growled again. "Why is that?"

"Apart from the injuries you've already recovered from, your eyesight intrigues me. My medicomp is far more advanced than what the outpost has, and can give a far better analysis. I'm curious how you've remained virtually undetected all these years."

"It's no surprise, I've kept to air-ducts and generally at the quiet hours."

"And what about at the terminal?" He continued after her puzzled look. "I don't think you know … Look at this." David scrolled through his tablet for a moment. "Here."

Leonie looked at a vid. It was the feed from a drone as it passed over the train. "I was lying right there," she said.

"You are. Look very closely." He paused the vid, expanding the image. "If you know exactly where to look, there was the vaguest outline of something."

Leonie's eyes widened in surprise. "I'm invisible?"

"Let's say very well camouflaged. You didn't know?"

"Not at all. I was just hoping no one would see me – obviously."

"I suspect that's been the case many times. Your subconscious can also control your abilities to some extent."

Again, a phrase from Styx came to mind – *anything you put*

*your mind to will work.* "How about when we get back you science the shit out of me!"

"Sure thing. I can't wait."

"Fair enough."

They finished their meals, and moved to the lounges while the droids cleaned up.

"I'll probably regret asking this, but how will your computer determine where Yarnik is?"

"Space is unimaginably big. Imagine these glasses are stars, and you are on Yarnik." He moved the wine glasses a foot apart. "While they'll move across the sky because of the planet's rotation, these two stars will always look the same to you in your lifetime here on Earth.

"But if you were a very long way away – want to move over by the door?"

Leonie stood and walked to the door. "Here?" she called out across the room.

"What do they look like now?" David asked in reply.

"Other than they're much smaller, I can only see one because the other is behind it."

"Good." He waved her back, returning her wine glass. "You *know* there were two stars because you have seen them, and then you moved to a known location, so you naturally assumed that one star was behind the other. Now, what if you'd didn't see those stars before, and the distance was far greater?"

"I think I need another wine." Leonie sighed.

Sussah passed the bottle over. "And to think, I'm going to get this every day."

"I know, dreadful." Leonie joined her in a laugh. "So, the stars we see from Yarnik could be these same stars overhead here, but from a very different angle."

"Precisely. The program will look at hundreds of thousands of combinations to determine where I would need to be to see your stars."

"And that would show you where home is?" Leonie sipped again. She noticed Sussah's eyes were heavy as another thought occurred to her. "If space is so big, and you haven't flown past Mars, other than the portal, how would you get to Yarnik?"

"A time-machine could do it."

"Oh, that again." Leonie drank her wine and nibbled some of the cheese. "How?"

"How, is difficult to explain. There is space and time. They are inseparable. Like every other celestial body, Earth moves through space. If I wanted to go to Earth twenty years from now, I'd need to know exactly where that planet would be in space in twenty years. If I travelled through time alone, without taking placement into account, I'd only find empty space. And the same if I travelled in space only. Both must be taken into account.

"I said the astrogation comp can determine what stars you could see where. So knowing the planet's movement and speed etc., I'd program the computer to determine how I'd see the stars from that point. Then I'd go to that point, but that is only the space component. I've still got the temporal component to work out."

"And that's behind that locked door?"

"You'll see when I'm finished. I'm having a few minor setbacks, but progress is being made."

"In the meantime, let's go and see Yarnik with your own eyes?" She turned to David. "When can we go?"

"Being more or less my own boss, how about now."

Leonie turned to Sussah. "Want to see home again? For a brief visit?"

"That would be so wonderful, and you say you charged it?"

"We'll see how long it lasts, I guess."

"What say we go and investigate this portal of yours? I'm sure mum shares my concerns with you *powering* it yourself. Show me how you do that, and I'll see if it can be *improved*."

"Yeah. Dying is so inefficient, Leonie," Sussah said.

"Better take some warm clothing. The weather there is much different."

# 38

## SKYLAND REVISITED

Dianah switched off her comlink. "I just got notification David has left the labs in his flyer and should be away for several hours. That'll give us plenty of time to check out this project, and to confirm the clone is exactly what we need. I'll just go and collect 'David'."

As the elevator approached the fifteenth floor, Brendon took a big, nervous breath and looked to Dianah then at the clone. The resemblance was uncanny. It was in every sense identical to David Osbourne. It was a perfect replica as long as no one asked it anything. All clones had vocal chords, but because of the urgency, this one had no concept of language or cognitive thought, it was simply an unprogrammed biological computer, with only basic functions; walk, breathe, blink.

"Where's he off to at this time of night?" Brendon asked.

"Who knows with Osbourne. He's up and about all hours." She saw his look. "Oh yeah, we're keeping tabs on him."

The lift doors opened. The passage was empty.

*Walk.* Brendon willed.

The David clone stepped into the corridor.

*Turn left.*

The pair followed, walking quietly down the corridor

towards SciCorp's main entrance. This corporate section was deserted at this time of night. An automatic sliding panel in the wall opened when sensing their movement. The recess within had a handprint recognition device for entry.

Brendon willed David to place his right hand in, palm down on the display and say the password.

*Archaeopteryx.* "Archaeopteryx," David repeated into the small mic.

The main doors opened without a hitch. The three walked in.

The apartment was a surprise to them. With so much wealth at his disposal, it was quite utilitarian in furnishings, and only a few pieces of art adorned the walls.

Brendon willed the clone to the door at the far end of a corridor. Behind these doors was David's latest work, a time-machine – or what he thought was a time-machine.

The security at the door required voice, palm and retina scan, all at the same time. He got the clone to stare into the camera as he put his palm on the sensor and spoke the code phrase *"Per ardua ad astra"*. A red light blinked. *"Per ardua ad astra,"* he repeated.

The door clicked. He willed the clone to enter and followed, closing the door behind him. *Stop.*

There it was. On the outside, the *Skydancer* looked like a standard space-yacht – sleek and fast, but the surface of this one had a very different finish. Normally such craft gleamed with a highly polished surface or flashy murals. The *Skydancer* was quite bland in a flat monotone grey.

The David clone, given no further instructions, stood by the door where he'd stopped after entering. Brendon and Dianah walked up the small ramp into the central passageway, which ran across the width of the ship, and two passageways to the front and rear.

"There's the column?"

"As the memory showed, in the centre of the ship, but against the front wall."

The dark grey column reached from floor to ceiling. Other

than a blank metal-like surface the control panel was the only adornment. It had a display, several dials and buttons. No lights showed, but it vibrated slightly.

A quick search to the rear showed a standard engineering section and cabins. Moving to the front revealed an extra control panel in the command centre. In the top right-hand corner was a red-button labelled 'Emergency jump only'.

"That's it, without doing a thorough search. I don't think it a good idea to touch it."

They wandered back to the unusual column. "If it works, it could be very interesting."

"We'll go back through your mind and see if we can understand how it works," Dianah suggested.

Brendon willed David to follow, and they made their way back to Dianah's apartment.

Later that evening, with 'David' in stasis in the HelixR R&D labs, Dianah and Brendon discussed the *Skydancer*. "Can we confirm, Alex doesn't need to know about this?" he asked.

"Of course. I don't think, with his paranoia, allowing him access to a time machine would be a smart move."

"Assuming it works," Brendon pointed out.

"This is David Osbourne we're talking about. If he's been to a pre-apocalyptic city, I have no doubt it works."

"But does it go forward? I don't recall seeing any future scenes in his mind."

"Maybe he hasn't been forward yet. Either way, let's not quibble; going back in time should be enough of a spectacular achievement."

"Maybe you could stop your father from being arrested," Brendon suggested.

"There's this paradox I recall from my studies about going back in time to change or modify an event, but if you did, the reasons for you to go back into the past wouldn't have happened, so you'd never go back in the first place, but if you didn't go back, then the event would happen ..."

"I don't understand."

"It's an age-old argument that what has happened, happened, and you can't change the past," Dianah explained.

"Too deep for me."

"Well, we can experiment with it once Alex's plan is implemented."

"And that reminds me, once the clone is gone, how do we then get back into SciCorp's labs?"

"I guess I better make an eye and right hand."

"You can do that?" Brendon asked.

"We won't need a complete clone. Growing body parts for organ transplant is standard. ReJuv can do a hell of a lot, but when it can't, we rely on DNA replication. You, on the other hand, will need a bit of homework."

"Me? Why?"

"David's vocal cords. Your voice is very similar. A few hours practice with voice recognition software and you'll be able to talk exactly like him."

———

David flew north when they left the tower. "Even for me, a ship heading west straight from the tower might draw attention, especially if it's done several times," David explained as he took off. "For now, we'll head northwest towards the badlands pit mines, then make a slight detour. Are we comfortable?"

"Surprisingly, yes. The seats mould to fit," Leonie answered.

"It's more comfortable than what I'm used to," Sussah added.

"I have a question," Leonie started. "What happens when you turn towards the portal. Won't sensors in the tower pick that up?"

"You may have noticed the lacklustre finish to the flyer?"

"Yes." Leonie and Sussah nodded.

"Surprisingly bland for such a speedy little craft, if any of the vids I've seen are anything to gauge by," Leonie observed.

"We have this new metal … though it has strange qualities. It is so dense and malleable, that even a small amount can be stretched and flattened into a foil or even a mesh. Some of my recent research has shown that when an electric charge at a specific frequency is applied to the mesh, it can disperse radar and light."

"Which means what, exactly?"

"It means we can be invisible."

"That's handy," Leonie agreed.

The flight to the portal was extremely fast. Leonie was amazed at the speed. Other than appearances, everything about it said sleek, efficient and expensive.

They landed on the edge of the pinnacle, with the tail section and some of the fuselage hanging over the cliff. Amazed at the portal, David offered to study it.

"Maybe study can come later," Leonie suggested, unclipping her buckle. "Do you think the flyer will fit?"

"I'll check the dimensions, but I doubt it." He raised the canopy and hopped out, sliding the short distance to the ground and walked the few paces to the portal. Sussah and Leonie followed.

After a closer inspection he shook his head. "Unfortunately, the dimensions aren't compatible." He studied the shimmering effect – a slight luminescence which made the area within the portal a shade lighter than the surrounding night.

He put his finger in briefly, feeling a very cold sensation. "Interesting," he muttered. Looking down he saw the spent solar batteries. "They're flat?" he asked. "Show me how you charge it."

Leonie dragged the closest battery closer and went through the motions. "I can draw the charge *through* me into the portal surface. I do this over and over until it is powered up. It could take more charge. I don't know."

From a pocket in the flyer, David pulled out a small tool and a clear plastic bag. He then tapped and scraped at the surface of the portal for a sample of the material, but nothing came off. "It sounds neither like stone or metal."

"My world has a lot of crystal, though I've not seen anything like that," Leonie told him.

"Either way, it's nothing I've seen before."

"If the flyer won't fit, we'll go on paw. The trip will still be cold and uncomfortable for a minute, and it will more than likely be cooler on the other side."

"We better grab our gear then."

Leonie flew up to the cockpit, grabbed her backpack, then tossed two jackets down. When she landed she handed him his heavy satchel.

With a remote, David closed the flyer canopy.

Sussah donned her jacket, rubbing her hands nervously. "I'm not looking forward to the trip, but can't wait to see Yarnik again."

"Shall we? I'll go first. Deep breath." Leonie flew into the shimmer.

"We'll cope." Sussah held David's hand and stepped through after Leonie.


Leonie zipped through the portal, the effects not as severe the third time through. She landed on the grass, surprised at the bright sunshine. There was a cool breeze as she scrunched her claws into the cool, soft turf, before moving back to the portal, in anticipation. She checked the charge on the torc. *All good.* She put it back.

A few minutes later, Sussah and David stepped through. David stumbled to his knees. Leonie caught him, so it wasn't a hard fall onto the paving.

"Ccold and … uncomfortabble is an understatement." David shivered.

Sussah hugged him, partly in concern but also because she was cold as well.

Leonie rubbed their backs and shoulders. "If you open your eyes, you might forget being cold. Welcome home, Sussah."

Sussah looked up and around. David got up off his knees. Leonie then assisted them over to the grass.

David immediately crouched and ran his hands through the green blades, feeling the texture and the dampness. The look on his face gave Leonie a warm, fuzzy feeling.

"Better than researching in a stuffy office?" she asked.

The trio remained silent, soaking in the moment.

"Let's go for a walk," she suggested.

Before they stepped off, David pulled a drone out of his satchel, tapped a few small buttons on its side and tossed it in the air. It buzzed as it powered up, hovering for a few seconds before rising to fifty metres and then heading off.

"It will go for two kilometres north, then do a full circle with me as the centre and return."

"This is a skyland. We're already about twice as high as your tower." She scrolled for the altimeter on her wrist-com. "Mine's not working."

"It's ok. The small drone computer will have compensated for it with its internal altimeter. I can see what it sees." His wrist-com displayed a holo of the view. "What ruins are they?" he asked, showing her the view as the drone whizzed past.

"I think they are the remains of Dromas. The belief is these skylands were a result of the Power Wars – or magic wars." At his curious look, she explained in detail about the wars and beliefs about the skyland origins.

She turned and walked through the wooded area to the nearest ruin, the one the l'ith had torn down when chasing her. There wasn't much to see, but considering David lived in a massive modern tower, he'd never seen rotting wood or decay before and thought it was all fascinating.

"Are you going to take a vid or pictures?" Sussah asked.

"No need, mum." He tapped his head.

Leonie chuckled. "Something else you might be interested in." She wandered over to a different section of the woods.

The carapace of the l'ith remained where it died. A subtle odour of decay lingered still.

"Think this will stay in your memory?"

"Undoubtedly." David looked in a daze as he got closer. "I've never seen anything like it … an ant, larger than an elephant, with two extra pair of legs. What's it called?"

"L'ithnamagri. From what I've heard, these and the wyverns are native to this world. Everyone else is from elsewhere. If we had the flyer, you could see them for yourself, the seven races here. You think I'm unusual, wait to you see the shapeshifters or the hroltahgs. If there *is* a next time, we'll bring mag-bikes. I know they fit through."

David was closely examining the l'ith. "This is all so utterly amazing." He knocked on the shell. "Hollow. How did it die?"

She pointed to the fire damage around the head. "I fire-blasted it, then gored it with a javelin."

"You did this?"

"A couple of glins'ool warriors helped. I was weaker then too. Not that I'd want to take one on now either."

After walking around the entire carapace, they strolled to the nearest edge, watching the landscape far below. Presently, the drone returned, landing just behind him on the grass. David picked it up and tapped further instructions, then tossed it over the edge.

"I'd like to see the structure underneath. See why the land around here can float."

"Crystals. There is a large amount of crystal in the ground."

"Intriguing," he said, looking at the vid feed.


They spent the better part of an hour walking around the skyland before returning to the portal. The trio was reluctant to leave.

"It will always be here. You can pop over any time, as long as it's charged." Leonie walked closer, examining the shimmering. "I'm trying to gauge how much charge is left to work out what it needs per transit. Since the last charge, it's had a round-trip with two people and a mag-bike, and now us three."

"Oh," Sussah said. "Leonie, here's your grav-belt. Where you left it."

"What's that?" David looked at the device Sussah brought over.

Leonie explained its origins, its initial purpose, and how she used it afterwards. "I'm guessing, but I believe this is how I learnt the basics of flying. A crystal powered it, now broken. And I learnt the fire-blast with a ring."

"Will you need this anymore? I'd like to study it." David held it in his hands, moving it around to look at it from every angle. "Interesting material. Any idea what it is?"

"None whatsoever." Knowing exactly the metal's origins, Leonie turned to hide her grin. "I'd be interested to hear what you find, though. It's all yours, but you're carrying it." She noticed some clouds drifting closer. "I reckon it's going to rain soon. Shall we go?"

David looked up. "Rain? I've not had it before."

Leonie stopped. "Of course you haven't." She sat on the pond wall where Sussah joined her. "We'll warm up and dry the moment we get home."

David stood there when the rain fell, putting his arms out, opening his mouth and sticking his tongue out to catch the cold droplets.

"Just a big kid, really," Leonie laughed.

"*My* big kid," Sussah sniffed.

**39**

---

## THE SUM OF ALL THINGS

"GOOD MORNING," DAVID GREETED LEONIE AND SUSSAH AS HE entered the kitchen. "I see breakfast has been made."

"These droids are remarkable. Your design?" Sussah asked.

"Only a modified program. They're pretty good cooks, but great surgeons too."

"Surgeons?" Sussah paused her eating.

"Oh yes. Fully programmable." He sat down beside his mother and tapped out his breakfast on the table menu. "Leonie, after breakfast, I'd like to run that diagnostic over you."

"Diagnostics? I'm not a machine." She eyed the droids moving about.

"My apologies. Bad terminology. How about a quick check-up. State-of-the-art medical software to make sure everything is functioning as it should be."

"It could be interesting. It might answer a few questions of my own too."

"And after, I'll get to work on a portal charging method. I had some ideas last night."

"That would be great too. The wilders aren't safe where they are."

"How will they get to the portal? It's not exactly easily accessible."

"I had initially considered using an aircraft to lift it and take it to them," she said. "Since the portal on the skyland works after moving around, I don't see why this one wouldn't work either."

"It would appear the location or orientation isn't paramount," David agreed. "If what you say is true – and I have no doubts it is – the portals were made before other species came to your world. How did it get here? If there are seven different species – seven different homeworlds – then only an advanced race could have created and placed them." He stopped as his breakfast arrived.

"I certainly haven't got a clue."

"And of course, the other question is why did they do this?"

They pondered this silently while consuming breakfast and fresh coffee.


"What do you hope to achieve with this examination?" Leonie asked as she climbed onto the medicomp. It didn't look too different from the Outpost 7 medicomp, other than being in pristine condition.

"It will give us a rundown on your overall physical condition. The advanced programming might pick up something not discovered by the older version." David adjusted the device and set the program. "Those outpost medicomps were already superseded when they were installed. Too expensive to put new devices out there, especially considering the minimal usage. You mentioned you had some questions?"

"I'm not what I appear," she said.

"You aren't?"

She laughed. "Maybe that depends on what you see." She stopped laughing. "What *do* you see, David?"

He looked at her for a long moment. "Distinct feline features – the eyes, claws, fur, whiskers, tail and ears ... but also definite female human features as well: facial features, breasts, general body shape, voice, but no clear distinction between; a subtle blend."

"Now I'm starting to sound like coffee. One of the races on Yarnik is the rrell. They are far more cat-like, but as you know there are seven races. I'm led to believe other than the main rrell-human traits you can see, I have illios and hroltahg DNA as well."

"You know about DNA? Did you learn about that here?"

"I learnt more about it here, but no. I was told by those that created me. I'm genetically engineered, as part of some damn experiment."

"Genetically engineered? How is that possible? Surely not magical?"

"I was *made*. They were using the genetic material of all the other races; mixing them up to see what they'd get. Trying to make something better for their own personal gain."

"You think you have other genetic material as part of you?"

"Yes. It would be good to know what and how. It might explain other things."

"What other things? The magic?"

"Maybe, I don't know, but I can heal faster ... maybe a bit like your ReJuv? I'm more agile than a normal rrell, and you know I have some telepathic abilities. My *mentor* told me it is very rare for anyone to be able to do all these things, yet here I am, flying and using fire and electricity like a powershaper. I can read minds, I can manipulate people's thoughts and actions to some extent. You know I can see things others can't. I want to know what I'm really capable of. Can you tell me that?"

David stood silently for a minute, considering. "I will. If not with this examination, I will develop tests to find out everything we can about you."

"I can't thank you enough. It's bugged me for a long time."

There was a ping.

"Done."

"That was quick?"

"I like to think it was more efficient. Let's get a coffee and see the results." He disconnected her and she stood up. "Leonie, you showed me a whole new world when I thought it was an impossibility for us today," he said as they left the medbay and strolled back to the kitchen."Helping you is the least I can do to repay you. Do you know who did this? How can somebody on a non-tech world know anything about gene-splicing?"

"We had some ruthless people running Delta. There's Lord Zander, but I've never met him, maybe when I was much younger, but I don't remember. Then there were two other associates. I think they did most of this without Zander's knowledge or approval. Their names were Lady Dianah and Lord Brendon."

"What?" David said, stunned. "That can't be a coincidence."

"What do you mean?"

"I know a Dianah and a Brendon." David grabbed two mugs and poured coffee.

Leonie gave him a description of the pair from her vague memories of two decades ago.

"I was going to tell you this later, but from what you just told me, now would be best." He took a deep breath. "We had intruders last night while we were on your world."

"Intruders? Here? I thought this place was secure."

"The only access granted is for three people, me, mum, and you." He put his tablet on the table showing a vid of the entrance.

Leonie looked to the ceiling, judging where the cam was placed by the angle. The door opened, and she saw David walk in. "That's you!"

"Keep watching."

Moments later, two more figures entered.

"That only looks a bit like Brendon, but that is definitely Dianah. Much younger though! How is this possible?"

"How is anything lately possible? We've done several *impossible* things; you do impossible things daily."

"Well, I don't want to brag," she tried to joke. "Are your Brendon and Dianah telepathic?" she asked.

"Can you tell visually? I've no idea otherwise." They continued to watch the three figures walk to the corridor. The camera followed until they were out of view but reappeared on the next one. "That's the entrance to my lab," he told her. The 'David' on the cam opened the doors and Brendon and Dianah followed.

"How do you know them? Have they read your mind? I can't, by the way. You've got some natural defence."

"It's not natural. When you mind-messaged me back in university, I then knew all the stories about telepathy were true, though I didn't know any telepaths before then. You know I remember everything. People will use this to their advantage if they can. With proof that telepathy is real, I endeavoured to work out how I could shield my thoughts. Eighteen months ago, TowerGov allowed me to work on one of their projects—"

"The new metal?"

"Correct. I said earlier this evening it has amazing applications. When I redesigned the wet-wiring, I incorporated a fine mesh of this new metal. It works." He pointed back to the vid. "I only met Brendon recently. He is Dianah's new partner– "

"As they were in Delta! What else?"

"And Dianah is involved with genetics. She runs HelixR."

"They clone animals for the zoo," Leonie said. *And I rescued Rhiannon from them!* "HelixR are using wilders for something."

Sussah came in at that point. "What's this about the zoo and HelixR?"

Leonie continued. "Yes, but years ago it also had a sister company—"

"GenLabs. Dr Stefan Felton ran it, as we both know!"

"How do you know about Felton?" Sussah asked. "You were only a boy then."

"I read about him." David looked away uncomfortably. "In my studies."

"There's something you're not telling me." She stepped closer. "Look at me, Davey. What do you know?"

"Have a seat, mum." David sighed, then told her how he

researched GenLabs' activities, found out about the cloning, and was responsible for Felton getting arrested, and the ramifications afterwards.

"You did it? Not Leonie?" Sussah turned to Leonie, who studiously examined the ceiling. "Leonie! You let me think it was you all this time?"

"Well, I *did* say I didn't do it."

"And you knew David did it, didn't you?" Sussah accused.

"Maybe. We had an agreement. There was no point with you being angry at him. I knew it would be alright in the end."

"How could you possibly know that?" Sussah asked.

"Lucky guess?" Leonie offered.

"Both of you should've told me." She wiped her eyes.

The three remained silent.

"Sorry mum. I was an angry kid at what he did to you," David said softly. "To us."

"Oh, Davey." Sussah hugged him. "You're an idiot."

He nodded, returning the hug. "I try to blend."

"So then," Sussah said when she pulled away. "Why were you talking about the zoo? What's that got to do with the examination?"

"We were discussing Leonie's origins. The examination might reveal some of it, but we will see. One other thing I've noticed is aging."

"I've seen the ReJuv injections in the bathroom. Why is that? You're only twenty," Sussah asked, a touch of concern in her voice.

"I have a condition – I age quickly. However," he continued as Sussah was about to say something, "I've noticed neither of you has barely changed in twenty years. I was stumped as to why, but after you told me about your transference I made a tenuous connection. You must have been pregnant during the transfer. I've yet to conduct testing on that, but now I think it's related."

"What does the aging mean then?"

"It's nothing to worry about, really. The only similarity to progeria is the actual aging effect, I don't have any of the other issues. The ReJuv, and the medicomp, keep me as you see. The up-side of this is you two are the opposite – barely aging at all."

"The powershaper that sent us here, she worshipped Eternix, the deity for Time."

"How many deities do you have on Yarnik?"

"There are eight major temples, based on the elements; Fire, Water, Life, death, Air, Earth, Spirit and Time."

"So, her deity was involved?" David shook his head.

"Not the goddess herself, but her power, Time in this case. I've seen various sects do things based on their element. The Temple of Woorin play with fire, the Temple of Opsyss play with the dead."

"Play with the dead? Surely not."

"Yes. Undead I think is a term used. I've killed the same assassin three times so far. I've not encountered her for twenty years now, so maybe she's staying dead." Leonie went on to describe her encounters with Evlin, the Jart'lekk assassin.

"This is ... incredible." David looked from Leonie to his mother.

"And it's taken us away from the other discussion," Leonie pointed out. "Dianah and Brendon. It's too coincidental."

"But how is it possible they got there? There's no ship capable."

"All I know is they arrived, crashing in some craft over a century before I was around."

"Over a hundred years?" David asked, surprised.

"Aren't there tower elites as old?"

"True, but we have ReJuv and advanced medication."

"We have gods and magic," Leonie countered. "And as we've seen, it works."

"Can you describe this ship?"

"As big as a whale, sort of dull-looking, like your flyer, but much larger. It was called the *Skydancer*."

David sat down heavily.

"What is it, Davey?" Sussah reached for him. "Are you alright?"

He looked dumbly from one to another. "Let me show you something."

Looking at each other quickly, Leonie and Sussah followed as David walked to the top secret project door.

"*Per ardua ad astra*," he spoke into the sensor. while he did the retinal and fingerprint scans. The door clicked open. He pushed it wide and waited, silent.

Leonie walked in, speechless.

Sussah squealed in delight. "You've got one of these?"

"Not for long, it seems," David said. "Mum, Leonie. Here's the *Skydancer*. My time-machine prototype."

"I don't understand," Sussah said, looking back and forth between them.

Leonie explained. "The rulers of Delta are Alexander, Dianah and Brendon. They stole this and, somehow, crashed near the original tower, where the palace now stands."

"How could they do that?" Sussah asked.

"With Leonie's Nightsky Orb and my astrogation program, I *will* find Yarnik. I *will* be visiting Delta. At some stage after that, they *will* steal it."

"Then you can stop them," Sussah said. "So they don't steal your work." She looked around in wonder.

"No. I can't do that," David stated.

"You have all the resources and credits you need—"

"Mum, it's not a matter of my ability to stop them, I *won't* stop them." He explained further as he led them up the ramp. "If I stop them, they won't do whatever it is they're going to do."

"Why is that a bad thing?"

"If I prevent them from stealing the *Skydancer*, they won't crash on Yarnik, Delta will not exist. It was their arrival that made Delta possible. If Delta doesn't exist, you or I won't exist. And since it has already happened, it can't be – must not be – stopped."

Leonie walked to the medicomp and looked around. "The last time I was in this room, I killed them. Right here."

"You killed Dianah and Brendon?" Sussah looked pale. "How …"

"They went back in time," David explained. "You said they crashed over a hundred years before you were born, but then you travelled here and stayed for twenty years."

"They were older when I saw them too."

"I can hazard a guess they were out of ReJuv. The medicomp can only do so much."

"Still not making sense to me," Sussah said, clearly flustered.

"At some stage soon," Leonie explained. "They will steal the *Skydancer*. They will travel *back* in time, to Delta."

"If they crashed, then something went wrong. I can assume they were stuck, unable to repair it."

"But it could still fly," Leonie explained it was inside the cavern under the palace. "Not a place they could have landed, since it didn't exist at the time." She continued her explanation. "It's because of their presence, Delta will be built. Dianah will carry out her experiments and I will be created. After eighteen years, when I find out more about *me*, I'll be tricked to come back, to this very room. Dianah and Brendon will trap me to get some genetic material before getting rid of me.

"We fight – they wouldn't know about my powershaping – though I was much weaker then. I blasted them before I left, then blew the cave up. A week or so after that, I meet Sussah. Then we get teleported from the palace to the skyland, then we turn up here."

Deep in thought, they left the *Skydancer* and walked back to the kitchen.

"You're saying Alexander Zodaich is Lord Zander?" Sussah asked. "Nicholai Zodaich's son?"

"Yes. He's paranoid now. I can only imagine how he must be being marooned for so long."

"And since Dianah is a geneticist working for HelixR …"

"As you'd expect from Stefan Felton's daughter."

"Then who is Brendon?"

"No idea. I only just met him and have never heard of him before."

"There are—"

"*Never* heard," David repeated.

"You said that," Leonie said.

"Because it's important. He isn't from the tower. No record of him anywhere." David paused. "We shook hands briefly two days ago. It's weird though. I thought there was some connection ... I felt *something*. A familiar bond ... I can't describe it, though I've read about something similar from our history." He paused in deep consideration. He turned to look at his mother. "You had twins."

The colour drained from Sussah's face. "How could you possibly know that?" Her voice trembled as she leant on the table.

"I can't explain it exactly – I was only a foetus, after all – but I have a definite recollection of another ..."

"I was unconscious ... I ... never saw him, only you." She sat down and told them both about her labour. "I was told he was stillborn."

"Did Harrond know?" Leonie asked, came over and held her hand when the first tears welled up.

She nodded, tears welling. "We kept quiet though. We couldn't afford any trouble of scrutiny. Excuse me." She got up and went to the bathroom.

"If he was stillborn ... I reckon he was smuggled out, not knowing who he really was. You don't know him because the wilders raised him." *I wonder if Rhiannon knows of him?* She considered before continuing. "When you and Brendon contacted each other, you felt it?"

"I felt something *familiar*." He shrugged. "That's the only way I can describe it." David sat silently for a while.

"Can I try to scan your mind?" Leonie asked.

"What?" His silence was broken by Leonie's question. "Sure," David waited.

Leonie concentrated. "Nope, nothing. Now, give me your hand." She put her paw out. "Now think of something." She held his hand. "You're thinking of a designing a new time-machine since this one will be stolen."

"So I can still be read—"

"With physical contact only. He scanned you the moment he shook your hand."

"It was only for a second."

"In a mind link, information can transmit very quickly."

"Especially if they know what questions to ask. Just before we shook, he asked what secret projects was I working on. I thought it was a joke at the time."

"So, they suspected you were up to something. Now they've confirmed it."

"What are your plans now?"

"No change, really. I still need to continue and do my experiments as normal, otherwise this will fail and none of us will exist."

"Okay, so how would they steal it? Can't they access the dock?"

"The dock is protected by lasers. If you'd used a ship to fly in, instead of *magically*, your onboard computer would have registered warnings. If you didn't comply, you'd get shot down. As you saw, the only access here is through the security door – voice recognition, password, retina and fingerprint scans. Each one in itself not impossible to do, but to do all three …"

"And yet …"

"They used a clone. It's what I would've done, and they have the resources to do it."

"Wouldn't it be easier if they simply controlled you?"

"I don't think they are anywhere near your strength."

"They aren't," Leonie confirmed.

"Then you have your answer – they cloned me. And when we shook hands, read me."

"What will they do with *you* you?" Leonie wondered.

"It would be too risky to keep me alive." He deliberated. "So, we'll have to make sure when they kill me I can die on my terms."

"You're calm about dying," Leonie observed.

"Not *real* dying, and worrying or changing my routine will alert them."

"How will they know how to use the time-machine?"

"Let's assume they've read what they needed. Can you imagine the power someone would have? A time-machine would be priceless to anyone. That's why no one knows about it, not even TowerGov."

"They don't?"

"None. You saw my flyer, it has stealth capabilities. Invisibility to radar," he explained. "They think I'm developing that on a larger scale – which I am. If TowerGov knew I was experimenting in time-travel, they'd want it for themselves, and the military.

"In the wrong hands, this could destroy or change history. And that, I will not allow. At least, not until I know how it works, how to police it and how to stop it."

"You can do that?"

"I'll have to, won't I?"

# 40

# SHIMMER EFFECT

"How about we go charge the portal?" David said as he emerged from his lab.

"You've got the charger working?" Leonie looked up from her breakfast. He looked dishevelled after two days of absence.

"I believe so, but we won't know for certain until we test it," he replied.

"And then the wilders can be evacuated."

"One thing at a time," David cautioned. "We can only plan on that after a successful recharging." He sat down and ordered his breakfast.

"You know, I can't believe how stupid I've been," Leonie complained.

"In what way?" David asked.

"Ever since we arrived here, I've seen signs that Earth was the origin of the *Skydancer* and Delta's rulers. The same medicomp in the outpost, the same language, the genetic research. We both knew of the cloning ten years ago ... and still nothing registered."

"You can't blame yourself. You were both thrown into a whole new world. It must have been an extremely traumatic experience."

"That argument is fine for the first few months, but remaining ignorant for *twenty years?*"

"Leonie, if you did anything different, then we may not be sitting here today. You knew how to recharge the portal, and maybe even had the opportunity to leave." He paused as his breakfast arrived. "You mentioned this was foreseen in a prophecy? Something I would have ignored previously, but there are too many coincidences. All I can say is – and it surprises me to even contemplate it – *something* is happening beyond our understanding … some grand plan. We're just playing our parts."

"Morning." Sussah entered wearing her bathrobe. "What are we playing?"

"The game of life," Leonie replied.


The *Skydancer* reappeared a few thousand metres above the portal. David descended, landing in the ravine below.

"That was incredible," Leonie exclaimed. "And way faster than the flyer."

Sussah nodded in agreement. Though she looked pale, the colour was coming back.

"You sure you can get all this gear up there?" David asked Leonie as they walked towards the central cross-passage. Various instruments, a large powerpac and a tool-box were secured to the wall with robust straps.

"As sure as you are about your recharger working," Leonie answered. "But, it will take a couple of trips."

"I'll stay down here for the moment," Sussah said.

"This shouldn't take long." Leonie lifted the powerpac and flew up to the portal, then repeated the process three times. "Your turn, David. Unless you want to climb?" When he shook his head, she lifted him like the powerpac and gently landed beside the rest of the equipment thirty-seconds later.

"Amazing," was all he said.

Leonie watched curiously as he set up the equipment. There

was a cable leading from the powerpac to two spring-loaded metal U-clamps, with a control box in-between. David opened each clamp wide enough to wrap around the outer half of the portal. Between the clamps lay a network of wire filaments. The result looked similar to the metal net wrapping the outer half of the structure.

"I'm not risking putting *through* into the portal in case it disappears," David explained. "As long as it has sufficient contact to the surface, it will suffice." He then set up a device on a levelled tripod. The device was then raised so it could be aimed at the centre of the portal.

"I'm taking readings of the shimmering now, and we can make comparisons while it's charging."

"How are you doing that?"

"Various ways; measuring light emission, reflection and refraction. That bowl of iron filings – simplistic but sometimes we can over-science things – will gauge any changes in the magnetic field. This device," he positioned then activated a large, black cylinder, "will detect any tachyons coming from the portal."

"I can see it. It looks like your force field back at SciCorp's dock."

"You can? Ok. I shouldn't be surprised. Well, if any tachyons come through, they will register here."

David stepped back to the portal and checked the metal web was in contact with the portal surface before adjusting the various settings on the control box. "Here we go." David flipped a switch, then slowly turned a dial, watching the small readout. He then went to the tripod and watched the readout.

"How long will it take?" she asked.

"At this stage, it's pure conjecture. First we'll see if there's an increase in the shimmer effect."

"And if there's no increase … then either it doesn't work, or it's at max already."

"Correct." Moving back to the powerpac, he said, "This pac is fully charged. Over time, we'll see if it decreases."

"It's like the powerpacs of the larger agtech machines."

"Yes. Good for a decade or so of constant use." He looked at the display on the side. After a few taps on the panel he said, "It's down a few amps, so something is happening. I could try charging at a faster rate, but safer is best for now if there's no urgency."

They returned to the *Skydancer* where David could monitor the various devices on his remotes while waiting and gave Sussah a progress report.

"What's the range of those?" Leonie asked, pointing to the readouts.

"It varies, but if it's line-of-sight and good weather, it can be a couple a hundred kilometres or so."

"So, we could visit the wilders and still monitor?"

"Certainly."

Leonie turned to Sussah. "How about we say hello to some friends?"

"Yes, please. Why did you think I came along?"


It took a few minutes to reach Westridge.

*Hi Rhiannon,* Leonie sent out a greeting. There was no response. "David, would a telepathic signal get out of your ship?"

"I'm afraid not. The meshwork I have coating the outside would prevent that."

Looking out the viewport, they saw everyone scatter.

"That confirms that, then." Leonie's breath fogged the glass.

Once they landed and the door opened, the three of them stepped out, looking around at the deserted area.

Leonie sent out another greeting. *Rhiannon, Lana, it's Leonie. Sorry about that.*

*Well, of course, it is. Hello, Leonie.*

*Some forewarning would have been appreciated,* Lana sent.

Not long after the landing the wilders emerged from the caverns and hiding places.

"I tried, but my thoughts couldn't penetrate the ship's hull."

"No harm done," Rhiannon replied, looking at the craft. "I'm surprised no one detected it."

"What about the radio?" Lana asked. "Did you think of that?"

David nodded. "Most certainly, but radio silence would be better."

"Sussah! I don't believe it," Lerry called out. He and Harrond came running.

Sussah turned just in time to be swept up in a bearhug by Lerry and then Harrond.

"What are you guys doing here?" Lerry asked.

"Recharging the portal *properly* this time." Leonie then explained how David had adapted a powerpac to charge the portal safely.

"I'm glad. You had us worried when you slammed into the cliff," Lana said. "You healed very quickly. I didn't think you'd make it."

"I've learnt my lesson," Leonie replied. "And I have Lerry and Harrond to thank for taking care of me." She noticed Harrond and Sussah had moved away and were talking quietly to one another. *That's nice to see. She hasn't had much reason to be happy for years.*

*Harrond has been remote too,* Rhiannon agreed. *They are good for one another.*

"How have things been here? Everyone settled in?"

"There are a few teething problems," Lana answered. "Too many extra bodies and cramped conditions."

"If the recharging goes according to schedule, we can start the transfer, then you'll have far more areas to live."

"I hope so, but I'll remain sceptical until proven otherwise."

"Fair enough."

"Would anyone like a tour of the *Skydancer*?" David asked, sensing a mood change with the group.

Several wilders nodded enthusiastically, including Lana.

"Aren't you coming?" Lana asked Rhiannon as David led them to the entrance.

"I'll be with you shortly," Rhiannon replied. "I'd just like to say hello again to Sussah."

David, Lana, and half a dozen wilders boarded the ship.

"Is she always such a pessimist?" Leonie asked after the group left.

"She is pragmatic, less of a dreamer than me," Rhiannon smiled.

"Less of a *seer*, you mean."

"These are trying times, and there has been increasing trouble from the badlands."

"Trouble? In what way?"

"Remember that large creature that we saw after you first arrived?"

"The wyvern, Noldor? Yes."

"He's back."

"He's not causing trouble, is he?" Leonie wondered how she could hope to battle with a large wyvern if she had to.

"No trouble, just sightings."

"It's got the pit mines upset though. They're sending out more patrols ... and that's where the problem lies." Rhiannon continued seeing Leonie's confusion. "More patrols means a greater chance of being spotted. There's been some random attacks in the north, just fly-bys, but there have been casualties."

"Serious?"

"Not yet, but it's only a matter of time before they make a concerted effort."

"Let's hope the recharging is successful," Lerry said.

Sussah and Harrond joined them. "Harrond is going to show me around Westridge," she said.

"Of course he is." Sussah blushed at Leonie's wink. "You've got quite a few years to catch up on."

"I'm sure the *tour* will be good for them both," Lerry said as they moved away.

"Hey, where's Bern? Is he okay?" Leonie asked.

"He's doing a run to Burraga. He'll be away for a few days."

"The mag-bike would do the return trip in a day."

"This is Bern we're talking about," Lerry laughed.

"I better have a look inside this *Skydancer*." Rhiannon smiled.

Leonie turned to lead the way. "David has made some modifications to it, but I'll let him explain." As she climbed inside she heard a cry and at the same time she felt a stabbing pain in her head. Spinning, she saw the seer buckle over and collapse. Leonie held onto the door as a wave of vertigo came over her.

Lerry managed to slow the seer's fall.

"I think there's been another attack," Leonie gasped. She slumped against the wall, images of mayhem and destruction beset her.

"Where?"

"I caught a bit from Rhi before she blacked-out. I don't recognise the area but saw wilders. Kanangra, at a guess. We need to get there. David!" she yelled. She heard the approaching footsteps.

"What is it?" he asked returning from the control room.

"I think Kanangra is under attack."

"We can be there in a few minutes. I better get everyone off."

"I'll do it," said Lana, behind him. She turned to gather the other wilders. "Tour's over," she called.

"Lerry, have you got any weapons here?"

"We still have some, from our escape. I'll grab them." The agtech rushed off to his accommodation.

"What happened?" Lana came over to assist, gently running her hands over Rhiannon's head and chest. "Her breathing is okay. Pulse is low—" She stopped when Rhiannon rose silently.

"I'll put her on the medicomp," Leonie suggested.

Lana followed as Rhiannon's body floated through the door.

"It's one of the newest." Leonie moved the seer into the medbay as the wilders were making their way down the passageway.

"I think she was overwhelmed by the trauma of Kanangra's attack."

"I sensed nothing." Lana looked doubtful.

"Because you were inside. The hull stops the signal." Leonie placed Rhiannon on the medicomp as David started working the controls.

"Lana, better get everyone prepared to leave. I don't know how long before we'll be back, but if everyone can get—"

"I understand." She was already out the door, herding the rest of the wilders. "We'll be ready."

Lerry came running back with several pulse rifles. "What about Harrond and Sussah?"

"Not enough time." She closed the hatch as soon as he was inside. "They'll be here when we get back."

With all the wilders off, and the agtech onboard, Leonie called to David, "Lerry can do that. Get us out of here."

"I got this," Lerry confirmed to David.

"Better hang onto something." David strode to the control centre.

Leonie tried stowing the weapons in a cupboard. They didn't quite fit, but enough to not be a hazard if the ship hit turbulence. She then grabbed a handhold and supported Lerry as he finalised the programming.

"Monitors say she's fine, but if what you say is true, then maybe she has some form of mental trauma. Shock, I reckon."

In moments, they were rising rapidly. Leonie staggered through to the control centre.

"You know where Kanangra is?"

"I gather it's north," he paused, pointing to the monitor. "And now we can see the blips on the scanner."

Four red blips were moving around an area two hundred clicks north.

"I know she's good, but I'm amazed Rhi picked up anything at that distance," Leonie said.

"Was it a telepath that sent it?"

Leonie shrugged. "I can only guess."

"If so, perhaps the trauma she felt was similar to an adrenaline boost for the mind, but not in a good way. We'll be there in six minutes."

"Six?" Leonie shook her head.

"And thirty-four seconds. She's not the fastest, especially at this low altitude."

"And these are the readouts for the portal?" She peered at some other displays to his left.

"They are. The powerpac is down four per cent, and the rate of discharge has virtually stopped, so I can assume the portal is almost fully charged."

"Maybe those clamps fell off?"

"Those green lights indicate a solid link. We're good to go."

"All we need to do now is work out how to move it."

"Already taken care of. I have a laser cutter in Engineering, as well as cable and heavy-duty clamps."

"You're thinking of everything."

"It's what I do," he replied calmly. "Almost there." He slowed the *Skydancer*.

Ahead, they saw smoke, and the flyers flying low over the rugged terrain, in large circles.

"Bastards," Leonie hissed. She moved to the exit.

"I found an area to land—"

"Not yet. When it's safe," she called back. She popped her head into the medbay. "How's Rhi?"

"Stable," Lerry answered. "What's happening?"

Leonie relayed the latest information. "I'm going out there. When we land, we'll need to bring any survivors on board."

Lerry unclipped from the chair and retrieved two weapons. He handed her one.

"I won't need that." She winked. "I haz skills."

Before Lerry could argue, she opened the door and jumped out, hastening to the closest flyer. As she approached, Leonie saw a motley crew of four men; a far cry from the soldiers she'd normally expect. No one was paying attention to anywhere else but the ground.

As she had done many times in the past in this situation,

Leonie held onto the roof of the flyer and scanned the pilot's thoughts – he was concentrating on looking for mutants. She delved into his mind, making him see mutants in one of the other flyers.

Cursing in shock, the pilot turned towards it and started firing the mounted gun. It was spinning and going down before her pilot was punched, breaking the mind link.

Before letting go the flyer, Leonie sent a small charge into the hull, shorting the circuitry. It dropped the thirty metres to the ground, then rolled into a ravine.

*Two down, two to go.*

She heard a faint staccato. On reflex, she soared into the sky and twisted towards the next craft now coming at her. She considered she'd probably be shot if these were professional soldiers.

Leonie zigzagged towards the flyer, then shot past to the left as an idea came to her. The flyer turned sharply to follow. She intended to try and get them to shoot at her when she passed between the two flyers, but they didn't fall for that. She flipped onto her back and EMP'd it, then turned to face the last one which was moving away fast. Now it was the pilot's turn to start evasive manoeuvring, having seen three of their number drop out of the sky in as many minutes.

Before Leonie could get close enough, it descended rapidly, landing hard in a rocky valley. She saw four figures jump out and run for cover among the crags. Deciding not to pursue them, she fireballed the flyer, then climbed higher, looking for the *Skydancer*. It was now on the ground near the remains of the wilder community.

Fearing the worst, she headed towards them.

As she landed beside the spacecraft, she saw people huddled in the shade of the cliffs. Lerry and David were with them, giving what aid they could. She walked closer, counting twenty-seven people, including four toddlers.

"How bad is it?" she asked.

"Not as bad as one might think," Lerry said. "With raids

happening more often, they were more or less prepared. Some of their dwellings were destroyed, but they were empty."

"Great to hear. Is this all of them?" She saw one of the adults limp over to her.

"You must be Leonie. We've heard so much about you," said one of the wilders. His body was mottled and discoloured.

"This is Maran, the Kanangra elder," Lerry introduced the man.

"Pleased to meet you, Maran." She shook his hand. "What happened here?"

"A couple of our elders were linking to communicate to Northridge when one of the flyers attacked."

"How are they?"

"Sadly, they did not survive." Maran took a deep breath. "It will be good to leave this place. Too many deaths of late."

Leonie nodded. "We need to get out of here. I hate to rush, but I can't say if any of those flyers called for back-up. Are your people ready?"

"Yes." Maran nodded. "We've been ready since we got the message about a gateway."

Leonie looked at them all. They were all staring back. There were two people stretched out on the ground. "Are they the elders?"

"No, those two are in shock, much like Rhi, I suspect. The others ..." he glanced to a smoking lean-to.

"I'm sorry." She looked away. "David, can they all fit in the *Skydancer*?"

"We'll have to make them fit," David joined them. "I'll go slow, most will have to sit in the passageways."

"Are you okay with that?" she asked David. "I seem to be taking over, but it's not mine to control."

"It's okay. I fully expected this would eventuate," David said. "Why are we still talking about it?"

Leonie laughed. "Well, let's get out of here. Maran, can you get your people to grab their belongings?"

"It will be done." Maran walked back to his community and spoke to them quietly. In moments they dispersed.

"Anything I can help with?" she called out to Maran.

"We are accustomed to moving at short notice. They will all be back very soon."

David packed up the first-aid kit while Lerry collected the weapons.

Even as they were walking back to the ship, some wilders returned with various backpacks, sacks and bed-rolls. There was a scream and yelling as they began to panic at the large, dark shape flying closer.

"It's okay, everyone. Keep moving to the *Skydancer*," Leonie called out. "I'll deal with this."

# 41

# EXODUS

Noldor landed with a crunch on the ground, careful not to damage the *Skydancer* in the confines of the narrow valley.

*Greetings, Leonie,* he sent.

*Hello to you too, Noldor.* Leonie felt the frightened stares at her back from the wilders. *What brings you here?*

*I have made a lair of sorts in a remote area, but now and then these annoying things intrude.*

An image of a flyer like the ones recently destroyed, appeared in her mind.

*They are a nuisance,* she agreed. *But with the whole world to choose, why here?*

*When I was alive back on my world, wyverns communicated frequently with hroltahgs. I became aware of the many prophecies they espouse —*

*Not you too?* Leonie shook her head. *I thought wyverns were smarter than that.* She started strolling around the area, inspecting the set-up the wilders had here.

*What can I say? I am an undead wyvern, transported to a new world through the powers of a god to assist an undead assassin in slaying you, the one entity purported to be central to many of these prophecies. Simple coincidence? To my thinking, there are too many threads here to ignore. So, yes, me too.*

He turned his head, his long neck snaking around to follow her.

*I have travelled this world; north, south, east and west,* Noldor continued. *While very different from my old world, it is not for me. I am alone and have been for the last twenty years.*

*You didn't think there would be another wyvern, did you?*

*Considering you humans are on my world, and here. I hoped ... but there is nothing for me. When I sensed your presence – much closer than usual – I thought it polite to meet.*

*You must be very lonely, to want to visit me.*

The wyvern inclined his massive head. *You are too hard on yourself. I'm surprised you are here.*

*Some of the people here had an issue with those flyers too.* Leonie indicated the ruins of the small community. *We came to help them.*

*And it would appear you have been successful.*

*Yes, but it shouldn't have to be this way. Now we're moving them to a safer place.*

*It seems these flyer-people are everywhere.*

*True, but we've found a way to return to Yarnik – to your world.*

*I can sense this new energy to the south. Is this by the same way of your arrival?*

*It is.* Leonie nodded, now considering his size. *Have you lost weight?*

*It is not something I've ever considered.*

*It's just that you look ... thinner. I'm wondering if you'll fit through the portal. How tight can you tuck in your wings?*

*Like so ...* Noldor brought his wings in and flattened them to his flanks.

*And if you can wiggle and flex a bit, then you just might fit.* She considered her next words. *Would you like to go back? It might be the end of you though.*

*One will not know until one tries. Either way, it is a risk I'm willing to take.*

*I guess you'll be dead, one way or the other.*

Noldor snorted. *I see why Dorn liked you.* He unfurled his wings in preparation for departure.

Leonie flew the short distance to the *Skydancer* door. The interior passageway was crowded, wall to wall wilders. She called out, hearing Lerry's voice in the distance.

"How's Rhi?" she asked.

"Recovered nicely. Ready to go now?"

"You guys going straight back to Westridge?"

"No. Rhiannon suggested we take them to Northcliff instead. We need to make certain they're okay and prepared. It's much closer, so they won't have to endure the cramped conditions for long."

"Good idea. I'm going to fly back with Noldor. We've got twenty years to catch-up on. I'll see you at the portal."

"I'll let David know. See you there."

Leonie waved and smiled at the staring wilders. She soared into the sky as Noldor cruised past.

*You asked them about me using the portal?*

*I wasn't seeking any permission. Regardless of what they say, this is our decision. Besides, you might not fit.*

The pair continued, a few thousand metres high.

*What became of Evlin?* Leonie across at him. Seeing him flying reminded her so much of Dorn, Slana and Faldo.

*As promised, I dropped her in the deepest ocean I could find. Using your units of measurement, it was several thousand kilometres away.*

*It's been two decades and no-show. It must have been enough. Thank you.*

*Again, like last time, your thanks is not required for what you did for Dorn and her younglings.*

The shimmering from the portal was far more intense than Leonie had ever seen, indicating David's genius.

*What do you reckon? Will you fit?* She moved the tripod device David had set up to measure the shimmer effect.

Noldor studied the portal. *As you say, it might be a tight squeeze, and I might lose a few scales, but I believe so.*

*Have you been to Fisbane before?* Leonie asked.

*In my youth. This is where it leads?*

*Yes, on a skyland in that region.*

*And you will be coming through too?*

*Just to confirm you got through, but I think I'm still of use here.*

*Is that to fulfil the prophecy?*

*I have no idea. I just feel there's more to do here. David is the key to this, I'm sure of it. At first I thought getting Sussah safe was it. But I see it was because of her pregnancy, which means David is important. Somehow we're to get everyone on Yarnik off. I have no idea how to do that, but if David is the genius everyone considers him to be, then he's the one to keep safe.*

Noldor lined himself up, lowering his head and keeping his wings tightly furled. He slowly moved forward, his whiskers almost touching the shimmering threshold.

*It will be cold, disorientating and very uncomfortable,* Leonie warned.

*I'm sure—* His thoughts cut off the moment his head disappeared.

It looked very weird to Leonie, like he was sinking, but horizontally. The wyvern's body kept moving forward at a sedate pace. There was a moment when the front edge of his wings clipped the inner edge of the portal, but a quick adjustment freed it and the wings scraped through. The shoulders were the widest part. Once they had cleared the portal, the remainder of the body slipped away.

Leonie picked up a couple of green scales that had fallen off and tossed them through. She then realigned the tripod before flying after him.


Expecting to arrive at the pinnacle, seeing the gathered wilders in the community clearing at Westridge was a huge shock to

Leonie on her return. It took a few seconds for her to take it all in.

Lerry burst out laughing at the look on her face. "We were wondering when you'd show up," he called out upon seeing Leonie's sudden appearance.

"I didn't realise I had been absent that long." Despite her surprise, Leonie had to laugh herself. "How long has this been here?"

"Only about half an hour." He described how he used the laser cutter to free the portal, and then David attached grapples and flew it here. "We were just finalising the first wave of evacuees."

"I wonder what would've happened if we crossed paths?" Leonie wondered out loud. She told him about Noldor going home. "It was a lovely day over there, so I took the opportunity to do a bit of flying with him. After he left, I spoke to a farmer who confirmed the area is Fisbane. The nearest town is Irinius." Leonie noted the sacks and crates of supplies. "Is that everything?"

"It's all we've got," Rhiannon said as she strolled up.

"Hey, you. Are you feeling good enough to travel?"

"I better be." Rhiannon nodded. *Truly, I'm well after the medicomp.*

*I was worried.* "Are Sussah and Harrond back?" Leonie asked Lerry with a smile.

"Yes, everyone's here, even the clones."

"And David's happy with the portal charging? Did Noldor's transit use much charge?"

"Some, but insignificant, and was quickly recharged."

"That's a relief."

The crowd parted as David arrived with Harrond and Sussah.

"You're back I see. Just in time for us to go," David said.

Leonie nodded, letting them know of the conditions on the other side.

"Shall we go through first?" Leonie asked Rhiannon.

The seer nodded. She looked tall and confident, her mind was surprisingly calm for someone who was going to use an alien device to span the galaxy. *I've experienced this several times in your mind, as well as Bern's and Sussah's. It will be cold, disorientating and uncomfortable for a few minutes. I'll cope.*

"Right then." Leonie turned to the others, watching expectantly. "See you all on the other side." She took Rhiannon by the hand. "Yarnik, here we come."

"Who's left?" Leonie asked Lerry, the last to come through. Rhiannon and Lana were organising the wilders into work groups, depending on their abilities. Some were lugging the heavier items towards the buildings, while those with less physical attributes were either foraging for anything useful, and some were simply exploring and collating everything and anything on the skyland.

"David's tweaking the powerpac, then he'll move on to Burraga. Sussah and Harrond are helping."

"Are those pulse rifles handy?"

"They should be in those red cases." He pointed, then strode towards it. "Lana ordered it through first, and put to the side and not to be moved. She can be quite forceful when she wants to be. Do you need them?" Lerry opened the box and pulled one out.

"Not me. You guys. It might be remote, but there's always the chance of large, nasty creatures turning up. If you don't see them coming, you might hear them. They sound similar to a flyer."

"I doubt we'll be seeing any flyers here soon. Bern told us about the shell he saw. Sounds ghastly."

"They're worse when alive. I'll head back and send Harrond through, so you have a couple of weapons ready, just in case."

"Good luck in separating those two." Lerry smiled.

"It's not as if Sussah can't stay here, or visit regularly."

"It took her a decade to visit, and that was while on the same planet."

"She wasn't with David then. Things are very different for her now." Leonie turned towards the portal. "I'll be back before we finish up."

"See you soon." He waved.

The trip to Burraga was swift and simple. When the *Skydancer* arrived, the wilders were waiting, all their possessions by their feet, and any supplies stacked to one side.

"This should be straightforward," Leonie observed.

"One can hope. I'll place the portal between those boulders, nearest the supplies." He pointed.

"I'll go out and make sure it doesn't spin." Leonie went to the side door and jumped out as soon as it opened. She flew down beside the portal, and as David hovered it into place, she kept it aligned at the best angle, so access was easiest. Once the portal was grounded, she removed the coupling. David then moved the ship to a landing area nearby.

Bern made his way through the staring crowd.

"Good to see you, Leonie." He gave her a brief hug.

"And you. You big oaf, I thought you were avoiding me."

"I reckon shifting to another planet still won't be far enough," he laughed. "How are things progressing?"

"All good. Once Burraga is through, we move to Northridge, and that's it."

"You must be Bern." David strode up to them. "You met them on their arrival. I guess I have you to thank for my existence."

"I gather you're David? You have your mother's eyes."

The two men shook hands. David turned to check the powerpac connections.

"Still good?" Leonie asked.

"Better than expected, to be honest. The recharging is still working efficiently, and the powerpac is still at eighty-seven per cent."

"I gather that's good? Sounds good to me, considering all the people and supplies sent through, and a wyvern."

"A wyvern?" Bern asked.

"Yeah. We ran into Noldor at Kanangra. It's a long story, but he's back on Yarnik now."

"Maybe we'll run into him one day?"

"You never know with wyverns," Leonie said.

There was a murmur among the crowd of wilders.

"Ah," Bern said. "This is Zarra, Burraga's elder." He introduced everyone.

"Are you all ready to go?" Leonie asked.

"We are," Zarra replied. "We cannot thank you enough for all you've done for us."

"Nonsense. Wilders were the first to help me when I arrived. It's the least I could do, besides, I'm just doing the leg work. This young man here is the brains behind all this."

David nodded. "Don't believe a word she says. None of this would be possible—"

"So," Leonie interrupted, "shall we get these guys through?"

The evacuation proceeded as planned. By late afternoon, all known wilders were on the skyland. Many of them were milling about the area chosen to set up their new community. There were several ruins nearby in better shape than others. Part of the structures were already in the process of repair with stonework or wood from the other buildings.

"We'll bring more supplies to you over the next few days. David has access to resources far greater than the agtechs, and I can assure you delivery will be swift and easier."

"Have you decided where the portal will be kept?" Lerry asked.

"David's chosen a spot he's sure will be ideal. It meets everyone's needs; totally secure, away from prying eyes, and still easily accessed."

"Sounds too good to be true," Lana said.

"I wouldn't believe anyone making promises like that either, except for when it's made by my son," Sussah replied.

"Where is this *ideal* place?" Lana asked.

"When David comes through, he'll let you know."

"We could step through and ask him. I don't know about you, but I for one need more assurances for the safety of the community." She started walking towards the portal.

"You think David hasn't got your safety in mind?" Leonie turned to her. "He is the one taking all the risks here. He is the one using all his resources directly under the eyes of the tower security to help you, and you have the nerve to question him?"

"As a wilder, we have learnt nothing from the tower is for free."

"Fair enough. I certainly won't stop you."

"Thank y—"

"But you should say farewell to your people, just in case."

"In case of what?" Lana asked, unsure.

"Until David reappears we have to assume the portal is in transit. You might end up falling several thousand metres."

"You're not coming?"

"I've no need. I'd trust him with my life."

*Lana, let's wait until David returns. Nothing will come of this. Once we stepped through, we said goodbye to Earth.*

Lana realised everyone had stopped to see the outcome of the confrontation.

"Well, if you can bring yourself to trusting someone that much, how could I not?" Lana walked back towards the crowd. "Besides, we have so much still to do here." She started organising the work parties.


A large fire had been lit, and many were busy preparing dinner. To one side, several wallabies were being prepared for the evening meal.

"Before we left, we hunted far more than normal," a wilder was explaining to Lerry. "If we took this many too regularly, the mob wouldn't have the numbers to be viable. It wouldn't be sustainable."

"Here he comes," someone called out.

After a few minutes, David strode into the firelight.

"I gather there was no problem?" Leonie greeted him.

David shrugged. "Nothing I didn't expect, but the portal is now safe and secure."

"There was a bit of concern about it," Leonie said.

"Not concerned, so much." Lana was nearby and approached. "We have a right to know where the portal is situated."

David looked to Leonie. "You want to tell them, or shall I?"

Many conversations died, sensing the answer would be important.

"It's your idea," Leonie answered.

"The portal is now in the tower, in my highly secure laboratory."

"What? Is that wise?" Lana asked. Many voices echoed her concern.

"You've gathered everything you could from your communities," Leonie called out. "There's no reason for anyone to return. Now you'll have access to the latest medical facilities, a guaranteed supply route for food and building materials.

"This way, you literally have the best of both worlds, and you have something no one in the tower has – clean, fresh unpolluted air, and absolutely no radiation."

The group murmured this news.

Rhiannon stepped forward. "Once again, we cannot express how much you two have done for us. This is far more than we ever could have expected."

"Then some of you underestimated us," Leonie smiled. "You have nothing to thank us for. Sussah and I wouldn't be here if the wilder community didn't help." She turned and walked into the darkness with David, leaving the wilders to their dinner preparations.

Leonie heard footsteps behind her as Sussah came running up.

"David, do you mind if I stay?" Sussah asked. "We've been apart for so long, and now we'll be in a position to visit each other any time."

"I want whatever you want." He reached for both of her trembling hands. "I dare say I'll be very busy with my research anyway."

"Oh yes, big corporation man that you are."

"What about you, Leonie?" Sussah turned to her friend.

Leonie had to refrain from smiling. "I think you should stay here. No one should have to live in that tower all day every day. It will be good for you to be back home … besides, I don't think I could put up with your constant pouting."

"I do not pout," she argued, pouting.

"My mistake." Leonie laughed.

"But what I meant, will you be staying?"

"I'll be back and forth."

**42**

---

## THE ATRIUM

The Atrium was the ceremonial seat of TowerGov. While much business was conducted behind closed doors for TowerGov members only, the atrium provided enough seating for all TowerGov representatives and all the Elite with their partners. Two thousand seats in a tiered semicircle around a dais, and under the gaze of a million citizens with the vision sent by a myriad state-of-the-art drones. The front of the platform was open, providing a view to the base level of the white zone, one hundred and fifty metres below.

Overhead, the large skylight showed a blue cloudless sky and filled the area with bright natural light. For several hours each day, while the sun was overhead, every floor received natural sunlight.

The dais jutted into open air. The two Primes sat in their finest regalia facing the tiered onlookers and awaiting the inductee. Under this much scrutiny, everyone was immaculately presented and proper decorum was paramount. Any display of untoward behaviour or disrespect was dealt with swiftly.

Today was an occasion for great celebration – the Induction Ceremony of a new member into the Elite. The inductee would rise on a mag-lev platform, stripped of the garb of non-elites and dressed in the silk robes of the Elite before floating out into the centre of the atrium.

As befitting their status, Dianah and Alexander sat in the front row nearest the dais.

Much to his preference, Brendon watched from the wings slightly off to one side and away from the fanfare where the most scrutiny would lie. The orchestra, cunningly situated in an alcove below the dais, started an energetic yet majestic tune. As the elevator began its ascent from the base, thirty floors below, the tempo increased, timed precisely to finish the moment the platform reached the dais.

All inductee suits were modified to allow easy removal, but to the untrained eye, David wore the typical one-piece suit of most tower citizens. He stood silently and solemnly as befitting the event on the rising platform. An inductee was advised to ignore the crowd, and remain motionless until the final presentation.

Brendon needed to concentrate, to get into David's mind the moment he was within reach. He had practised a few times, but in the controlled environment of HelixR labs, and all had worked well enough. His ear-filters would dampen most sounds so he could concentrate, allowing only the voice of Dianah in case there were any changes.

The plan was simple, and yet the result would be devastating to everyone. It would be history-making.

There. He felt the familiar mind connection to the clone of David as it came into range. While he was now in full control, Brendon stayed dormant in the clone's mind and would only act at the precise time for maximum impact.

The praise and cheering from the thousands of viewers on the surrounding balconies rose in volume as the platform passed each level. With a quick look at his watch, Brendon confirmed the platform would arrive in thirty-five seconds.

The music would stop and the two Primes would stand. One would silently strip the inductee, and the other would clothe them in the new Elite attire. Who took what role was dependent on the gender of the inductee; in this case, the Prime Director would strip and the Prime Lady would dress.

The music built up, getting faster. Ten seconds.

Nicholai held Veronica's hand, preparing to rise; a new ceremonial robe draped over her left arm.

The head and shoulders of David's clone appeared. Five. Four. Three. Two. One. The platform stopped. The music stopped. The two Primes stood and stepped closer. The crowd roared. Nicholai smiled benignly, moving behind David and reaching around to the front to tear the subtly modified suit down the middle, stripping him naked. Now Veronica stepped forward and raised her arms to drape the robe over David's head and around his shoulders.

Dianah nodded. The signal for Brendon to act.

The clone raised its arms. It grabbed Veronica's hands and, dragging the Prime Lady with him, stepped backwards forcefully into Nicholai Zodaich, Prime Director of Blue Mountains Tower.

Momentarily stunned, screaming and shouting burst from the crowd. As they were programmed to do, the vid-drones buzzed as they followed every movement. Brendon removed his mind from that of the clone, the sensation of falling making him woozy even though he was still firmly in his seat. Any sudden movement or sound was lost in the ensuing cacophony from the shocked crowd.

All three fell. And all three screamed.

Dianah, white and rigid, dared not move. She had just conspired to murder her mother; her flesh and blood. And for what? Because her mother didn't mourn enough for her father?

Alexander, eyes glinting in the joy of success, jumped from his seat, not in horror but to witness the fall of his uncaring and unloving father.

Tumbling and spiralling, pirouetting around each other, one moment their robes fluttering behind like streamers, the next moment pushed firmly against their body or tangling flailing arms, the trio, plummeted the one hundred and fifty-metres to the ground where they died messily on impact.

———

Brendon witnessed the mayhem erupt around the atrium. Drones still buzzed overhead. Any vid footage of the Elite's reactions to the deaths of the tower's Primes would show to those viewing that in reality, the Elite were no different than any other citizen. All were capable of grief, being shocked and horrified, and dying.

As many Elites jumped from their seats in consternation and distress as those that were frozen in place for the exact same reasons. Those in front risked falling themselves as they moved forward to the edge of the balcony.

Brendon slowly got to his feet and pushed his way through the panicked crowd to Dianah, her face ashen, her eyes red. Reaching for her hand, he pulled her to him and together, silently they left Alexander alone. Brendon noticed her trembling. Yes, she wanted her mother dead, but it was still her *mother*. "Remember, you did this for the father you loved and adored," he whispered in her ear.

The only reaction was a firmer handgrip.

TowerPol met them halfway down the stairs. They spoke to Dianah. They were going to conduct a thorough investigation into this tragedy. Her only response was a nod. Several officers became a security contingent to escort them back to their apartments, the others pounded up the stairs to speak with Alexander. While not formalised in the last three minutes, he was the sole heir to the Zodaich estate and was the Prime-elect. To all intents and purposes, their new boss.

Exactly as planned, it was an open and shut case, though the scandal would rock the tower for decades. How could an Elite –

albeit an inductee and one of the most intelligent rising stars in the tower – succumb to something so base as murder?

To the rest of the tower, Alexander had locked himself in his suite for solitude while recovering from the tragic loss. In reality, he was rejoicing at the spectacular result of the perfect plan. Other than Dianah and Brendon, only senior officials involved directly with the investigation were allowed entrance to the suite.

"What now?" Brendon asked when they were alone.

"There will be a week of mourning. After which, I will be made Prime. Then I will ensure you are completely and fully documented as a Citizen and sibling to David Osbourne. There may be initial ramifications and gossip, but that'll pass."

"Gossip? About what?" Brendon asked.

"You had a twin sibling. No one else in over two hundred years has had a full brother or sister. But even so, it was short-lived. Now, you are just as normal as everyone else."

"And I'll be Second Prime," Dianah added. "Since mother was the Prime Lady and partnered to Nicholai, I take her role until Alexander becomes partnered. Assuming that ever happens."

"What's to be done with the real David?"

"I'm on my way to take care of him," Alex said. "My men should be there by now."

"You're going in person?"

"For this? You bet. I want to see the look on his face when he realises who beat him." Alex started walking to the door.

"I think it's unwise to let your ego interfere with common sense."

"Dear Dianah, I'll be Prime in a few days. Who can stop me?" Alex left the suite.

"Did he forget we just killed the current Prime?"

———

While the specific venue was a surprise, the outcome wasn't; making the murder-suicide such a public event left no doubt to David what would happen next. The only other surprise was why they didn't act sooner.

On the vid, the hall monitors he'd tapped into showed three men approaching.

"Leonie, are you on?" David spoke into his comlink.

*"I'm here."*

"They're at the door, setting charges." He watched their actions through the vid.

*"Too bad you couldn't install lasers in the corridor. Are you okay?"*

"Nervous, but it will work out."

*"There's a flyer approaching,"* Leonie informed him.

David walked to the shimmering dock entrance to look outside. "So there is." A light blinked on the adjacent wall. "The proximity alarm has been triggered. They'll be getting a warning now. If they continue to approach—"

Laser cannons on each side of the dock entrance instantly powered up. A stream of rapid pulses from each drowned him out. He watched the flyer explode and disintegrate, shrapnel flying in all directions including the dock. As the pieces struck the kinetic force field, their movement slowed dramatically. Some of the fragments of metal dropped to the floor while the bulk of the fuselage fell out of sight.

*"My way's quieter,"* he heard Leonie say. *"That will bring attention."*

Behind him, he felt the force of the explosion as the front door blew in. The thugs entered, weapons drawn.

"They're inside," he said softly as he turned to face them. "I'll keep the link on."

"Stop there!" one thug yelled, pointing the gun at him.

"What's the meaning of this?" David feigned surprise.

"Shut up and keep still."

The two other thugs moved closer, each covering a side of the entrance.

"If it's credits you want—"

"I said shut up."

"You realise security will be here any minute?" David stepped backwards through the entrance, putting the kinetic field between him and the weapons.

"You're wrong. It isn't *security* that's coming." The first thug strode closer.

At that point, Alexander walked in.

"Ah, of course, Alex," David said. "I should have said *insecurity*."

"Your wit won't save you this time," Alex said.

"You'd be surprised."

"I would be. Unless you can fly, you have nowhere else to go." Alex smirked.

"I guess congratulations are in order. Even I didn't think you'd stoop as low as patricide."

"Oh, but it was *you* who killed my father. It's all on vid, and almost a million citizens witnessed it. You've already died, so you won't be missed." Alex looked around the sparsely furnished apartment. "Minimalist." He shrugged. "Would you mind telling me the code to—" His link chimed. Irritated, he clicked it off.

"I'll wait," David said. He stepped a few more paces. "Mind if I enjoy my last few breaths of fresh air?"

"Keep still!" the thug yelled.

Alex turned to face his henchman. "It's not as if he's going anywhere, fool." Alex then walked towards David but stopped at the entrance. He ignored the link as it chimed again.

"You should come outside, enjoy the sunshine?" David kept edging backwards. He briefly looked back to avoid the metal fragments.

"No need. I must say, I'm disappointed. With all your resources, getting to you was too easy." Alex stopped at the threshold of the entrance door.

"Not for the occupants of this flyer." David indicated the hot metal remains scattered across the dock landing pad.

"I was hoping for more of a challenge, Alex continued, "but

not to worry, I get to watch you die again." Alex's link chimed again. "What is it!" he snapped. The blood drained from his face when he heard the other voice in his earpiece. He turned to the door as he heard a commotion outside.

"Sir, people are heading this way," one of his men called out. "Dianah and a big guy. Looks like security is after them."

"Quick, let them through and cover them," Alex ordered.

"Right." The henchman tapped his colleagues on the shoulder. They disappeared down the corridor.

"Sorry David, I would've loved to see you jump on your own volition.' Alex raised his pistol and fired.

David dropped to the deck and rolled over the edge.

"Well, I'll—" Alex paused, momentarily surprised. He shook his head then turned towards the front door as Dianah and Brendon burst in, panting.

"What's going on?" Alex snapped.

"Nicholai's alive!" Brendon gasped.

"What? He can't be!"

"I guess we we're not the only ones using clones," Dianah gasped.

"Frag that old man! Why did you come here?"

"Osbourne has a ship we can use."

Alexander turned to the small flyer by the door. "That thing? We'll be lucky—"

"No. His secret project," Brendon interrupted, pushing past. "This way." He led them to the lab entrance housing the *Skydancer*.

"You got the eye, Dianah?"

"And the hand. Lucky I was near the labs when the shit hit the fan."

"Eye? Hand? What the frag are you—" Alex's mouth hung open when Dianah pulled a hand out of a pocket. "You're crazy," he finished.

Placing the hand flat on the panel, Brendon spoke into the com while Dianah held the eye to the sensor. The doors to the labs clicked open.

"There's a ship in here. His pet project." Leaving the eye and hand on the panel, she darted inside, the two men hot on her heels.

Alex's jaw dropped when he saw the sleek vessel.

"How the hell do we get this outside?" he shrieked, arms flaying about in panic. "How the hell did he get it *inside*?"

Shouts and cries of pain from the corridor encouraged them to get on board. Dianah headed straight to the control room and activated the door closing sequence.

Alex glanced curiously at the grey, metal pillar in the central passage. "When were you going to tell me about any of this?" He glared accusingly from one to the other when they got into the control room.

"This would be the appropriate time," Dianah replied.

"Can either of you fly this thing?" He glanced between Dianah and Brendon.

They shook their heads.

"Lucky I have a few hours on a simulator, but there's no way in hell this can get out through those doors." He pointed through the screen. "Oh, that's fragging great!" A dozen security guards ran in and surrounded the ship, weapons drawn.

"Shit," Dianah swore, looking outside.

"Is this thing armed or armoured?" Alex paced.

Brendon paused before answering. "No." He looked around the controls. "But I think I know how to get us out."

"How, genius? You just said you didn't have a clue how to fly."

"This spaceship does more than fly."

"What are you gibbering about?" Alex asked.

"This is a time machine. When would you like to go to?"

"When?" Alex frowned at the concept. "What the hell do you mean *when*? Now!"

"Ten years? Twenty?"

"You are both crazy."

"That's still too soon," Dianah answered. "Statute of liability and all. Make it fifty years."

Alex followed, muttering, as Brendon walked back to the central passage.

Brendon studied the console on the pillar. He closed his eyes to think. When he opened them, he tapped a few numbers on the pad, turned a dial. He then lifted a spring-loaded safety-cap and pushed the exposed button.

"I think that's it." He walked back to the control room.

*"You have two minutes to surrender, or we'll blast our way in,"* they heard a voice say over a link.

Looking outside, a senior officer raised two fingers.

Alex showed him one.

They heard a faint hum and felt a slight vibration.

"Now what?" Alex looked around. The screen started going white, making the outside look foggy. In moments it was all white, now softly reflecting their images. He decided to sit down. Dianah and Brendon both grabbed a seat each, strapping themselves in.

The vibration increased. Their ears popped and all three felt a dizzying sensation and a whole-body experience with pins and needles.

Suddenly there was silence. The vibrations and sound ceased; the white screen faded to black.

"What the frag!"

The vast, empty blackness of space surrounded them.

# THE END


*continued in Book 3*
**Ripples in Time**


**Please consider leaving a Review**
Help other readers find this epic fantasy series by leaving a review on Amazon, Goodreads, or any other website. Even simple ones like a star-rating really help with a book – and an author's – success.

# END NOTES

## Characters

### Yarnik

**Leonie**: a hybrid (rrell/human) female, thief. Agile, black fur, violet eyes, heals fast, excellent senses, faster than average, stronger than average, 6′, 160lbs

**Jade**: human, female, Taker Guild Master, Leonie's boss and friend/mentor

**Feiron**: illios (shapechanger) (aka Hectr Cerrin, aka Drial)

**Sussah**: human, female, friends of Leonie

**Styx**: hroltahg, becomes Leonie's telepath trainer/mentor, from Reenat

**Dwer**: hroltahg, from White Cliffs, Qelay

**Riff**: hroltahg, from White Cliffs, Qelay

**Lord Zander**: human, male, ruthless overlord of Delta city-state

**Lord Brendon**: human, male, partner to Dianah, co-ruler of Delta city-state

**Lady Dianah**: human, partner to Brendon, co-ruler of Delta city-state

**Evlin**: human, female, Jart'lekk assassin

**Philbert**: human, Tesakian, wyvern trainer. Resides Hell's Maw

**Dorn**: female wyvern, green, and mate to Noldor. Leonie's telepath trainer/mentor. Resides Hell's Maw, Philbert's ride

**Noldor**: male wyvern, green, and mate to Dorn

**Slana**: young wyvern, green, sibling to Faldo, resides Hell's Maw, Feiron's ride

**Faldo**: young wyvern, green, sibling to Slana, resides Hell's Maw, Leonie's ride

**Ro**: human, male, Jade's 'bodyguard', plainsman from the Northern Reaches

**Netoha**: human, female, Ro's partner, plainswoman from the Northern Reaches

**Tipp Nul Chor Tukk**: glins'ool, male, high-ranking bard from Reenat

**Captain Jorak**: human, male, captain of the *Tearful Revenge*, from Ghalena

**Lemnon**: human, male, High Priest for the Earth Temple, Delta

**Kendallarnick**: vorien, male, High Priest for the Water Temple, Delta

**Felice**: human female, High Priestess to the Temple of Life

**Coundar**: human, male, High Priest of the Woorin Temple in Delta

**Lothas**: human, High Priest of the Temple of Opsyss in Delta

**Alen**: human, male, priest of the Temple of Opsyss in Delta

**Tirruk**: human, male, Priest of the Temple of Opsyss in Delta

**Mage Kormal**: human, First Mage of Delta

**Niaarin Grigorid**: rrell, female, Second Mage of Delta, from Ghalena

**Phelicks Grigorid**: rrell, male, Niaarin's son, city guardsman in Delta, from Ghalena

**Levan Macreedy**: human, male, Captain of the city guard, Delta

**Lews**: human, male, city guardsman, Delta

**Oren**: human, male, city guardsman, Delta

**Regor**: human, male, city guard sergeant, Delta

**Gruy si Ferik**: glins'ool, male, warrior, Talon from Nest Snarr, Tana Keep

**Wyth**: glins'ool, female, warrior, Tana Keep

**Sera**: glins'ool, female, warrior, Tana Keep

## Earth

**Bern**: human, male, wilder runner messenger from Jenolan community.

**Clara**: human, female, elder of Jenolan wilder community

**Lana**: human, female, elder of Westridge wilder community

**Jojo**: human, female, child, Jenolan community

**Rhiannon**: human, female, wilder/mutant, seer, elder of Jenolan wilder community

**Zarra**: human, female, elder of Burraga wilder community

**Lerry Carter**: human, male, agtech from Blue Mountain Tower, life-partner to Maz

**Maz Carter**: human, female, agtech from Blue Mountain Tower, life-partner to Lerry

**Harrond Carter**: human, male, agtech from Blue Mountain Tower, son of Maz and Lerry, arranged partner to Sussah

**David Osbourne (Carter)**: human, male, son of Sussah, genius, inventor of a time-machine

**Nicholai Zodaich**: human, male, partner to Ivana, then Veronica, 1st Prime of Blue Mountains Tower

**Ivana Zodaich**: human, female, (clone), life-partner to Nicholai, Blue Mountains Tower

**Alexander Zodaich**: human, male, (aka Lord Zander) son of Nicholai and Ivana, Blue Mountains Tower

**Veronica Felton/Zodaich**: human, female, partner to Stefan, then Nicholai, Blue Mountains Tower

**Stefan Felton**: human, male partner to Veronica, father of Dianah, Blue Mountains Tower

**Dianah Felton**: human, female, (aka Lady Dianah) daughter of Stefan and Veronica, Blue Mountains Tower

**Brendon**: human, male, (aka Lord Brendon) wilder/mutant from Burraga wilder community, unknown twin of David, Blue Mountains Tower

**Redmond Collins**: cloned male, servant to Veronica Felton

**'Ivanas'**: 'collective noun' for several clones based on Ivana Zodaich

**'Redmonds'**: 'collective noun' for several clones based on Redmond Collins

### Races of Yarnik

The bulk of the populace inhabits the Shak'aran continent, however a few groups of seleth and rrell have favoured the more arid conditions of Ghalena, a continent to the south.

**humans**: fair skinned, bipedal, generally head and facial hair (males), average senses, strength and speed, 4'5"-6'5", 110-230lbs

**rrell**: (feline): generally bipedal, fur (can run faster on all four paws), any solid colour: white, brown, grey, ginger, black, but may have dual or tri-colours (rare), whiskers, claws, keen smell, acute hearing, highly agile and dexterous, acute hearing and vision/night vision. Between 5'-6', 80-150lbs, possibly telepathic

**illios**: (shapeshifter): greyish blobs (natural form), potentially can form many shapes (can't change mass), average senses, telepathic immunity, regenerative ability, 1'-7' (shape-dependant), average senses

**hroltahg**: (rollos): very heavy/dense individual, grey to black, 100% powerful telepathy (no eyes, nose, mouth, ears), very heavy: 250-500lbs, ball-shape approx. 1'-2' diameter

**seleth**: (reptoid): bipedal, scales/thick skin, variations of mottled green or brown (black or white rare), 150-350lbs, 4'-5', acute smell and taste, very strong, poor reflex and speed, possibly telepathic

**vorien**: (mermen/women): bipedal, fine scales, any colour/combination, fins, acute smell and taste in water/poor on land, can survive on land for several hours, slow on land, fast in water, 100-300lbs, 4'-6', possibly telepathic

**glins'ool**: (avian): bipedal & wings feathers, fast and agile (better in the air/flying), any colour combination, 50-100lbs, 4'-6', possibly telepathic

**gryphon**: large, fierce flying creatures

**wyverns**: indigenous to Yarnik, bipedal & wings, long necks, spiked tail, various solid colours (offspring lighter shade than parents), all telepathic, keen senses, can fly/glide all day, 2000-4000lbs, 40'-80'

**l'ithnamagri**: indigenous to Yarnik, ant-like, ten legs, mandibles, black, 500-800lbs, acute smell/hearing and vibration senses, poor eyesight, very fast, very strong, telepathic/pheromones. Three sub-types: Queens, drones and hunters (capable of flight)

## Locations of Interest

### Yarnik

**Yarnik**: the world

**Shak'aran**: major continent, includes countries: Athglenn, Lyhosa, Tesak, Fisbane, Ertuk, Gruarch, In'sha, Central Steppes, Northern Reaches, Shattered Isles

**Ghalena**: arid continent to the far south across the Gratharg Expanse

**Delta**: rogue 'city-state' trading port in southern Athglenn, at the mouth of the Urmaq River

**Reenat**: capital city of Athglenn, seat of the true rulers of Athglenn

**Plenari**: capital city of Tesak, built on and around the massive trees of the Tesakian

**'The Web'**: poor quarter of Delta, generally for downtrodden, outcasts and misfits

**Portside**: western side of Delta harbour, for more prosperous traders, merchants and families

**Dockside**: eastern side of Delta harbour, for smaller, less prosperous traders and merchants

**Indras**: rural town on the North Road, half way to Qelay on the Urmaq River

**Hell's Maw**: volcano in the Central Ranges, lair to wyverns

**Central Ranges**: vast mountain range stretching from far north coast to south coast, also called 'Spine of the World'

**Qelay**: major rural city in Athglenn, halfway to Reenat. Head of the Urmaq River

**White Cliffs**: resort especially designed to cater for hroltahgs, located in Qelay

**Swangrove**: small rural town north of Indras on the Urmaq River

**Urmaq River**: Largest river in Athglenn, from springs in Lake Urmaq to south coast

**Deraz River**: small tributary feeds into the Urmaq River

**Vale of Dromas**: a region in the centre of the continent. Fabled to be home to the original and ancient city of Dromas

**Skylands**: hundreds of these sky islands of many and varied sizes, float high around the Shak'aran sky

**Ghalena**: southern continent. Very arid, mostly desert

**Luminor & Luxor**: twin moons orbiting Yarnik, believed to eclipse approx. every 100 years

**Diphei**: Yarnik's sun, closest star of the binary-star system, G-type star

**Zastre**: the other star of the binary-star system, much larger and hotter. The elliptical orbit of Diphei will bring it (and Yarnik) very close, resulting in extreme temperatures

## Locations of Interest

### Earth

**Blue Mountains Tower**: a megabuilding housing over a million people, east coast of New South Wales, Australia

**Atherton Tower**: a megabuilding housing over half a million people, Atherton Tablelands, Far North Queensland, Australia

**LA 3**: a group of megabuildings housing over two million people, west coast of California, United States of America

**Jenolan**: wilder community, New South Wales, Australia

**Westridge**: wilder community, New South Wales, Australia

**Kanangra**: wilder community, New South Wales, Australia

**Burraga**: wilder community, nearest to the badlands, New South Wales, Australia

**Northcliff**: wilder community, New South Wales, Australia

**Badlands**: area west of the mountains, most radiated region in New South Wales

**Badlands Pit Mines**: open mine nearest meteor impact site, New South Wales, Australia

**Outpost**: domed structures surrounding the vast crop fields of the towers, used by agtechs when on duty

# ACKNOWLEDGMENTS

No book can be accomplished without the tireless efforts of friends and trusty beta-readers. To that end, I'd like to extend my humble thanks to Pete Aldin, Stephen Kerwin, Aaron Cordy, and Lani Retter for their time and risking their sanity.

I'd also like to thank Belinda Crawford for her artwork for the series covers;
https://www.facebook.com/groups/designedbyboots/
and Barbara Holten for her editing prowess:
https://barbarajholten.com

And finally but most importantly, my wife Morag, for putting up with my absent-minded rantings, and our daughter, Meredith – for putting up with me, and also *her* mum for putting up with my absent-minded rantings.

And Alex, our British Short-Hair cat.

# ABOUT THE AUTHOR

Andre Jones made his debut appearance (unless you believe in reincarnation – in which case this is his third) in Wollongong, NSW Australia and has managed to stick around for 58 years… so far.

Okay, okay … enough of the third-person stuff…

My parents were Dutch immigrants, and since I had a gloomy and challenging childhood, (and I've forgotten most of it) I immersed myself with drawing, reading and sometimes writing. As a child, I devoured the works of Enid Blyton before progressing to Tolkien, McCaffrey, Asimov, Heinlein and Bradbury. As a young adult, I got lost in many and varied roleplaying games, including: MERP, GURPS, Harn, Skyrealms of Jorune, Cyberpunk, good old D&D *(and its many variants)* and Traveller. (I can't get into these new card games) … and also spent far too much time on video games like Skyrim (but no regrets).

This 'not so interesting' life led me to various occupations: Security Officer, Police Officer, Park Ranger and finally as a Petty Officer Electronics Technician in the Royal Australian Navy for 18 years *(sadly, my role-playing stopped there)*.

Currently residing in Melbourne with my lovely – and very understanding – Scottish wife and a British Shorthair cat, I'm now a retired Navy Veteran with the opportunity to write, role-play, draw and potter to my heart's content.

# ALSO BY ANDRE JONES

## The Seven Portals Series

Book 1

**City of Bridges**

Book 2

**Shadow of the Tower**

Book 3

**Ripples in Time**

## AND BY A A JONES

## The Misadventures of Biff and Tiff

Book 1

**Gnome Henge**

Book 2

**Lost Fairies**

www.ingramcontent.com/pod-product-compliance
Lightning Source LLC
Chambersburg PA
CBHW020003120726
47903CB00004B/1109